Praise for *The Right Sort of Man*

"Stellar . . . Both leads are complex, well-developed characters, whose penchant for humorous byplay never comes at the expense of the plot . . . Fans of Maisie Dobbs and Bess Crawford will be delighted."
—*Publishers Weekly* (starred review)

"Fans of M. C. Beaton will relish the wit, and followers of Susan Elia MacNeal and Jacqueline Winspear will enjoy the depth and the period detail. Readers will want to get on the reserve list for the next Iris and Gwen adventure!"
—*Booklist*

"The Right Sort Marriage Bureau's debut is exactly the right sort to have readers hoping for a second date!"
—*Kirkus Reviews* (starred review)

"Sparkles with excellence as the author devises a first-rate plot, invests her heroines with depth and charm, paints an atmospheric portrait of postwar London, and provides a bit of romance."
—*The Free Lance-Star* (Fredericksburg)

"With a fun historical setting and two witty heroines, readers will enjoy this duo."
—*The Parkersburg News and Sentinel*

"Brimming with wit and joie de vivre but sneakily poignant under its whimsical surface, *The Right Sort of Man* is an utter delight and a fantastic kickoff to a new series."
—*BookPage*

"The plot moves quickly, well paced with unexpected twists. There are moments of lightheartedness and moments of deep emotion, adding depth and dimension and lifting this book well out of the field of run-of-the-mill historical mysteries. The dialogue is fast

paced and funny, with some of the best one-liners I've seen in a novel."   —Historical Novel Society (Editors' Choice)

"Full of heart, astute, and darkly comic, *The Right Sort of Man* is a keenly observed historical mystery set in post-WWII London about two women, a former intelligence agent and a war widow, who join forces and set up a marriage bureau with the mission to knit lives together, while grappling with their own pasts."

—Cara Black, *New York Times* bestselling author

"*The Right Sort of Man* is the right sort of book! I loved every minute of this delightful adventure with two thoroughly modern women fighting for a place in a rapidly changing world. Can't wait for the next installment!"

—Victoria Thompson, bestselling author of *Murder on Union Square*

"Rarely have I seen a novel that manages to be so charming and so substantial at the same time. *The Right Sort of Man* does more than nail post-WWII London in pitch-perfect setting and language—it introduces a female dynamic duo with whom I very quickly fell in love. The end of this book left me with a single thought: When can I read the next Iris and Gwen adventure?"

—Lyndsay Faye, author of *The Gods of Gotham* and *Jane Steele*

THE RIGHT SORT OF MAN

ALLISON MONTCLAIR

Minotaur Books
New York

Published in the United States by Minotaur Books, an imprint of St. Martin's Publishing Group

www.minotaurbooks.com

Excerpt from *A Royal Affair* copyright © 2020 by Allison Montclair

Designed by Devan Norman

The Library of Congress has cataloged the hardcover edition as follows:

Names: Montclair, Allison, author.
Title: The right sort of man / Allison Montclair.
Description: First edition. | New York : Minotaur Books, 2019.
Identifiers: LCCN 2019004332 | ISBN 9781250178367 (hardcover) |
 ISBN 9781250178374 (ebook)
Subjects: | GSAFD: Mystery fiction.
Classification: LCC PS3613.O54757 R54 2019 | DDC 813/.6—dc23
LC record available at https://lccn.loc.gov/2019004332

ISBN 978-1-250-62141-2 (Minotaur Signature)

Our books may be purchased in bulk for promotional, educational, or business use. Please contact your local bookseller or the Macmillan Corporate and Premium Sales Department at 1-800-221-7945, extension 5442, or by email at MacmillanSpecialMarkets@macmillan.com.

First Minotaur Signature Edition: 2020

10 9 8 7 6 5 4 3 2 1

FOR MY NIECE, SUSANNAH—

MAY SHE FOLLOW IN MY FOOTSTEPS,

OR BETTER YET, RUN ON AHEAD!

ACKNOWLEDGMENTS

Many bits and pieces of research, not to mention larger chunks, came from books, articles, photographs, and newsreels too numerous to mention. However, the author owes a particular debt of gratitude to the following:

Mark Roodhouse, *Black Market Britain: 1939–1955*

Ina Zweiniger-Bargielowska, *Austerity in Britain: Rationing, Controls, and Consumption, 1939–1955*

Alan Palmer, *The East End: Four Centuries of London Life*

David Hughes, "The Spivs," in Michael Sissons and Philip French's (eds.) *Age of Austerity*

Carol Kennedy, *Mayfair: A Social History*

Patricia Baker, *Fashions of a Decade: The 1940s*

Ruth Adam, *A Woman's Place, 1910–1975*

Martin Pugh, *Women and the Women's Movement in Britain, 1914–1959*

Tom Harrison, *Living Through The Blitz*

Martin Stallion, Secretary of the Police History Society

And her handy, dandy, foldable 1946 London Bus and Tram Map, with which she guided Gwen through her misadventures. Iris, of course, did not need a map to find trouble.

The author takes full responsibility for any errors made. Indeed, she will immediately launch into a ghastly display of sobbing upon confrontation with any such, so please be kind.

Women want such unlikely things—
romance and adventure and excitement—
but what's the use?

—E. M. DELAFIELD, *TO SEE OURSELVES* (1930)

AN INTRODUCTION FROM THE AUTHOR

There is a technique that will supposedly trigger creativity in a writer. It is a list of words and phrases used as random prompts. Take the next one on the list, and use it like an electric cattle prod to goad your muse into action. (I can speak from personal experience that the word *tequila* is not a helpful prompt, although to this day I have only the fuzziest recollection of how I learned that. But trust me on that one.)

A more professional and constructive prompt come from Keith Kahla, my editor supreme at Minotaur Books. He invited me to lunch out of the blue and I, trusting soul that I am, readily agreed, happy at the prospect of catching up with him. I am a devious, cunning, and occasionally murderous person when I write, but blissfully oblivious when it comes to the machinations of others, especially when they are offering to feed me.

Sure enough, after pleasantries were exchanged, family histories were updated, and carbs were consumed, Keith said, "So, I've just read a book about a marriage bureau in London that was started up and run by two women in 1939. I thought it might be an interesting setting for a mystery, and I thought you'd be good for it."

"Oh?" I replied.

"Oh!" shouted the muse.

And we were off and running. Iris and Gwen sprang into my mind fully formed on the ride home and immediately began talking to each other (Iris more rapidly). This was a good sign. I once heard an interview with the great Elmore Leonard in which he said that he couldn't start writing for a character until he knew what its name was. For me, it's the voices, the speech patterns, that drive them in my mind. When they are fully formed, the voices will tell me about their needs, their desires, the pasts they reveal, and the pasts they conceal. When it's going well, it feels less like writing and more like I am listening and recording what they are saying. If pressed, I would say that Iris's voice was derived from the young Glynis Johns with a touch of the more madcap Katharine Hepburn, while Gwen is more Madeleine Carroll—only taller.

I moved the setting to the postwar period for various reasons, the principal one being that I did not want to write a wartime novel with our intrepid heroines sneaking around after curfew, tiptoeing through the bombs, and so forth. Postwar London was a fascinating place. The city was recovering from the Blitz; a Labour government had taken over with Clement Attlee succeeding Churchill as prime minister; rationing was still in effect; a young princess was being courted by the man she would eventually marry; and the Cold War, the nuclear age, and television were all set to change the world as they knew it.

And it was a fascinating time to be a woman. Women had been given opportunities in wartime that they would not have had otherwise. They took their places in factories, filled every administrative post that didn't involve combat, broke codes at Bletchley Park, parachuted behind enemy lines as spies, commanded anti-aircraft batteries, and died by the hundreds in transport ships sunk by enemy submarines. The postwar demobilization drove many of them back to a prewar existence, ceding their newfound positions and skills to the lads coming home—but not all of them, and many seeds were planted that would change their roles in British society.

Fortunately, there is ample documentation of these changes available to the modern researcher. I am of the generation that used microfilm readers, and this dormant skill was revived as I spooled through *The Times* of London, scanning the daily events for each month I was re-creating (a speedier process than you would expect, as newsprint rationing restricted the daily papers to eight to ten pages). Both stories and adverts were mined. Newsreel footage from the period is accessible on the internet, and of course, there are books. Of particular use were the oral histories of life in the Blitz compiled by the Mass Observation Project, and by Anne de Courcy, whose interviews with women in *1939: The Last Season* and *Debs at War* were a gold mine of information. Perhaps my greatest discovery was a reproduction of the London bus and tram route map for 1946, available for a small fee. (Thanks again, internet!)

To be a historical fiction writer is to live in terror. People are fiercely possessive of their slices of history. There are tiny little fiefdoms over which obscure academic wars are being forever waged. Pick the smallest plot of dirt you can find on the globe and the smallest sliver of time it passes through, and you will find that you have stumbled into several competing dissertations, and all of these people know far more about the subject than you do, unless you happen to be one of these current or future PhDs who dabbles in fiction writing on the side.

I am not an academic, thank goodness. I once attended a history conference that had the very democratic thought of including both academic and popular topics. Imagine middle-aged scholars of the Middle Ages milling about with fans of Middle-earth, and you'll have the general idea. I had to present a paper on a topic related to a book I was working on, and I was quite nervous, figuring that I was going to be surrounded by people who spoke Old English and Ecclesiastical Latin at the table. I was sitting in the communal lunchroom opposite an intense young woman, bemoaning my trepidation over trying to sound knowledgeable in front of people who actually were, and she glared at me and snapped, "Well, at least your career doesn't depend on it."

Well, yes and no. I may not be an academic, but I feel I have an obligation as a creator of worlds to Get Things Right. And that's what I enjoy about writing historical fiction. I have, as Douglas Adams once wrote, "endless fun doing the little fiddly bits around the fjords." I come across countless obscure nuggets of information or long-discarded bits of slang that have triggered plot points, moments of dialogue, or random thoughts for the characters.

I am, as of this writing, five-eighths of the way through Book Three of the adventures of Sparks and Bainbridge, still happily ensconced in 1946. I hope to get to 1947 soon. And in 1948 comes the London Olympics. There's bound to be some trouble there. We shall see.

Until then, thank you for reading.

Sincerely yours,
Allison Montclair

CHAPTER 1

Tillie climbed the stairs from the Bond Street Station out to Davies Street, blinking in the afternoon light. She had directions, but the directions were from Oxford Street, and she didn't know whether that was to the right or left. She felt like the overwhelmed child that she had been the first and last time she had come to Mayfair, when her dad took her on a special shopping expedition after a rare successful day at the track. She dragged him into shop after shop, looking at all of the clothes, the toys, the sweets, her voice a non-stop series of squeaks and squeals while her dad beamed at the happiness he had produced all because the favourite in the fifth race at Kempton Park had snapped a foreleg and the long shot managed to skirt the subsequent pileup of horses and jockeys and push its nose past the other survivors. Two horses were put down after that race, and three jockeys went to hospital, but Dad came out of it forty quid ahead, so tragedy be damned.

She wasn't even certain what he had bought her that day. Some pretty printed dress, she thought. Probably from Dickins and Jones. One that she outgrew within months, because Dad would never think of buying a size or two up, but that day was still the best of her life. So far.

Dickins and Jones was bombed during the Blitz. She read about it the morning after it happened, thinking about being there with Dad back in—'28? '29? She cried when she read about it, cried like she was a little girl again, she who had never shed a tear when friends and family were lost. It was as if the Germans had attacked her best memory.

There it was, on the left. Oxford Street! She reached into her handbag and pulled out the scrap of paper with her directions.

It was June, 1946. The war was over, and Tillie La Salle had come back to Mayfair to shop.

Only this time, she was shopping for a husband.

A right, two blocks, and another right brought her to her destination. She gawked when she saw it. It wasn't the appearance of the building itself that caused her astonishment. It was very much an ordinary, turn-of-the-century structure with bricks of a dull, almost muddy red, four storeys with not much in the way of falderal in the edging of the windows or the parapets. But it was the only building still standing on this particular block. On both sides, piles of rubble and a few ruined walls lay where similar buildings once stood, bracing their surviving neighbour. To the right, a solitary bulldozer was scooping up shattered pieces of brick, concrete, and wood and unceremoniously depositing them into a waiting lorry.

She walked past, wondering which phase of the German air assault had devastated this particular block, and what quirk of Fate had missed leveling the very building containing the goal of her journey.

The driver of the lorry was leaning against the cab. He caught sight of her, then took off his twill cap and waved.

"'Allo, gorgeous!" he shouted. "Give a working man a smile!"

"You don't look like you're working at the moment," she replied.

"They also serve who stand and wait," he said. "Fancy a cuppa?"

"Some other time," she said.

"Name's Frank," he said, giving an exaggerated bow. "I'm here all week."

"Save some love for the wife," she advised him.

He laughed and replaced his cap, his wedding ring prominent.

She sighed and continued to the building. On the front by the entry was a small collection of signs advertising the occupants. Amidst a few drab placards for accounting and typing services was a cheerful light green one with large hand-painted yellow letters reading, THE RIGHT SORT MARRIAGE BUREAU. MISS IRIS SPARKS AND MRS. GWENDOLYN BAINBRIDGE, PROPRIETORS.

Tillie hesitated, then thought how easily she had just been accosted in the street by a married man.

"No faint heart, Tillie," she admonished herself. "This is why you came."

She took a deep breath, then walked through the door.

There was no reception, merely a cramped hallway with a daunting set of stairs to the right and a narrow passageway directly ahead that vanished into darkness with alarming rapidity. An elderly, unshaven man in dingy overalls was mopping the floor. She ignored him and turned her attention to the building directory.

"If you're looking for a husband, they're on the top," called the custodian, his sporadic yellow teeth flashing in what she assumed he meant to be a friendly smile.

"I see that," replied Tillie, spotting a smaller version of the green placard. "Thanks. Don't you think there ought to be more light down here?"

"No point," said the custodian. "It's all vacant, innit?"

She took the stairs, initially at a nervous trot to get away from the gloom of the ground floor and the vaguely menacing demeanour of the custodian. By the time she reached the top, her pace had slowed considerably.

This hallway was brightly lit, however, and in the middle of it, she saw yet another green sign proclaiming her journey's end. She paused to catch her breath, then walked up and rapped on the door.

The woman who opened it was her height, a brunette maybe six or seven years past Tillie's twenty-two. She gave her a quick, inquisitive look, then smiled.

"Miss La Salle, is it? Come in, come in."

Tillie found herself ushered in and plopped onto a wooden chair that creaked ominously. There were two desks in front of her on either side of a single window. They looked like they themselves had served during the war, perhaps seeing combat in some skirmish against German furniture, and now sat battered but unbowed, the one on the left jammed against the wall for partial support, a book stuffed under one leg which was noticeably shorter than the others.

The room itself was painted the same soothing light green as the placards. On the wall to the right hung photographs of happy couples at their weddings, with announcements from the *Guardian* and the *Evening Standard* taped to their frames. There was an ancient filing cabinet in the corner that could have told tales from previous wars to the two desks.

"How do you do, how do you do?" rattled off the woman. "I'm Iris Sparks; call me Sparks, everyone does. So nice to meet you, and you're perfectly on time. You made it up the steps, hurrah! The first hurdle on the path towards happiness is those steps. They've been wonderfully firming for my legs, I must say. I've lost eight pounds since we started up. This is Mrs. Bainbridge, my partner."

From behind the desk on the left, a very tall woman rose gracefully and came over to shake her hand.

"How do you do, Miss La Salle?" she said.

Tillie tried not to gape. Mrs. Bainbridge was elegant, blond, and wearing an impeccably tailored silk suit that must have been sealed in a cedarwood closet for the duration of the war to have been resurrected so perfectly. The woman had a patrician air that was completely out of place in this small, solitary office, yet seemed wholly at ease in spite of it. She could have stepped from the pages of the *Tatler,* or been the slumming aristocratic sidekick in a Jessie Matthews musical, lacking only the art deco sets for the appropriate back-drop.

Sparks noticed the young woman's attempts not to stare and grinned.

"Impressive, isn't she?" she commented. "Don't worry, she's one of us."

"I'm sorry," stammered Tillie. "I didn't mean to be rude."

"Not at all," Mrs. Bainbridge reassured her as she resumed her seat. "Now, you are looking for a husband."

"That's right," said Tillie.

"Then you've come to the right place," said Sparks, sitting on the edge of her desk and picking up a pair of typed forms. "Business first. Before we ask you a single question, we want you to know what you are committing to, and more important, what services we provide. We are a marriage bureau, one of two such in London, licensed to arrange meetings between eligible single people. For an initial fee of five pounds, you receive our unwavering efforts to find you a suitable husband. We currently have eighty-three single men on file, as well as ninety-four women, all of whom have been subjected to questioning by Mrs. Bainbridge and myself—"

"Which is rigorous," interjected Mrs. Bainbridge.

"As you will see for yourself," continued Sparks. "We cannot, of course, guarantee that marriage will result from this."

"Or that happiness will result from marriage," added Mrs. Bainbridge. "That would be up to you."

"But we've already had seven weddings result from our efforts in the three months since we've opened," said Sparks.

"Seven!" exclaimed Tillie. "In only three months? Such short engagements!"

"The war is over, and people want to start normal life up again in a hurry," said Mrs. Bainbridge. "And there has been so much loss and devastation—"

"Oh, yes," said Tillie. "It's amazing this building's still up."

"Incendiaries to the left of us, doodlebug to the right," said Sparks. "Yet here it is, and here we are."

"It's why we chose this location," said Mrs. Bainbridge. "Something about it says *hope,* don't you think?"

"It does," agreed Tillie. "I hope there's some hope left for me."

"For five pounds, there will be," said Sparks. "Now, there's one more part of the contract, and this is the catch. Should you end up marrying a man who you met through our efforts, then each of you will pay us a—call it an achievement fee."

"How much?"

"Twenty pounds."

"Twenty quid?" exclaimed Tillie.

"Each," said Sparks.

"That's an awful lot," said Tillie.

"But don't you see, that's the incentive for us to work so hard on your behalf," said Mrs. Bainbridge. "It will be in all of our best interests to find you the right sort of man."

"Moment of truth, Miss La Salle," said Sparks, holding up the papers in her hand. "Five pounds and a signature, and we shall commence your quest for matrimony. Are you with us?"

"Well," said Tillie, considering. "It can't be any worse than what I've been going through."

"It will be so much better," said Mrs. Bainbridge confidently.

"Right," said Tillie, opening her handbag.

She counted out five pounds and handed them to Sparks.

"Bravo," said Sparks. "Come sign your contracts. There's one for you, one for our files."

She handed her a pen and vacated the desk so that Tillie could sign. Tillie looked over the contract carefully.

"One question," she said. "How do I know you don't grab the best boys for yourselves?"

"We have a firm policy of never dating clients," said Sparks. "We even put that in the contract. Item seven."

"You really did," marveled Tillie. "It seems like you thought of everything."

She signed them both, then handed them and the pen to Sparks.

"Well done," said Sparks, sitting behind her desk and taking out a steno pad. "Now, let's find out more about you. We have your name, and you gave me your address when you phoned for the appointment. Ratcliffe Cross Street. That's in Shadwell, yes?"

"Shadwell born, Shadwell raised, and I work there as well," said Tillie.

"You like it there, do you?" asked Sparks.

"I want to get out of there as soon and as fast as I can," said Tillie fervently. "I will settle for a lesser man if he lives far from Shadwell. Find me a farmer up north, and I'll learn to herd ducks with a willing heart."

"I don't think we have any duck-herding farmers at the moment," said Sparks.

"I'll take any spare dukes or millionaires you have lying about, then," said Tillie.

"I'm afraid we're fresh out," said Mrs. Bainbridge, smiling.

"Let's start with the basics," continued Sparks. "Religion?"

"Church of England," said Tillie.

"Looking for the same?"

"I suppose. I don't go enough. I wouldn't mind Catholic, if he's Continental and a gentleman."

"So, French, Italian . . . ?"

"I've got some French in me."

"We suspected as much from the name," said Mrs. Bainbridge.

"Yeah, that's a dead giveaway," said Tillie. "A couple of Free French soldiers tried chatting me up, but I don't speak a word of it. Didn't stop them from trying, though, did it?"

"So, Catholic acceptable," said Sparks, writing it down.

"But not Irish," added Tillie hastily.

"But not Irish," repeated Sparks.

"I mean, I don't want you to think—"

"My dear, we do not judge," said Mrs. Bainbridge. "Your preferences are respected here."

"Right," said Sparks. "Education."

"In school until I was fourteen. Wasn't good at it, and my family needed me to work, so I quit and got a job."

"And you're currently working in Shadwell."

"Yes. At a dress shop."

"Do you sew, then?" asked Mrs. Bainbridge. "Make alterations and such?"

"We have a tailor," said Tillie. "He's the owner and does all that. I can help out in a pinch, but mostly I'm the shopgirl. I show the ladies the styles, make recommendations, keep the books."

"You're like us, only with dresses," commented Sparks.

"Although we don't offer alterations," said Mrs. Bainbridge. "Perhaps we should."

Tillie giggled at the idea, and she and Mrs. Bainbridge began trading suggestions that quickly became ridiculous. Iris took the opportunity to jot down a quick assessment of their new client.

Certainly a pretty girl, she thought. Bright-eyed, naturally perky when she smiled, good teeth when she laughed, although she was missing one on the top left. Iris wondered what circumstances led to that blow to the mouth. Miss La Salle knew how to wear makeup to good effect, just the right amount of powder and rouge without being garish or common. Nice raspberry red lipstick. And her clothes—the jacket was a lovely light blue cloth bolero with an abundance of white trim; her collar was of a cheerful polka-dotted pattern; her kiltie was a riot of pleats, stopping below the knee, with a good set of taupe nylons clinging to a good set of gams. And sensible shoes, as a shopgirl must have.

"Now, as to the type of man you are looking for," Sparks said. "You mentioned wanting to abandon Shadwell. How far would you be willing to go?"

"How far can you send me?"

"Australia," said Sparks.

"Australia?" exclaimed Tillie.

"India. Burma. Africa . . ."

"We have several clients who were here for the duration of the war, and wish to return home, a blushing bride by their side," added Mrs. Bainbridge.

"Oh," said Tillie. "I never even thought . . . I mean, my Mum and Dad are still here. If anything happened to them . . ."

"Then you'd want to be able to see them quickly," finished Mrs. Bainbridge. "We understand entirely. Family is important."

"To some," said Sparks. "Age?"

"Not, you know, doddering about. Fit. Able. I'm not a nurse-maid, am I?"

"Certainly not," agreed Mrs. Bainbridge. "Any limit?"

"I suppose forty? Fortyish?"

"Ish," muttered Sparks, writing it down.

"Now, this one is somewhat delicate," said Mrs. Bainbridge. "Most of our bachelors served our country. Not all of them emerged unscathed. We have men who lost limbs . . ."

"Oh, dear," said Tillie.

"We have a lovely gentleman who was badly burned," said Sparks. "It's startling when you first meet him, but within minutes of speaking to him, you completely forget about it."

"So, our question is would you consider one of these wounded or disfigured heroes?" asked Mrs. Bainbridge.

"I know that I'm supposed to say yes, of course," said Tillie. "That I would do anything for the lads. But I'm the one who would have to live with them forever, aren't I?"

"You are," said Sparks.

"I'd like, you know, I'd like a bit of something to look at while I'm doing the wifely duty," said Tillie. "It's what they want from me, so why shouldn't I be the same?"

"You're saying that looks are important," said Mrs. Bainbridge.

"I suppose they shouldn't be," said Tillie. "But I've had men chasing after me since I was too young, and it had nothing to do with my personality."

"Wouldn't you rather be wanted for your personality?" asked Mrs. Bainbridge.

"Yeah, I would," said Tillie. "It's why I came here, isn't it? And I know that I just said I want a man who looks all right, so bad on me for being confusing. He doesn't have to be a heartstopper. I just want something more than the bare minimum. And if he's missing a leg, he won't even be that."

"We'll see what we can do," said Mrs. Bainbridge. "Any other physical preferences?"

"All of his hair still on his head," said Tillie promptly.

"Noted," said Sparks. "Height?"

"Be hard to find one shorter than me," said Tillie.

"Oh, no, it isn't," said Sparks. "We have several."

"Well, save them for the girls who like short men," said Tillie.

"Right," said Sparks. "If they run to fat . . ."

"We all will eventually," said Tillie. "With luck and no rationing. I don't mind a bit extra around the waist."

"Interests? Hobbies?"

"Never had time or money for any," said Tillie.

"Anything you don't want in a gentleman?"

"No gambling. No drinkers."

"Smokers?" asked Sparks.

"As long as he shares," she said, grinning. "Ciggies are my secret vice."

"Right, that should give us enough of an idea to pair you up with someone," said Sparks.

"How long will it take?" asked Tillie.

"We'll be in touch with a suitable candidate by this afternoon's post," said Mrs. Bainbridge. "You should be hearing within two to three days."

"That quick?" exclaimed Tillie. "I won't even have time to get my hair done."

"Your hair looks fine," Mrs. Bainbridge assured her.

"Oh, Lord, I'll be in all of a dither waiting," said Tillie. "It's rather exciting, isn't it?"

"That's all part of the experience," said Mrs. Bainbridge, rising to shake her hand once more. "So nice to have met you, Miss La Salle."

"Likewise," said Tillie. "Ta ta."

"Ta ta," said Sparks.

Iris watched Tillie leave, then drummed her fingers on her desk.

"What?" demanded Gwen.

"A hunch," said Iris, getting up. "Be right back."

She walked out of the office and peered down the stairwell. Tillie was one storey down.

"Miss La Salle," called Sparks.

Tillie looked up at her in surprise.

"One last question, if you could wait one second," said Sparks.

She hurried down the stairs to where Tillie was waiting, then looked around to make certain they weren't being overheard.

"Yes?" said Tillie.

"Stockings," whispered Sparks.

"What?"

"Help a girl out," said Sparks conspiratorially. "I ruined my last pair, and I'm short coupons. Have you got a place?"

"It's illegal," said Tillie indignantly.

"Come on," said Sparks. "Everyone's got a fiddle. I'm desperate for them."

"You'll find me a nice bloke?" said Tillie.

"I have the perfect match in mind already," said Sparks. "You'll like him, I promise."

"Well," said Tillie, biting her lower lip while she considered. Then she smiled. "All right, then. There's a pub called Merle's on Wapping High Street. There's a spiv named Archie, usually sits at one of the tables in the back with his mates. Tell him Tillie sent you, and he'll fix you up."

"Thanks," said Sparks. "You're a lifesaver."

"Anything else?"

"No," said Sparks. "Back to work for me."

"Ta, then. Remember, no short men!"

"No short men."

"If I wanted a jockey, I'd go to the Derby," said Tillie, and she disappeared down the stairwell.

Iris climbed back to their office and returned to her desk. She moved her Bar-Let typewriter to the center of the desk, then rolled a piece of foolscap into it.

"Did your hunch prove correct?" asked Gwen.

"It did," replied Iris as she began typing her notes of the interview.

"What was it about?"

"Her stockings."

"Were her seams not straight?"

"The seams were straight," said Iris. "The girl is crooked."

"I thought so as well," said Gwen. "Something about her struck me as shady."

"She's a shady lady from Shadwell," sang Iris. "And you oughter see her shimmy and shake!"

"The music halls lost so much when you retired," murmured Gwen. "How did her stockings set off your alarms?"

"That she had them. And that skirt—more pleats than a dozen honest English girls have, much beyond regulation."

"I never thought about that," said Gwen.

"Well, let's be honest, dear, you have a ton of clothes—"

"Certainly not."

"All that I'm saying is that having used most of my coupons on this tweed suit, which I needed for this venture of ours, I am painfully aware of when another girl shows up wearing something non-reg. You, with your fabulous pre-wardrobe, are not."

"I could loan you—"

"No, thanks," said Iris. "I would have to stand on Miss La Salle's shoulders to fit into one of your lovely frocks."

"I was going to say stockings."

"Same problem," sighed Iris. "Oh, if I had your legs, I could get places in half the time. Why did you think she was—oh!"

There was a man standing at the door, wearing a dustman's coverall, his cap in hand.

"Sorry, didn't mean to intrude," he said. "Is this all right, or do you need to make an appointment?"

"You've just made one," said Mrs. Bainbridge, stepping from behind her desk to usher him in. "I am Mrs. Bainbridge. This is my partner, Miss Sparks."

"How do you do?" said Sparks.

"'Ow d'you do?" returned the man. "Name's Alfred Manners, though me mum says I got none, ha ha!"

"Ha ha," echoed Sparks.

"How may we help you, Mister Manners?" asked Mrs. Bainbridge, directing him to the chair.

"I been passing by, regular-like," he said, sitting down. "Keep seeing the lovely green sign, think to meself, Alf, maybe they got a girl for you."

"Maybe we have," said Mrs. Bainbridge.

"So, I finally decided to see what's what," he said.

Then he looked at them expectantly.

"What's what is we are a licensed marriage bureau," said Mrs. Bainbridge. "We have a growing clientele of both sexes, and we seek to find couples who would be amenable—"

"Amenable. What's that?" asked Manners.

"Compatible," said Mrs. Bainbridge, pausing as he continued to look at her blankly. "Suitable for each other."

"The Right Sort!" he said, brightening.

"Exactly," said Mrs. Bainbridge. "Now, there is an initial fee—"

"How much?"

"Five pounds, then—"

"Five quid!" he exclaimed. "Just to meet a girl? There's mott shops that charge less."

"Not just any girl," continued Mrs. Bainbridge determinedly. "One that we believe will match up with your personality and preferences."

"Are you saying I got preferences?" said Manners indignantly.

"What you prefer, what you like in a woman," said Mrs. Bainbridge as Sparks suppressed a grin.

"Oh," said Manners. "Think you could fix me up with that bird who just left? She was a bit of a looker, no argument."

"Which bird?" asked Sparks.

"The one what was 'ere before," said Manners.

"Mister Manners, we maintain the privacy of our clientele," said Mrs. Bainbridge. "As we would maintain yours should you choose to join us."

"I don't have five quid on me," said Manners.

"Then let me provide you with one of our adverts," said Mrs. Bainbridge, taking one from a pile on her desk and giving it to him. "Should you wish to avail yourself of our services, you may make an appointment."

"Right," he said, taking it. He glanced over the two of them appraisingly. "Are you two on the list?"

"We are not," said Sparks quickly.

"Pity," he said, leering. "But never say never, right?"

"Good day, Mister Manners," said Mrs. Bainbridge. "We hope to be hearing from you shortly."

He put his cap back on, touched two fingers to the brim in salute, then sauntered off.

They waited until they heard his footsteps fade down the stairwell.

"Never," said Gwen.

"Never, never, never," said Iris, and the two of them began to giggle.

"Oh, dear, he was dreadful," said Gwen. "I'll bet you tuppence he doesn't come back."

"No bet," said Iris. "No woman is worth five pounds to him."

"You know, I believe that is the first conversation that I've ever had with a dustman," mused Gwen. "It's wonderful how broadening an experience this life is. He smelled much better than I would have expected."

"We're in Mayfair," said Iris, finishing her notes. "Even the dustmen are upper-class."

"Mott house," said Gwen thoughtfully. "Is that what I think it is?"

"What do you think it is?" asked Iris innocently.

"A, um, a house . . ."

"A house is a house, certainly," said Iris.

"Of—ill repute," finished Gwen, blushing deeply.

"Ill repute?" gasped Iris. "You mean—a bordello?"

"Well—"

"A brothel?"

"Stop it."

"A whorehouse!" wailed Iris melodramatically, pressing the back of her wrist to her forehead and swooning in her chair.

"You're making fun of me," said Gwen. "You knew what it was right away."

"I did," said Iris. "But I have the benefit of a Cambridge education."

"Which class did you learn it in, I wonder?" said Gwen. "Are you done with that form?"

Iris pulled it from the typewriter and handed it along with Miss La Salle's signed contract to Gwen, who read them over, then paper-clipped them together and put them inside the file cabinet in the corner behind her.

Iris took a pair of index cards, then placed a piece of carbon paper between them. She rolled them carefully into the typewriter, then typed in a short summary of Miss La Salle's preferences and incidentals. When she was done, she separated them.

"Your turn for the carbon," she said, handing the bottom one to Gwen. "Now, tell me—why did you think she was wrong?"

"Something about her responses," said Gwen. "Not that she was lying so much as she was leaving some things out."

"Do you think she warrants further vetting?" asked Iris.

"I don't think that she's an adventuress," said Gwen. "But we do want to make certain we're not foisting a criminal upon anyone. We have our reputation to maintain."

"I'll make some calls," said Iris. "Should we hold off on the matching?"

"No, let's go ahead," said Gwen. "We promised her a quick result. If your friend with the police finds anything, we can always contact the gentleman candidate and cancel. I will say, she speaks well for one of her background. I would have expected some dropped h's."

"She has aspirations to higher things," said Iris. "Right, let's get cracking, shall we? Miss La Salle is Female Candidate Number 102."

They each wrote it on their index cards, then placed them in green metal index boxes labeled F. Then they each moved another box labeled M in front of them.

"Ready?" asked Gwen.

"Ready," answered Iris.

"Then begin," said Gwen. "And no short, bald Irishmen, as tempting as that would be."

Iris began looking through her cards at the eligible bachelors. She found one she thought might do, pulled out the card and studied it, then placed it to the side. She glanced over at Gwen.

"No peeking," said Gwen without looking up.

They each proceeded until they had three cards in front of them. Iris gave her group one more perusal, then switched the second and third ones. Gwen waited, her order undisturbed.

"Shall I go first?" she asked.

"Please do."

Gwen held up a card.

"Sydney Collins," she said.

"Interesting," commented Iris. "Yes, I can see it now. He didn't leap out. Right, my third choice is Morris Cannon."

"Hmm," said Gwen.

"You don't like him?"

"I think we can do better."

"Give me your second choice."

"Alex Renbourn," said Gwen.

"Mine as well," said Iris, grinning and holding it up. "Are we about to have a great-minds moment?"

"Let's savour it, shall we?" suggested Gwen.

She took her final card, clutched it to her bosom, closed her eyes, and inhaled deeply. Then she turned it towards Iris.

"Yes!" cried Iris, holding hers up. "Dickie Trower!"

"I love it when this happens," sighed Gwen. "Now, tell me why you chose him."

"He's an accountant, but he comes from working-class people," said Iris. "Not a snob at all. He's shy with women—remember how he kept blushing being in the room with the two of us? But he's also on the move up, so Tillie will be more than happy to hitch her wagon to his rising star, or whatever that expression is."

"You make it all so mercenary," complained Gwen.

"I call it practical," declared Iris. "It's a step up for him, and she

keeps the books at her shop so she'll impress him with her econ-
omy as well as her looks. Now, on what ethereal plane did you put
them together?"

"I think she's a diamond in the rough," said Gwen. "Mister
Trower, underneath his shy exterior, can see the real value of people.
He will see hers."

"But you thought she was shady."

"I think she's had a hard life," said Gwen. "I think that she'll be
forever grateful to him for making her a better one."

"Then we are agreed."

"We are," said Gwen, reaching for her stationery. "Could you
pass me a sheet of carbon?"

"Press hard," intoned Iris. "You are making a copy."

Gwen wrote out a letter to Mister Trower, detailing how to contact Miss La Salle, then sealed the original in an envelope, which
she addressed and stamped. She put the copy in the cabinet with
Mister Trower's file.

"Earned our pay today," she commented.

"Which reminds me," said Iris, gathering Tillie's banknotes.
"Do you want a George or an Edward?"

"Which Edward?"

"The Eighth."

"George, then."

"Right. One for you, one for me, three for the kitty."

She handed a pound over to Gwen. Then she crouched under
her desk and slid open the false panel concealing their strongbox.
She unlocked it, let the three pounds fall into it, then relocked it
and closed the panel.

She straightened up, then looked at her watch.

"Shall we close up?" she asked. "No more appointments."

"Might as well," said Gwen.

They collected their coats and left, Iris locking the office
behind her.

"Walk with me as far as the park," Gwen asked as they emerged from the building.

"Gladly," said Iris.

They walked to Oxford Street, where there was a post box on the corner. Gwen popped the letter to Mister Trower inside, then set off to the west. Iris had to walk quickly to keep up with the taller woman, but Gwen noticed and slowed her pace.

"Thanks," said Iris.

She took a deep breath and looked up at the clear sky, then sighed.

"Here we are, two girls in Mayfair with the evening ahead of us. It's the height of the season, and we're both going home," she said. "How sad is that?"

"We're not girls anymore," commented Gwen.

"Neither are we old maids," said Iris.

"Speak for yourself," said Gwen.

"Stop that immediately," Iris said. "All right, say it's seven or eight years ago. What would you be doing right about now?"

"I'd be changing from a cocktail dress into an evening gown," said Gwen, looking dreamily out into the distance.

"Which one?"

"The Molyneux, I should think. It was made of crêpe-de-chine the colour of sea-foam, which brought out my eyes smashingly."

"And where would you be going?"

"Oh, to some ball or other. Lady Londonderry's, Lady Cunard's, maybe one of Mrs. Corrigan's bashes at the Dudley House. Ever go to those?"

"One," said Iris. "Had an encounter with the son of the American ambassador there. He was over visiting, an absolutely scrumptious lad. Fairbanks had thrown him a party, I think at Grosvenor House, but I missed that one. I spent half the party at Mrs. Corrigan's getting my date drunk enough for me to ditch him so I could slip off with the American."

"Did you succeed?"

"I can tell you nothing about the second half of the party."

"Naughty girl," said Gwen. "Which fiancé was that?"

"I was between fiancés at the time," said Iris. "I don't even remember who I came with. Someone rich enough to get me into the party, but too dreary for me to leave with. Oh, no! What is it?"

Tears were streaming down Gwen's cheeks.

"I was wearing that dress when I met Ronnie," she whispered.

"Oh, golly," said Iris, seizing her hands. "I didn't mean to—"

"No, no," said Gwen. "It was a lovely memory. I miss him so much."

"I know, darling," said Iris.

They came to the northeast corner of Hyde Park, where the Marble Arch stood proudly and incongruously in what was essentially a glorified roundabout. Batteries of anti-aircraft guns still remained in place on the park grounds, their barrels pointed at the eastern skies.

"I think I'll walk through the park while we still have the light," said Gwen.

"Be careful, dear," said Iris.

"I will. See you tomorrow."

"Gwen, let me find you someone," Iris said impulsively.

"I can't possibly—"

"It's been two years," urged Iris. "You can't keep on like this. No one will think the less of you if you begin a new chapter."

"I can't," said Gwen. "Let's keep helping others write their own books, all right?"

"All right," said Iris. "And remember our watchword: The world must be peopled!"

"The world must be peopled," echoed Gwen, smiling.

They went their separate ways, Gwen through the park, Iris heading north.

* * *

It was pleasant enough, Iris thought, to stroll through Marylebone with the air finally cooling down as the sun began to set. Her flat was in a brick block on Welbeck Street, just past Bentinck. She was on the third storey, which meant no balcony but some late morning sun if she chanced to be home on a late morning.

She climbed the stairs, turned her key in the lock, stepped inside, then paused, wrinkling her nose slightly.

There was an unfamiliar scent in the air. An eau de cologne, but not one she recognized.

She dropped her keys noisily into the dish on the table in the hall, the sound covering for her easing a stout cricket bat from the umbrella stand. She gripped the handle with two hands and stepped into the sitting room.

It was empty. Which, she realized uncomfortably, left only the bedroom.

She took a deep breath, then kicked the door open and sprang inside, ready to send the intruder's head across the boundary.

The man in her bed looked up at her, then at the bat.

"I thought your game was golf, Sparks," he said calmly, setting down the book he was reading when she came in.

"Left the mashie at Grand-Dad's," she returned, panting slightly. "You had better not have lost my place."

"*Traitor's Purse*," he intoned dramatically. "Campion with amnesia. Far-fetched from the start. Where've you been all day?"

"Work."

"You poor dear! Any business?"

"One new customer, one unlikely potential. How are you?"

"I am not quite certain yet. Are you going to put the bat down?"

"I haven't entirely given up on the idea of braining you."

"Fair enough. There is a present for you on the bureau."

She glanced over to see a small embossed box. Still holding the bat raised with her right hand, she opened the box and peeked inside.

"Vol de Nuit!" she exclaimed.

"Guerlain's back in production," he said.

"Lovely. I accept your offering, Andrew, and will place my bat gently on the floor as a gesture of good faith. Is that your cologne I've been smelling?"

"Yes. Thought I'd go back to it now that they're making it again. What do you think?"

She came over, sat on the bed and sniffed his neck, then rested her cheek on his bare chest and gazed up at him.

"It's nice enough," she pronounced. "But I like your natural scent better. When did you get in?"

"This morning."

"You should have told me. I could have met you at the airfield."

"First, I didn't fly into Croydon. Second, my comings and goings are not meant to be general knowledge."

"Your damn protocol plays havoc on a girl's nerves. You've been in Cologne and Paris, based on your shopping spree. Where else?"

"Can't tell you. Let me help you with that."

"Thanks. Does Poppy know you're back?"

"Rang her up. Told her I was exhausted from the flight and would be staying in town."

"Mistress before wife. I'm honoured."

"You're not my mistress. You're my lover."

"Same thing."

"Not at all. A mistress is in it for the money. A lover for love."

"You pay for the flat."

"So that there can be love."

"Does Poppy get a bottle of Vol de Nuit?"

"Wouldn't suit her. I got her Mitsouko."

"How very even-handed of you."

"I got her a smaller bottle."

"Now, you've made me love you again," she said, sliding under the covers next to him. "Are you, by the way?"

"Am I what?"

"Exhausted?"

"No," he said, pulling her to him. "But I hope to be."

CHAPTER 2

She opened her eyes to see him lying on his side looking at her, smiling when he saw she had come awake, that smile that still set her heart racing whenever she saw it. She started to say something, but he put a finger to her lips and she stopped. Then he opened his mouth and the blood came pouring out, pooling onto the bed, spilling over the sides, filling the room, drowning her . . .

Then she awoke for real, her heart pounding for all the wrong reasons, the twin bells on her alarm clock rattling away on the nightstand. She slapped at it repeatedly until it quieted.

Next to the clock was Ronnie's photograph in its silver frame. He wore the dress uniform of the Royal Fusiliers, and he had the same smile that he had in her dream.

That uniform hung in his wardrobe by the wall. It wasn't the one he wore when the mortar shell found him in Monte Cassino.

Two years, three months, and four days ago.

She hadn't had that dream in a while. She had thought she was over them. Maybe she should take one of Doctor Milford's powders.

But they interfered with her work, and she was a working woman, now.

So, up and at 'em, Gwennie, as Ronnie used to whisper when the baby started crying in the middle of the night.

The same baby, who was no longer a baby, who was running down the hallway, if footsteps were anything to go by. Towards her room.

She grabbed a tissue and quickly wiped away her tears. Then the door burst open and Little Ronnie leaped onto her bed into her embrace.

"Good morning, my darling," she said, covering his face with rapid kisses until he nearly went into hysterics.

"Good morning, Mummy," he chirped. "Agnes says we're going to the museum today. Can you come?"

"It sounds wonderful," said Gwen. "But Mummy has to go to work."

"Oh."

"You and Agnes will have a lovely time," promised Gwen. "And tonight, you tell me everything you learn about dinosaurs and bears and narwhals."

"What's a narwhal?"

"A creature that swims in the oceans with a sword for a nose," said Gwen.

"A nose-sword! Do they have duels?"

"Only in matters of honour," said Gwen. "Now, you go have a proper breakfast. It's a very big museum, and you need your strength."

"Yes, Mummy!"

He jumped off the bed.

"Wait!" commanded Gwen.

He stopped and turned and looked at her.

Ronnie's face. Sometimes, it was all she could do not to burst into tears when she saw him.

"Give Mummy a kiss," said Gwen. "Then you may go."

He jumped back onto the bed without hesitation and planted his lips on her cheek with a resounding smack. She hugged him, hugged him hard, then when he began to squirm, released him to the wild.

She washed and dressed, then went down the back steps to the breakfast room. Prudence, their cook, poked her head out of the kitchen.

"Good morning, Mrs. Bainbridge," she said. "What would you like?"

"Just tea and toast," she said, sitting in the seat by the window. "Is Lady Carolyne up?"

"Her Ladyship was at a dinner party last night," said Prudence. "I don't expect she'll be on her feet much before eleven."

"Thank you, Prudence."

Gwen tried to restrain her relief at not having to make polite conversation with her mother-in-law.

She picked up the *Guardian* and scanned the headlines. Trouble in Greece. Iranians protesting Soviet troops remaining on their soil. Agitation in Palestine. And rationing, rationing, always rationing. Stern platitudes from Atlee that left no end in sight, and labour troubles in the States threatened to slow down the vital shipments of wheat.

Prudence returned with her own personal shipment of wheat in the form of two slices of toast. Gwen picked one up.

"Prudence, how much does this weigh, do you think?" she asked.

"Loaf's a pound," Prudence said promptly. "We generally slice twelve to the loaf, and that's sixteen ounces to the pound, so about an ounce and what? A third, I suppose."

"So if they reduce the daily amount to nine ounces, as it seems they will, I may still have my toast and tea?"

"Yes, Ma'am."

"Maybe we should thin our slices down."

"I will have to ask Lady Carolyne before I do that, Miss. Unless you would like to."

"I think that Lady Carolyne will take the suggestion more seriously if coming from you than from me," said Gwen. "This is your bailiwick, after all. Don't tell her you spoke with me about it."

"Very good, Ma'am. Will there be anything else?"

"No. Thank you, Prudence."

She finished her breakfast, made some last-second adjustments to her hair, then topped it with a pale blue beret. She picked up her handbag, then walked out of their house into Kensington.

The dream bothered her. It meant something was wrong. Not in any predictive manner—she knew better than that—but something unpleasant was simmering just below the surface of her psyche, waiting to erupt.

It was the shock of Ronnie's death, they told her when she was strapped to that gurney in the sanitorium. The shock leaves traces behind. We can calm you down, they said. In time, they said. But there may be further episodes.

She was there for four months, and when she came out, Lord and Lady Bainbridge had assumed custody of her son, and it would take a court order to reverse that. The solicitor with whom she had consulted looked at the records of her stay in the sanitorium, then folded his hands and said, "Oh dear, oh dear, oh dear."

So she lived in the Bainbridge house, a very large, very well-appointed house indeed, and watched her son as he basked in the care of a governess and a tutor, and was allowed to interact with him as much as a mother might while having absolutely no maternal authority over his existence whatsoever. And she thought if she hadn't been driven mad before, this velvet prison might very well do the trick on its own.

Which is why, when a chance encounter with the impetuous Iris Sparks led to this preposterous idea to start a marriage bureau, she had leapt at the opportunity.

They had met at a wedding, of course. One of Ronnie's unit, and the groom and the best man, as well as many of the guests, wore the dress uniform of the Royal Fusiliers. A pavilion had been set up on the sward next to the church, and waiters stood with trays carrying glasses of champagne—real champagne, carried up from who knows what secret hoards. It was all she could do not to gulp hers down on the spot. She summoned her willpower, always tenuous in moments like these, and held the glass decorously in one gloved hand while the rest of the guests sauntered in. Tom Parkinson, the best man, stepped forward.

"Ladies and gentlemen," he said. "I have been with George through Dunkirk, Tunisia, and Italy. I have seen him charging through heavy machine-gun fire to take one hilltop after another from the Eye-Ties, and never have I seen him so nervous as I did this morning prior to walking down that aisle."

There was an appreciative chuckle from the assemblage. He turned to the bride.

"And never have I seen him conquer anything more worth conquering," he said. "Emily, whatever miracle brought the two of you together makes me believe that hope has been restored from the horrors we have been through. I wish you all the happiness that you deserve. Ladies and gentlemen—I give you Captain and Mrs. George Bascombe. To the bride and groom!"

"To the bride and groom!" echoed the crowd.

"To the bride and groom!" Gwen whispered softly.

She noticed a short, intense brunette woman looking at her. She was wearing a royal blue dress with padded shoulders, cut just above the knee. She saw Gwen returning her gaze, and walked over.

"Apologies," said the woman. "I was admiring your gown. Absolutely smashing."

"Thanks," said Gwen. "Haven't worn it in years. Slipped right into it without a struggle."

"Lucky you," said the woman. "I've been waiting for them to get on with the toast so we can start drinking properly. I'm trying to remember how many glasses of champagne I can have before I start speaking honestly."

"Ah," said Gwen. "I should stop at two, then. Three glasses usually do me in, and I have a few inches on you."

"Pity," said the woman. "I'm on the second now."

"Still safely in the throes of mendacity?"

"I think so. I'm Iris, by the way. Iris Sparks."

"Gwendolyn Bainbridge. Call me Gwen."

"Nice to meet you. Bride or groom?"

"A bit of both, really," said Gwen. "I'm the miracle."

"Excuse me?"

"What Tom said—a miracle brought them together. It was I."

"Well done, then," said Iris, tapping her glass against Gwen's in tribute. "I must ask, how did you see them as right for each other? Don't get me wrong, I love Em, but she's always been the horsey sort, riding to hounds in the country and all that. George is a brave lad, certainly, but he's never been part of that world. His people are factory folks. Pots of money, but still, not the horsey sort at all. And the height difference—did you think she needed a jockey?"

"Are you sure that's not your third?" asked Gwen.

"Yes, that was catty, wasn't it? It's been a while since I've had any decent champagne. I shouldn't be behaving badly just yet. All right then. Why him for her and her for him?"

"I knew George before the war," said Gwen. "He wanted to be an artist. Did you know that?"

"I never knew him before they got engaged."

"Well, George has an eye for the beauty that lies underneath. Emily never saw herself as beautiful. She's always been taller than everyone, and it made her feel awkward about herself. I thought George would see her, really see her, and that she had never been seen like that and would completely blossom under his gaze. Look at her now. Would you ever have said that she was a beauty before today?"

They turned and looked at the newlyweds who were feeding each other cake. Emily was laughing, and seemed to take in the sunlight and turn it into something even more golden.

"You're right," said Iris. "Never saw her like this. I don't think anyone did. Besides you."

"And now George," said Gwen, starting to sniffle.

She grabbed at her handbag and pulled out a handkerchief.

"Damn," she said, as the tears ran down her cheeks. "Weddings. Always get me."

"Here, let me," said Iris.

She took over the dabbing and effected some quick repairs to the makeup.

"Thanks," said Gwen. "I must look a horror."

"Your horror is better than most of my good days," said Iris. "Do you know, I was at your wedding?"

"Were you? I don't recognize your name."

"June of '39, wasn't it? I was a guest of the official invitee. My first fiancé was some second cousin once removed of your husband. Ronnie Bainbridge is your—oh, no!"

She had set off the waterworks again.

"Oh, golly, I didn't mean—damn, I've put my foot into it, haven't I? When?"

"March, '44," said Gwen shortly, wiping her eyes. "Monte Cassino. He was in the Fusiliers with Tom and George."

"I am so sorry," said Iris. "I didn't know. There have been so many."

"It's all right. His cousin didn't tell you?"

"I lost track of him after we broke the engagement."

"Yes, you did say 'first fiancé,' didn't you?" said Gwen, the tears subsiding at last. She gave her eyes one last wipe, then tucked the handkerchief into her sleeve for quicker access.

"Right, the fiancé once removed," said Iris.

"There was another?"

"One or two more," said Iris. "Yet here I am, going stag. Or doe, I suppose."

"No one in your life currently?" asked Gwen.

"No."

Gwen looked at her keenly. "No," she said finally. "I don't think that's true. Are you a prevaricator by nature, or is it a hobby?"

"Still on my second glass," said Iris lightly. "Shall I have another and tell you the whole sordid tale?"

Gwen shook her head. "I'm sorry, it's really none of my business," she said. "I was sizing you up to see if I knew anyone suitable. I have this compulsion to match people up."

"Have there been others besides George and Em?"

"Oh, yes. I've got a knack. My goodness, I've been rattling on about myself, haven't I? Where do you know Emily from?"

"Boarding school and Cambridge," said Iris. "Lost touch during the festivities of the last few years, but she reached out to me after the engagement."

"Really? Why then?"

"Truth be told, she wanted me to do a little quiet digging into George's background to make sure there were no family skeletons lying in wait."

"Is that something you normally do?"

"Well, no, but I'm naturally nosy and I've got some helpful connections."

"Friends in high places?"

"And low. The latter are sometimes more useful."

"I take it there were no skeletons."

"None. Not even the tiniest phalange. He's one of the good ones."

"I sensed that," said Gwen.

"Then we have approval from both your ethereal plane and my jaundiced underworld," said Iris.

"We make a good team," said Gwen, holding up her glass.

"Good on us," said Iris, tapping hers against it and finishing it. She glanced at the bar reluctantly. "I had better pretend I have some self-control. Shall we get some cake?"

"By all means," said Gwen. "Would you care to meet up sometime after today?"

"I would be delighted," said Iris, pulling a small notebook and pencil out of her handbag and handing it to her.

They exchanged numbers, then headed for the cake.

They had lunch two days later, and by the end of it had planned The Right Sort. Neither could remember who was the initiator of the idea, which is why they both knew it was perfect.

Gwen didn't need the money, although it was nice to have. She needed the occupation to fill the empty hours that she once hoped would be spent with a loving husband raising their perfect child.

Children, if all had gone to plan, but the war had other plans, didn't it?

Three months later, it was with these gloomy thoughts that she climbed the four flights to their office, to find that Iris had got there first and was busy scribbling away on her pad.

"Good mornin', pardner," she drawled as Gwen hung her beret on the coat-tree. "Nice of you to mosey in."

"I am two minutes early," she said. "Why are you a cowboy today?"

"I saw a Western last night," said Iris. "It put me in the mood."

"What are you working on?"

"I am indexing our clientele by height," she said. "Our Miss La Salle was so insistent about it. It got me to thinking we should list everyone by physical characteristics as well as everything else."

"I suppose so," said Gwen, sitting behind her desk.

"You don't sound enthusiastic," said Iris.

"Just tired," said Gwen. "I had a bad night."

"What was the matter?"

"I dreamed about Ronnie," said Gwen. "It was a nightmare. It felt like a premonition."

"Of what?"

"If I knew, I'd do something to stop it," said Gwen. "It's all silly nonsense, I know."

"My Auntie Elizabeth used to have dreams that she thought were prophecies," said Iris thoughtfully. "She'd dream about a goat falling over a stile, or some such, and cry, 'There will be calamity! Mark my words!' And maybe the next week someone would bark their knee on a car door, and she would scream, 'Aha!'"

"I fail to see the connection between the two," said Gwen.

"Oh, there absolutely was none," said Iris. "Which is why I'm saying . . ."

"Someone's coming," Gwen interrupted her.

"Prophecy?"

"No," said Gwen. "I can hear them on the stairs."

"Oh, yes," said Iris, sitting up straight. "More than one. Curious."

A man appeared in the doorway wearing a brown wool suit. He had brown hair, greying at the temples, matched by an equally grey mustache.

He was followed by a younger man dressed similarly. A good-looking fellow, Gwen thought, if he smiled. He certainly wasn't smiling at the moment. The two of them were followed by a uniformed constable.

She glanced over at her partner, who was staring at the second man with an expression of bemused shock.

She knows him, realized Gwen. Well, best take the initiative.

She rose to her feet, letting her height impress them.

"Good morning, gentlemen," she said in her politest tone. "I am Mrs. Gwendolyn Bainbridge. How may we help you?"

"Then she's Sparks?" asked the older man.

"She is," said Sparks. "Who is he?"

"Detective Superintendent Philip Parham, Central Office, CID," he said, flashing his identification card. "These are Detective Sergeant Kinsey and Police Constable Larkin."

"I am so pleased to make your acquaintances," said Mrs.

Bainbridge. "I take it that none of you are looking for a wife at the moment."

"Hardly," said Parham. "We're here about a Matilda La Salle, better known as Tillie La Salle. I believe the two of you know the young lady."

"A client of ours," said Mrs. Bainbridge. "Has she made a complaint?"

"She has cause for one," said Parham. "But I'm afraid she's in no position to file it. She was murdered last night."

"What?" exclaimed Mrs. Bainbridge.

"Oh, the poor girl," said Sparks. "What happened? Do you know who did it?"

"Not yet," said Parham. "We came here hoping to find out."

"Here? Why here?" asked Mrs. Bainbridge.

"Because you may have introduced her to the man who killed her," said Parham. "So we'll have to have a look at your files."

"Our files? Oh, no, that's quite impossible. You shan't," said Mrs. Bainbridge. She stood in front of the file cabinet. She wondered for a moment if it would be more effective if she flung her arms to its sides to protect it further, but settled instead for folding them in front of her while assuming an expression of what she hoped was stern reprimand.

"Shan't?" repeated Parham. "She actually said 'shan't,' didn't she, Kinsey?"

"She did, sir," said Kinsey.

"Why shan't we?" asked Parham.

"Our clientele come to us on matters of great personal intimacy," she said. "We regard these matters as confidential. So you may neither willy nor nilly ransack these people's lives."

Parham stepped between the desks to face her, which had the additional effect of trapping her in the small space behind hers. The other two policemen watched.

"Constable Larkin," he said.

"Sir," replied Larkin.

"Mrs. Bainbridge has brought up confidentiality as a barrier to our investigation."

"So it would seem, sir."

"This seems an opportune moment to test your knowledge of confidentiality as it applies to police investigations. Are you up to the task?"

"I believe I am, sir."

"Name the various forms of confidentiality."

"Well, sir, there's the confessional."

"Very good, Constable. We may extend that to religion in general."

"Yes, sir. That seems fair."

"Now, do you observe any confessional here?"

"I do not, sir."

"Any vestments on the ladies standing before us? Any of the more obvious accoutrements of holiness?"

"No, sir. But they might be one of those modern religions."

"Constable, you rightfully rebuke me for my narrow view of the topic. Mrs. Bainbridge, are the two of you in fact running a religious order here?"

"I'm afraid not," she replied. "Perhaps we should."

"Then that's out. Constable, what else?"

"Medical privilege, sir."

"I see no indications of any such practices here, Constable," said Parham. "Although one might make the case that they treat maladies of the heart."

"You're enjoying this, aren't you?" remarked Mrs. Bainbridge.

"Indeed I am, Mrs. Bainbridge. Next, Constable?"

"Er, I believe that attorneys and their clients have that special relationship."

"They do, they do, Constable," beamed Parham. "You are doing exceedingly well. And once again, the lack of a legal license on display would rule that out. Now, the final one."

"It's on the tip of my tongue," he said. "But I cannot think of it."

"Come, come, Constable. The most common one."

"Ah, yes. The marriage bed, sir."

"Precisely. And in fact, the least likely one, given the professed occupation of these ladies. If they were married to their clients, then it would be rotten luck for all the poor sods who come in here expecting matrimonial opportunity."

"And bigamy, sir."

"That, too, Constable."

He turned back to Mrs. Bainbridge.

"Therefore, I must ask you to step aside, Mrs. Bainbridge," he said, no longer in a bantering mode. "Any further obstruction will be regarded—"

"My father-in-law is Lord Harold Bainbridge," she said. "He would take it very badly indeed—"

"Is Lord Harold Bainbridge affiliated with the London Metropolitan Police?" asked Parham.

"Well, no. But he's tremendously influential."

"Not with me, he's not."

"Excuse me," said Iris. "Would you all mind keeping it down for a moment? I have our solicitor on the telephone."

They turned to look at her sitting calmly at her desk, the receiver against her ear.

"Hello," she said. "Is that you, Sir Geoffrey? It's Sparks. Iris Sparks, yes. How are you? It's good of you to come to our aid so quickly. We are having a bit of a contretemps with the local constabulary. No, no, I didn't do anything. This time. They're investigating a murder case, and they wish to poke through our files sans warrant. Yes, I suppose it does sound rather exciting from your end, but we are in the thick of it. What do you advise?"

She listened for a moment.

"That's an excellent question," she said. "I shall ask."

She placed her hand over the receiver.

"Detective Superintendent, are Mrs. Bainbridge and I suspects?" she asked.

"Certainly not," said Parham.

"Is he telling the truth, Mrs. Bainbridge?" asked Sparks.

"He is," she said, studying his face so intently that he shivered for a moment.

"Sir Geoffrey? He says that we are not. He sounded very firm about it. I'm inclined to take him at his word. You do. Very good, Sir Geoffrey. Thank you for your time. Give my love to Samantha."

She hung up, then nodded at Mrs. Bainbridge.

"He believes that a proper warrant would have been the better part of practice," she said. "But in light of the urgency of the matter, he suggests that we assist them in their inquiries."

"Very well," said Mrs. Bainbridge. "Detective Superintendent, how may we help you?"

Parham turned to the others and raised his eyebrows in exasperation. Kinsey shrugged and Larkin remained stone-faced. Parham turned back to Mrs. Bainbridge.

"We need to know the names and addresses of all the men you set her up with," he said. "And view any correspondence."

She turned, opened the top cabinet, and pulled out the file for Dickie Trower.

"She signed with us Monday a week ago," she said, handing it to him. "This was our first match for her. But I doubt that he's your man. There's not a speck of evil or violence in him. I will vouch for him myself."

"So will I," said Sparks.

"Unfortunately, we must be the judges of that," said Parham. "I must direct you to have no contact with him until we have completed our investigation. Thank you, ladies."

He handed the file to PC Larkin, who wrote out a receipt and handed it to Gwen.

"One more thing," said Parham. "You list yourselves as proprietors on your sign."

"We do," said Mrs. Bainbridge.

"A term reserved for men, I believe."

"Proprietresses is so awkward to say," said Sparks.

"And proprietrix sounds vaguely—illicit, don't you think?" asked Mrs. Bainbridge.

Kinsey, standing behind Parham, smiled briefly.

"Well, I don't like it," said Parham.

"We shall endeavour to carry on under the weight of your disapproval," said Mrs. Bainbridge, humbly casting her eyes downwards. "Good day, gentlemen. Good hunting."

"Detective Superintendent," said Sparks. "Might I have a word with the Detective Sergeant for a moment?"

Parham glanced at Kinsey, who shrugged noncommittally. "Be quick about it," he said, and he and the constable left.

Iris looked at Kinsey for a long moment. He stood there, expressionless.

Smooth man, thought Gwen. And he is choking on his anger under that smooth demeanour.

"Hello, Mike," said Iris.

"Sparks," he returned.

Gwen sat down quietly and watched.

"I never thought I'd run into you in your professional capacity," said Iris.

"I never thought I'd run into you at all," he said. "Complete coincidence, or the vicissitudes of Fate. Our squad was up on the rota. How long have you been at this?"

"Three months."

"Doing well, is it?"

"Tolerably well."

"Hmph," he said, looking around. "The irony of you brokering marriages does not escape me."

"I knew you were going to say something along those lines," she said. "Speaking of which, I hear congratulations are in order."

"You know," he said warily.

"Beryl Stansfield."

"You can leave her name out of this and all future conversations," he snapped. "I will not have you—"

"I was going to say well done," she said softly. "If I had been given the task of finding you the best possible match, Beryl would have been at the top of the list."

"Oh," he said, more confused than mollified. "Well. Thanks, then. Better than the last one, certainly."

"She certainly is," agreed Iris.

"Is that it?"

"That's it," said Iris. "I am glad to see you doing so well. I mean that."

"I'd best be off," he said, stepping to the doorway.

"Mike?"

"What, Sparks?" he said.

"How was Miss La Salle killed?"

"Stabbed," he said. "Once through the heart. It was neatly done."

"Stabbed through the heart," she repeated.

"Yes," he said. "Which is why I disagree with the Detective Superintendent about ruling you out as a suspect."

Iris smiled at him, a hard, brittle smile that made him shrink a little.

"Go catch your murderer, Mike," she said. "And don't come back here until you've learned better manners, or I'll tell your mother that you've been bothering innocent girls."

"I'll give Mrs. Bainbridge the benefit of the doubt," he said. "But you, sweetheart, are no innocent."

He turned and walked out.

Gwen looked at Iris, who was still staring at the vacated doorway.

"And that was—" began Gwen.

"Fiancé Number Two," said Iris.

"The One Who Got Away."

"Something like that," said Iris, sitting back down.

"He doesn't like you."

"Not without reason," said Iris.

"Do you want to talk about it?"

"Can't," said Iris. "War stories."

"Which you will never tell."

"Someday, when we're old," said Iris. "And probably not even then."

"What did you think of Parham?"

"Not my type," said Iris. "Likes to show off to the subordinates and bully women. Didn't strike me as a man with much real imagination."

"He seems like someone who forms a theory first, and then goes looking for facts to fit it," observed Gwen.

"Mike, on the other hand, has an imagination," said Iris. "Too much of one, as I recall."

"Iris," said Gwen. "Tell me this isn't our fault. Promise me that we are not in any way, shape, or form responsible for that poor girl's death."

"How would we be?"

"If Dickie Trower did it, and we introduced them—"

"He's a false trail," said Iris. "We both know he wouldn't hurt a fly. He's just the first lead and the easiest one. They'll rule him out by tomorrow morning, mark my words."

"But if we're wrong—"

"We aren't."

"How can you be so certain? How much do we truly know about people after just one interview?"

"More than most, dear," replied Iris. "I did follow up with some informal vetting when we met him, and he came through with flying colours. More important, you thought him a decent chap, and I have absolute faith in your perceptions."

"There's always a first time," said Gwen. "Damn. What if this was what my dream was about?"

"Piffle. In any case, there is nothing we can do, so let's see what their investigation turns up."

It only proved to be a matter of hours. Both ladies looked up as a clatter of footsteps approached from the stairwell. Then Kinsey, Larkin, and a third man burst through the doorway.

"Hands off that typewriter," commanded Kinsey, pointing at Sparks who froze, fingers poised over the keys.

"It's the Drudgery Police, Gwen," she said out the side of her mouth. "We're done for!"

"Thank goodness you got here in time, gentlemen," said Mrs. Bainbridge. "We were in danger of actually getting some work done today."

"Move away from the desk, Sparks," said Kinsey.

"What on earth for?" exclaimed Sparks.

"We need to fingerprint your machine. Godfrey, take Miss Sparks's exemplars."

"You will do nothing of the kind!" she protested as the third man opened a leather-bound box and removed a printed form and an ink pad. "Would you mind explaining this?"

"We have arrested Richard Trower for the murder of Matilda La Salle," said Kinsey.

"I don't believe it," said Mrs. Bainbridge. "Has he confessed?"

"I'm not at liberty to say," said Kinsey.

"That means no," said Sparks. "Upon what evidence have you charged him?"

"We found a bloody knife under his mattress," said Kinsey.

"And have you—I don't know what the proper terms are," said Mrs. Bainbridge.

"Matched it to her blood type," said Sparks.

"Our initial tests were positive," said Kinsey.

"You still haven't said what this has to do with my poor Bar-Let," said Sparks. "I will vouch for her. She's been to Cambridge, served valiantly during the war, and has done yeoman's work—"

"Yeowoman's work," corrected Mrs. Bainbridge.

"Yeowoman's work here. Plus, she can't walk. It's a tragic story."

"You promised us complete co-operation in this matter," Kinsey pointed out.

"We were told that we weren't suspects," said Mrs. Bainbridge.

"There's another piece of evidence," said Kinsey. "Godfrey?"

"Yes, sir," said the third man.

He took a small jar of white powder from his kit.

"You've been typing today?" he asked Sparks.

"Obviously," she replied.

"Won't bother with the keys, then," he said.

He sprinkled the powder liberally on the sides and back of the typewriter, then blew off the excess with a small, rubber bulb. Dozens of prints, smeared and overlapping, covered the surface.

"I really ought to clean her once in a while," sighed Sparks. "Never occurred to me. Sorry, old girl."

Godfrey pulled out a camera and photographed each side.

"Right," he said, sliding the ink pad over to Sparks. "Hold out your right hand first."

He took each finger, rolled it in the ink, then onto the rectangles designated for each digit.

"You're quite gentle with a lady's hands," observed Sparks. "You could take a few lessons from him, Mike."

"As long as you're co-operative, I'm gentle," said Godfrey, repeating the process with her left. "I've broken a finger or two in my time with less co-operative people."

Sparks held up her blackened fingertips for Mrs. Bainbridge's inspection.

"What do you think?" she asked.

"That colour doesn't go with your outfit," said Mrs. Bainbridge.

"Now, Mike, what is this all about?" asked Sparks. "What is this evidence?"

"Your Mister Trower claimed he never had his meeting with the late Miss La Salle," said Kinsey. "He had arranged it, but then he received a letter saying it was canceled."

"A letter? Who from?" asked Mrs. Bainbridge.

Kinsey gestured to Larkin, who removed a manila folder from an attaché case he was carrying. He opened it on the desk. Inside were a sheet of stationery and an opened envelope.

"That's our letterhead," said Sparks, peering at them.

"Mrs. Bainbridge, is this your signature?" asked Kinsey.

She looked at it closely.

"It is a close facsimile," she said. "But it isn't mine."

"How can you tell?"

"Because I never signed that letter. I've never signed any typed letter. I've never used that wretched machine."

"Now, now," said Sparks. "Don't be mean to my Bar-Let. But she's correct, Mike. Anything from me is typed, because it's more businesslike, and my handwriting is atrocious, as you well recall."

"I do," said Kinsey. "So were some of the sentiments expressed."

"Mrs. Bainbridge, on the other hand, has exquisite penmanship, the mark of her superior breeding and upbringing."

"Thank you," said Mrs. Bainbridge. "So, every letter leaving my desk is hand-written. That letter did not come from either one of us."

"But the stationery did," said Kinsey.

"Stolen, perhaps," said Sparks.

"Would you mind providing a typed letter for comparison?" asked Kinsey.

Sparks looked at the half-completed letter in the Bar-Let, sighed, then unscrolled it.

"I'll have to do it fresh," she grumbled. "I can never line them up properly once they're removed."

"You're assisting Scotland Yard in a murder investigation," Kinsey reminded her.

"Yes, yes, I know," she said, rolling a fresh sheet in. "You want 'A quick brown fox?'"

"All the letters, capital and small," he said.

She typed them out rapidly, then whipped out the sheet and handed it to him. He placed it next to the one in the folder.

"Mister Godfrey, if you wouldn't mind," said Kinsey.

Godfrey reached into his case and produced a magnifying glass.

"I say, Holmes," murmured Mrs. Bainbridge.

The technician pored over the newly typed sheet, then over the letter.

"I would say they both came from the same machine, sir," he said.

"May I?" asked Sparks, holding out her hand.

Godfrey looked at Kinsey, who nodded. He handed the magnifying glass to Sparks, who looked at the letter in the folder.

"The nick in the capital *R*; the smudge in the lower-case *e*, that matches," she said. "And—yes!—the wobble in the *w*. It's a fair cop. My Bar-Let is the culprit. But I never typed this, and neither did Mrs. Bainbridge."

"How did Trower duplicate her signature? Has he received other correspondence from her?"

"Certainly," said Mrs. Bainbridge. "You saw them in our file."

"So Trower would have had a facsimile to work with," observed Kinsey.

"So might anyone if they were using our office," said Mrs. Bainbridge. "All they would have to do is go into our filing cabinet and take one to copy."

"An excellent point," said Kinsey. "Godfrey, print the filing cabinet. And you might as well take exemplars from Mrs. Bainbridge while you're at it."

"Oh, dear," said Mrs. Bainbridge in dismay. "I just did my nails this morning."

Sparks smirked as Godfrey inked her partner's fingertips.

"This does wash off, doesn't it?" asked Mrs. Bainbridge as he rolled them on the form.

"Eventually, Ma'am," he said. "It takes some scrubbing. A little alcohol helps."

"In so many things," said Sparks.

He dusted and photographed the filing cabinet, then stepped back, satisfied.

"I don't understand why Mister Trower would go to all of this trouble," said Bainbridge, staring disconsolately at her blackened fingertips. "He could have just said she called him to cancel."

"He needed a plausible reason to say he never met up with her," said Kinsey.

"Did he tell you that?" asked Sparks.

"He hasn't told us anything."

"Good for him," said Sparks.

"Are you siding with a murderer?" asked Kinsey. "Not that it would surprise me in your case."

"I'm siding with Dickie Trower," said Sparks. "I still don't think he did it."

"Who else would know that you had set him up with Miss La Salle?" asked Kinsey.

"Anyone she told," said Mrs. Bainbridge. "She must have friends or family in whom she would confide. Have you spoken to them?"

"No," said Kinsey. "We found your information in her handbag at the scene, along with a note in her handwriting with the time and place for the date. He must have contacted her by telephone."

"If someone went to all the trouble to send himself a letter establishing a weak alibi, then he would have been smart enough to get rid of the knife," said Sparks.

"Maybe," said Kinsey. "But murderers, in my experience, tend not to be the clearest of thinkers."

"Whose prints are on the letter?" Mrs. Bainbridge asked Godfrey.

"Not my department," said Godfrey. "We have a specialist."

"A dactyloscopist," said Sparks, savouring the word as it rolled off her tongue.

"Very good, Miss," said Godfrey. "Not many know that."

"You'll find that Miss Sparks likes to show off," said Kinsey. "She thinks her brain is better than most others."

"If you're through, may we clean up?" asked Mrs. Bainbridge. "It's disconcerting to the clientele when one's office looks like a crime scene."

"We're done," said Kinsey.

"Mike, I'd like a quick word with you," said Sparks. "Alone."

"Where alone?"

"Come with me," she ordered.

He followed her into the hallway, then down to the landing just below.

"What is it?" he asked when they stopped.

"I need to have your word that our fingerprints will be destroyed after you rule us out," she said.

"Left yours on another crime scene somewhere?" he asked.

"I'm serious, Mike," she replied, not taking the bait. "I can't have mine on file."

"Why not?"

"I can't tell you."

"Oh, there it is," he sighed. "Your explanation for so much of your life. I'm beginning to think they really were on a body some-where. Perhaps more than one."

"I'm asking you to trust me on this, Mike. Please."

"Trust with me, once destroyed, is difficult to regain, Iris."

"Ah, you do remember my first name. I was beginning to wonder."

"I have been trying to forget everything about you," he said wearily.

"No one forgets me," she said. "Will you promise to destroy our fingerprints?"

"I can't make that commitment."

"Mike, I am asking as a favour to me."

"Oh, that's lovely," he said, laughing bitterly. "Your days of ask-ing favours have long vanished."

"Well, then we're finished here."

They walked back into the office. Mrs. Bainbridge raised an eye-brow slightly in question. Sparks shook her head.

"I guess this is farewell, then," said Mrs. Bainbridge. "I would offer to shake your hands, but I don't want to get ink all over them."

"We'll forego the niceties," said Sparks. "Good-bye, gentlemen. Come again when you have more red herrings to chase."

"Thank you for your assistance, ladies," said Kinsey.

"Good-bye," said Godfrey.

They left. Iris waited until the constabulary clatter faded down the stairs and out of the building.

"Toss me the key, would you?" she said. "I need to get these stains off my fingers."

Gwen pulled the lavatory key and threw it to her. She stared moodily into space until Iris returned, contemplating her finger-tips.

"Here's the smell of the ink still!" cried Iris. "All the perfumes of Arabia will not sweeten this little hand! Do we have any perfumes of Arabia, by the way?"

"None," said Gwen, taking the key from her. "My turn."

"Take this," said Iris, tossing her a small bottle of nail varnish remover.

She walked down the hall to the lavatory, unlocked it, then scrubbed as hard as she could until the ink was gone. Her fingertips looked red and raw when she was done. Looking at them, she had a sudden impulse to jam her nails into her arms until they bled. She gripped the sides of the sink, her breath coming in shuddering gasps. She held on until the attack subsided, then splashed some cold water on her face and neck.

The face that stared back from the mirror looked like a dead woman. She took a deep breath, pinched her cheeks to give them some colour, then walked back.

She was halfway there when she remembered that she hadn't locked the lavatory door. It was silly, taking these precautions, but they had been drilled into her by Mister MacPherson, the custodian, so she went back and locked it. The physical act of turning the key set her mind to work, and she walked slowly back to the office, pursuing the train of thought.

She heard her partner's voice speaking softly as she reached the door. Iris was on the telephone. She signaled for silence when she saw Gwen in the doorway.

"Yes. Yes, that would be fine," she said. "No, we certainly don't want that matter coming to light. Thank you so much. Yes, we must do that soon. Good to hear your voice as well. Good-bye, sir."

She hung up, then smiled.

"What was that all about?" asked Gwen.

"I wanted to make sure our fingerprints were destroyed once they've eliminated us," said Iris. "I had to go over Mike's head. Several heads over his head, in fact."

"He won't like that," said Gwen.

"No, he won't," said Iris, "but his happiness is no longer my charge."

"He seemed a solid sort," commented Gwen. "A good man in a difficult job."

"He's solid enough," agreed Iris. "Solid to the point of rigidity. He needs to be more flexible if he's to rise in this world."

"So you think Dickie Trower is innocent," said Gwen.

"I do," said Iris. "God help him, because the police certainly won't."

"Then we should help him," said Gwen. "We should find out who really did it."

CHAPTER 3

W e should do nothing of the sort," said Iris. "We'd be inter-
fering in a police investigation. We are not equipped—"

"You are," said Gwen.

"I most certainly am not. What gave you that idea?"

"You're smart. Much smarter than most. And you know a great deal about many things that would help us find the truth of this matter."

"You're daft, my dear," began Iris, then she stopped as Gwen's face flushed. "Oh, God. Forgive me, please. I know you hate to be called names."

"No, no," said Gwen, breathing slowly to calm herself. "I'm being—sensitive. One of my faults."

"One of your strengths, rather," said Iris. "*Sensitive* is certainly a word no one has ever applied to me. I'm the proverbial bull in the china shop."

"Cow," said Gwen.

"I've been called that a few times in other contexts," said Iris. "I wonder why only bulls qualify for that expression?"

"Because males blunder about and do more damage," said Gwen. "A cow in a china shop would look at the lovely patterns and think about having some tea. With milk. Look, here's a thing that bothers me. That stationery was ours. How did whoever forged that letter get in here?"

"Picked the lock," Iris said promptly. "The lock on our office door isn't that difficult if you know what you're doing."

"You could pick it, couldn't you?" asked Gwen.

"Er, maybe," said Iris.

"You can," Gwen stated confidently. "Part of that war-time training you never talk about? Or was that at Cambridge as well?"

"I can't—"

"You can't answer that, I know," said Gwen. "So, our murderer has both forgery and lock-picking amongst his skills. Is that a common combination in your experience?"

"Not usually," replied Iris. Then she shot Gwen a dirty look. "In my experience," she repeated, "your interrogation skills can be impressive. You've got more out of me than anyone."

"I see you more than anyone," said Gwen. "I know you better, even with your secrets. So, who would have done this? Who could have killed that poor girl?"

"We don't know enough about her to speculate," said Iris. "My instinct would be a jealous lover."

"Mine as well. Which means we need to find out more about Miss La Salle."

"No, we do not. It's not our business."

"If they hang Dickie Trower, will you rest easy in that belief? We must investigate."

"My goodness," said Iris, staring at her in astonishment. "When did you turn into Bulldog Drummond?"

"It's the right thing to do. And I can't do it without you."

"No," said Iris. "And that is my last word on the subject. I have a letter to retype, and a typewriter to clean and console, and a business to run."

"Which reminds me—we should return Miss La Salle's fee to her family."

"Oh, hell!" cried Iris in chagrin.

"You know that we should."

"Yes, yes," said Iris. "It's absolutely proper. I wish that she hadn't been our only new customer in the last week and a half. And I wish I hadn't celebrated that fact by treating myself to a night out."

"Are our funds so short?" asked Gwen in concern.

"Well, we still haven't received our marriage fee from the Cornwalls," said Iris. "In fact, that was the very letter I was working upon when we were so rudely interrupted."

"They still haven't paid? Did you not send them the Inquiry Polite?"

"A week ago," replied Iris, rolling a fresh sheet of paper into the typewriter. "I am now working on the Rebuke Stern, but I have a bad feeling about them. They both seemed dodgy."

"Which is why we thought they would suit each other," remembered Gwen. "What comes next if the Rebuke Stern produces nothing? The Threat Litigious?"

"I was thinking that we should go straight to Sally," said Iris, typing away furiously.

"Oh, dear. Not Sally."

"You disapprove?"

"You know how I feel about Sally. Sally unnerves me."

"Sally unnerves everyone," said Iris. "That's the point of Sally."

"Promise me you won't resort to Sally until we see the results of the Rebuke Stern," said Gwen.

"I promise," said Iris.

She finished the letter, signed it with what she hoped was an angry signature, then sealed it in an envelope. She held it in her hand for a moment after she affixed the stamp.

"Did you notice the postmark?" she asked thoughtfully.

"What postmark?" asked Gwen.

"On the fake letter to Dickie. It wasn't from around here. It was from the Croydon Post Office."

Gwen thumbed through her file box and produced Dickie Trower's card.

"He lives in Croydon," she said. "What do you make of that?"

"If he wanted to fake a letter to himself as a plausible excuse for breaking the date, he'd be more likely to mail it in his own neighbourhood," said Iris. "That would make certain it was delivered more quickly."

"Do you think the police will have come to that conclusion already?"

"Most likely," said Iris.

Gwen looked dolefully at the fingerprints and powder covering the filing cabinet.

"We have no cleaning supplies," she noted. "I'm going to borrow some from Mister MacPherson."

She went down the steps, lost in thought, and sought out MacPherson's rooms in the basement. A sporadic trail of bare yellow bulbs buzzing in their sockets lit the hallway and the doors concealing the boiler and the electricals. Gwen had only been down here twice, the first time being when the custodian had given them the tour of the building and insisted on showing them the equipment stored for its maintenance. Equipment that she almost never saw put to actual use since they had moved in.

She also knew there was a thriving community of rats down there, and she hoped to make her visit short.

She came to MacPherson's door—badly in need of painting, but who would care to inspect it? It did have an actual brass plaque, with "Angus MacPherson, Senior Custodian" engraved on it.

She was unaware of the existence of any junior custodian during their tenure there. Perhaps he had been taken by rats, or lived some Renfieldian existence in the shadows behind the boiler.

She rapped lightly on the door. There was no reply. She knocked again more firmly, and there was a sudden strangled cry and a crash.

She went through the door quickly to find the old man getting up from the floor beside a camp cot at the rear of the room.

"Don't you know better than to disturb a man when he's sleeping?" he roared.

"My apologies," said Gwen. "I didn't know that was on your agenda."

"For future reference, I have a bit of a kip in the late morning," he said. "I am not to be disturbed then except for the direst of emergencies."

"Duly noted," said Gwen. "I confess that this is not such an occasion."

"Social visit, then?" asked MacPherson.

She thought that she detected a hint of hopefulness in the question.

"I'm afraid not," she said. "I was wondering if I might borrow some cleaning supplies. Nothing too toxic or industrial, please."

"Cleaning supplies?" he repeated. "What's the nature of the befoulment of my property?"

"Your property?"

"Mine to manage. Was there an accident?"

"No. We had a visit from the police."

"The police?" he exclaimed, his eyes narrowing in suspicion. "I thought you were running a respectable establishment."

"We are," said Gwen. "But one of our clients—well, that's neither here nor there. Do you have anything suitable for cleaning metal surfaces?"

He went over to a shelf holding a number of spray bottles and selected one. Then he plucked a rag from a hook on the wall and handed them both to her. She accepted the rag gingerly, wondering if it might more likely transfer grime to a surface than remove it.

There was an array of keys hanging from hooks below the shelf.

"You have a spare set for our office?" she asked.

"For every office," he said. "Why?"

"In case I ever mislay mine," she said. "It's good to know about. Thank you, Mister MacPherson."

She climbed the stairs.

"It's late afternoon, isn't it?" she asked when she walked back inside their office.

"It is," said Iris. "Why?"

"Mister MacPherson exists in a different time zone than we do," said Gwen. "Or else he is a prodigious napper."

"Either explains much," said Iris. "Drink would explain more. Would you like me to do that? I suspect that you've never cleaned fingerprints before."

"I have to learn sometime," said Gwen.

She sprayed and wiped down the file cabinet, then handed over the bottle and rag to Iris who tenderly applied them to her Bar-Let.

"Where would Dickie be now?" asked Gwen, watching her.

"Jail," said Iris. "Bound over for Assizes or Quarter Sessions, I suppose. I don't know which handles murder cases."

"Will he have bail?"

"I doubt it."

"Which jail would he be kept in?"

"Brixton, I should think."

"Right," said Gwen. "How do I get there?"

Iris looked at her partner appraisingly. Gwen was sitting up straight in her chair, staring out the window, seeing something other than the view of the sunlight waning over London.

"It's so interesting that you think I know the answer to that," said Iris.

"You're the one with friends in low places," Gwen reminded her. "And Cambridge. I thought between the two, you might have visited the Brixton jail upon occasion."

"I'm more of a Wormwood Scrubs girl," said Iris, opening a drawer. "All the best criminals go there."

She pulled out a folded map and handed it across.

"Time to learn the bus routes, dear," she said.

"Thank you," said Gwen, unfolding and studying it carefully. "I'll be coming in late tomorrow."

"Oh, golly," sighed Iris, staring at the vastness of the empty space between them and the door. "I do hope that I can handle the rush of business. Give Mister Trower my regards."

"I will," promised Gwen.

Iris lay next to Andrew, her mind elsewhere despite his thoughtful ministrations.

"Your name came up today," he said.

"Did it? Casual reminiscences? Nostalgia for pre-war party girls?"

"The Brigadier says that you telephoned. He wanted to know more about what you were doing with this business enterprise of yours."

"He asked you?"

"He did."

"He knows about us. Damn."

"It's his job to know about the people working for him. And the people who used to work for him. Especially when they get involved in murder cases."

"Are you interrogating me on his behalf?" asked Iris, shoving his hands away from her and sitting up. "Your technique is wanting."

"You've never complained about my technique before," he said, grinning. "No, I'm not interrogating you. I'm merely curious as to why you didn't mention the murder. I would think it would be the principal topic of discussion."

"I didn't see that it would set the proper mood," said Iris. "I wanted to make love, not talk about dead girls."

"Still—"

"I only have you for a few nights out of a blue moon," said Iris. "I want to make the most of them. And I don't like the Brigadier knowing about us."

"He approves, for what it's worth," said Andrew. "He'd rather my infidelities be with one of us than, say, a fetching Russky lass."

"He still thinks of me as one of us? One of you, I should say?"

"As he put it, you're family."

"Oh, I dislike that intensely," she said, hugging her knees to her chest. "It makes this all sound incestuous."

"Well, I don't think of it that way," said Andrew. "So, what was the murder about? Did you do it?"

"Stop," said Iris. "It isn't a joking matter. One of our clients, a young woman, was stabbed to death a few days after signing with us. They arrested the man with whom we arranged her first date."

"And you feel responsible."

"I do not. People kill each other occasionally, and that's got nothing to do with me. It happened, they arrested someone, and it's all over but the hanging."

"Unfortunate. How is your partner handling the situation?'

"Oh, God, she's convinced that the fellow is completely innocent. She wants us to drop everything and go investigate it."

Andrew began to laugh.

"What?" Iris asked, glaring at him.

"Just picturing the two of you, banging about where the police fear to tread," he said. "Has she any skills in the area?"

"Apart from a frighteningly accurate ability to read people, none," said Iris. "But she also has something I've never had and never will have."

"Which is?"

"Goodness," said Iris simply. "She's a good person. She's actually a good person. I'm in business with a good person. Me. Who is not a good person. Who is neither a person who is good nor good at being a person. It's laughable that I'm mixed up in the marriage-making business. Mike was right."

"Mike? Which Mike?"

"Ah, the gentleman perks up. I didn't tell you the worst part."

"Worse than a girl getting herself stabbed to death?"

"All right, not as bad as that. Among the investigators is one Detective Sergeant Michael Kinsey."

"Really? How extraordinary! How was the reunion?"

"Tense. Tortured. Everything one could have hoped for upon encountering an ex-fiancé."

"No forgiveness for your—indiscretion, then."

"Not likely in this lifetime or the next. He saw what he saw, drew the logical conclusions, and that was an end to it."

"And you've never explained the truth to him?"

"Said explanation is covered by which section of the Official Secrets Act again?"

"I'm sure the Brigadier would bend the rules for you on that."

"And I'm just as sure that he would then hold it over me for the rest of my life. I don't care to owe him that favour. Besides, if Mike were really the man for me, he would have accepted the situation, stiffened the old upper lip, forgiven me my obvious wartime lapse, and taken me back. Since he did none of those things, he clearly wasn't worth any more effort on my part. To hell with the bastard."

"There's my girl," said Andrew admiringly. "Never let sympathy get in the way of getting the job done."

"That was not one of your better sweet nothings, I must say."

"It brings me to my next topic."

"Which is?"

"The Brigadier would like you back."

"Back? You mean—"

"Back in the field."

"Which field?"

"Germany, for starters."

"Doing what?"

"Working under me," he said. "And don't make the obvious

joke. You'd be ideal. The opposition has never seen you. You're fluent in all the necessary languages, you've already had most of the training, and the best part is we could see much more of each other than we do now."

"Except the Russkies would know about me inside of one clandestine rendezvous," Iris pointed out.

"Not if we're careful."

"There's always a careless moment in these matters," said Iris. "You'd be making more mistakes with me more available to you. I'm surprised the Russkies haven't stumbled onto this little love nest by now."

"Yet they haven't."

"Andrew, you know why I can't do this," said Iris. "The real reason."

"Oh, bollocks, Sparks. You don't have to get on a plane to get there. Take the bloody ferry and a few trains. It would be less obvious an entrance, anyway."

"It's not the flying, Andrew," said Iris, looking away. "It's all of it. Facing where the girls all died without me."

"That wasn't your fault, Sparks," said Andrew. "None of it."

"But I should have been with them. Maybe I would have spotted that damned traitor. Maybe I could have saved them."

"Or maybe you would have died along with them. What's the point of beating yourself up about it now?"

"I'm sorry, Andrew," said Iris. "It's just that the trial's coming up soon. It's been bringing up much that I've been forcing down, and I'm not enjoying it one bit. Tell the Brigadier thanks, but no thanks, all right?"

"Don't make this your final decision," Andrew urged her. "You were made for this work."

"I don't know what I'm made for," said Iris. "Now, do me a favour."

"Anything. What is it?"

"Shut up and make me forget about all of this."

"Gladly."

And for a while, she did. But after, when he lay sleeping next to her, she stared up at the darkened ceiling and saw the faces of dead girls.

CHAPTER 4

G wen unfolded the Greater London bus map at the breakfast table and studied the intricate tangle of red, blue, and green lines. She had not wanted to admit to Iris her unfamiliarity with the city in which she had grown up, married, and attempted to raise a child, but she had in fact never thoroughly explored it. Indeed, it wasn't until late wartime that she had traveled by means of either Tube or bus. All of her journeys had been effectuated by either chauffeurs or cabbies, and she paid little attention to the routes involved. She had a vague idea where the East End lay, or at least that section where the Cunard ships had carried her off to other worlds when she was growing up. She knew Wimbledon, of course, but the majority of the interconnected sections of the city were more foreign to her than, say, the opulent houses of Biarritz or the slopes of Gstaad.

She didn't know where Brixton was. She didn't even know which part of the map she should be searching. She settled for methodically tracing her finger back and forth across each section, trying to find the name.

Prudence came in with the teapot.

"Going on a trip, Ma'am?" she asked.

"Prudence, do you know where Brixton is?" asked Gwen, giving up.

"Brixton, Ma'am?" asked Prudence, coming to peer over her shoulder at the map. "That's south. There, Ma'am. See where Battersea Park is? To the right and down."

"Oh, yes, thank you," said Gwen. "Now, how would I get there from here? This map is like finding intersecting strands of spaghetti in a pot."

"Oh, I wouldn't know that," said Prudence. "I don't go to Brixton. Let me fetch Albert for you."

"No, I don't want to trouble—" Gwen began, but Prudence was already out the door in search of the chauffeur.

Gwen sighed and stared at the map some more. She found Croydon, where she had her fateful encounter with Iris at the wedding. Where Dickie Trower lived as well. It wasn't far from Brixton. She wondered if any of his family or friends were visiting him.

If they even knew of his predicament. She wasn't certain that she would tell anyone if she was in his position. The shame and embarrassment of being arrested and locked up, even if one was innocent. Of being strapped to a gurney—

She shook off that memory, and was composedly sipping her tea when Prudence returned, Albert in tow. He was a short man in his early sixties who had driven three generations of Bainbridges in a series of expensive cars for over forty years. He was still buttoning his black uniform jacket when he came in.

"Good morning, Ma'am," he said giving her a brief salute. "Going to Brixton, are we? Will you be there long? Lady Carolyne needs me to take her to the plant later. I can bring the car around—"

"Oh, I wish you hadn't gone to this much trouble," said Gwen. "I was only asking which bus route takes one there."

"Bus?" The concept seemed to flummox him. "You're taking the bus?"

"If I can figure out the route," she said.

"Well," he said, coming over with Prudence to look at the map. "I'm not much of a bus-taker. It all depends where in Brixton you wish to go."

"It's an address on Jebb Avenue," she said.

"Jebb Avenue?" he said, looking at her sharply. "If you don't mind me saying so, Ma'am, you shouldn't be going there. That's where the prison is, isn't it?"

"Is it?" she asked with what she hoped was innocent ignorance. "Well, I shall certainly avoid that. I meant to say, an address near Jebb Avenue."

"There's a Tube station at Brixton Market," he offered, stabbing at the location. "Might be the quickest."

"Not the Tube," she said with a shudder.

"Bus, then," he said, peering at the map. "Funny, I haven't taken a lot of buses since I've come to this house. But to get anywhere, you have to figure out where you want to be, then trace it back to where you are. There's the 133, but that goes over London Bridge, that's too far. Lots of Green Line buses—you can catch one of them by Westminster, Baker Street—oh!"

"Yes?"

"The 159. That looks like your best bet. You can catch it at Trafalgar Square or Westminster—"

"What on earth are you all doing?" came a voice from behind them.

The three turned with a collective guilty start. Lady Carolyne stood in the entrance to the room. She was wearing a black silk kimono with a scarlet sash to match the lining visible in the sleeves, decorated with a scene of snow-covered evergreen branches with a mountain looming in the background, thrusting imperiously upwards, perhaps that famous one that everyone referred to but whose name Gwen could never remember.

Lady Carolyne's head perched atop this Japanese scene, her expression colder than the mountain cap hovering just below her bosom. Her eyes were less bleary than Gwen was accustomed to seeing this time of morning, at least on the rare mornings when Lady Carolyne emerged at all. There must have been no dinner party for her to attend last night, leaving her to drink at home. She tended to drink less when someone else wasn't footing the bill.

She was a woman somewhere past fifty, the actual distance being an official secret clouded in a haze of denial. Even in her most hungover states, she never left her dressing room less than perfectly made up. Yet even the strongest of powders and creams were powerless to force her normal expression from its perpetual scowl, which at the moment was directed at the three aspiring navigators.

"Good morning, Lady Carolyne," said Prudence, curtseying quickly.

"Good morning, Madam," said Albert.

"Well?" huffed Lady Carolyne. "Must I repeat my question?"

"Begging your pardon, Ma'am," said Prudence. "We were trying to figure out the best route to Brixton."

"Brixton? Why on earth would anyone want to go to Brixton?"

"I have some business there, Lady Carolyne," said Gwen.

"You?" said Lady Carolyne suspiciously. "What manner of business?"

"I am visiting a client."

"A client? Do you actually mean that this ridiculous enterprise of yours requires you to travel to Brixton?"

"It's to celebrate an engagement," said Gwen blithely. "She invited us, and we like to show the flag at these successes. It's good for business. I could scoop up half of the bridesmaids as future prospects if all goes according to plan."

"An engagement party in the morning?" scoffed Lady Carolyne. "Unheard of."

"I don't disagree, but she works evenings, so she had to make it early," said Gwen. "In any case, Prudence and Albert were helping me with the route. Do you know which bus would get me there the easiest?"

"Never been on a bus in my life," said Lady Carolyne. "I don't approve of them. I don't approve of people who take them. If you wish to travel to this party, have Albert take you in the car."

"No," said Gwen.

"No? Why not, for Heaven's sake? What is the point of having a car? What is the point of having Albert, for that matter?"

"That's a good point," said Albert, grinning.

"I won't waste the petrol for this when there are other perfectly good means of getting me there," said Gwen.

"I would not describe our system of public transportation as either good or perfect," said Lady Carolyne. "Not to mention that you will be exposing yourself to all manner of filth and disease—"

"Goodness!" exclaimed Gwen. "I'm not going to the tropics, I'm going to Brixton!"

"It might as well be the tropics," sniffed Lady Carolyne.

"It is to the south," observed Albert.

"You're not helping," whispered Prudence.

"Lady Carolyne, I don't mean to argue with you," said Gwen. "My mind is made up. I will be perfectly safe. I will pay my respects to the ladies, have some tea and cakes, leave a few flyers, and be back at my office by noon. You need not concern yourself with me."

"I do not wish to concern myself with you," returned Lady Carolyne. "But you insist on making yourself a concern. Very well, go to Brixton. Keep dabbling in your little business venture. It matters not to me. Albert, you may bring the car around at eleven."

"Yes, Ma'am," he said.

"And Gwendolyn?"

"Yes, Lady Carolyne?"

"We will be discussing another matter later. Spare me some time this evening if you have no other pressing social engagements."

"It shall be my great pleasure," said Gwen, wondering what was in the offing.

Lady Carolyne turned and strode from the room, revealing in her wake a vertical display of Japanese ideograms whose meaning was understood by none in the household but which no doubt was disapproving.

"Anyway, I'd take the 159," said Albert as if there had been no disruption.

"Thank you, I shall," said Gwen, rising from the table. "I will see you tonight."

She was at her dressing table, in the midst of applying her lipstick, when there was a soft tap at the door. She turned to see Millicent, the upstairs maid, peering at her.

"Begging your pardon, Ma'am," said Millicent timidly.

"Yes?"

"I was overhearing what everyone was going on about, and forgive me if I'm wrong, but if it is the jail you're going to, then there's a better route."

"Let's say for the sake of argument that I was," said Gwen, smiling. "How should I go?"

"You should take the tram," said Millicent. "The Number 20. You can get it right out of Victoria Station, and it will take you down Brixton Hill to Jebb. There's a stop there."

"Thank you, Millicent. That would save me a bit of a walk, not that I mind the exercise."

"I used to visit my uncle there," said Millicent. "He was—well, I don't like to say, and that was—"

"There is no need to explain any further," said Gwen.

"I like the trams better, anyways," said Millicent. "It's because of the electrics—there ain't any fumes like you get with the buses. And it's quieter—you can sit up top, and the city rolls right past you like a movie."

"One must get a lot of thinking done," commented Gwen wistfully.

"Well, maybe in short bursts, but the clangers will keep you from doing it too long. But it's the best way to get there, if you're asking me."

"Thank you, Millicent. I will give it a try."

Millicent turned to leave, then turned back.

"Is it a gentleman friend?" she whispered hopefully.

"No, Millicent," said Gwen. "And don't spread any rumours."

"All right, Ma'am."

So her morning walk was to Victoria Station, which brought up memories of taking the boat-train to Dover and Calais when she was young. And later on her honeymoon, blissfully, ecstatically ensconced in a private room on the train to Rome, arriving without seeing one whit of scenery.

A blast of a car horn brought her back to her purpose. She took a direct route to Victoria, avoiding her recent tendency to make sudden turns and explore streets she had never seen, or had seen but didn't know exactly where they were before. These small, tentative deviations from her path gave her a tiny sense of adventure, a secret rebellion against the straightforward course that her life had taken.

This deviation, however, was not a small one. She was amazed, somewhat appalled, yet also delighted at how easily she had lied to her mother-in-law this morning. The very idea of deceiving this overbearing overlord of her existence would have caused her panic a few months before, yet there she was, rattling off her improvised story without a moment's hesitation. She never knew she was capable of lying so fluently.

It was the positive influence of Iris, she decided. Another benefit to working with her on a daily basis. She was nowhere near Iris's league when it came to invention on the spur of the moment, especially when an unhappy customer or an irate merchant called, but she was improving. She was still bubbling over their confrontation with Parham. She felt that they had scored their share of points in the encounter, even if they ultimately were forced to capitulate to his demands. And if they succeeded—

Succeeded in what, exactly? Exonerating Dickie Trower? Was that really her intent?

Was this trip necessary?

Bulldog Drummond, Iris called her. Well, Drummond wouldn't hesitate if he were in Gwen's shoes.

She briefly pictured Ronald Colman as the intrepid hero wearing her heels and laughed to herself at the image.

She reached Victoria Station, then walked around it to where the trams came in. The Number 20, Millicent had said. Gwen located the stop and stood on the queue with others bound for Brixton. The tram pulled up, a cheerful red and white double-decked affair with an advert for Saxa Salt plastered on the side between decks. The door opened and a stream of passengers hurried off into the early morning. Gwen waited until the rest of the queue had clambered aboard, then purchased a ticket from the conductress who stood outside the doorway.

"I'm going to Jebb Avenue," Gwen whispered. "Could you let me know when we come to it?"

"We all have our crosses to bear, don't we?" replied the conductress, winking at her sympathetically. "Plenty of seats up top, Madam."

Gwen climbed the narrow steps to the upper deck, clinging to the rail with a death grip until she found her footing. She took a seat by a window. The doors closed, the bell clanged, and the motor engaged with a low rasp that rose in pitch like a hand-cranked siren. The tram bumped through a series of switches, then they were off, barreling down Vauxhall Bridge Road, the rest of London peeling away as they rose towards the crossing of the Thames.

She had never seen the river from this vantage, looking over the walls to see its broad expanse curving away on both sides. She wanted to press her nose against the glass like a schoolgirl. Why had her parents never taken her on the tram before, even on a lark?

She felt giddy with discovery. There was the Chelsea School of Art, where she and her friend Marilyn had daringly taken Life Drawing classes without telling their parents exactly what that entailed. And the Tate—even from here, she could see the wartime damage. She hoped that the paintings had been removed before the bombs hit. She had a mental image of a sullen group of landscapes and portraits, queued up to board a train to the country where they would be condescending to the local village paintings.

She was saddened when the tram descended to the south bank, plunging her back into the streets of—which neighbourhood was this? She consulted her map quickly. Lambeth, she supposed. Yes, the sign at the turn said South Lambeth Road. She tried to think if there was ever an occasion for which she had come to Lambeth. She couldn't think of any.

The tram bells rang with frequency once they were in South London, interrupting her train of thought. Her tram of thought, she corrected herself. The upper deck seating allowed her to peer over the temporary wooden walls thrown up in front of burnt out storefronts and abandoned houses. Some buildings showed their façades bravely to the passers-by, with nothing but ruins behind.

Some days, she felt the same way.

She tried to distract herself with a brief fantasy that Ronald Colman was on the seat next to her, beginning an inappropriate flirtation in the relative privacy of the upper deck.

The clangers went off, the tram jerked to a halt, and Ronald vanished like mist.

There was more bomb damage to be seen, and the upper deck provided glimpses over the temporary fences erected to block the views from the sidewalks. The randomness of the attacks was very much in evidence—one theater stood completely intact next to the remains of another, its stage still standing, waiting for an audience that would never come. Adverts clung hopefully to crumbling walls—Bisto, the meat-flavoured gravy powder! Ovaltine gives health and vitality! McNish Whisky!

There was no new whisky to be had yet. The daily papers carried adverts from the distilleries urging patience to their customers and bidding them to wait for the start-up for new production, once there was sufficient grain available to divert to less essential goods, although Lady Carolyne might beg to differ as to the relative necessity of whisky.

A few arcing turns brought them to Brixton. Quin and Axtens, Ltd., a department store, had once taken up an entire block at the corner by the turn. Now, it was just a set of walls and vaguely Romanesque columns. SMARTEST DESIGNS AND BEST VALUE proclaimed a surviving sign.

Maybe again, some day.

The columns forced her into a memory of walking through the Roman Forum with Ronnie, their first emergence from the hotel where they began their honeymoon proper. Where he leaned her against a column and kissed her, and said, "Our love will outlast all of this. I promise."

She would never go to back to Italy, she thought. Not even if there were a thousand years of peace.

The conductress poked her head up the stairway.

"Your stop's coming, Madam," she said.

Gwen collected herself and moved forward, glancing back for a moment to see if Ronald (she thought that they must be on a first name basis by now) was still there, maybe with one hand up, giving her a rueful wave. But the seat was empty.

The tram lurched to a halt, and Gwen descended the stairs.

"Thank you," she said to the conductress.

"Wipe your face, dearie," replied the woman. "They need us looking proper cheery, no matter what, right?"

Gwen put her fingertips to her cheeks and felt the tears.

"Thanks again," she said, stepping onto the street.

The tram set off, its bells clanging merrily away. Her heart strings remained unzinged. She pulled out her handkerchief and wiped her cheeks.

It was a short walk down Jebb Avenue to the prison, the brick walls looming some twenty feet over the sidewalk, festooned with barbed wire at the top. She could hear shouts echoing from inside, the sounds of men marching to nowhere. Prisoners being exercised in the yard, she guessed. Like they were horses in a stable.

The entrance was a large, wooden door, arched on top, set into several layers of brick. A smaller door set into it was opened by a guard, and she was admitted to the gatehouse area. A large metal gate separated her from the main courtyard. In the distance, she could hear the marching prisoners more clearly, the shouted commands of the keepers: "By the left march!" "Four, all correct, sir!"

She saw a sign for visitors, and went to sign in. The guard looked at her with studied blandness.

"Who are you here to see, Ma'am?" he asked.

"Dickie, or I suppose Richard Trower," she said, stammering slightly. "I believe that he came in yesterday."

He consulted a list, running his finger down it, his lips moving silently.

"Indeed he did," he said, stabbing at a name at the bottom. "You're right quick off the mark. Fine, wait for your escort. Trower's in A-Wing. We have to call a matron to search you first."

"Search me? Do I look dangerous?"

"No, Ma'am, and that means you could be carrying all manner of contraband. Step inside there."

She went into a small room with a chair in one corner and

waited. After what seemed an eternity, a uniformed woman with a bored expression stepped inside.

"Right," she said peremptorily. "Coat off, handbag open. Turn to the wall."

Gwen complied, blushing furiously as the woman ran her hands down her sides, then up her legs.

"First time here, I take it," commented the woman.

"Yes. How did you know?"

"The girls visiting their men usually wear something more— well, they like to put on a bit of a show, if you know what I mean."

"Do they?"

"Oh, yes," said the woman. "Quite the spectacle in a few cases. You must be a do-gooder."

"I try my best," said Gwen.

"Good for you," said the woman with no indication of meaning it. "You can put your coat back on. Follow me."

There were corridors, and locked doors, and more corridors and locked gates. Finally, she was led into a small waiting room where three other women sat on wooden benches. They looked at Gwen, craning their heads upwards to register how much closer to Heaven her blond tresses were than theirs.

"Well, you'll 'ave no trouble seein' 'im," said one, and the others cackled.

"I'm sorry?" said Gwen.

"Oh, you'll see," said the woman. "First time, love?"

"Yes," said Gwen.

"What's 'e done, then?"

"Nothing," said Gwen firmly. "It's all been a terrible mistake."

"Oh, love," said the second one sympathetically. "It's just the latest mistake."

"Mrs. Corcoran?" called a guard, standing at the far door.

"Time for me fifteen," said the first, standing up, adjusting her clothes, and throwing her shoulders back. She waited until the guard turned to lead her inside, then quickly unbuttoned the top two buttons of her blouse and followed him, turning her head to throw a wink at the others.

"How long 'as yours been 'ere?" asked the third woman.

"Just since yesterday," said Gwen.

"Married, are you?" she asked, glancing at the ring.

"Yes," said Gwen. "I mean, no. Not to him."

"Oooh, it's like that?" said the second woman.

"No, it's not like that at all," said Gwen. "He's a—"

She was about to say "client," but there had been enough misunderstandings for one brief encounter.

"He's my cousin," she said. "Aunt Mary was too distraught to see him, so I'm representing the family."

"Oh, that's nice of you," said the third woman. "I wouldn't visit my cousin if they were 'angin' 'im the next day."

"But you'd go to the funeral," said the second woman.

"Just to make sure 'e was dead," said the third, and the two of them snickered.

It didn't take long for the first woman to emerge, surreptitiously buttoning up her blouse.

"See you next week," she said to the others.

"Ta ta," they returned.

The guard brought each of them in after Mrs. Corcoran left. Finally, it was Gwen's turn.

"You're new," said the guard as he brought her to another room. A metal door with a sliding viewing grille was set into the wall.

"Yes," said Gwen. "What do I do?"

"Leave your bag on the table," instructed the guard. "You go in. You stand away from the mesh. You do not attempt to put anything through the mesh. Try it, you'll end up in the women's wing over there. Once the doors close, you have fifteen minutes, not a second more. Understood?"

"Understood," said Gwen.

He pressed a button on the wall. She heard a buzzer go off in the distance. Then a green light went on, and he opened the door.

"I'll be watching," he reminded her.

"I know," said Gwen, and she stepped into a small, dank room with thick stone walls, only a bare, yellowed bulb providing light.

There was a wall in front of her that stopped at about five feet. Over it, a window looked into a room symmetrical with the one she was in. The window was covered on both sides by wire netting, held in place by thick, metal staples. There was a small wooden step stool in front of it, but Gwen didn't require it to see into the other side. That must have been what Mrs. Corcoran had meant.

A door opened in the opposite room, and Dickie Trower walked in. He looked through the window, his pupils widening as they became accustomed to the change in the lighting. His jaw dropped as he saw his visitor.

"Mrs. Bainbridge?" he said in amazement. "Is it truly you?"

Dickie Trower was a slight, slender man. He had sandy hair that he normally combed back and slicked down with Morgan's, emphasizing the beginnings of his widow's peak, but it was currently pomade-free and unruly. He was wearing clean but shabby brown prison garb, and had some two days' stubble sprouting from his face. He looked like he hadn't slept for the same amount of time. A whiff of carbolic soap floated through the mesh, and she forced herself not to crinkle her nose at it.

"Hello, Mister Trower," she said gently. "How are you holding up?"

"How am I—you know why they put me here, don't you?"

"They said that you killed a woman. Miss La Salle."

"I didn't!" he cried, his face contorting in pain. "I never even met her. I got the letter from your office saying the date was off."

"We never sent it," said Gwen.

"Then how—?" he asked, and he began pacing furiously back and forth. "Who did this?"

"I don't know," said Gwen. "What can I do to help? Have you a solicitor yet?"

"Mum and Dad are searching for one," he said. "But they're expensive. And there's no bail. I've gone from a no-name accountant to Public Enemy Number One. Me!"

"I'm so sorry," said Gwen.

"Why did you come, Mrs. Bainbridge?" he asked abruptly. "You're the first person to come see me here. My friends—they aren't as good friends as I would have hoped."

"We just—" she began, then corrected herself. "I felt that I was somehow responsible for getting you into this situation. We set up the encounter, and someone must have taken advantage of it to kill that poor girl and throw the blame on you."

"You really think that I'm innocent," he said in wonder.

"I know that you are," she said.

"How? How could you possibly be certain?" he asked, almost laughing in disbelief. "You don't really know me, or what I'm capable of doing."

"I have very good instincts about people," she said, smiling for the first time. "I am almost never wrong."

"I need you on the jury," he said. "I need twelve of you."

"Good women and true," she said. "Please, what else can I do? I would like to help in some fashion."

"Look, there is one thing—no, it's too much to ask."

"Ask," she said.

"It's Herbert. I'm worried about him."

"Herbert?"

He looked embarrassed.

"Herbert is my goldfish," he said. "I had just finished feeding him when the police burst through my door. It's been two days. I was wondering if you could visit him. You'll have to speak to Mrs. Dowd, she's the landlady."

"Why did you name him Herbert?"

"He—well, when I got him, he looked like a Herbert, so Herbert he was."

"I will visit Herbert immediately," promised Gwen. "How will Mrs. Dowd know that I have your permission?"

"I'll write you a note," he said.

There was a banging on the door behind him.

"Time's up!" shouted the guard on that side.

"That was never fifteen minutes!" protested Gwen.

Trower shook his head vehemently.

"It doesn't matter," he said. "I can't thank you enough, Mrs. Bainbridge."

"Good-bye, Mister Trower," she said. "I will come visit you again."

He turned to leave, then turned back.

"Tell me, Mrs. Bainbridge," he said hesitantly, then he stopped.

"Yes?" she encouraged him.

"The girl. Miss La Salle. Was she pretty?"

"Very pretty, Mister Trower," she said softly. "I think you would have liked her."

"I can't help thinking about it," he said, shaking his head in sorrow. "What if she had been the one for me? What if she had been my one real chance for happiness? And now she's gone forever, and I'm here."

"You won't be here for long," she said.

"You can't possibly know that," he said. "Good-bye, Mrs. Bainbridge."

He turned and walked through the door.

The door on her side opened behind her, and the guard beckoned to her. She walked out and collected her handbag. As she did, another guard came in, holding a folded scrap of paper.

"He wanted you to have this," he said. "Bending the rules, but he seems a decent chap, considering what he's done."

She took it from him and read it quickly. It was a note to his landlady, along with his address. She folded it again and placed it inside her handbag, then pulled out her bus map.

"Excuse me, gentlemen," she said, unfolding it. "Which tram does one take to get to Croydon from here?"

CHAPTER 5

The Bar-Let echoed extra loudly without Gwen in the office. The silence when Iris had completed the letter was even more deafening.

She sorted the morning mail into two small stacks—one for clients' responses, one for bills and business. She picked up her letter opener, then on a whim put it down and pulled out a folding knife from her handbag. She flicked it open with practiced ease and began slicing open the envelopes.

When she had finished, she balanced the knife point-down on the tip of her finger and eyed a spot just above the light switch by the doorway. She wondered if she could hit it from where she sat. She gripped the knife by the handle and drew back her arm.

Then she remembered the security deposit, and gently folded the blade back into the handle and put the knife back in her handbag.

A dart-board, she thought. We could put it behind the door, out of sight of the clientele—

Footsteps from below, ascending the steps, then stopping.

Come up, come up! she prayed. Give me something to do!

They resumed, then stopped again, and this time she heard a man panting for breath.

Well, it won't be someone in shape, she thought. Certainly not the return of the dustman. What was his name again? The man with no—Manners! That was it, Alfred Manners. She was disappointed at his failure to apply for their services. He was a nice-looking chappie under all of it. She was sure that she could find him—

The footsteps made it up to the landing just below, then paused again.

You're almost there, thought Iris encouragingly. One more flight to happiness!

The steps resumed and reached her hallway. Iris stood between the two desks, her hand folded primly in front of her, prepared to greet whomever Fate was about to provide.

Fate lurched through the door in the form of a corpulent man in his early forties, his hand dabbing at his face with a handkerchief that had been in use far too long without laundering.

"Hello," he gasped, still panting. "Need a moment."

"Please, sit," she said, indicating the chair. "Would you like a glass of water?"

"God, yes," he said, plopping onto the chair which held bravely under the onslaught.

She filled a glass from a pitcher on the windowsill and brought it to him. He took it and gulped half of it down gratefully.

"How do you do?" she said, holding out her hand. "I'm Iris Sparks. Welcome to The Right Sort Marriage Bureau."

"Carter," he said, switching his glass to his left hand and shaking hers with his right. "Phillip Carter."

The hand was still profusely sweaty. She kept her expression as bland as possible while he continued to shake hers, then extricated herself and sat behind her desk.

"I don't have an appointment, sorry," he said.

"We can squeeze you in," said Iris, taking her handkerchief and wiping her hand discreetly under the desk. "Let's get you settled, then we'll go over the preliminaries."

"I think I've recovered," he said. "Lord, I was not meant for climbing."

"Then we'll eliminate all of our mountaineering enthusiasts from consideration immediately," said Iris.

"Have you any of those?" he asked with interest.

"Two that I can think of offhand," she said.

"My, my," he said. "Maybe I should consider them. Opposites attracting, and all of that. I could be their mountain."

"We are a little more specific in our matchmaking process than that," said Iris.

"How does it work?"

"We conduct an extensive interview—"

"We? Who's we?" he interjected. "There's only you."

He was looking at her closely. A small alarm went off in her head.

"My partner stepped out for a few minutes," she said, smiling. "She should be returning in a moment."

She slid her bag closer to her chair with one foot, calculating how quickly she could retrieve her knife, flick it open, and throw. Less time than it would take for him to cross the space between them?

Easy, Sparks, she admonished herself. Don't make assumptions without evidence.

But what if the man who killed Tillie La Salle wanted to come for her next? said the part of her brain that maintained the alarm.

"Now," she said, starting her routine while keeping a wary eye on the potential client/potential murderer, "we are a marriage bureau, one of two licensed to arrange meetings—"

"They have licenses for that?"

"Every commercial establishment must be licensed," she said. "If I may continue—"

"What sort of training do you have to have?" he asked. "I mean, are there courses of study? Professional certifications and that sort of thing?"

"When there are, I expect that we will be the ones teaching the courses and certifying the students," said Iris, picking up her pad and pencil. "Time for me to ask the questions. We conduct a thorough screening of our clientele, as you are about to discover. Shall we proceed?"

"Well—"

"Good," she chirped. "First, your name."

"I gave you that already."

"You must forgive me," said Iris. "I am a creature of habit. Downright obsessive in my routines. Name?"

"Phillip Carter."

"Is that with one *l* or two?"

"Two," he said, hesitating for a moment and gulping down some more water.

She looked at the hand holding the glass.

Right, she thought.

"Phillip, two l's, Carter," she repeated, jotting it down. "Occupation?"

"File clerk."

"With what firm?"

"Bourne and Dudley, on Montague Street."

She sighed and placed the pad and pencil on her desk.

"Mister Carter," she said, folding her hands and looking at him sternly. "You have given me three lies on the first three questions I have asked. However will we be able to complete this interview, much less place you with an eligible woman, with this behaviour?"

"What do you mean, lies?" he asked indignantly.

"Your name, your occupation, and place of employment," she said, ticking them off on the fingers of her left hand. "Every single one of them a lie. Not to mention the ultimate deception of coming in here under false pretenses."

"Which would be—?"

"You're already married," said Iris.

"Says who?" he demanded.

"Says the mark on the knuckle of your ring finger," she said. "You scraped it when you removed your wedding band."

"I'm divorced," he said. "It wasn't easy to get it off."

"It will be very easy for your wife when she finds out that you're here," said Iris. "That scrape is fresh. And it seems to me that I know your face, but a thinner version of it."

"Yeah, maybe," he said. "Maybe I know a younger, prettier version of yours as well."

"Impossible," declared Iris. "I get prettier every day."

"But not younger."

"I'm working on that one," she said. "Who are you? Wait a tick—"

A memory of a scrum of faces under cheap fedoras, garishly lit by flashbulbs going off like ack-ack guns, rude questions shouted by several at once, pads out—

"You're a reporter," she said, her heart sinking.

He bared his teeth and pulled a pad and pencil of his own from inside his jacket pocket.

"Well done, girlie," he said. "Gareth Pontefract's the name. The real name."

"You're with the *Daily Mirror*," she said. "I remember you. Not fondly."

"Yeah, I remember you, too," he said. "Hilarious to see you running a marriage bureau. You ruined more than your share."

"What are you doing here?"

"Come to talk about Tillie and Dickie, London's Tragic Sweethearts," he said. "How you set her up for her last date on Earth. I'd say his as well, but maybe he'll have a few dances in the yard once he's out of solitary."

"I have nothing to say to you."

"How did you select him? Do you keep the stabbers separate

from the stranglers? Do you rank the girls based on whether they can fight back or not? I hear he's a wee lad. He must have needed the advantage."

"Get out."

"Not until you answer my questions."

"You are now in my business office without my permission," she said. "Sounds like trespassing to me."

He stood and positioned his bulk between the two desks, blocking her exit.

"What're you gonna do about it, girlie?" he leered. "Be nice to me, and I'll make you look good in the story. Shock and horror, innocently used by depraved murderer, all that guff. I can make you or break you."

She looked him steadily in the eye and contemplated her options: shoes on or off? Off, she decided, silently easing her feet out of them.

She rose, then sat on the corner of her desk, crossing her legs. He looked at them.

"Now, Mister Pontefract," she said demurely. "We don't want to be threatening helpless, solitary women, do we? I'm sure that's not how your mother raised you."

"I don't leave until I get my story," he said. "And there's nothing you can do about it."

"There are several things I can do," she said. "Let's try this one."

She swung her legs over the front of the desk, planted her hands on either side, and propelled herself off the desk onto the floor behind him. As he turned, she caught his right wrist with her right hand, placed her left palm firmly above his elbow, then pulled back and twisted the arm.

He gave a shout of anguish, his pencil clattering to the floor. She continued to apply the pressure, and he dropped to his knees to ease the pain.

"This is your writing arm," she observed. "I suppose that it would be difficult for you to do your job if it was broken."

She released his elbow and quickly grabbed his fingers and bent them back.

"Do you type your stories yourself?" she asked. "Or do you get a nice little girlie to do that for you? One who needs the job so badly that she won't complain if you subject her to your gross affections once in a while?"

"You're a lunatic!" he shouted, then cried out as she bent the fingers back some more.

"I really don't respond well to criticism," she sighed. "It's a fault, I know, and I fully intend to work on it. But until then, Mister Pontefract, I must ask you to leave. Take your pencil and pad, by all means. Mind the door! Here we are at the steps. You should find going down them a good deal easier than coming up. Or I could simply throw you down the stairwell. Your choice—which shall it be?"

"You're gonna love my story," he growled.

"I vaguely recall that your prose style lacked a certain elegance," she said. "But perhaps you've improved. Shall I send you my comments tomorrow?"

She released him. He adjusted his jacket, then stormed down the stairs.

She listened until she heard the front door open and close, then sat on the top steps and stared out the window opposite.

"Damn," she said. "Damn, damn, damn."

Trams were her new favourite thing, decided Gwen from the top deck of the 42 as it trundled her further southwards to Croydon. This time of day, there were fewer passengers and stops to interrupt her reveries, so Ronald Colman was making considerable progress in his advances. His perfect, pencil-thin mustache grazed her neck as his lips pressed against the nape. It tickled a little. She tried to get her own Ronnie to grow one once, but he insisted on waxing it, which looked and felt ridiculous, so she made him shave it off.

You're a bully, he said teasingly as she stood in the bathroom doorway, watching him lather his upper lip.

Tears again.

Idiot, she thought, dabbing at them. When will this stop?

They reached the Combe Road Terminus, and a helpful bobby pointed her towards the street where a goldfish awaited her mission of mercy.

Croydon had been hit harder in the Blitz than most neighbourhoods. They had the airport and the factories, and a fair number of errant bombs and rockets had plunked down in the commercial and residential sections. Entire blocks had been reduced to rubble and broken beams; the rowhouses dotted with burnt-out wreckages amidst the intact, like a prize-fighter with missing teeth.

Dickie Trower's street, on the other hand, was untouched, as if God had decided to keep one example of a British commuter neighbourhood absolutely pristine. Victory Gardens grew in front of the semi-detached houses, tomatoes ripening on the vines, marrows lurking menacingly under their leaves like swollen, green sharks. Every fifth house, a white waste bin stood where food scraps could be saved for feeding pigs. A pair of twin girls, too young for school, chased a rabbit around a wire-enclosed pen while another rabbit watched nervously from the top of a wooden ramp leading to a small hutch. Gwen stopped and watched them for a moment, wondering what it was like to raise girls. Just as noisy as boys, if these were any to go by.

Trower's address was at the end of the lane. A park lay beyond it, much of it taken up by allotments for community gardens. It will be nice when it goes back to its original purpose, thought Gwen. When there's food enough again that we can all start enjoying life like we used to.

The house itself was different than the others in that it stood alone, with a tower on the side facing the park. Built between the wars, she guessed. Much of this neighbourhood seemed recent, slapped together to take advantage of the improved railways after the previous war, notwithstanding the mock-Tudor exposed beams on the garrets meant to give one a sense of history. There was a chicken coop out back—she could hear them contentedly clucking away from the street. She opened the gate and walked up the short front walk, noting with approval the tea-roses growing on either side of the front door. She took a deep breath and rang the bell.

The door opened, and a woman in a housedress covered with an apron looked up at her in surprise and suspicion.

"Who are you?" she demanded.

"Are you Mrs. Dowd?" asked Gwen.

"I might be, and then again, I might not," said the woman. "Who are you?"

"My name is Gwendolyn Bainbridge. Mrs. Gwendolyn Bainbridge. I am here on behalf of Mister Trower."

"Dickie? He's not here. You can't see him."

"I've just come from visiting him, Mrs. Dowd, if that is who you are," said Gwen, removing the letter from her handbag and handing it to her. "He asked me to look in on Herbert."

Mrs. Dowd read the letter and clapped her hand to her mouth.

"Oh, that silly fish!" she exclaimed. "I had forgotten all about him!"

"May I come in?"

"Yes, you had better. Oh, dear, I hope he's all right. With all of the excitement and the police rummaging through everything, he had gone plumb clear out of my mind. Poor Dickie will never forgive me. This way, Madam. Do I call you Madam?"

"Mrs. Bainbridge will do, thank you," said Gwen as she stepped across the threshold.

The entrance hall was small but neat and well-lit. A side table nestled against the wall, holding a small pile of letters. Gwen saw that the top one was addressed to Trower.

"His room is in the garret," said Mrs. Dowd, leading her to the steps. "Watch your head—it sticks out on the turn. The ceiling, I mean, not your head. Never a problem for me and Dickie—Mister Trower, I should say."

She hustled up the steps, which were covered with a worn, dark red paisley-patterned carpet. Gwen had a chance to observe her better as the older woman made each turn. She appeared to be around fifty, guessed Gwen. Or a hard forty-five. She kept her hair in a neat bun, not a strand sticking out. There were grey streaks amidst the brown, and her face, devoid of makeup, showed signs of strain.

"I have a perfectly good lodger room on the second storey," said Mrs. Dowd as they circled the landing to the stairs to the garret. "But Mister Trower wanted the top one. He liked the quiet, and there's a view of the city out the front window. More of a chore for me, of course."

She paused when she reached the door and fumbled in her apron for a key.

"I cleaned it after the police were done," she said, unlocking the door. "Such a shambles they made of everything. I washed the sheets, except for the bottom one. The police took that one."

"Why, do you suppose?" asked Gwen.

"Looking for blood," said Mrs. Dowd.

"But wasn't the woman killed elsewhere?" asked Gwen. "I wouldn't think that Mister Trower would be able to bring her here without you noticing."

"Not likely," sniffed Mrs. Dowd. "I hear every creak of board and bedspring in this house. He wouldn't get anything by me. Not that he'd try, of course. This is a respectable household, and

Dickie's a good boy, he knows the rules. There's the fish tank on the desk by the window. Poor little creature—he must be on his last legs."

Gwen peered into the tank. A solitary goldfish swam slowly about a tiny underwater landscape consisting of a miniature farmhouse surrounded by fenced paddocks and tiny metal horses, cows, and sheep. The fish dwarfed the pastoral scene like a flying leviathan. It looked up at her with what she thought was a forlorn and reproachful expression.

"He does look like a Herbert," said Gwen.

"Doesn't he?" agreed Mrs. Dowd. "I can't say why, but there it is—Herbert the fish. That's his food in the tin."

Gwen espied the small, round King British Fish Food tin next to the tank. There was a tiny pewter spoon next to it.

"I don't know how much Herbert eats," said Mrs. Dowd. "He's probably extra hungry."

"Two spoonfuls should do it, I imagine," said Gwen, unscrewing the lid. She dipped the spoon in and sprinkled the dried flakes into the tank, then repeated the process.

Herbert's placid demeanour changed immediately to one more predatory, his tail waving frantically as he darted back and forth in pursuit of the flakes drifting slowly through the water.

"My, he is a hungry little thing, isn't he?" laughed Gwen.

"He is," agreed Mrs. Dowd. "Well, you've done a good, Christian deed there, and that's no lie. May I fix you a cup of tea?"

"I would be most grateful," said Gwen. "However, before I leave Herbert, I wonder if you know when the water in the tank was last changed."

"This Sunday past," said Mrs. Dowd. "Dickie changes it every Sunday without fail. He's so good to that fish. 'He's my best mate, Mrs. Dowd,' he tells me at dinner. 'He listens to all my troubles and never doubts me for an instant.'"

"We could all do with a Herbert in our lives, couldn't we?"

"Well said, Mrs. Bainbridge, well said," applauded Mrs. Dowd. "Now, come downstairs and tell me how he's doing."

Gwen glanced around the room before she left. It was small and neat, much like Mister Trower. Mister Trower normally, she thought, not like she saw him today. A single bed with a hand-made quilt was against the far wall. On the nightstand was a blue and white ceramic jug and two glasses, and a framed black and white photograph of him standing between what must have been his parents. A small shelf over the bed held a collection of cheap editions of Dickens and Thackeray.

Mrs. Dowd held the door so that Gwen could go down the steps first, then came through and locked the room behind her.

"He's paid through the end of the month, of course," she said as she followed Gwen downstairs. "After that, I don't know what to do. I don't want to rent out the room while he's in jail, but I don't know how long that will be."

"I hope not too long," said Gwen.

"Of course, I'm not making him meals or doing his laundry, so there's a savings," said Mrs. Dowd. "You sit, dear. I'll be back in two shakes."

The parlour was small and crowded with furniture, leaving little room for Gwen to maneuver. She felt like a growing Alice trying to find a good fit for her long limbs. She sat first on a low divan, but it put her with her knees sticking higher than her lap. She shifted over to one of a pair of high-backed upholstered chairs, its edges dotted with round brass buttons, like a doorman's uniform at Claridge's.

There were photographs everywhere—on the tea-table, the mantelpiece, and so crowding the walls that the broad blue and yellow stripes of the wallpaper were barely visible. Most were of Mrs. Dowd in younger days with a man who Gwen assumed to be Mister Dowd. Mrs. Dowd was smiling in every picture, a petite young woman filled with happiness and hope, traits not much in evidence in her current persona.

Gwen wondered if Mister Dowd, so present in the pictures, was still in the present picture.

She also wondered if living without happiness and hope would turn her into a Mrs. Dowd someday.

There were two stacks of magazines on a side table, *Good Housekeeping* and *Woman's Own*. She picked up the most recent issue of the latter, and became engrossed in an article about new books for children. Little Ronnie had become addicted to repeated readings of the Worzel Gummidge books after hearing the story on the Children's Hour, and Gwen was on the lookout for anything new, just for variety's sake. She was halfway through the article when Mrs. Dowd returned, carrying a tea tray.

"Earl Grey all right?" she asked.

"It's fine, thank you," said Gwen.

"How do you like yours?"

"Milk, please."

"Do you take *Woman's Own*?" asked Mrs. Dowd as she poured.

"I do not. It looks like a very informative magazine."

"Oh, I couldn't live without it," said Mrs. Dowd enthusiastically. "You'd think that housekeeping was stuck in the last century, but they keep finding better ways to do everything. And Mary Sedley's advice column—have you read Mary Sedley?"

"I have not."

"Wonderful. Much more practical than the usual Agony Aunt columns, which I cannot tolerate. My morning ritual after breakfast dishes is to prop me feet up, turn on the Light Programme, and read an article or two."

"Sounds heavenly."

"I swear I'd be barking if I didn't have it. It gets too quiet around here. Now that it's back to how it was, anyhow."

"It was rather noisy for a while, wasn't it?" agreed Gwen.

"Oh, you don't know half!" laughed Mrs. Dowd. "I had a cat, he would go absolutely wild when the Wailing Winnies went off. And

I couldn't take him to the bomb shelters—he wouldn't stay put. I had to leave him here, and he would scratch the place up something awful."

"Poor thing," said Gwen. "What happened to him?"

"He ran off," said Mrs. Dowd. "Least, I suppose he did. I came back, he wasn't here. Never saw him again."

"I'm sorry."

"Well, good riddance to bad rubbish. Funny thing is, I got him to keep me company after Mister Dowd did the same thing. Ran off, I mean. Unlucky in men am I."

"Oh, dear," said Gwen. "Is that him in all of those photographs?"

"Yes. Handsome devil, wasn't he?"

"He was."

"We were quite the picturesque couple," said Mrs. Dowd, picking up one showing the two of them in a café. "This was our first date. He brought his camera along to commemorate it, can you fancy that?"

"Very romantic."

"Oh, he was that," said Mrs. Dowd. "Swept me right off my feet, and it was a long time before they touched ground again. It was good when it was good, but then it wasn't. And now there's Dickie gone. I still can't believe he's a murderer."

"Neither can I," said Gwen firmly.

"If you don't mind my asking," Mrs. Dowd began hesitantly, "how do you know him? How did you know he was—taken away? It hasn't been in the papers yet."

"He was—he is a client of mine. Of ours, I should say."

"Client?" repeated Mrs. Dowd, her eyebrows raising.

"My partner and I operate a small business concern," said Gwen. "Mister Trower came to us seeking—"

"You don't have to tell me anything else," huffed Mrs. Dowd. "Well. To think that I have been nursing this, this viper in my very household. To think that I, a respectable woman, would have sitting in her parlour a, a, oh, I cannot even say the word!"

Gwen looked at her in shock as the import of the other woman's words became clear to her.

"Mrs. Dowd!" she exclaimed indignantly. "I don't know what you are thinking, but you have clearly mistaken my meaning. What sort of woman do you take me for?"

"Well, I'm sure I wouldn't take you for—what's that?"

Gwen handed over her business card. Mrs. Dowd took it and read it over several times, then put her hand to her breast.

"Oh. Oh, my word," she said. "I am so, so sorry. Forgive me. Good Lord, what you must think of me."

"Perhaps I should have made it clear who I was from the start," said Gwen graciously.

"Well, this explains it," said Mrs. Dowd. "You're the tall one."

"I usually am," said Gwen.

"No, I mean when he came back from his first meeting there, he couldn't stop talking about the two of you, especially you, dear. He was very complimentary."

"That's sweet," said Gwen. "He's a lovely lad. We were hoping to find him someone. We thought we had. Then all of this happened. I don't know what to say. We're still reeling from the shock."

"I don't know how it works in the courts," said Mrs. Dowd. "Does he get out on bail?"

"I think not," said Gwen. "It's a serious matter."

"Well, murder generally is, isn't it?"

"Yes, of course. Do you know anything that would be of help to him?"

"Me?" said Mrs. Dowd in surprise. "Why would I know anything?"

"Well, something that might convince the police that he didn't do it."

"I'm sure I told them everything I know," said Mrs. Dowd, sipping her tea thoughtfully.

"The night it happened . . . was he home?"

"Well, at first, yes," she said. "But I went to bed early. I thought he had as well."

"And you would hear if he went out after, wouldn't you?"

"Yes, well, you would think so. But I was very tired that night. We both were—we remarked on it. He was talking about the canceled date, I remember. He was very put off about it."

"Was he?"

"Oh, yes. 'I suppose she decided I wasn't good enough,' he said. It was a disappointment."

"I'm sure it was," said Gwen. "Did he seem particularly angry about it?"

"I don't like to say," said Mrs. Dowd shortly.

"Oh, dear," said Gwen, her heart sinking. "I do hope that it wasn't him."

"He's been such a lonely boy," said Mrs. Dowd. "He had all sorts of expectations built up. Kept talking about this girl as if his whole life was waiting to start on that night, and then he got that letter. The look on his face—heartbreaking."

"I'm so sorry."

"Well, he's still got his room waiting for him," said Mrs. Dowd, brightening. "At least, until the end of the month, he does. And his laundry done, so that's a load off for me, and now that you've reminded me about Herbert, I'll have him waiting for him as well. So, it should all be fine, shouldn't it?"

"I only wish I knew," said Gwen.

"I'm glad you reminded me about that fish," said Mrs. Dowd. "It will give me something to do. Someone to take care of. That's all we need when all is said and done, isn't it?"

"Yes," said Gwen. "It truly is."

Mrs. Dowd gave her the issue of *Woman's Own* to read on the trip back, and Gwen became quite absorbed in it, reading articles with expert tips on beauty, fashion, and baby care, all of which concerned her, as well as on cooking, furnishing, and housekeeping, of which she had little to no experience whatsoever.

I must learn these things, she thought. I must learn them if I am ever to—

Ever to what? Take Ronnie out of Kensington Court to live with her on their own? Could she do that? Not just legally, and there was already one whomping great hurdle to leap, but could she manage even a smallish household on her own?

She was not without financial resources. Her husband had left her something. She wasn't sure of the details, but there was a family lawyer managing it. But there was much tied up in trusts and holdings, and what with her in-laws seizing custody of her son and an unsympathetic guardian being appointed by the court for Gwen herself after her stay in the sanitorium, she wasn't certain how much she could access, or what legal battles would be triggered by any attempts to do so on her part.

What would she require if she succeeded? She would at the very least need a governess to take care of Ronnie while she went off to The Right Sort every day. And a maid and a cook. Or a maid who could cook. Or a cook/maid/governess, if there was such a thing.

Oh, wait, she thought. There are such things. They're called wives.

Maybe she could ask Iris to find her one. She had already offered to find Gwen a husband, so it would only be a matter of changing one little word in the request. She smiled at the idea.

Yes, she would take a wife to handle all of the household matters. And drop Ronald Colman a line to see if he would occasionally squire her about town—oh, wait. He was married to that Benita Hume in real life, wasn't he?

She detested real life some days.

She reached Victoria Station and exited the tram. She glanced at her watch. It was already after one. She hurried to catch the bus to Oxford Street, then walked quickly to the office.

She hoped that Iris had managed all right in her absence. It was the first time that she could remember that either of them had been alone there for that long. Having both there continuously was a comfort, even when there was little to do. She knew that Iris was self-sufficient, fully capable of taking on all comers. Gwen doubted that she would be the same in similar circumstances. A woman alone can be—

"Mrs. Bainbridge!" shouted a man. "Mrs. Bainbridge! Over here!"

She looked up, startled, and a flash bulb flared from across the street.

"Give us a smile, love!" shouted a man with a camera as he quickly replaced the bulb.

"There they are, the jackals," said her mother. "Now, my girl, let's give them a good show. You don't want to see yourself looking fearful in the morning tabloids."

Gwen straightened her shoulders and gave him a brilliant display of perfect teeth.

"Lovely!" shouted the photographer, bringing his camera up.

She held her magazine in front of her face right as the flash went off. The photographer muttered an imprecation.

"Gwen!" called Iris, lurking behind the partially opened front door. "Do not engage! In here! Now!"

"Mrs. Bainbridge!" shouted a heavyset man next to the photographer. "What is your comment on Tillie La Salle's murder? Why didn't you properly investigate Dickie Trower before sending her to her death?"

"What?" cried Gwen, stumbling for a moment as she reached the door.

Iris stepped forward and grabbed her arm, steadying her, then hauled her inside with a strength Gwen didn't know that she possessed and slammed the door shut.

"The press," gasped Gwen in shock.

"I am aware," said Iris. "That was Gareth Pontefract. Do you know of him?"

"That greasy little toad from the *Daily Mirror*?"

"The same. He paid us a visit while you were away."

"Oh, dear God!"

"Have you recovered enough to climb the steps? We need to have a little war conference."

"I'm all right. Lead on, Captain."

"Never reached that rank," said Iris as she started up.

"What rank did you—"

"Can't tell you."

"I should have known that would be the answer," said Gwen.

Gwen sat down and took the glass of water that Iris poured for her with a silent toast before drinking it.

"Tell me what happened," she said.

Iris filled her in, leaving out the details of her near-assault.

Gwen looked at her closely when she was done.

"How did you get rid of him?" she asked.

"I asked him to leave, and he left," said Iris smoothly.

"Did you hurt him much?" asked Gwen, smiling slightly.

"Ah, maybe a little," confessed Iris. "His pride more than anything. No lasting damage."

"Pity," said Gwen. "So, Captain—"

"I already told you—"

"I believe that you merit a field promotion under the circumstances," said Gwen. "So, Captain, how much trouble are we in?"

"Once it hits the papers, I expect the phone to be ringing off the hook with clients wanting their money back."

"Do we have to give it to them? Wait! Someone's coming."

"By God, if it's that Pontefract fellow again, I swear I will not be held accountable for the consequences this time."

The steps increased their pace.

"That's not him," said Iris.

"How do you know?" asked Gwen.

"That pace would give him a heart attack before he reached the landing. I wish it were him, given that."

The door was shoved open, and Detective Sergeant Michael Kinsey strode into the office.

"Sparks," he spat. "A word with you. In private. Now."

Iris leaned back in her chair and folded her arms.

"Is this official police business?" she asked.

"It is not."

"Then I am not speaking to you if you're behaving like this."

"And I'm not leaving her alone with you if you are going to continue exhibiting these poor manners," added Mrs. Bainbridge.

"I am afraid that I must insist," said Kinsey.

"You are in our office," Mrs. Bainbridge pointed out. "You have no authority here."

"And, short of a warrant, none over me," said Sparks. "Now, take your ill manners and go away."

Kinsey's face was a mask of suppressed rage. Then with a supreme effort, he took a deep breath and drew himself up.

"Miss Sparks, forgive me," he said. "May I please speak with you in private on a matter of some personal urgency?"

"Much better, Detective Sergeant," said Sparks. "Mrs. Bainbridge, I am going to accompany him to the third floor. Will you please mind the office until I return?"

Mrs. Bainbridge looked back and forth at both of them, then nodded slowly.

"Of course, Miss Sparks. It will be my pleasure," she said.

Sparks stood up and walked to the door, then stood there.

"Well?" she said expectantly.

He turned, flustered, and held the door open for her.

"Thank you, Detective Sergeant," she said, and then exited the office gracefully.

He looked down at the floor for a moment, then followed her.

"Round one to Sparks," Gwen whispered to herself.

The third floor corridor was lit only by one bulb and the sunlight coming through the window opposite the landing. Sparks led him there, then turned to face him, her back to the wall. She waited, saying nothing.

Kinsey looked at her, his face now unmasking the fury within.

"Who was it?" he demanded.

"Be very specific with that question, Mike," she said. "There are many ways to answer it."

"Who did you call to get us to back off?"

"I have no idea what you mean."

"Bollocks!" he said, and she put her hand to her mouth, feigning shock at the language. "Parham received a call from someone. Someone he wouldn't identify, even to me, and I'm his right-hand man."

"I don't know who called him, Mike," she replied.

Technically the truth, she thought. There would have been a string of intermediaries.

"Where the hell did you get that kind of pull?" asked Kinsey. "How is it that you know someone with enough clout to make us put on the kid gloves when we handle you?"

"I would not have expected you to own a pair," said Sparks. "I don't think they would go with that suit, but fashions are capricious, aren't they?"

"The capricious one is you, Sparks," he said. "Always have been. I should have known that before I—"

"Before you dropped me?"

"Before I asked you to be my wife," he said.

"You should have accepted me for who I was," said Sparks.

"I didn't know who you were," said Kinsey.

"Yet you proposed, which was incautious of you. And I said yes, which was ridiculously conventional of me."

"Then I caught you with that Spanish bloke when I came back on leave. What was I to think? Especially after what you said."

"What did I say, Mike?"

"As I stormed away, I heard him ask you who I was. You said, 'Just a boy from years ago who thought he had some claims on me.'"

"I didn't know you understood Spanish," she said, looking away into the dark corridor. "I'm sorry that you heard that."

"What was going on there, Sparks?" he asked. "Did I completely misread the situation? Was it truly an innocent matter?"

"I won't tell you, Mike."

"I'm seeing all of this in a new light," he said. "You told me that you were some form of lowly clerk in the War Office. But now I find you have access to people powerful enough to stop Scotland Yard from checking into your background."

"My background has nothing to do with the death of Matilda La Salle," she said. "That's where you should be directing your efforts."

"That case is solved."

"No, it isn't," she said. "You know it in your bones. You are probably a very good detective, Mike. Trust your instincts on this one."

"I trusted them when I dropped you," he said. "Did I make a mistake?"

"No," she said softly. "I'm unreliable, untrustworthy, and guilty of everything that you think I did and more. You're better off without me."

Quicker than thought, he stepped forward, took her in his arms, and kissed her.

Her first impulse was to throw him down the stairs.

She resisted it, and let the kiss flood through her. After an eternity, she placed her palms on his chest and gently pushed him away.

"I've already had to manhandle one fellow who tried to get fresh with me today, Mike," she said. "Don't make me get rough with you."

"I can take anything you can give," he said.

"I am not in the giving vein today," she said.

She pulled her handkerchief from her sleeve and wiped her lipstick from his mouth.

"You're getting married in a few weeks," she added. "Or had you forgotten?"

He didn't say anything.

"Well, I hope that adequately addresses your inquiries, Detective Sergeant," she said, tucking the handkerchief back in. "Will there be anything else?"

"I have nothing else," he said.

"Then I have one question for you."

"Yes?"

"Did you tip off the press about The Right Sort? Maybe after becoming furious at being shut down from looking into my life under the pretext of investigating a case your superior regarded as solved?"

"I would never do that, Sparks," he said. "Not even to you."

She fervently wished that she had Gwen there to read his face on that answer.

"All right, Mike," she said. "Go catch Tillie's murderer."

"That case is closed," he said. "I'm moving on."

"Then move on," she said. "I hope that the wedding goes smoothly. I hope that she makes you happy."

"Thanks," he said, turning towards the steps down. Then he turned back to look at her.

"That fellow I caught you with," he said. "Is he still part of your life?"

"No," she said.

"Good," he said.

She watched as he went down the stairs, disappearing from view as he made the turn, the steps fading until she heard the front door open, then slowly close on its own. Then there was silence.

"No," she said to the silence. "That man is no longer part of my life, Mike. Or of anyone's life. Including his own."

CHAPTER 6

Gwen watched without saying a word as Iris returned, opened a bottom drawer, and pulled out a bottle of whisky. She held it up to the light and inspected it, then waved it in Gwen's direction. Gwen held out her glass and held up one finger.

Iris poured her a drink, then one for herself. Then she held the glass up to the window, thought for a moment, then doubled it.

"Are we toasting anything?" asked Gwen.

"To, to," muttered Iris. Then she raised her glass high.

"To hell with all of it!" she shouted, and she tossed back half of the contents of her glass.

"To hell with all of it," echoed Gwen, sipping hers. "Do you want to talk about it?"

"Not really."

"He tried to kiss you, didn't he?"

Iris's hand went immediately to her lips.

"Is it that obvious?" she asked, reaching for her handbag. She opened the lid to reveal a small mirror and studied her mouth critically. "Yes. He tried to kiss me. Succeeded, too."

"I thought that he might."

"You could have given me some warning."

"What was I supposed to say? 'Look out! He has lips! And he's going to use them!'"

"You don't have to be—"

"Or, let me think, I believe that I still remember my semaphore training from the Girl Guides," continued Gwen.

She stood and flung out her arms in a series of angular poses.

"I don't know semaphore," said Iris, looking at her in alarm.

"D, A, N, G; E, R!" Gwen chanted. "L, I, P, S!"

"He might have noticed you doing that," said Iris. "He is a detective, after all."

"Was it a good kiss?" asked Gwen, resuming her seat.

"Went through me right down to my toes. I saw our entire relationship flash before my eyes. Mostly the boudoir moments."

"I am surprised that you let him."

"He caught me off guard."

"No," said Gwen, shaking her head. "You're never off guard."

"Ahhhgg!" cried Iris in exasperation, burying her head in her arms on her desk. "Stupid! So bloody, bloody stupid!"

"Was it because he's getting married?" asked Gwen. "Did you want to punish him for being with someone else?"

"Why are you torturing me?" asked Iris, her face still down and her voice muffled.

"Why are you torturing yourself?" returned Gwen.

"I can torture myself as long as I want," said Iris, pushing herself back up. "I still won't talk."

"Of course," said Gwen, unconvinced.

"Tell me about your visit with Trower," said Iris.

"Changing the subject won't make it go away."

"This is the subject. This is the only subject from now on. You spoke with him."

"Yes," said Gwen, and she filled Iris in on the details of her morning.

"Herbert," said Iris when she was done. "I should have suspected there would be a Herbert. Trower seemed like the goldfish-owning type."

"Seems like the type, dear," Gwen corrected her. "He's not dead yet."

"I have but one question for you," said Iris.

"Fire away."

"You looked him in the eye. Did you believe him when he said he didn't kill Miss La Salle?"

"I did. And I do. I unreservedly believe that he is an innocent man. Do you think that you can persuade Scotland Yard of that?"

"Not based only on your assessment, no. They've closed the case."

"Then it's up to us to put things right," said Gwen. "Are you willing?"

Iris sat silently, her eyes focused on a point far beyond the confines of their office. Gwen waited, patient and still in her chair.

"I have no faith in humanity, not one speck," said Iris abruptly. "And I might have been like that even before the bloody war came and confirmed everything that I have ever suspected about people. I have ruined every romance I have ever had and have spent far too much time railing against the general unfairness of life."

"If you're expecting me to disagree about the unfairness of life, I have had much more experience with that than you," said Gwen.

"I know, I know," said Iris. "I'm off on one of my solipsistic rants, forgive me. You want to investigate this matter because it's the right thing to do. What a lovely idea. Lovely, lovely, lovely."

"Don't belittle me."

"I'm not. What I'm trying to say is that I'm not like you. I'm destructive. Towards the world and towards myself. I'm Queen Midas with an acid touch instead of gold. Even my attempts to—to do whatever I was trying to do during the war—"

"Which you can't talk about."

"Which I can't talk about, which I ended up cocking up miserably on at least two—"

She stopped, pounded both fists on the desk, and roared in rage. Paper clips bounced everywhere.

"I survived the damn thing, and then I met up with you and suddenly, I'm doing something positive," she said. "Something I can take pride and comfort in, and say, how about that, Iris is looking out for others for a change, not to mention earning her own keep. And I'm doing it with another female of the species, a superlative example of womanhood—"

"Stop immediately," commanded Gwen.

"I mean to say that I signed on for this insane enterprise of ours because, among other reasons, I was sick and tired of being under the collective thumb of the men in my life. I wanted to gain control over my existence, and now that is all being threatened because some deranged man stuck a knife in an innocent girl."

"Or perhaps not so innocent."

"Or perhaps not so innocent," conceded Iris. "But short of being a murderess herself, she didn't deserve to be stabbed to death on a night meant for hope. And we certainly don't deserve to be dragged down because of it. If Dickie Trower goes to the gallows, the scandal will throw our brave little bureau into financial oblivion. We've been backed into a corner, and when I'm backed into a corner, I fight and I fight dirty and with any weapon I can get my hands on."

"Good," said Gwen.

"The first thing I'm going to do is call Sally, because if our business is going to fizzle out after that article breaks, then we're going to need that forty quid from the Cornwalls to tide us over."

"Oh," said Gwen. "Oh, dear. Has it come to that?"

"It has. And if I'm going in with you on this investigation, then I need to know you're with me on every step of the way, including Sally."

"Anything left in that bottle?" asked Gwen.

Iris pulled it out. This time, Gwen held up two fingers.

"Your turn to toast," said Iris after she poured.

Gwen held up her glass.

"To saving Dickie Trower," she said. "And maybe ourselves along the way."

Iris tapped her glass against Gwen's, and they drank them down.

"What's our next step after calling Sally?" asked Gwen.

"We need to find out more about Miss La Salle," said Iris. "I've already made some inquiries. There's going to be a viewing starting at four. Shadwell address. I'll go—"

"We'll go," said Gwen firmly.

"No," said Iris. "This isn't what you do. I can blend in and winnow out information. I've had training. You'd stick out like a sore thumb. A very tall sore thumb. More of a sore middle finger."

"Lovely metaphor, thanks very much," said Gwen. "But I repeat, we'll go. We are in this together, we shall investigate it together. You need me. I'm a better judge of people than you are, and I'm not basing that solely upon our comparative romantic histories. You know this to be true."

"How are you in a fight?" asked Iris.

"Will it actually come to that?"

"We'll be chasing down someone who stabbed a girl through the heart. It might actually be dangerous."

"'Your hands than mine are quicker for a fray. My legs are longer though, to run away,'" quoted Gwen.

"'I am amazed and know not what to say,'" responded Iris immediately. "I played Hermia at Cambridge, you won't sneak any *Midsummer* lines by me. Seriously, any oomph when you swing those long limbs of yours?"

"Haven't been in a fight since childhood, but at least we won't be going in unaware. Forewarned is forearmed in our case."

"And we have four arms between us, so there's that," said Iris. "All right. Come to the funeral parlour with me. But follow my lead. Let me do the talking."

"I've never been able to stop you," said Gwen. "Fine. You talk, I'll observe."

"Good," said Iris.

She picked up the phone receiver and dialed a number.

"Sally? It's Sparks," she said. "We have a job for you."

Celia Cornwall, née Maitland, was happily spooning warm milk over the scalloped potatoes when the doorbell rang. She hesitated, wondering if she should finish the task and plop the dish into the oven before the milk cooled down. Maybe the matter on the other side of the door was something that could be handled briefly, or politely put in abeyance until she finished.

The bell rang again. The ringer held it longer this time. It sounded insistent.

She sighed, put down the spoon, and went to open the front door.

Her first view was of a man's chest, bulging in a broad charcoal grey suit jacket with white stripes that looked like they were carefully drawn on with chalk and ruler. The red silk handkerchief folded perfectly in the pocket matched the tie, and the shirt looked tailored—well, it would have to have been, given the size of the man it enclosed.

She had yet to see his face, but a voice drifted down from above, and she looked up to see him smiling down at her. It was not a nice smile.

"Mrs. Cornwall?" he asked. "Do I have the pleasure of addressing Mrs. Celia Cornwall? Formerly Miss Celia Maitland of East Ham?"

"Y-yes," she stammered. "I am Mrs. Cornwall. Who are you?"

"Forgive my manners, Mrs. Cornwall," he said, removing his trilby. "My name is Salvatore Danielli. My friends call me Sally."

"What do you want?" she asked.

"Right to the point, very good," he said, beaming. "First of all, may I congratulate you on the happy occasion of your recent nuptials. I wish both you and Mister Cornwall joy and long life."

"Thank you," she said automatically. "Now, if you'll excuse me, I'm making dinner—"

"I won't be long, I assure you," he said. "Now, I am here on a somewhat delicate matter, that being the debt that you and Mister Cornwall, Aloysius, is it? Yes, Aloysius. A debt, as I was saying, of forty pounds that you owe to the source of your marital bliss, that being The Right Sort Marriage Bureau."

She meant to slam the door in his face, but he seemed to have foreknowledge of her design. He merely rested one of his massive hands lightly on the open door, and she found that she could not budge it.

"We do not owe them anything," she said. "Aloysius? Aloysius! Come down, darling. There's a man at the door."

"What is it? What is it?" came a querulous voice from above, and Mister Aloysius Cornwall came downstairs. He was a scrawny fellow, still in his stocking feet and in need of a shave. He stood next to his wife and gaped upwards at their visitor.

"What is the meaning of this?" he asked.

"Mister Cornwall, perfect," said Sally. "I was just informing your wife of my intention to collect the marriage fee of twenty pounds each that you now owe The Right Sort Marriage Bureau as a result of their successful efforts on your two behalves. They need to be made whole by your payment. I believe two behalves make a bewhole, don't they?"

"What?" spouted Mister Cornwall. "They expect us to pay forty pounds? They had nothing to do with this. We met independently of them. Quite the chance romantic encounter."

"Ah, but there is correspondence indicating the contrary," said Sally. "And even without it, your claims will stand you to no good stead in a court of law."

"Why? Why wouldn't they?"

"If you will review your contracts, and copies of both with your signatures remain with the bureau, you will find that the language of Paragraph Eight explicitly states that the fee shall be paid upon marriage to *any* other client of The Right Sort, irregardless of the number of introductions made or the amount of work done by the bureau. This is plain and simple English. You both signed contracts earlier this year. You are both clients, and were at the time that you exchanged vows in the eyes of God and England. The language of Paragraph Eight, you will find, is binding and all-encompassing, and any efforts to forestall the payment will only amount to unnecessary legal expenditure on your part."

"You're bluffing!" sputtered Mister Cornwall.

He seized the door with both hands and attempted to force it shut. Sally looked at him with pity. Mister Cornwall put his shoulder into the effort. The door remained motionless.

"Mister Cornwall, I do not bluff," said Sally. "A man of my size is sadly deprived of the gift of subtlety. I am here to facilitate a process in lieu of court action. My clients would very much like to avoid legal proceedings. I myself have come to have a healthy respect for the courts based upon some previous experiences which I would rather not detail, and I suggest that it would be in your benefit to avoid the same."

"I don't have the money on me," said Mister Cornwall, giving up his efforts and puffing heavily.

"Now, I didn't expect that you would, what with me showing up on your doorstep unannounced-like," said Sally. "My arrangement with The Right Sort covers three visits. The first, which is happening as we speak, is, shall we say, informatory in nature. The second, which will be at this time tomorrow, will be confirmatory. I shall arrive, you shall fork over the forty quid, and bygones will be themselves again. Have I sufficiently explained everything? Do you have any questions?"

"You said three visits," said Mrs. Cornwall.

"The third visit only becomes necessary if there is an unsatisfactory conclusion to the second," said Sally.

He put his trilby back on his head at just the right rakish angle and gave it a gentle tap to secure it.

"You really don't want that third visit," he said, no longer smiling. "Good day to you both."

He released the door, turned, and strolled away. The Cornwalls stared after him.

"I don't think informatory is a proper word," said Mister Cornwall.

"Shut up," she hissed. "Just shut up, will you?"

Gwen left a message with Percival, the Bainbridge butler, that she would be returning later than usual. Then they closed up shop and she allowed Iris to haul her to the Tube.

"Do you know Shadwell?" she asked Iris as the train left the station. "I don't think that I've ever set foot in it."

"Yes, you think Mayfair is the East End, don't you?" teased Iris. "I, on the other hand, know London inside and out. I used to go with my mum to the East End when she handed out pamphlets."

"What sort of pamphlets?"

"Birth control. She had a doctor friend who had set up a clinic in Wapping, so she would walk around all the East End neighbourhoods, me in tow."

"It must have been quite an education."

"Oh, yes," said Iris. "When people pointed out the incongruity of her promoting birth control while accompanied by her daughter, she would tell them that I was the single best argument for not having children that anyone could possibly make."

"Ouch."

"It was meant as a joke," said Iris.

"Not a good one."

"Maybe not, but that's how she was. She once told me that I was conceived the day that women got the vote."

"Really!"

Iris beckoned to Gwen to stoop so that she put her mouth by her ear.

"And that she was on top," she whispered, and it was all Gwen could do not to lose her composure on the train.

They got off at Stepney Green. Iris glanced around once to get her bearings, then set off confidently down Mile End.

"The Chapel of Rest is at Grimble and Sons," she said. "It's a ten minute walk from here. Ten for me, anyway. Probably five for you. Could have got off at Whitechapel, but this is a more interesting route."

"And no danger of meeting that Jack the Ripper fellow."

"Hmm, he'd be fairly up in years by now if he's still gadding about. I think we could outrun him."

"Why doesn't Shadwell have its own stop?"

"It used to."

"When did it close down?"

"In 1941. Which is also the answer to why."

"Oh. What family did Miss La Salle have?"

"Mum and dad, two other sisters," said Iris.

"And we are?"

"Friends. Acquaintances, rather. For now. People she met along· the way, come to pay their respects, thought she was loads of fun, dressed fabulously."

"So, not mentioning The Right Sort at all."

"I have a feeling that might get us hung from the nearest yard-arm," said Iris. "Fortunately, nobody knows us there. We pay our respects to the family, then I will chat up some of her friends, get the lowdown."

"Your accent changed in midsentence," observed Gwen.

"Got to sound local, dun I?" said Iris. "Can you sound less posh?"

"I will endeavour to try," said Gwen.

"And that would be sounding more posh," said Iris. "Hunch your shoulders and slump a bit as well."

"What on earth for?"

"So that you look less like someone used to holding a proper seat on a horse and more like someone who grew up in a cramped room with an outhouse in back."

"Like this?" Gwen offered, bending at the waist and contorting her torso as she walked.

"Don't overdo it, Quasimodo," cautioned Iris. "Just be less like you."

"Some days, I wish I was," said Gwen.

"One more thing. The ring."

"The ring?"

"The antique heirloom on your finger. I'm no appraiser, but it must be worth more than your average East Ender makes in a year. Pop it into your bag for now."

Gwen looked down at her wedding ring. For an instant, she saw Ronnie sliding it onto her finger. Her fist clenched, then relaxed. She eased it off her finger and placed it securely inside her handbag.

She felt exposed.

Grimble and Sons was a two-storey brick building with a workshop and stables attached in back. Iris and Gwen glimpsed the tops of the old horse-drawn hearses over the gates to the driveway, but there was a pair of Daimler hearses parked in front. A sign over the large windows on the right proclaimed, "Grimble and Sons. All funerary services. Burials and cremations. Embalming available."

There were two entrances. The one on the right led to the commercial side, where display coffins waited on trestles for future occupants, English elm, Canadian walnut, oak, and mahogany gleaming from French polishing. The other entrance, surmounted with a stone cross over the lintel, led to the Chapels of Rest. Three placards inside the front window indicated the current loved ones in temporary residence before transport to their burial grounds.

"Miss Matilda La Salle, Chapel Two," read Iris. "Deep breath, Gwen. Look sad."

"No difficulties there," said Gwen.

They entered. Chapel Two was on their right. A young man, no more than sixteen, stood by the doorway. He was dressed in classic undertaker's garb, a black suit that must have been passed down from previous and slightly larger Grimbles dating back to the prior century, surmounted by a top hat with a veil gathered in back. He maintained a solemn look that was as unsuitable to his youth as the suit was to his frame.

"Welcome, ladies," he said, opening the door. "We are sorry for your loss."

"Thanks," said Iris.

She entered, with Gwen following, clutching her handbag in front with her elbows drawn into her ribs to bring her shoulders down.

The chapel was not ostentatiously decorated. It was an interior room, so no stained-glass depictions of saints or holy scenes graced the walls. A simple cross hung on the wall behind the coffin. The family had opted for English elm, and the smell of linseed oil and freshly sawn wood drifted towards Iris and Gwen as they approached.

There were other mourners scattered amongst the pews, some in prayer, some chatting away as if they were oblivious to their surroundings and the occasion. Iris marked them as targets of inquiry. Two young women were ahead of her, about the same age as Miss La Salle.

But they could still get older, Iris thought gloomily.

She waited in the short queue to the coffin, crossed herself, and pretended to pray for a moment. The two women were standing by the coffin, peering down at the corpse.

"They laid 'er out nice," murmured one. "Din't overdo the powder. She'd 'ate looking too done up."

"Too true," agreed the other. "Although I dunno that she'd 'ave picked that outfit, given the choice. She oughter 'ave gone with the green one. She wouldn't be caught de—"

She stopped herself barely in time, her hand flying up to her mouth.

Gwen looked over Iris's shoulder at the late Miss La Salle. Grimble and Sons had done good work. Her hair was styled beautifully, just like in the black and white photograph that was up on the easel next to the coffin. She was wearing the same bolero jacket and kiltie combination that she had on when she had come to their office.

A lifetime ago, thought Gwen.

"Ooo, that lipstick always looked good on 'er," said the first woman.

"What's that, the raspberry?" asked Iris.

"I think so," said the second, leaning over to peer at it.

"I wanted to borrow that one," said Iris. "She said not likely. Said it was 'er favourite, and 'ard to come by, what with the extra tax."

"Oh, she 'ad her ways of gettin' around that," said the first woman. "Don't think I know you. I'm Elsie."

"Fanny," said the second.

"Mary," said Iris. "That's Sophie be'ind me."

Gwen gave a timid wave.

The women turned to the family who were sitting in a front pew, silent and stunned. They passed through them, issuing a series of muttered "So sorry's" without engaging at length. Gwen was grateful for the cover the two women gave them. Iris managed to guide them to a back pew. Gwen sat across the aisle, watching as people drifted in and out.

"How did you know 'er?" asked Elsie.

"Run into 'er every now and again," said Iris. "On the town and all. First time we met, a couple of French soldiers tried to chat us up. Thought we were together. We let 'em."

"Oh, I think I 'eard about that," said Fanny. "They thought she was French 'cause of the name."

"And we din't savvy a word," said Iris. "We just kept nodding and they kept buying us drinks. Then we staggered off our separate ways. Most fun I 'ad in the war was with 'er that night. After that, we sorter looked out for each other when we'd run into each other dancing and the like. So I thought I'd pay me respects. 'Ow about you?"

"Oh, we're Shadwell girls," said Elsie. "Known 'er for donkey's years."

"Knew 'er," amended Fanny.

"Right, knew 'er," agreed Elsie, and the two lapsed into solemn silence.

Which lasted for a second.

"I wonder if Roger is goin' to show," said Elsie.

"'E'd 'ave a bloody nerve to put 'is face inside," said Fanny darkly. "There's other coffins what's available."

"Who's Roger?" asked Iris, trying not to sound too eager. "Family?"

"Should 'ave been," said Elsie. "If 'e'd a done as 'e oughter, which 'e din't."

"Ah," said Iris, nodding wisely. "Never knew about 'im. After me time. They together long?"

"Long enough," said Fanny. "Long enough for 'er to think they were going to be cut and carried. But 'e drops 'er. I blame 'im for what 'appened to 'er."

"Likewise," sniffed Elsie. "If she weren't so set on showing 'im he made a mistake, she wouldn't 'ave gallivanted off to that lonely 'earts place and get 'erself ripped."

"Is that 'ow it 'appened?" asked Iris. "Why'd he scarper?"

"She thought 'e was using 'er," said Fanny. "That 'e was just a low-down spiv aiming to get a leg up."

"And she was goin' to 'elp 'im? What was 'er fiddle?"

"I don't like to say," said Elsie. "Not speaking ill, and 'er still in the room."

Gwen listened, trying to sort out the slang when it came up. She didn't want to stare at them while they were talking. She turned back to watch as a few elderly women paid their respects.

She never had the chance to bury Ronnie, she thought. He was in the Cassino War Cemetery in Italy. His parents had spoken about having him exhumed and brought back to be placed in the family vault, but had been dissuaded by his commanding officer in the Fusiliers. She had overheard two of the servants talking about it when she finally was released from the sanitorium. Something about there being not much left to bury after the shell blast hit him.

Hearing that almost sent her back to the sanitorium.

Someone tapped her on the shoulder. A man sat next to her, holding a handkerchief out. She looked at him in confusion, then instinctively felt her cheeks.

Tears again. Of course.

She wiped her face, then handed it back.

"Des," said the man. "Tillie's me cousin."

"Sophie," she said, hesitantly.

A dockworker, she guessed from his clothes. He wore a brown peacoat over a ratty grey sweater, a grey cap with a short black brim, and black rubber wellies. He had grey-green eyes that reminded her of the ocean on a cloudy day.

"Did you know her much?" asked Des.

"Not really," she said. "Met her once."

"Only once?" he said in surprise. "And you came?"

"I liked her," said Gwen. "She was so lively. And then I heard about—it's such a waste. I wanted to come. I can't even say why."

"You're not from 'ere," he observed.

"No."

"Where'd you get them posh tones?"

"Kensington," she said. "Upstairs maid growing up. They expect you to talk proper like them."

"That right? Then 'ow did you meet Tillie?"

"I left, went to work in a department store," Gwen improvised. "I work there with—"

She momentarily drew a blank on Iris's alias.

"With Mary," she said, summoning it. "Tillie came in. She knew Mary from somewhere. She wanted to buy a hat, something feathery. We got to talking, hit it off, met up after for a drink. Never did sell her that hat."

"She liked to shop, but she didn't like to spend 'er own money," he said, chuckling quietly.

"She said she worked in a dress shop, too," said Gwen. "Was that right?"

"Oh, yeah. Tolbert's, over on Martha Street. 'E's probably broken up over it. Thought the world of 'er."

"Sweet on her, was he?"

"Well, no thinking that," said Des. "Old Tolbert 'as to be sixty if 'e's a day, and 'e ain't been a day in many a day."

"She must have been a good worker, then."

"I expect," said Des. "You coming to the funeral?"

"I don't think so," said Gwen. "I had to beg them to let me off early to make this. Where is she to be buried?"

His eyebrows raised at the phrasing.

"She is to be buried at Bow," he said. "She is to be transported by one of them Daimlers out front, with us walking be'ind. She would've wanted the old 'orse-drawn 'earse with the black feathers and the crape in the tails and Old Grimble leadin' the way with the top 'at and the big wand, but 'orses cost more."

"Sounds like that would have been grand," said Gwen.

"Yeah, well, waste of money on brown bread, innit?"

"I wish I could come."

"There's gonna be a bit of an 'ale and 'earty after if you can make it," he said.

"Where?" she asked, her mind scrambling to figure out what that meant.

"Merle's. That's over on Wapping High Street. Come raise a glass to 'er."

"I'll be there," she promised. "Thanks for the hanky."

"Don't mention it," he said, tucking it away.

She saw Iris rising and shaking hands with Elsie and Fanny. She went over to join them.

"You don't 'alf waste any time, do you?" said Fanny.

"Yeah, it's the quiet ones what they like," added Elsie. "If I could keep me mouth shut, I'd 'ave better luck."

"If wishes were 'orses," sighed Fanny. "Been setting me sights on that one for ages."

"I wasn't trying—" Gwen began.

"We know," said Elsie. "Ones like you don't 'ave to try, love. Makes it 'arder for the rest of us, picking through the leavings."

"Nice meeting you," said Fanny. "See you tomorrer at Merle's, then?"

"Count on it," said Iris. "Come on, Sophie. Let's 'oof it back to the station before it gets dark."

"Ta ta," said Gwen.

They walked out.

"Ale and arty?" asked Gwen as soon as they were safely out of earshot.

"Put the h's back in," said Iris. "Then think of a rhyme that makes sense."

"Hale and hearty. Oh! A party?"

"Well done."

"Context is all," said Gwen. "I needed you to interpret."

"You needed me to chaperone," teased Iris.

"It wasn't like that."

"Why not?"

"It was in a chapel of rest, for goodness' sake! With the poor girl lying not twenty feet away!"

"Never stopped any red-blooded man from approaching a fair maid."

"I am no fair maid to be approached."

"Fair matron, then."

"Low blow."

"They're the only kind I can land on you," said Iris. "Learn anything useful?"

"I got the name of the shop she worked in. Tolbert's on Martha Street."

"Martha Street, Martha Street," mused Iris. "I think that's just north of the railway. Might be worth a little shopping expedition."

"How about your new friends? Anything more about Roger?"

"Oh, you heard that? Yes, that was interesting. Poor Tillie came to us on the tail of being dumped."

"I wonder if we could find out more about him. His last name might prove useful."

"My thought as well. Hence the hale and hearty. Or 'ence the 'ale and 'earty, I should say."

"Two late nights in a row. Oh, God!" exclaimed Gwen. "I completely forgot!"

"Forgot what?"

"Lady Carolyne. I was supposed to have a talk with her after work. She'll be furious."

"A talk about what?"

"I don't know. Her talks are never about anything I want to hear. And now I've given her the advantage by being late."

"Want me there?"

"No," said Gwen. "I have to deal with this myself."

"Then I shall lend my shoulder for you to cry on in the morning."

"I'll have to lean down considerably."

"And volley returned. That's my girl."

"So, Captain, what is our next move?"

"We can try Tolbert's tomorrow afternoon. Then head on to Merle's, if you fancy a drink with your new suitor."

"What about The Right Sort?"

"I don't expect business to be booming tomorrow," said Iris gloomily.

CHAPTER 7

I t was past seven thirty when Gwen reached Kensington Court. At the last second, she remembered to replace her wedding ring. She slipped inside the house as quietly as she could, wondering if dinner was already over. They ate earlier now that Little Ronnie was joining them at the table. She had no time to change. She'd have to go with her workday suit, which would surely arouse some comment on Lady Carolyne's part.

To her dismay, Percival, the butler, was standing in the front hallway when she came through the door.

"Good evening, Madam," he said. "I trust that your day was satisfactory."

"Thank you, Percival," she said, unpinning her hat. "I hope that you haven't been waiting here just for me."

A faint grimace flickered over his face, then disappeared.

"Lady Carolyne is expecting you," he said.

"I am aware."

"She has been expecting you for some time. She is in the library. Please follow me."

He turned to lead her.

"There's no need for you to—" she began.

"Please follow me, Madam," he repeated without looking back.

He led her the short distance down the main hallway and knocked lightly on the second door to the right. There was a muffled bark from within. He opened the door.

"Mrs. Bainbridge has arrived," he announced.

The formality of the moment did not bode well, she thought. She gathered herself up and walked passed Percival into the room.

The library at the house held a collection of antique volumes bound in leather, with titles in Latin, German, and English embossed in gold leaf. The oldest, most priceless members of the collection were locked in a glass-doored mahogany cabinet perched on a quartet of elaborately carved legs. The rest of the books, merely valuable, ran across two sides of the room. There was a reading nook at one end with a tea table next to it, and a fireplace at the other with a marble mantelpiece, over which a painting of the current Lord Bainbridge glared down on everyone and everything, maintaining vigilance while his model in life was off inspecting their holdings in East Africa.

In all the years that Gwen had lived in this house, she had never seen anyone reading any of the books mouldering on the shelves. Ronnie, when he had first shown her around the place, shuddered with mock revulsion when she asked if he liked to read in there.

"God, no!" he had exclaimed. "With the Pater glowering down like that? I'd be terrified of leaving the slightest nick in the most unread tome in the place. He'd find it like a shot, and out comes the belt. No, I was happiest curled up in my secret hidey-hole in the attic with Ashenden or Hornblower."

Lady Carolyne sat in one of a pair of matching armchairs by the fireplace. She did not deign to look in Gwen's direction when she entered. There was a decanter of sherry and one glass on a small table between the two chairs.

There was no fire.

Gwen hesitated, then went to take the chair opposite Lady Carolyne. She sank deep into the cushions. The arms felt like they were trying to pinion her down.

"Good evening, Lady Carolyne," she said.

"You're late."

"I telephoned. There was a funeral."

"A funeral?" responded Lady Carolyne, jerking her head towards Gwen. "Whose?"

"One of our clients," said Gwen. "It was unexpected."

"And you went to solicit the bereaved for business?"

"To pay our respects, of course," said Gwen. "Anything else would have been inappropriate."

For example, pursuing a highly speculative murder investigation, she thought with a pang of guilt.

"An engagement party in the morning, a funeral in the evening," said Lady Carolyne. "A true panoply of human existence in one short day. It's too bad that you couldn't pick up a christening during tea."

"I—"

"Yet no actual weddings, which I understood to be the point of your vacuous little enterprise," continued Lady Carolyne. "An unprofitable day overall, I would say."

"Some are better than others," said Gwen. "Is this the matter which you wished to discuss with me?"

"No," said Lady Carolyne. "It concerns your son."

"Ronnie? Is anything wrong?"

"Not a thing," said Lady Carolyne. "However, Lord Harold and I have been discussing his schooling."

"Yes?"

"I received a letter from Lord Harold confirming our plans. We have decided to send Ronnie to St. Frideswide's School. It was where his father went, where Lord Harold went, indeed, where Bainbridge men have gone for generations."

"But that means sending him away," protested Gwen. "You can't do that. He's only six."

"As to what we can or cannot do, let me remind you that we are his guardians, not you," said Lady Carolyne. "The manner of his education falls to us. Being tutored at home is too limiting. He must receive proper instruction if he is to take his rightful place in the world."

"I don't disagree, but St. Frideswide's—it's terribly far. There are many fine schools right here in London—"

"There is a tradition to be upheld," said Lady Carolyne. "You, like myself, have entered into this family from the outside, and by doing so, you have agreed to be bound by the family traditions."

"I by no means agreed to have my only son sent two hundred miles away when he's only six years old. What mother could possibly agree to anything so cruel?"

She regretted the words as soon as they came out of her mouth. Lady Carolyne looked at her with cold fury in her eyes.

"So, I am cruel now," she snapped. "I am a villainous woman because I allowed my son to be given the benefits of one of the finest schools in England, one which turned him into the superb man that he was. I must disagree with your assessment of my maternal skills. And if you were so concerned with your child's upbringing, then you would scarcely be playing at this silly business venture. You would be at home, helping to raise him—"

"Which you won't let me do!" shouted Gwen, rising to her feet.

"Which you are incapable of doing," said Lady Carolyne. "If you think for a moment that we would entrust our grandson, the only child of our only child, to the care of a woman whose emotional instability—"

"My husband was killed. His loss destroyed me."

"You did not see us overreact to his death like that," said Lady Carolyne. "We grieved, yes. We mourned, certainly. Then we carried on, and it was fortunate for you that we did. Who would have taken care of your child if it hadn't been for us?"

"Lady Carolyne, I can never repay you for what you did," said Gwen. "But I am past that episode—"

"Are you?" scoffed Lady Carolyne. "I doubt that anyone would view your current behaviour as that of a respectable widow and mother. Certainly not anyone in a court of law."

"He is my child," said Gwen. "You've already taken away my rights as his mother. Please, Lady Carolyne, he is all I have left of Ronnie. If you send him away, there will be nothing for me here."

"Be that as it may," said Lady Carolyne. "The family traditions will be upheld. When Ronnie takes his place as a Bainbridge man, it will be with a St. Frideswide education."

"You don't care about his happiness," said Gwen. "All you care about is turning him into another figurehead for the family holdings."

"He is the heir now that my son is dead," said Lady Carolyne. "It should not have fallen to him so early. It should have been Ronnie. My Ronnie. I never thought life would be like this, but we must make the best of what it provides."

"This is not—"

"There will be no more discussion on this matter."

"When?" asked Gwen in despair. "When does he leave us?"

"The autumn term," said Lady Carolyne. "I am done. Good night."

Gwen walked slowly to the door, nearly blinded by her tears.

She staggered upstairs in search of her son. He was in his playroom, drawing on his pad with crayons.

"Mummy!" he cried when he saw her standing at the doorway. "You missed dinner. We had mutton."

She knelt, and he flew into her embrace.

"I'm sorry, my precious darling," she said, kissing him on the forehead. "Mummy had to work late tonight."

"Did anyone get married today?"

"Not today," she said, releasing him. "But soon, I hope. What are you drawing?"

"I'm making a story," he said excitedly.

"Show me."

He held up a picture of a yellowish fish, with a long nose. No, more of a tusk.

"Is that—is that a narwhal?" she said.

"Yes!" he said proudly. "That is Sir Oswald the Narwhal. He swims in the Arctic Ocean, saving the world and fighting the Nazis."

"He sounds like a very brave and noble fish," said Gwen.

"He's not a fish," said Ronnie impatiently. "He's a mammal."

"Is he really?"

"He's a type of whale. That's what the second part of his name means."

"*Whal* means whale? I must say, that makes sense. I never knew that. Then what does *nar* mean?"

"It means corpse," said Ronnie.

"What?" exclaimed Gwen, stiffening involuntarily. "Goodness gracious, why?"

"The colour," said Ronnie. "The sailors thought it looked like a floating dead thing. Isn't that strange?"

"Very strange," said Gwen, stifling the dread that this innocent drawing was now creating in her. "Well, you must tell me all about Sir Oswald's adventures. How did he become knighted?"

"It happened when he was very young," said Ronnie. "They live a long time, narwhals do. They stay with their mummies because they have to nurse, like baby cows. Did I nurse when I was a baby, Mummy?"

"Of course," said Gwen. "I took very good care of you. We were out in the country then."

"Are we going back there this summer?"

The question caught her by surprise. She had been so wrapped up in The Right Sort that she had not thought about any summer plans. And now that Ronnie was going to be leaving in the fall, this would be their last time together until the holidays.

"I'm not sure, darling," she said. "I'm working now, so I might not be able to go, or at least, not for very long. I will discuss it with your grandmother."

"It's all right if we don't go," he said, turning to his drawing.

"You don't mind me working, do you?"

"Why would I mind?"

"Because it's the first time I've done that since—well, really the first time ever."

"All the other people here work, don't they? Except for Grandmother, of course."

"Yes, I suppose that's true."

"Only you don't work for Grandmother."

"No," said Gwen. "I don't."

"We should tell Grandmother to get a job," said Ronnie.

Gwen gave an involuntary snort at the thought, then hugged him.

"You are a marvelous boy," she said. "Now, tell me more about Sir Oswald."

"I think he needs a helmet," said Ronnie, studying the picture critically.

"I think you're right," said Gwen.

Andrew was stretched out on the divan in the sitting room when Iris returned to her flat, his stockinged feet up on a cushion, his boots standing at attention on the carpet beside him. He looked up from the book he was reading.

"I didn't know you were coming in tonight," she said, dropping her handbag on the table.

"Wanted to finish this," he said, holding up the Campion. "Still don't believe a word, but it's entertaining enough. You're getting in later than usual."

"I was out investigating."

"So you've turned detective after all. Good for you. What changed your mind?"

"A visit from the press," she said, sitting on the edge of the divan next to him and kicking off her shoes. "Move over and I'll tell you all about it."

He listened intently as she recounted her visit from Pontefract.

"You should have called me," he said. "We could have tried to quash the story."

"No, that would have made matters worse," she said. "Once the terrier has seized the rat in its teeth, it won't cease worrying it."

"What are you going to do when the paper comes out?"

"Weather the storm the best we can. Maybe the free publicity will help in the long run."

"You don't believe that."

"No, I don't," she said glumly.

"Still, I wish I could have seen you buffeting that fellow about," he said. "His pride must be below his ankles now."

"It was surprisingly satisfying," she agreed. "Less so when Mike Kinsey showed up later."

"Did he? Why?"

"He was unhappy over having the Brigadier lower the boom on him. He was all gung-ho for digging into my background."

"Did you appease him?"

"I doubt it," she said, not wanting to go into the discomfiting details. "I wish I could set things right there."

"If you turn up someone who is not the man they've already

charged as the killer, you won't be endearing yourself to him or the Yard."

"Oh, God. That's true, isn't it? Well, there's no turning back now."

"Of course there is. You could leave it all alone."

"Then Dickie Trower hangs for a crime he didn't commit, my bureau goes down in flames, and the man who killed Tillie La Salle remains free to do it to some other poor girl."

"Unless he was satisfied with just the one," commented Andrew. "This sort of thing is usually personal."

"I agree," said Iris. "Still, one would hope for—no, that's a silly, Pollyannaish thing to think."

"Hope for what?"

"Justice," said Iris. "But we both know that there is no such thing in this world."

"It's only a fancy word for vengeance, anyhow," said Andrew.

"I'll settle for vengeance," said Iris grimly. "It's better than nothing. Dear Lord, this is setting the wrong mood again. I'm sorry."

He leaned over and kissed her neck.

"Does that help?" he asked.

"It's a start. Keep at it, soldier."

"Shall we continue this in the other room?"

"I'd rather not waste time moving," she said. "By the way, you're still wearing clothing."

"A problem easily remedied."

Gwen, thinking ahead to the 'ale and 'earty, pulled out one of her Utility Collection dresses, not wishing to draw attention to anything that would mark her as someone capable of affording more. The "Margo," they had called it, one of the approved designs. She had used eleven precious coupons for it in '45, the first thing she bought when the war ended. It was of a muted rose, with enough trim detail on the bodice to make it interesting without going over the fabric limits, and a large pocket into which she made sure to place a clean handkerchief, given the unreliability of her tear ducts. The skirt had a few wide pleats which allowed some swirl as she walked.

She left early, sneaking into Ronnie's room to kiss him on the cheek before he woke. She skipped her morning toast, having only a cup of tea to sustain her. She walked through Kensington, then took the long way around the perimeter of Hyde Park for the added exercise.

She carried the borrowed issue of *Good Housekeeping* to use as a shield should there be any photographers lurking about the office. She poked her head around the corner of her street to reconnoiter before walking down it. Sure enough, a man with a camera with a large flash attachment was hiding ineffectively in a doorway across from their building.

"Did you know that we have a back entrance?" said Iris behind her.

Gwen nearly jumped out of her Margo.

"Please don't ever do that to me again," she said when she recovered.

"Sorry," said Iris, clearly not meaning it.

"How did you know I would be coming this way?"

"You are a creature of habit," said Iris. "I, on the other hand, never take the same route twice in a row. Follow me."

She led Gwen back half a block, then ducked down a narrow alleyway, past dustbins and piles of scrap lumber. She came up to a wooden fence and slid aside a loose board. She stepped through, then held it open as Gwen did the same.

They were in the rear of the lot where the building next to them had been demolished. The rear wall still stood in part, giving them cover from the street.

"Aren't we trespassing?" asked Gwen as Iris replaced the board.

"Technically," said Iris. "Mind your footing. There are some dodgy bits back here."

She strode confidently through the rubble, reaching the rear of their own building. Gwen picked her way carefully after her, trying to place her feet in the same locations so as not to twist an ankle or damage her stockings. Iris walked down a narrow stone ramp to a door marked *Deliveries*. She pulled out her keys from her handbag, riffled through them, then selected one. She unlocked the door and held it open.

"It's dark," she said. "Go straight ahead. You'll see the light by the stairwell."

"I didn't know we had keys to this door," said Gwen as she entered. "I didn't know this door even existed."

"We didn't have keys," said Iris, shutting it behind them and locking it. "I made a copy of Mister MacPherson's spare."

"When?"

"When we first moved in. Here's another one for you. You'll need it now that you're a fugitive from the press."

"You're very prepared. Were you anticipating a need for a way to sneak into our own building from the beginning?"

"No," said Iris. "I was anticipating the need for an escape route."

"Why? An escape from what?"

"You weren't in London during the Blitz. I was. You always need an escape route. Here's the stairs. Let me get the light."

Gwen looked upwards to where distant daylight glimmered somewhere.

"I feel like—who was the girl Orpheus fetched up from Hades?"

"Eurydice."

"I had better not look back," said Gwen as she climbed the stairs.

"Orpheus was the one who looked back," said Iris. "Because he couldn't resist her beauty and mostly because, being a man, he couldn't follow even the simplest of directions."

"If it had been you, would you have looked back?" asked Gwen.

"I've never loved anyone so much that I would go to Hades for them. How about you?"

"If I found him in Hades, I would stay there," said Gwen.

She reached the ground storey and risked a peek out the front door.

"He's still there," she said. "Looking both ways."

"Good," said Iris. "Let's get to work."

The telephone was ringing when they opened the door to their office. Iris dashed to her desk and snatched the receiver up.

"The Right Sort Marriage Bureau, Sparks speaking, how may we help you?" she said. "Ah, Miss Sedgewick, how are you? What? The article in the *Mirror*? Yes, I've seen it."

Gwen looked at her in dismay. Iris pulled a clipping from her handbag and handed it to her. On top was a picture of Gwen, her expression startled, as she was walking to work the previous day. A headline read, PROCURESS OF DEATH!

"No, utter nonsense," continued Sparks. "Don't give it another thought. You want what? Well, I'm afraid that we can't do that. It's in your contract, look at Paragraph Nine. No, it's nonrefundable. What? Stuff and nonsense! Seriously, what are the chances of us having two murderers amongst our clientele? No, I'm not saying Mister Trower is a murderer, quite the contrary. I'm certain it was a misunderstanding—don't believe what you read in the papers, especially the *Mirror*. Don't worry, Miss Sedgewick, I'll find you one who won't kill you. Good-bye."

She hung up.

"Although, God help me, I might change my mind," she muttered.

The telephone rang again.

"It's going to be a long morning," sighed Iris as she answered.

Gwen read the article rapidly, then again more slowly.

"'Slumming society girl,'" she said when Iris hung up. "How dare he?"

"He makes his living daring such drivel," said Iris. "That was Terence Robicheaux on the phone. Same conversation, different register. I wish I had a phonograph and a record I could play with my response for each of these."

"At least the photo wasn't clear," said Gwen. "Thank goodness my face was in motion. I wonder if they'll dig up any of my old society shots from their archives."

The telephone rang again.

"Shall I take this one?" asked Gwen.

"No, you're still in a state of high dudgeon over that article," said Iris, answering it. "Hello, The Right Sort Marriage Bureau, Sparks speaking."

"Hello, Sparks, it's Jessie Kemp. I've got that information you wanted."

Iris momentarily drew a blank, then remembered.

"Yes, yes, Jessie," she said, grabbing her pad and pencil. "What's the verdict?"

"Only mildly criminal," said Kemp. "Matilda La Salle, also known as Tillie, no other known aliases. Nicked once in September, '44, using fake clothing coupons. Got off with a fine and seems to have walked the straight and narrow since, or at least has got away with anything else. Think she's still marriage material?"

"Not anymore, but not because of that," said Iris. "Was she charged with anyone?"

"As a matter of fact, she was," said Kemp. "An Elsie Spencer. Why? Is she another candidate?"

"Not yet," said Iris.

"Anything else?"

"Not a thing. You've been grand, Jessie. Thanks awfully."

"Just find me a good one, Sparks. Mum's been pressuring to set

me up with a widower who dribbles soup in his beard. I'm contemplating throwing myself in the Thames as an alternative."

"Don't do either, Jessie. I'm on the case. I'll be in touch soon.
Good-bye."

She hung up.

"What was that all about?" asked Gwen.

"My source with Records at Scotland Yard," said Iris. "Miss La
Salle was caught with counterfeit clothing coupons two years ago.
Skated with a fine and a wrist slap."

"So your instincts about her were correct," said Gwen.

"Maybe," said Iris. "She had an accomplice."

"Who?"

"Our new best friend Elsie."

"Really? That's too bad. I liked her."

"Just because she tried to pull a fast one once doesn't mean that
she's rotten to the core," said Iris.

"No, I know that," said Gwen. "How does this affect things?"

"We're searching for another reason why someone would want
to kill Miss La Salle," said Iris. "Jealous lover is one possibility,
but if she was tied into counterfeiting, that could be another."

"Counterfeiting clothing coupons hardly seems like a scheme
worth murdering anyone for."

"Maybe not," said Iris. "But we should follow up on everything
we have—"

"Which is not much."

"Are you giving up already?"

"No, of course not," said Gwen. "So we visit the shop where she
worked this afternoon, then go from there to the pub?"

"That's the plan," said Iris.

"What about the bureau? Do we close early?"

"Perhaps I could help you with that," said a man's voice from
the doorway.

"Sally!" exclaimed Iris, running up to give him a hug.

"Hello, darling," he said, squeezing her as lightly as he could, which nevertheless produced a muffled *oomph* from her. "Oh, dear, I'm so sorry. No ribs broken, I hope?"

"Not this time," she said, extricating herself. "You remember Gwen, don't you?"

"Mrs. Bainbridge, a pleasure to see you again," he said, stepping into the office and extending his hand.

Gwen placed hers in his, feeling like a child shaking hands with a grown-up.

"It is nice to see you as well, Mister Danielli," she said politely.

"How did it go with the Cornwalls?" asked Iris.

"Oh, it was simplicity itself," he said. "I put on my second-most fearsome persona. I thought I'd save the full growly monster for the finale, if it should come to that. But I doubt that it will."

"Wonderful," said Iris.

"You didn't hurt—anything, did you?" Gwen asked hesitantly.

"No damage done, neither to human nor property," said Sally. "I have a return engagement at dinnertime to collect your well-gotten gains."

"Less your commission."

"I have not forgotten," he said. "Now, as to your immediate problem, what is the situation and what may I do to help?"

"We are investigating a murder," said Iris.

"How very public-spirited of you," said Sally. "Why?"

"You haven't seen the *Mirror* by any chance, have you?"

"My sweet girl, do you possibly believe that I would ever bother with that trashy tabloid? You don't mean to tell me that you're in it?"

Iris filled him in on the relevant details.

"My, my, ladies," said Sally, his face creasing in sympathy. "You have been through it. So, you need a secretary for the afternoon, do you?"

"Yes, in a nutshell," said Iris.

"I could be bounded in that particular nutshell," said Sally.

"You? Goodness, darling, I could scarcely ask you to sit here and answer the telephone for four hours."

"Why not? What other use for my skills are there today? My dear, I am at your disposal. What's the drill?"

The telephone rang.

"Watch and learn," said Iris as she answered it.

Sally listened intently as she placated yet another worried client.

"Sounds simple enough," he said. "Paragraph Nine, was it?"

"Yes."

"I'm getting to know your contract better than you. Appointments?"

"In the unlikely event that there are any, here's the book. Try and make them for the mornings this week, as we expect to be out sleuthing in the afternoons."

"Sleuthing," said Gwen. "I like that."

"It does sound quite thrilling, doesn't it?" said Sally. "And if any intrepid reporters show up at your office door, what are my standing orders?"

"Break out that most fearsome persona," said Iris.

"Lovely," he said. "I've been wanting to put that one to the test. I quite hope they do show up now. Ladies, you have yourselves a secretary. May I have the use of your typewriter? I'm working on a new play."

"Of course," said Iris, taking up his massive hand between hers. "But no pounding. The poor girl's had a rough week."

"I am capable of the utmost delicacy when the situation demands it," he said, kissing her hand gallantly. "I shall return at one."

He turned to Gwen and repeated the gesture. She accepted it without flinching. Then he left.

"How do you know him exactly?" she asked when he had gone.

"Cambridge," Iris replied. "Then we worked together during the war."

"And I will question you no further," said Gwen. "We are now in the no-point-in-asking territory."

"Thank you."

"What's remarkable is how he showed up on our doorstep without either of us hearing him come up the steps. It's as if he manifested himself in response to our wishes."

"I have often suspected him of being a genie," said Iris.

"Is the fearsome aspect only an act?"

"Not at all. He's decorated. Parachuted behind enemy lines, blew up an astonishing number of targets. We used to joke that he could bring a bridge down merely by jumping on it, but we would never say it to his face. He's sensitive about his size."

"And he's a playwright?"

"He hopes to be. I thought his student work showed promise."

"He seems quite devoted to you," said Gwen.

Iris shrugged noncommittally.

"When you write your memoirs, send them to me first," said Gwen. "If there's anything left after the censors get through with them."

"Hey, did you hear that?" asked Iris.

"Hear what?"

"The sound of the telephone not ringing for five minutes now. Maybe we're out of the woods."

"Not everyone reads the *Mirror*," Gwen reminded her. "I pray that no one connected to Lady Carolyne does."

"Ah, yes. How did last night's meeting go?"

"I don't want to talk about it," said Gwen.

"That bad?"

"You have your private matters, I have mine," said Gwen.

"Fair enough," said Iris. "Shall we get to work at long last?"

"Please."

"I drew up a cheque for Miss La Salle's family. I had it with me yesterday, but there was no opportunity to leave it. Would you write them a note? You do that sort of thing so much better than I."

"Because of my handwriting?"

"Because you're more sympathetic," said Iris.

"Very well," said Gwen, grabbing a sheet of stationery.

Sally returned at ten minutes to one and wedged himself carefully behind Iris's desk.

"Here's the key so you can lock up," said Iris, tossing it to him. "Same time tomorrow?"

"And tomorrow and tomorrow," he said as he scrolled a sheet of paper into the typewriter. "Good hunting, ladies. Tantivy, tantivy, and all that."

"Tantivy, tantivy," replied Iris. "Thanks, Sally."

The two women paused to look out the window from the stairwell landing.

"Persistent, isn't he?" commented Gwen as she spotted the photographer.

"And he's multiplied," said Iris, indicating a small knot of reporters nearby.

"I nominate the back door."

"Seconded. Carried unanimously. We'll dispense with the recording of the vote."

They descended to the basement. Mister MacPherson, who was mopping the floor, looked up at them in surprise.

"Do you need anything?" he asked, clearly hoping that they didn't.

"We're going out the back door," replied Iris.

"The back door? Why?"

"We like the view," explained Gwen.

This time, Iris led Gwen to a different section of fence directly to the rear. She eased another board out of the way.

"It's convenient how many loose boards there are," commented Gwen as she passed through it. "Surprisingly poor craftsmanship among our local fence-builders."

"I may have loosened a few," Iris admitted as she replaced it.

"You are hereby banned from all zoos until this reckless habit of yours has subsided."

"I wish you had told me that before," said Iris. "There'll be hell to pay when those lions get out. Now, let's discuss our next cover story."

"We're not going to be Mary and Sophie? I like Sophie."

"You can be Sophie when we go to the pub later. But first . . ."

Tolbert's Fine Clothing was tucked in a vaulted space under the rail line, the broad arch covered with a wooden plank sign. The store was the only one open along this stretch, its desperately optimistic display sandwiched between a storage facility and a boarded up print shop whose own signs had faded badly. In the large windows adjacent to the entryway, men's suits a small step up from demob outfits hung on one side, while this year's Utility Collection draped a trio of headless female mannequins in the other.

Martin Tolbert was in the rear of his shop, surrounded by dress dummies of a variety of sizes and builds. He sat at a broad work table with a sewing machine at one end and an overlocker at the other. He squinted as he teased out the fabric in the waistband of a pair of grey flannel trousers. There was barely enough to support the necessary inch to let out as requested by the customer. He sighed and began to reconnect the new seam in back.

There was a tinkling of bells. Mister Tolbert perked up at the prospect of speaking to a live human being, even perhaps making a sale. He poked his needle into a faded green pin-cushion, slapped the bits of thread from his apron, and hobbled through the curtained doorway into the front of the shop.

A tall blond woman with an imperious expression was inspecting the rack of women's clothing. A smaller brunette woman stood behind her, nervously fiddling with her handbag.

"Are you sure that this is the right location, Lucy?" demanded the tall woman. "This hardly seems the type of store that would carry what I need."

"It's the address she gave me, Miss," squeaked the shorter woman. "There ain't no other dress shops on this street."

"There's barely any more street on this street," scoffed the first woman. "It hardly seems long enough to merit a name. But then neither do you, yet you have a name, don't you, Lucy? So I suppose even this alleyway could have one."

"Ha, ha, very good, Miss," said Lucy.

Mister Tolbert cleared his throat. They turned to look at him.

"Good afternoon, ladies," he said politely. "Welcome to Tolbert's Fine Clothing. I am Martin Tolbert, owner and proprietor. How may I be of service to you?"

"Well, it's like this," began Lucy.

"Lucy, I am perfectly capable of explaining the matter without your interference," interrupted the other woman. "Here is the situation, Mister Tolbert. I am a tall woman."

"I noticed that right away," said Tolbert.

"How very observant of you," she said icily. "As you well may imagine, we tall women have been unfairly neglected by the fashion industry. I've taken the step of writing several letters expressing my dissatisfaction with the situation, but to no avail. My maid has been on the lookout for dress shops that have the means to accommodate me."

"And I suddenly remembered I 'ad this friend what works 'ere," added Lucy excitedly. "'Aven't seen 'er in ages, but I thought she'd be able to 'elp out Milady."

"Never refer to me like that in public!" snapped the tall woman.

"Sorry, Miss," said Lucy, crestfallen.

"By God, I don't half wonder why I didn't give you the sack years ago," said the tall woman.

"No, no, Miss, it was a slip of the tongue, it won't 'appen again," Lucy assured her. "You won't give us away, will you, Mister?"

"I don't even have a name to give if I wanted to," said Tolbert. "Fortunately, I do have a few outfits in your size, and of course, if any tailoring should be necessary, I could do it right here in the shop."

"Very well," said the tall woman. "I assume that Lucy's friend will be assisting in the measurements? It would hardly be appropriate for me to allow you to do them."

"Um, my assistant is—truth of the matter is, she no longer works for me."

"Oh, no!" exclaimed Lucy. "You let 'er go? Why?"

"Not let go, not exactly," he said, stammering slightly.

"Well, what then?" asked the tall woman.

"I'm sorry to tell you that she—she's passed on, I'm afraid," said Tolbert.

He pulled out a scrap of cloth from his apron pocket and quickly wiped away the tears that were forming.

"She died," said the tall woman, looking at him intently. "That's too bad. What happened?"

"Someone killed her," he said. "Stabbed her."

"Oh, my God!" exclaimed Lucy. "Poor Tillie! When?"

"Just the other day," he said. "They arrested the man who did it."

"A lover?" asked the tall woman.

"She—it wasn't her lover, not that she had a lover, she had another fellow she'd been seeing for a while," he said. "Roger."

"Oh, I think I met 'im once," said Lucy. "Short, on the dumpy side? 'Ad curly brown 'air?"

"Oh, no," said Tolbert. "This was a tall fellow. Bit of a scoundrel, I thought. I kept telling her he wasn't good enough for her, but she wouldn't listen to me."

"Not Roger Oliver?"

"No, his last name is Pilcher."

"Like the fish?"

"No, like, eh, like Pilcher. Rhymes with filcher."

"Ooo, was 'e one, then? Is that why 'e wasn't good enough for 'er?"

"This is really none of your business," said Tolbert. "Would you like to see our selection of tall sizes?"

"Yes, I would," said the tall woman.

"I have some in back," he said. "I'll go fetch them for you."

He disappeared behind the curtains.

"So far, so good," whispered Iris. "When he comes back, try one of the dresses on in the changing room, and I'll keep up the conversation."

"Right," said Gwen.

"Where on earth did you get this gorgon persona from?"

"We have a gorgon at home. I married her son."

Iris stifled a laugh.

Tolbert returned holding three outfits on hangers. He had to hold his arm up over his head to keep them from trailing along the floor.

"Now, this one's by Creed," he said, holding up a black shirt-waister. "It's made of rayon—"

"I detest rayon," said Gwen. "And I'm not planning to go to any funerals, thank you. What's next?"

He held up a jacket and skirt combination. The jacket was of a medium blue cotton, with three large navy blue buttons down the front, cinched at the waist with a cloth belt. The pencil skirt was also navy blue, ending below the knee.

"I don't know," said Gwen. "I think I would be mistaken for a police constable wearing these colours."

"No, we don't want that, do we?" said Tolbert. "Well, I have this."

He held up a pink, floral print dress.

"That's not bad," said Gwen, taking it from him.

"There's a mirror over here," he said, pushing a wheeled rack of blouses out of the way.

She held it up against her body and turned in both directions, examining it critically.

"Where's your changing room?" she asked. "I must see this one on."

"In the back," he said, holding open the curtain. "Bit of a shambles in there, I'm afraid. I'm at loose ends with the girl gone."

"So I see," said Gwen as she went past him. "Well, make do and mend, as they say. Lucy, I shall be back in a minute."

"Yes, Miss," said Iris.

She waited until she heard the changing room door close, then heaved a sigh of relief.

"I'm sorry to be so much trouble, Mister," she whispered. "She's a piece of work, there's no denying, and there ain't enough make do and mend in the world to fix it."

"Not at all, not at all," said Mister Tolbert reassuringly. "We all have our challenges in life. I'm sorry to break the news about Tillie to you."

"I can't believe it," said Iris. "I saw her only last week. It's what put the idea of bringing Milady, uh, Miss Amalia—"

"Oh, Amalia is it?"

"There I go again," said Iris ruefully. "All chatter, no stops. You see, the thing is, she's run through all her clothing coupons."

"She has? Then what's the point of this expedition?"

"She 'as the notion that she needs a new dress for the summer parties, and she needs it yesterday," said Iris. "Tillie said that maybe we could work something out."

"There are laws, you know," said Mister Tolbert. "We could get into trouble."

"I don't think anyone would come looking 'ere, would they?" asked Iris. "It's an out-of-the-way location. That's why I thought it might be the right place. It would mean a lot to me, Mister Tolbert. It would take her off me back for a month if she found something she liked. Could you give a girl a break? Tillie would 'ave."

"Tillie did not always walk the straight and narrow," said Mister Tolbert. "Not in commercial matters, certainly not in affairs of the heart."

"But you knew what she was on about, din't you?"

"I indulged her," he confessed. "She was a ray of sunshine in here. But now that she's gone, I'm not sure that I want to take the risk."

"Even if we sweeten the pot?"

"The fines I would incur would be more than I make in a month," he said.

Gwen took a quick look around the workshop after changing into the dress. She didn't know exactly what to look for. She had hoped that Tillie had left something behind, maybe even had her own locker, but no such luck.

There was a desk in the rear with several thick ledgers piled on top. There was not enough time to go through them, nor, she realized, would she know what any irregularity would look like if it was in there, even if it was outlined in red ink with several arrows pointing at it. She silently slid open a few drawers.

In the second one, Tillie's face looked back at her. And again. And again.

Different pictures, modeling various dresses, smiling just enough so that the missing tooth didn't show.

And beneath those, more pictures of her. Wearing less. Much, much less. Still smiling. There were pictures of other women as well.

She closed the drawer and returned to the front of the shop. She paused as she passed through the curtains to inspect them.

"These were blackout drapes, weren't they?" she asked.

"Perfectly reusable," he said. "Easily done."

She stepped in front of the mirror, looked at herself, then turned away and looked back over her shoulder.

"You look like something out of a magazine, Miss," said Iris. "Like that Deborah Kerr."

"I've got at least six inches on her," said Gwen. "I'm one of the taller English roses you'll find. Still, I like this. With tailoring, how much?"

"The problem, as I have been explaining to your young lady, is the coupons," said Mister Tolbert.

"I might be willing to compensate you for that problem," said Gwen, looking at the mirror but watching his reflection instead of her own.

"I am afraid not, miss," he said. "The new coupon books come out in a month. If you like, I could set that one aside for you until then."

"I can't wait that long," said Gwen. "The season is well upon us. We shall move on in our quest. Lucy, I shall return."

She vanished through the curtains.

"I'm sorry about all this," said Iris. "I wish I 'ad known about Tillie before. You 'aven't found a new girl yet? Never know with Milady if I'm suddenly going to be in need of a job again."

"Not yet," he said. "Things are tight right now. I'm trying to manage on my own until the end of the month. Things should pick up for me in July, if you're looking then."

"You wouldn't know any shops around 'ere where we might 'ave a go without scruples?"

"I am afraid not," he said.

Gwen returned.

"Good day to you, ladies," he said, offering his hand.

Gwen looked down at it in disdain, then turned and swept out of the shop.

"Oh, dear, she is truly in one of her little states," said Iris, taking his hand and shaking it enough for two. "Thanks awfully."

She hurried out of the store.

"Goodness, that was rude at the end," she said when she caught up with Gwen.

"I don't like that man," said Gwen.

"Even so, common decency—"

"He deserves none. He is an indecent bounder."

"Based on what? Your soul-piercing gaze?"

"I found a little shrine to Tillie inside his desk," said Gwen. "Photographs. Some of them worthy of French postcards."

"Oh," said Iris. "Now I have this urge to wash my own hands very thoroughly. I wonder if that's how Tillie kept him happy while dealing on the black market."

"Is that what she was doing?"

"He didn't deny it."

"But he's not willing to do it on his own," said Gwen. "At least, not with us. I found his reluctance unconvincing."

"Maybe one needs to be introduced by someone in on the scheme. Do you think they were lovers?"

"No," said Gwen. "But he wasn't hesitant about expressing his disapproval of Roger Pilcher."

"Rhymes with filcher. At least we have a last name to match the first. That should put us a step closer to finding him."

"Yes," said Gwen. "And there's one more thing. Mister Tolbert's tailoring skills are excellent."

"Why is that of interest?"

"His workroom. Filled with any number of sharp objects. He'd be good with a knife."

CHAPTER 8

T he walk to the pub took them south towards the river. Gwen was silent.

"Penny for your thoughts," said Iris.

"I was thinking how nice it was to try on clothes again," said Gwen. "To do something ordinary for once, even if it was in the course of something so strange. To think that I would have to undertake a murder investigation to bring some normality back into my life."

"It's been seven years of insanity," agreed Iris. "I had hoped that it would go back to the way it was once the war ended, but it hasn't."

"Now here we are, going to a party for a dead woman we barely knew," said Gwen. "What's bizarre is that I haven't been—my God, it's the first party I've been to apart from a few weddings since Ronnie died. No, even before that. Not since we evacuated from London. And we're going under false pretenses to gather information from people we would never be with socially otherwise."

"Speak for yourself," said Iris. "I've spent the odd night out in a dockside pub before."

"Any pointers for the uninitiated?"

"Nurse your drink and don't get backed into a corner," advised Iris.

"That was just as true in Mayfair," said Gwen. "What should I do when we get there? Follow your lead again?"

"It might be better if we split up," said Iris. "Get people talking about Tillie. It shouldn't be difficult—it's why they're coming. Avoid the maudlin reminiscences, try to steer them to the juicier parts of her life."

"We should have a signal," said Gwen. "In case of trouble."

"Good thinking," agreed Iris. "Right. We'll use the double brush to the ear."

She turned to Gwen and brushed her hair back behind her ear, as if she were restoring a wayward strand. Then she repeated it.

"Right or left, depending on where you want me to look or go," said Iris.

"That seems simple enough," said Gwen, duplicating the gesture. "And if we should have to leave in a hurry?"

"Follow with a touch to the nose. That will mean, 'Sorry, must dash!' Then we meet outside."

"What if we get separated? Or there's something serious happening?"

"The nearest police station is straight down Wapping High Street, maybe five blocks. We'll rendezvous there. Oh, you still have your ring on."

"Thanks," said Gwen, stopping to remove it.

She placed it in her handbag, then held out her hand and inspected it.

"This makes me fair game," she said.

"Have some fun while you're at it," suggested Iris. "Flirting will bring out the talk in the lads, and talk is what we're after."

"What we do, we do for England," said Gwen solemnly.

Iris grimaced for a second. Gwen noticed it.

"What?" she asked.

"Nothing," said Iris.

"It's not nothing," said Gwen. "It's what I just said, isn't it?"

"Someone said that to me once before," said Iris.

"I take it it didn't go well after that," said Gwen.

"No, it didn't," said Iris.

Then she forced a bright smile.

"Here we are," she said. "Let's give 'em a good show."

Merle's was on the Thames side of the street, a three-storey building with the pub on the bottom and rooms to let above. Wide bay windows on either side of the entrance framed clusters of dockworkers and merchantmen, pints in hand. The women inside were outnumbered and very much in demand. One looked out the window, saw the two of them, and waved. It was Elsie, their new friend.

"You made it!" she shouted over the din as they entered. "I was wondering if you were gonna show."

Gwen looked around. The bar was a long, well-worn slab of oak with a century's worth of spills scrubbed into it. Hurricane lanterns hung from hooks on the walls and chains bolted to the ceiling, and the few visible table tops sat on old wooden casks that might have been rolled down a plank from a pirate ship once upon a time.

Elsie was with Fanny and another girl, fending off the more aggressive males while staking claim to the table. She beckoned Iris and Gwen over.

"This is Becky," she said. "Another friend of Tillie's. Becky, the short one's Mary and the tall one's Sophie. We met 'em yesterday at Grimble's."

"Niceter meetcha," said Becky.

"Likewise," said Iris. "Did you go to the funeral? 'Ow was it?"

"Me and Elsie went," said Fanny. "Decent turnout. No one got pissed first, so proper decorum was observed for a change."

"I 'ad to tend to me mum," said Becky. "She's been off 'er feed. But Dad got 'ome in time, so I came 'ere for the festivities."

Elsie suddenly looked up at Gwen and grinned mischievously. Gwen wondered at it, then started as someone tapped her on the shoulder.

She turned to see the ocean in a man's eyes.

"You came," said Des, smiling. "I din't think you would."

"You invited me," said Gwen, smiling back.

"Not every invitation gets accepted in life," said Des. "Since we're celebrating Tillie, and because you'll be needing to toast her in a few, may I buy you a drink?"

"Please," said Gwen.

And before she knew it, his hand was on the small of her back, guiding her away from the other women and towards the bar.

It was like an electric jolt to her spine, feeling the touch of an unfamiliar man's hand. Since Ronnie's death and her time in the sanitorium, the only physical closeness she had known was with the men who had danced with her at weddings, and they had either been relations or members of Ronnie's unit, which meant that they had held her at a respectful distance while looking at her with barely suppressed pity. But this man whom she had only met yesterday guided her with an easy authority that she found herself welcoming even as her conscience whispered caution.

"What are you 'aving?" he asked. "I'm guessing you're not a pint of pigs type."

"Oh, you'd be surprised," she said. "But if they can come up with a fizzy lemonade with gin, that would do me nicely."

"Oy, Kit!" he called to one of the bartenders. "Pint of Burton and a fizzy lemonade with gin for the lady."

"Righto," said the bartender.

He placed the drinks in front of them. As he did, a burly man in his fifties started pounding on the bar for attention. The room gradually quieted down.

"My name is Tom La Salle," he bellowed. "We are gathered 'ere on account of my niece, Tillie, who we sent to be with the Lord this

afternoon. That bloke there is Fred, who is the only man not drinking tonight."

He pointed to a serious young man seated by the bar, holding a
derby upside down.

"'E's collecting for the family," said Tom. "In addition, part of
the proceeds from the bar is going in the 'at, so drink up, lads and
lasses. If Tillie were 'ere, she'd be leading the pack of you, singing
the loudest and dancing the 'ardest. Raise your glass to 'er, and let
the party commence."

Glasses and mugs shot up in tribute.

"And the next time I toast my Tillie is the day that little bastard
swings for it," shouted Tom, and there was a roar of approval from
the room. "To Tillie La Salle, may she be dancing in 'Eaven!"

"To Tillie!" people shouted.

Des clinked his mug against Gwen's glass, and they drank. He
drained his beer in one go. Gwen had a sip, letting the tartness of
the lemonade roll around her tongue.

"Another, Kit!" shouted Des, and another pint appeared in front
of him.

"Ever been 'ere before?" he asked.

"Never," said Gwen. "This isn't still Shadwell, is it?"

"Nah, it's Wapping 'ere, but we been coming to Merle's forever. There's a verandah out back with a nice view. Care to take a
butcher's?"

"All right."

Once again, she was brought expertly through the crowd. She
caught a glimpse of Iris watching her with one eyebrow raised.
Then she lost sight of her as they crossed through the back room
and out a doorway.

Iris raised her pint in the direction of her vanishing friend.

"Des is a fast worker," she commented.

"Fair smitten, that one is," said Fanny.

"What's 'e do, then?" asked Iris.

"Carpenter down at the docks," said Elsie. "Good catch for a girl, if you ask me. Your friend could do a lot worse."

"She going to be all right out there with 'im?"

"Aw, 'e's a proper gentleman," said Elsie.

"More's the pity," sighed Fanny.

"That's all right then," said Iris. "So this is Merle's. This is the place what Tillie told me about."

"That right?" asked Elsie. "What'd she tell you?"

"I don't know that I should say, 'er being gone and all."

"Now, there ain't nothing you could tell us about Tillie that would surprise us," said Elsie.

"Not a thing," said Becky.

"Well, we were talking about stockings," said Iris.

"Oh, is that all?" laughed Elsie. "Not like it was anything shocking then."

"'In olden days a glimpse of stocking . . .'" Becky sang.

"Now, don't you start," said Elsie. "She starts singing now, she'll be up on the bar screeching 'er 'ead off by the end of the night."

"You 'ave no appreciation for me talents," sniffed Becky.

"I would if you 'ad any," retorted Elsie. "So, what about Tillie and stockings?"

"Oh, just that she said she could put me on to a bloke 'ere what sells 'em on the QT," said Iris. "I was looking for some. I 'aven't got a decent pair left."

"'Fond of fun as fun can be,'" Becky sang. "'When it's on the strict QT!'"

"There she goes again," sighed Fanny. "You might as well get up on the bar now, love, and save us the suspense of wondering when."

"So, you know the bloke she was talking about?" asked Iris, trying desperately to keep the conversation on track and with no further song cues.

"Yeah, I know 'im," said Elsie. "Name's Archie."

"That's the one," said Iris. "I couldn't remember the name. Is 'e around and about?"

"Archie usually don't come in 'ere this early," said Elsie. "I'm surprised Tillie mentioned 'im. I thought they was on the outs."

"Another boyfriend?"

"Oh, no," said Elsie. "No, more of—well, I don't like to say."

"Ow, come on," urged Iris.

"No, it's 'er party," said Elsie. "We shouldn't be disrespectful of the departed so fresh in the ground."

"No disrespect intended," said Iris. "But it sounds like there's a tale to be told there."

"I'm not the one to be telling it," said Elsie. "Look, if you're after stockings, give me your number and I'll give you a call. I can set you up with Archie."

"Don't 'ave a phone at 'ome," said Iris. "You give me your number, and I'll call you from the box on the corner."

"Give 'er mine, too," said Fanny.

Iris slid a paper and pencil over, and Elsie wrote down the numbers.

"What do you think?" asked Des.

The verandah projected out eight feet from the rear of the pub, hovering over the top of the wall holding back the Thames. Below her was the exposed muddy bank, strewn with stones and scraps of lumber. A small group of boys was playing by the riverside, throwing sticks into the current and chasing them down to the dock to the left.

Gwen stepped forward gingerly.

"You can come all the way out," said Des, walking out to the rail. He thumped it confidently. "It's solid. I should know—I built it."

"Well, in that case," said Gwen.

She walked forward to the rail and leaned against it, gazing down the river. On both sides, cranes spiked into the air, idle for the moment. The remains of burnt and bombed wharves protruded from the water like the hands of drowning men. Some, more encouragingly, were being rebuilt. A few late tugboats chugged by, heading back to their home docks. The sun was off to the right, getting lower.

"Where do you work?" asked Gwen.

"Off that way," he said, pointing to the left. "Got a new shop on Benson Quay. We opened up again a month ago."

"Congratulations. Where was the old shop?"

"Near there. Took out by a heavy bomb in '40."

"I'm sorry."

"Well, could've been worse. They came at night, so most of us was down shelter. 'Ad a mate, Andy, wasn't so lucky. 'E was a fire watcher. Building 'e was on collapsed with 'im on it."

"I'm sorry," she said again, then she shook her head.

"What's wrong?" he asked.

"All of our stories nowadays end up with someone saying, 'I'm sorry,'" she said. "It wears you down."

"It does, dunnit?" he agreed. "What kind of story would you like to 'ear?"

"Tell me about Tillie."

"Ah, that one," he laughed. "She was a tough one, she was. Give you an example, we useter bunker down at the Tilbury Shelter when things were 'ot and 'eavy during the Blitz. You know that one?"

"No."

"Well, it's this massive warehouse up between Cable and Commercial, where Whitechapel comes up against Aldgate. The basement is enormous, and 'as these big arches 'olding up the girders, so as bombproof as bombproof could be. It wasn't an official shelter, but we would cram ten thousand in there every night."

"Ten thousand! Goodness, that's a city in itself."

"It was that," he said. "People even brought 'orses down, which didn't make the air any better. So, they put up all these wooden platforms to keep you off the damp, and there was no official types running anything, so we ran it ourselves, unofficial-like."

"How did that work out?"

"Better than you'd expect, given 'uman nature," he said. "Rule was, long as you got in and laid out your blanket somewhere, that spot was yours. We used to send the kids on first, loaded up with blankets, so we could grab a decent location, not too near the entrance, not too near the lavs, and as far away from the 'orses as possible.

"So, one night, we're coming in after work, and Essie, that's me little sis, comes running up in tears, saying that some toughs had taken over our place. Now, there's just a few of us adults there at the moment, and I'm the only Johnny on the spot. I got me toolbox with me, so I take out me biggest 'ammer in case I need to, you know, persuade anyone."

"Oh, dear."

"But before I can even get started, Tillie barges forward, all five foot nothing of 'er. She's not even seventeen then, I think. She goes up to the biggest tough there screaming bloody murder and says if 'e and 'is lads don't vacate right away, she's going to cut off 'is—"

He stopped before he completed the sentence.

"There is a lady present," he said, grinning. "I can't tell you the whole story. But you get the gist."

"I do," said Gwen. "Was the threat effective?"

"It was," he said. "We told 'er after that the RAF were calling the Spitfires by the wrong name. They should've been calling them Tillies."

"I wish I knew her better," said Gwen.

"She was a pistol and an 'alf, all right," said Des.

"I wonder why she wanted to get out of Shadwell," said Gwen.

"What makes you think she did?" asked Des, looking at her curiously.

"Well, she went to that marriage bureau, didn't she? Sounds like she wanted a fresh start somewhere."

"Yeah, a lot of good that did 'er," said Des gloomily. "Tillie bombed some bridges 'erself, from what I 'eard."

"How?"

"Well, you know about Roger?"

"The girls told us about him. Ex boyfriend?"

"Yeah, she was 'ead over 'eels," he said. "Roger shows up after demob, tall, dark, and 'andsome, and before you know it, she's talking about turning over a new leaf and settling down. Then 'e up and quits 'er."

"Why?"

"She said 'e was using 'er because 'e knew she was in with this spiv named Archie. She introduces 'im, they start palling around, and before you know it, Roger's wearing a chalk-striped suit and running errands after dark."

"And Tillie? Was she working for Archie?"

"She was, but I 'eard she wanted out," said Des. "Maybe she thought if she could find a nice bloke from somewhere else, maybe she could marry 'im and put it all be'ind. And look where it got 'er."

He shook his head.

"This is not the conversation I wanted to be 'aving," he said. "I take a girl out 'ere for the view, and I sail us right into the doldrums."

"I like the view," said Gwen.

"It's the best view on the river," he said. "If you 'appen to fancy cranes, that is."

"I've decided that I like cranes, now that I've seen them up close," she said.

Good Lord, Gwendolyn! she thought. Laying it on rather thick, aren't we?

But he was smiling at that.

"What's your story, then?" he said. "I can't figure 'ow a looker like you 'asn't been snatched up by now."

"Someone did," she said.

"Ah, that's what it is," he said. "You lost someone."

"Yes," said Gwen.

"I imagine 'e was a good one to 'ave won you over," said Des. "What was 'is name?"

"Ronnie. We were married five years. Almost five."

"Well, 'ere's to Ronnie," he said, holding up his pint. "'Ere's to Ronnie, and Andy, and Tillie, and all the ones we lost."

"To the ones we lost," said Gwen, tapping her glass against his.

"And to the new ones we find," he added, smiling at her.

She drank to cover her confusion, her feeling of betraying Ronnie. This is nothing, she told herself. This is harmless. Nothing will come of it. Nothing could. I barely know him.

But would you like to know him better? asked a voice from somewhere inside her that she hadn't heard from in a long time.

She turned back to look down the river.

"You can't see the Tower Bridge from here," she observed.

"That's around the bend," said Des. "It's a nice walk down the street, if you fancy one."

"Not tonight, thanks," said Gwen.

"Maybe sometime else, then?"

Only a walk along the river, said the voice. *Safe as houses.*

"All right," she said.

Safe as houses in a Blitz.

"I'll need your number," he said.

"We don't have a working telephone right now," she said. "Give me yours. I'll call."

"I've 'eard that line before, you know," he said. "It generally leads to disappointment."

"I promise that I'll call," she said.

But I will end up disappointing you anyway, she thought, as he wrote his number down.

"Well, speak of the Devil," said Elsie. "There's Archie coming in now with an 'ole passel of wide boys. We'll be drinking deep tonight, girls!"

Iris turned to see a powerfully built man push through the door. He was six feet, wearing a double-breasted American-style lounge suit, with a dark purple shirt and an extra-wide kipper tie, the knot bulging loose and large below his throat, a diamond stickpin impaling it halfway down. He walked as though he expected the crowd to give way before him, and they did. He went up to Tillie's uncle Tom and shook his hand firmly, then made a brief circling motion with his forefinger to the bartender, who refilled Tom's drink in an instant.

Archie pulled a roll of banknotes from his pocket and tossed a tenner into the hat, then strode past Elsie's table into the back room along with his men, who were similarly dressed but careful not to match their boss in flamboyance or opulence. Seconds later, a group of men hurriedly exited the rear room, clutching drinks in their hands, hastily throwing on their jackets. The evicted customers from Archie's regular table, guessed Iris.

"No Roger," said Fanny. "Not surprised."

"So, you want to be introduced?" asked Elsie.

"'E doesn't 'ave the stockings with him, does 'e?" asked Iris.

"No, don't be silly," laughed Elsie. "But if I introduce you, you can work out a time and place."

"All right," said Iris.

"Guard our seats with your lives," Elsie instructed the others. "And no singing, you!"

"Spoilsport," muttered Becky.

Elsie led Iris through the crowd to the back room, where Archie sat at a corner table commanding the view of the room. He was regaling his boys with a story while a beleaguered barmaid attempted to take their orders. He looked up and beamed as Elsie approached.

"There's my best girl," he said. "Give us a wet one, gorgeous!"

Elsie leaned down and planted her lips on his as his companions cheered.

"And what have you brought us?" he asked, glancing past her at Iris. "A lovely thing in a small package, I'll warrant."

"This is Mary," said Elsie. "Friend of Tillie's from days gone by, come to pay 'er respects."

"'Allo," said Iris.

Archie looked her down, then back up. Iris met his eye boldly, a slight smile on her lips.

"You're a shy one, then," said Archie. "Knew Tillie from where?"

"Here and there, different places," said Iris. "Places where a girl could get a laugh and a drink for the price of a smile."

"Sounds like Tillie, all right," said Archie. "Never 'eard 'er mention you, though."

"You must 'ave a few friends she didn't know about," returned Iris. "She told me about you, though."

"Yeah? Nothing good, I expect," said Archie.

"Oh, it was very bad indeed," said Iris. "So bad that I said to meself, 'Mary, you 'ave to come see this fellow in the flesh and see if 'e is what Tillie said 'e is.' I was 'oping she'd fix me an intro, but things went south before she could."

"Well, 'ere I am, bigger than life," said Archie, leering at her. "What's the verdict?"

"That depends," said Iris.

"On what?"

"On whether you can help a girl in distress."

"I admit, I am a sucker for a sob story," he said. "Tell me all, and per'aps I will be your gallant knight for these perilous times."

"It's me legs," said Iris.

"What about 'em?"

"They get so cold, and I've got nothing left to warm them with," Iris purred. "Tillie said you could line me up with some nylons."

"I might know a fellow," he said. "Elsie, my pet. Go see what's 'olding up our pints while I 'ave a chat with your friend."

The commotion caused when Archie and his men commandeered the back room caught Gwen's attention.

"Who are they?" she asked.

"Ah, them," Des said shortly. "They are men to be avoided. That's Archie, the one I was telling you about."

"You've had your run-ins with them, I take it."

"They are part of the cost of doing business around 'ere," said Des. "I try to keep to the up and up. It ain't always easy. Look, there's Elsie and your friend."

Gwen watched the interaction between Iris and the spiv, trying to read their lips, their expressions.

"What do you suppose she wants from the likes of 'im?" asked Des.

"Knowing her, anything is possible," said Gwen.

Then a movement at the entrance to the room caught her attention, and she stepped back from the window in surprise.

Alfred Manners, the dustman who never returned for his interview, was walking into the room. Only he wasn't wearing a dustman's coverall this time. He was sharply dressed from the deep turn-ups of his trouser cuffs to the top of his trilby hat.

"Do you know the man who just walked in?" she asked.

"I do," said Des grimly. "And if 'e didn't have the rest of 'is gang 'ere, I'd be throwing 'im over this 'ere railing into the river."

"Why?"

"That's the bastard what dropped Tillie for the bad life," said Des. "That's Roger Pilcher."

CHAPTER 9

From her vantage point, Gwen could see Pilcher but didn't have the right angle to catch Iris's eye. She would have given anything for a pair of semaphore flags.

"Des, may I beg a large favour of you?" she asked.

"What's that?"

"There's a man in there I recognize," she said. "A man who I'd like to avoid. Would you be so kind as to shield me while we walk through to the front room?"

"Of course," he said.

He opened the door and stepped through it. She slipped in behind him, keeping out of Pilcher's sightlines. Iris saw them come in and smirked as Gwen took Des's proffered arm and nestled affectionately into his shoulder. As she did, Gwen brushed back her hair with her left hand, then repeated the gesture quickly. She followed by scratching her nose briefly.

She walked with Des like that past Pilcher, who didn't give them a glance. As they exited the back room, Gwen chanced a look back. To her dismay, Pilcher was moving directly towards where Archie was talking to Iris.

"Successful evasion?" asked Des.

"So far, so good," said Gwen. "Thank you."

"Right. Shall I walk you 'ome and make sure you get there safe?"

"I have to wait for Mary," said Gwen.

"But if the feller comes out 'ere and sees you . . ."

"What else can I do?"

Des glanced back into the room.

"You go outside and wait over by the phone boxes," he said. "I'll wait for 'er and tell 'er to meetcher there. You can duck around the corner if you need to 'ide."

"That should work," said Gwen. "But if she gets into any trouble . . ."

"Why would she be getting inter trouble?" he asked. "You're the one with the troubles."

"Good point," said Gwen. "Right, let her know I'll be waiting for her. And thank you."

She waved a quick good-bye to Fanny and Becky, and left, her heart pounding.

Iris's first thought when she saw her partner cuddling with Des was a mixture of surprise and approval. Then she saw the hand signal and shifted her alertness, already at a high level, into the red zone.

She couldn't turn away from Archie to see where the danger lay. She was still on her feet, which meant it would be marginally easier to escape than if she had been sitting. But which way? Back through the crowd of Archie's boys towards the front, hoping she could burst through before they were aware of her intent? And wasn't that where the new danger, whoever it was, would be standing? How would he react to her sudden flight? Exit, pursued by a spiv? Perhaps she could make a mad dash to the verandah instead, hoping there would be some means of climbing down from there. But what if there wasn't one? A dramatic dive over the railing into the Thames?

She hoped that the tide was in if it came to that.

She decided to wait and brazen it out before doing anything rash.

"'Allo, look what the cat dragged in," said Archie, looking past her. "The old scoundrel 'imself. What do you say, Rog? Come meet an old friend of your dead ex."

This gave Iris a chance to turn and see who she was dealing with. Her eyes came face to tie with a stylishly dressed man. She looked up with her best smile, then froze as she saw Alfred Manners, the nice-smelling dustman from the other day.

From right after they parted with Tillie.

Only Archie had just called him Rog?

Alfred Manners was Roger Pilcher. Roger Pilcher had followed his ex-girlfriend, Tillie La Salle, to The Right Sort. Roger knew that Tillie was looking to find a new man. And no doubt knew exactly what Iris was doing in the pub tonight.

The dive over the railing now seemed like a very viable option.

"You know 'er, dontcha?" asked Archie.

"Remember me, Rog?" said Iris. "Mary. We met at that pub over in Stepney. You were with Tillie, I was with an American G.I. named Harry. Sorry to 'ear about Tillie."

"What are you doing 'ere?" he asked.

"Looking for stockings and a good time, but mostly for stockings," she said. "You working for Archie now?"

"Yeah," he said. "Yeah, I'm working for Archie now. What's it to you?"

"Makes no difference to me," she said. "Nice to see you again. Give us a ring sometime."

"So you know 'er," said Archie.

"Yeah, I know 'er," said Roger. "She's a friend of Tillie's."

"Then she's a friend of Archie's," said Archie. "Now, it's past me regular business hours, Mary, but come by tomorrow and we'll see what we can do about warming up those pins of yours."

"Is afternoon all right?" asked Iris.

"Any time before five," said Archie. "Come close to quitting, we can maybe step out, put them to the test with a little dancing."

"Can't tomorrow night," said Iris. "But if you think you can keep up with me on a dance floor, we'll make a date of it for later. Where do I go?"

"There's a warehouse on Wapping Wall on the side opposite the river, third one past Monza Street. You know it?"

"I know the street. I'll find the warehouse."

"If you see the pub—"

"The Prospect of Whitby?"

"Yeah, that'd be the one," said Archie, approvingly. "If, like I said, you see that, you've gone too far."

"It wouldn't be the first time I've gone too far," said Iris, winking at him. "Tomorrow, then. Niceter meet all of you. Rog, nice to run inter you again."

"Likewise," said Rog as she walked by him.

She intercepted Elsie in the front as she was returning, the other girls in tow.

"I got to 'ead on," she said. "I met the legendary Roger."

"Oh, did you?"

"Yeah, only turns out I 'ave met 'im before," said Iris. "I must've been three sheets that night, or I would've remembered."

"All right," said Elsie, unconcerned. "You call me sometime and we'll do it up right, all right?"

"I will," promised Iris. "You see where Sophie got to?"

"She came back with Des," sad Fanny sorrowfully. "Progress 'as been made, if you ask me."

"I saw that," agreed Iris. "Well, I 'ope you 'ave the same luck."

"Not likely with this lot," said Fanny. "Ta ta."

"Ta ta," said Iris.

She looked around the pub quickly. No sign of Iris, but there was Des, who gave her a meaningful nod. She went up to him.

"Sophie saw someone in 'ere she didn't want to see," he said. "So, I sent 'er to wait for you by the telephone boxes down the corner."

"Thanks, and thanks for watching out for 'er," said Iris.

"She's worth the watching," said Des. "Night, then."

"Night," said Iris.

She walked out of Merle's and kept herself from breaking into a run. Gwen peeped out from a phone box as she crossed the street.

"You made it out alive," she said. "I didn't know what else to do. I was going to give you another minute, then phone for help. Are you all right?"

"I'm all right," said Iris. "I'm not quite sure what just happened."

"Alfred the dustman is Roger the ex," said Gwen. "And Roger the ex works for a black marketeer."

"Who Elsie and Tillie also worked for," said Iris. "Come on, let's walk and figure this out."

They walked down Wapping High Street. They got about half a block when Iris lifted her head and listened.

"We're being followed," she said.

"Yes, you are," said a man.

They spun to see Roger Pilcher standing behind them.

"Mrs. Bainbridge, Miss Sparks," he said, nodding to each in turn. "What a lovely surprise."

"For all of us, I'm sure," said Gwen.

"I'd like to know what you think you're doing, poking around my business," he said.

"We weren't poking around your business," said Iris. "We were poking around someone else's business, and you popped up unexpectedly."

"Is that right?" he said. "And 'ose business were you poking around in?"

"None of your business," said Iris.

"Why did you come to The Right Sort?" asked Gwen.

"Why does anyone?" he asked. "I was looking for love. That's what you sell, ain't it?"

"You were following Miss La Salle," said Gwen.

He shrugged.

"I was curious," he said. "Wondering what she was all about. She was acting mysterious about something. So, you're poking about in 'er life, are you?"

"Is that a problem?" asked Iris.

"I would say, yes, that is a problem," said Pilcher. "It doesn't 'ave to be. But if you show up 'ere again, it will become very problematic indeed. And I 'ave a solution for problems like you."

"That sounds like a threat," said Gwen.

"It very definitely was a threat," said Iris. "Do you feel threatened?"

"Not particularly," said Gwen. "It's two against one, after all."

Pilcher smiled unpleasantly, then pulled a switchblade with a staghorn handle from his waistband. With the press of a button, the blade snicked open, gleaming in the light from the street lamp.

"How about now?" he asked.

"Yes, I confess it, I do feel threatened now," said Gwen, backing away.

"I don't," said Iris.

"But he's got a knife," pointed out Gwen.

"So do I," said Iris as she pulled it from her bag and flicked it open.

Pilcher looked momentarily nonplussed.

"Not what you expected, is it?" said Iris. "You think when you pull a knife on a girl, they'll do what you say, don't you?"

"Please," said Gwen. "Could we all take a deep breath and pause for a moment?"

"Don't make this worse for yourself," said Pilcher.

"Worse?" scoffed Iris. "I think I've made it considerably better. Now, do we really need to escalate hostilities from here?"

"I'm warning you," said Pilcher.

"Warn me all you like," said Iris as she started to circle to the left, the knife rock steady in her grip.

"Look, this is very exciting, and I can't wait to go home and write it all down in my diary," said Gwen. "But could you both put away the cutlery before someone actually gets hurt?"

"You first," Iris said to Pilcher.

"Not bloody likely," he returned.

"Very well, if you're going to behave like children, I shall be forced to take action," said Gwen.

The other two turned to look at her as she opened her handbag and rummaged through it.

"And what 'ave you got in there, a Tommy gun?" asked Pilcher.

"Oh, blast, where did I put it?" muttered Gwen. "It's always on top when I don't want it, and now that I—ah, there you are!"

She pulled out something small and silvery and held it up triumphantly.

"I have a whistle," she announced. "It's a very good whistle, and I have excellent lungs, so if you don't put those knives away immediately, I shall wake every dog inside of a mile, as well as any bobbies within earshot. I understand that the Wapping police station is not too far away, but you know this neighbourhood better than I do, so you tell me if that is the case. Well?"

Pilcher looked back and forth at the two of them, then folded his blade back into its handle and slid it into his waistband.

"Don't come back 'ere," he said, his finger raised in warning.

Then he turned and walked back to the pub. He gave them one more glance before disappearing inside.

"Well done," said Iris.

"Iris, put that knife away," said Gwen sternly. "Now."

Iris looked at her partner's expression, then meekly folded up her knife and placed it back in her bag.

"To be fair, you still have your whistle out," she said.

"And it will stay out until we reach the train," said Gwen, turning and walking down the street. Then she stopped, and looked back at Iris.

"And in exactly which direction is the damn train?" she shouted.

"Right," said Iris, hurrying to catch up with her. "This way, Milady."

"Fine. Let's go."

"What is the matter with you?" gasped Iris, rushing to keep pace as Gwen strode angrily along.

"With me?" exclaimed Gwen. "How about you? You could have got yourself killed, pulling a stunt like that. More to the point, you could have got me killed!"

"I was protecting us—"

"You were doing nothing of the sort," said Gwen. "You took a situation that we could have talked our way out of in numerous ways, and went straight to armed combat."

"I warned you that this could be dangerous."

"There's unavoidable danger that happens because it finds you, and there's avoidable danger that happens because you decide to prod it with a sharp stick. What were you thinking, goading him on like that?"

"You were goading him, too," said Iris defensively.

"I was merely standing up for myself," said Gwen. "I did nothing to provoke him. What did you hope to accomplish by bringing a knife—my God, Iris! You have a knife! How long have you been carrying that around?"

"Since '37," said Iris. "Want to see me hit that sign from here?"

"You're insane," said Gwen. "I've roped my fortunes to a madwoman."

"I thought you knew," said Iris.

"I know better than to pull knives on people, and I'm the one who was in an asylum!" shouted Gwen.

"You were? You never told me about that."

"No, I didn't," said Gwen. "It was none of your concern."

"No, but still—I'm your friend, you could have—"

"Friend? How long have we known each other?"

"Well, I was at your wedding, but—"

She blanched as Gwen glared at her.

"All right, actual friendship," said Iris hurriedly. "From when we met for lunch after George and Emily's wedding."

"Which makes it five months," said Gwen. "We've known each other for five months, we've been working side by side for three. We've chatted about everything but our recent history. What I know of your life during wartime has been censored more than the Vatican Library. So yes, I have a past that you don't know about. I was in an asylum. I cracked up when Ronnie died. They pieced me back together, more or less, filled me with arcane potions, cleared me for some aspects of my life, and were quite enthusiastic about me working with you. 'Good girl,' said my doctor. 'Takes the old noodle off what's troubling it, what?'"

"Your doctor talks like that?"

"Shut up," said Gwen. "So, there we were in our ramshackle office in our decrepit building, spreading happiness and joy and making a few bob into the bargain, and now we're investigating a murder and consorting with spivs and being accosted by switchblade-wielding thugs in the middle of the docks—"

"We're not in the middle of the docks," said Iris.

"You did hear me say 'shut up,' didn't you?"

"Sorry. Carry on."

"And I see for the first time that you are a woman who wants nothing more than to dive into danger at the drop of a hat, dragging me kicking and screaming behind you. I suspect you of instability, Iris Sparks."

"You wouldn't be the first," said Iris. "But you're missing the big picture."

"Which is?"

"Which is we now know that Miss La Salle's ex followed her to our establishment, even to the point of coming into our office under false pretenses."

"So we're talking about that now?"

"Are you done yelling at me?"

"Have you learned the error of your ways?"

"Oh, yes, Mama," burbled Iris. "I promise that I will never pull a knife on a man again."

"Very good."

"Unless he deserves it."

"Were you ever properly spanked as a child?"

"I wasn't. That came much later. Now, back to Mister Pilcher trailing Miss La Salle to our office. I think that somewhat unusual behaviour for someone who has supposedly dropped her for better things."

"Not very ex-y at all," said Gwen. "And now he's worried about our investigation. You still haven't told me how you extricated yourself from the hands of the angry mob. I expected to see at least one pitchfork sticking out of your derrière when you came out."

"You make it sound more exciting than it was," said Iris. "I heard Archie greet 'Rog,' turned around, and there was our dustman, dressed spivvily. I thought the jig was up, but threw him a line like I'd met him before as Mary."

"And?"

"Then the miracle happened," said Iris. "He played along."

"He did? Why?"

"That's what flummoxed me," said Iris. "He could have got me out of the way right then and there, and made sure Archie would never give me the time of day again. But he didn't."

"Maybe he has something he's hiding," mused Gwen. "Hiding even from Archie. And giving you up would have raised too many questions."

"Interesting thought," said Iris. "Maybe he and Tillie had some game going on under Archie's nose. Maybe the breakup was staged to throw him off the scent. Maybe it went wrong, or she double-crossed him, or he needed her out of the way to keep Archie from tumbling it. Which means that we now have ourselves a suspect!"

"With two possible motives—jealousy and greed. Good work for a night in a pub, I say."

"And I nearly got to cross swords with a possible murderer, which is more fun than I've had in a while."

"It's all fun and games until someone gets stabbed through the heart," said Gwen. "What do we do with this—follow up with Mister Pilcher?"

"We have enough to bring to Parham, I think."

"He won't lift a finger," said Gwen. "You should contact—"

"No."

"You should contact Mike Kinsey," Gwen persisted. "He'll listen to you."

"Damn, damn, damn," groaned Iris. "All right. I'll call him first thing. Now, let's talk about the most important event of the evening."

"Which was?"

"Did you get a date with Des?"

"Don't be ridiculous."

"I'm not. He's taken a shine to you, and I didn't see you fending him off with any great determination."

"I was flirting with him to get information about the case," said Gwen. "Nothing else."

"Do you have his number now?"

"I took it to be polite," said Gwen. "No more than you would have done."

"He seems like a nice fellow," said Iris. "A diamond in the rough, wouldn't you say?"

"Iris, how could I possibly date someone from the docks?" asked Gwen. "For all of his manners, his gentle nature, his—"

She stopped, blushing.

"His what?" asked Iris. "His beautiful eyes? His muscled physique? What were you going to say next in your litany of praise?"

"I like him," admitted Gwen. "But it could never work. I've already lied to him about who I am and what I do. It would be a cruelty for me to lead him on any further."

"So have yourself a fling and be done with it," urged Iris. "We're entitled to a little fun every now and then."

"Even if it's at the expense of someone else?"

"It'd be fun for him, too, don't you think?"

"What I think is that I am not like you in this respect," said Gwen. "I am not being disapproving, mind you, but I've never been—"

She paused, not wanting to complete the sentence.

"Promiscuous?" said Iris. "Is that the word that you hesitate to apply?"

"You're not promiscuous," said Gwen. "You're adventurous."

"Oh, I like that," said Iris. "Puts more of a positive spin on my self-destructive behaviour."

"And you haven't been all that adventurous since I've known you, have you?"

"Good Lord, I had two broken engagements and all that Mayfair had to offer between the sheets. What more do I have to do to convince you?"

"Oh, I'm not saying that you weren't like that once," said Gwen. "But the war changed you, didn't it?"

"It changed all of us," said Iris.

"I happen to believe that there is currently only one man in your life," said Gwen. "And that you only see him every now and again."

"What makes you think that?"

"Well, you've been much happier in the mornings these past few days. You were last like this about two months ago. In between, you were quieter. One might even say moody."

"My moods shift with the phases of the moon," said Iris airily. "You have proved nothing. What other evidence do you have?"

"You've been wearing Vol de Nuit recently," said Gwen. "Not every day. But you sneak off to the lav on certain days, often coinciding with some tiny additions of frill to your standard wardrobe. Given that Guerlain's generally not available here, I surmise that your fellow is a traveler to the Continent. Since he was there for a lengthy stay, he is probably someone either diplomatic or military."

"Heavens," exclaimed Iris in chagrin. "You've figured all that out from my perfume?"

"I love Vol de Nuit," sighed Gwen. "Ask him to pick me up a bottle next time. He's married, isn't he?"

Iris didn't answer.

"He is," said Gwen sadly. "If he wasn't, you'd be dropping hints about him right and left, even if you were lovers without benefit of clergy. Another area of your life that you keep secret. It's a wonder that you don't burst."

"Is your psychiatrist any good?" said Iris. "Maybe we could go together."

"I don't trust him, to tell you the truth," said Gwen. "He was hired by my mother-in-law."

"Interesting. Well, I am impressed with your analysis. I will neither confirm nor deny its accuracy, but your skills are formidable. Nevertheless, your attempt to divert me from the Des situation is for naught. I think that you should consider giving him a tumble just to get yourself back on the horse."

"What a horrid metaphor."

"You might accidentally enjoy yourself, darling."

"No doubt. But again, no thanks."

"Don't you miss it?" asked Iris curiously.

"It? You mean sex?"

"Yes, I mean sex. I mean what you've had before on at least one occasion, which I cleverly deduce from the fact that you have a child. It's part of our life."

"It was," said Gwen. "Very much so."

"So don't you have longings for more?"

"Of course I do," said Gwen sharply. "I miss it. I miss it because I miss Ronnie, and it was all bound up with loving him. If he was alive today, I would be waiting every night in our bedroom in indecent poses while draped in the sheerest of silks, presenting tableaux that would make a French postcard blush. I would seek out forbidden books containing exotic Oriental techniques and I would learn them all, because I do miss it, and he was It, It with a capital *I*. Every moment alone with him was ecstasy, and there is no possible way that it will ever be like that with anyone else ever again. I want Ronnie. I want him so badly that it hurts, it physically hurts me, do you understand? So, no, Iris, I am not interested in a little fun, as you put it. I don't want fun. Fun will only be a disappointment."

Iris said nothing, but reached out, took her friend's hand, and squeezed it gently. Gwen gripped Iris's hand hard, then hung on to it until they reached the train.

Andrew was in her flat when Iris walked in. He looked at her face, then grinned.

"You've been up to something, haven't you?" he asked.

"I have been up to many things," she declared proudly. "I have put my undercover skills to good use. I have successfully impersonated an East Ender, I have infiltrated a den of gangsters, and I almost got into a knife fight. Now, I would like to put on a fabulous frock, get you into a dinner jacket, and go out on the town. Belle Meuniere for a thick, juicy black-market steak, then dancing at the Bagatelle."

He came forward and took her in his arms.

"I don't have a dinner jacket here," he said.

"I know," she said, holding him close.

"The steaks at Belle Meuniere are actually well-disguised horse meat," he said. "The secret is the sauce."

"Damn."

"And I can't be seen with you in public."

"I know, I know," she said, pulling herself away from him.

"I have brought things in tins and a decent claret to share," he said.

"After," she said, grabbing him by the tie and leading him into her bedroom.

Gwen walked through the front door of the house, her mind still racing with the day's events. Inside the front hallway, Percival stood on the same spot on which he had stood the night before.

"Good evening, Madam," he said.

"Good evening, Percival," she replied. "Is standing guard now a regular part of your duties?"

"Lady Carolyne wishes to speak with you," he said. "She is in the library."

"Déjà vu," she said under her breath.

"Excuse me, Madam?"

"Isn't this where we came in?"

"It is not for me to say, Madam. Will you follow me, please?"

She sighed and walked down the hallway behind him. He knocked on the door, then held it open for her.

Lady Carolyne sat in the same chair by the fireplace in which she had sat during the previous evening's haranguing.

"Mrs. Bainbridge is here, Lady Carolyne," announced Percival. Then he closed the door behind Gwen.

Gwen took a deep breath and walked over to the other chair.

"You wished to speak to me, Lady Carolyne?" she asked.

Her mother-in-law did not reply. Instead, she held up a newspaper, the front page facing Gwen.

"Oh," said Gwen weakly. "I didn't know we took the *Mirror*."

CHAPTER 10

A slumming society girl who made her fortune marrying the sole heir to Bainbridge millions,'" read Lady Carolyne. "'Now, she fixes up other social climbers with ambitions of joining their betters. Unfortunately, her latest customer, a lovely East End lass, met her Waterloo in the guise of a petty Croydon Lothario by the name of Dickie Trower.'"

She tossed the newspaper into the fireplace.

"Utter trash," she said. "With you wallowing right in the midst of it. Working with murderers, are you?"

"I don't believe that he did it," said Gwen.

"He's been arrested for it, hasn't he?" sniffed Lady Carolyne. "Scotland Yard seems to think he killed that poor girl."

"I know what they think," said Gwen.

"How?"

"Because they interviewed us, of course," said Gwen. "How do you think they got on to poor Mister Trower?"

"Poor Mister Trower, is it?"

"We think he's innocent."

"We? You mean you and that sordid little minx you work with?"

"Don't you dare call her that!" said Gwen. "You have no right to belittle my friends."

"I have no right? My dear daughter-in-law, let me remind you that you live under our roof, purely upon our charity. If I wish to describe that wretched Sparks woman in that manner, then I shall. Given her record of broken engagements and God knows how many affairs—"

"Leave her out of this," said Gwen. "You don't want me under your roof? Then give me back my child and I will happily leave here."

"That will not happen," said Lady Carolyne. "And considering the tarnishing of the Bainbridge name by your conduct, I do not see that you have any hope of improving your chances in the future."

"What if Dickie Trower turns out to be innocent?" asked Gwen. "What if we are right?"

"And the rest of the world is wrong? Doubtful to say the least. Who is going to take his side?"

"We are," said Gwen. "We already have."

"Two silly girls against the world," scoffed Lady Carolyne. "What could you possibly do to change this?"

"Investigate," said Gwen. "Find the truth."

"Nonsense."

"We've already begun," said Gwen.

"What? What do you mean, you've already begun?"

"We are investigating the—situation," said Gwen.

She was going to say "case," but realized how strange it would sound.

"Investigating?" laughed Lady Carolyne. "First you thought you could be a businesswoman. Now, you fancy yourself a detective? Utter madness!"

"Nevertheless—"

"Madness," repeated Lady Carolyne more thoughtfully. "I am beginning to wonder . . ."

"Wonder what?" asked Gwen, a sudden chill falling over her.

"I wonder if perhaps this behaviour of yours is symptomatic of a deeper mania," said Lady Carolyne. "When is the last time you spoke with Doctor Milford?"

"Two weeks ago," said Gwen.

"Before all of this happened," mused Lady Carolyne. "No wonder that he missed the signs. I think that I shall have a little talk with him."

"Stay out of that," said Gwen. "You have no right to interfere with my treatment."

"My dear, it concerns the welfare of your child," said Lady Carolyne blandly. "I would be in dereliction of my duties as his guardian if I did not see to the mental welfare of his mother. Perhaps more extensive measures need to be taken."

"You cannot—"

"It would be such a shame if the *Mirror* were to hear about that portion of your past," continued Lady Carolyne. "We've managed to keep it from the press so far—"

"You wouldn't dare," said Gwen.

"I will make an appointment to see Doctor Milford," said Lady Carolyne. "I will listen to what he has to say. It would be in your interest to co-operate. I am done with you. Go fetch Percy and tell him that I am going out tonight."

Gwen stood, on the verge of screaming at the other woman, then forced it back down and fled the room.

"You were particularly enthusiastic tonight," commented Andrew.

"Was I?" said Iris.

They were sitting side by side on her bed, propped up against the pillows, eating something grey and fishy straight from the tins. Two partially filled glasses of claret sat on the nightstand.

"You came in keyed up," he said. "I felt positively overwhelmed by the onslaught. Remarkably enjoyable, by the way."

"Thank you, kind sir," she said, digging out some more and shoving it into her mouth greedily. "Any idea what this was when it was alive and swimming?"

"I suspect whale of some kind," he said. "Thank God for the claret. Otherwise, we'd be revisiting the flavour all night."

"You're staying overnight?"

"I'm flying back tomorrow," he said. "Told Poppy it was an early plane, so staying in town was the easiest way."

"Awfully short notice. When did you find out?"

"Last night."

"So, this is our farewell fling," said Iris.

"Yes."

"And you're spending it with me instead of your wife. I'm flattered."

"I much prefer it here," he said.

"Did you give her a proper send-off as well?" asked Iris, reaching over him for her wine glass.

"Excuse me?"

"Fulfill your husbandly duties," said Iris, taking a sip. "Give her something to remember you by while you're off fighting the secret wars."

"That's really none of your business," he said.

"None of my affair, you mean," she said. "Oops, sorry. I'm the affair, not her. I forget that sometimes. Especially when we're in the throes of it."

"Where did this come from?" he asked. "Are you having second thoughts about our arrangement?"

"Long past second," said Iris. "Deep into double digits by now."

"What brought this on?"

"I watched Gwen turn down a perfectly good opportunity to lose herself to a very acceptable specimen of the male species tonight."

"So?"

"So her reasons spoke of her love, her loss, her mourning—her passion."

"Passion."

"Yes, passion," repeated Iris. "What am I to you, Andrew? Is this passion?"

"I've told you that I love you," he said. "Many times."

"In here," she said. "In one or two other rooms before you arranged for this flat. Would you say it outside?"

"Where?"

"I don't know. Piccadilly Circus. On the Serpentine. In Covent Garden. Shouted from the rooftops would be nice."

"I've told you—"

"That you can't be seen with me, I know," said Iris. "The question for me is can there be passion when there is also caution and secrecy?"

"You agreed to all of this when we began," said Andrew.

"I did," said Iris. "Part of the thrill at the time was the clandestine nature of it all. I said yes, and I think that I have held up my end of the bargain adequately."

"More than adequately," he said. "God, now it's sounding entirely mercenary. What is it that you want?"

"Would you consider divorcing Poppy and marrying me?" asked Iris.

"Are you proposing, Sparks?"

"I asked you a question."

"Would I consider it? Yes."

"Consider," she repeated. "Damn that word. It gives you all manner of escape routes, doesn't it?"

"You and I always need room for a fast exit, don't we, Sparks?"

"All right. Let me ask this properly. If I said that I wanted you to marry me, would you? Would you divorce Poppy?"

He didn't reply.

"It's astonishing how a man who risks life and limb nearly every day for his country could be such a coward," she said bitterly.

"That's not fair," he said. "My marriage is complicated."

"And I am simple," said Iris. "I am a simple woman with simple needs, but I'm wondering if I should be asking for complexity. I look at Gwen and all that she has had and lost, and how it's nearly destroyed her, and do you know? I envy her. She's had more happiness in a few short years with one man than I have had in all of my life, and I don't know if I can even attain that anymore."

"Did you ever have a chance for it with any of them?" he asked.

It was her turn to be silent. He laughed, suddenly.

"Mike," he said. "Mike Kinsey."

"Maybe," she said. "I didn't realize it at the time if so."

"He comes back into your life, betrothed to another," said Andrew. "As a result, you are filled with regrets for what might have been, but what in actuality probably would not have been. And all of those regrets are now being projected onto me."

"My regrets about you are entirely independent, I assure you."

"Right," he said, getting up.

"What are you doing?"

"Getting dressed. Leaving."

"I thought you were going to spend the night."

"So did I," he said, grabbing his shorts from the floor and pulling them on.

"Where will you stay?"

"I'll find a nice hard chair at the airfield and have a kip there until my plane," he said.

She watched him as he dressed, sipping her claret. He finished, then picked up his glass and downed the rest of his.

"I was wrong," he said, staring at the dregs. "The bad taste doesn't go away."

"When do you return?" she asked.

"Don't know. It doesn't matter. Look, if you want to reconsider what you and I have said tonight, that's fine," he said. "But if you wish to see other men while I'm gone, feel free."

"That was about the worst thing you could have possibly said to me," she said.

"The rent on the flat is paid for through the end of the year," he said, picking up his bag. "I'll hang onto my key for now, if you don't mind."

She waited until she heard the door open and close behind him, then got up to make certain that it was locked. Then she poured the remainder of the claret into her glass and gulped it down.

She woke the next morning sprawled across the bed, her head throbbing. She made herself coffee instead of her usual tea. It didn't help.

She decided to see Mike Kinsey in person rather than call him. Telephones could be hung up. Of course, he could refuse to see her, but she liked her chances better if she could confront him directly, especially if there were other witnesses around forcing him to be polite.

She took the bus to Westminster, got off before the bridge, and walked down Victoria Embankment to the entryway to New Scotland Yard. The two old buildings with their rounded brick towers projected an air of solidity, but Mike was in the newer Curtis Green building.

She walked through the arches to the interior, staying to the side in case any Flying Squads had to peel off in their Wolseleys, but it was relatively quiet. A constable at the front desk directed her to Mike's office, which was the anteroom to Parham's in the Homicide and Serious Crime Command. She saw her ex sitting behind a desk, typing laboriously away at some report.

"You still can't type any faster than that?" she remarked.

He looked up at her and grimaced.

"What do you want, Sparks?" he asked.

"To make your life easier," she said.

"Then turn around and walk away."

"I need to talk to you about something," she said, taking a seat by his desk. "I figured that if we met on your turf, there would be no unseemly displays."

"That is something for which I should apologize," he said. "It was an unforgivable action on my part."

"And yet, I forgive you," she said, reaching across his desk and grasping his hand for a second. "Given all that I need to be pardoned for, one kiss—a very good kiss, by the way—is scarcely worth mentioning."

He pulled his hand away, sat back in his chair, and looked at her.

"You're not here about that, are you?" he asked warily.

"What makes you say that, Detective Sergeant?"

"You came here and you're being nice to me. Which means that you want something."

"Yes, Mike, I do. As much as I would like to reminisce about the good times, I am here about the present. I have a new suspect for you for the murder of Matilda La Salle."

"No, no, no," he said. "That's over and done with. We got our man."

"And the Yard is never wrong."

"We have the knife. We have motive and opportunity. It's a strong case."

"Still circumstantial."

"Not our problem. We have enough to charge him, and we have done so."

"What if I told you of someone with stronger motives, a longer history with her, and, moreover, a criminal background?"

"If you're thinking about any of that gang of spivs she used to run with—"

"Not just any of them. A particular one. One who followed her to our office, who had a relationship with her before she decided to seek greener pastures, who saw our setup and could therefore figure out how to use our files to divert Mister Trower from his date. And who also would have known Trower's address from those same files, which would have given him a chance to plant the murder weapon in such a blindingly obvious place."

"You're saying a spiv showed up—"

"On our very doorstep, right after she left, probably listening as we interviewed her."

He picked up a notepad.

"Tell me," he said.

She recounted what she knew about Manners/Pilcher, leaving out the near knife fight. When she was done, he stared at the pad, then slid it across.

"Sign that," he said.

She read it over, then put her signature at the end and dated it. She gave it back to him.

"I'm not saying you're correct," he said. "I still don't think that there's anything here. But I'll look into it."

"Thank you, Mike," she said. "I appreciate it. I honestly thought you would put up more resistance."

"Whenever I resisted you, you would bring out the wheedling tone," he said. "I thought we could forego that dance for once."

"I never did!"

"Every single time," he said. "I don't think I could take the wheedling tone anymore."

"I had no idea I was such a terror to you," said Iris, getting to her feet. "Well, that's all I have. You will call me if you turn up anything?"

"I will," he promised, coming around the desk to hold the door for her. "And Sparks?"

"Yes?" she said, turning back to him.

"It's good to see you again," he said. "Regardless."

"Likewise, Detective Sergeant Kinsey," she said. "Now it's back to the matrimonial mines for me."

She gave him a bright smile that she didn't feel, and left.

She sat by a window on the bus, staring at the parade of Londoners going about their lives.

Andrew was gone, maybe for good. Mike was getting married.

She was twenty-nine, and this was how things were.

She wondered how Sally's second visit to the Cornwalls had gone. The Right Sort dearly needed the cushion that payment would provide if they were going to survive any lengthy period without new customers. At least their investigation was over, and they could concentrate on the business of matching up potential couples. Unless those potential couples refused to accept their introductions for fear of filleting.

One good thing, she thought. I would like one good thing to happen to me today.

Maybe she would keep her appointment with Archie and buy a new pair of black market nylons. Maybe she'd take him up on his offer to go dancing. Dancing with a gangster might be exactly what she needed.

God. How had she turned into a woman who thought that dancing with a gangster was what she needed?

Still.

It might be fun.

Gwen had her box of index cards open on her desk when Iris finally arrived at the office.

"There you are," she said. "I have been thinking about Mister Robertson. I have some candidates in mind for him."

"Any new business?" asked Iris.

"A few more attempts to cancel," said Gwen. "I assured them that even if they wanted to give up on their chances for a lifetime of happiness, we certainly would not."

"Any word from Sally?"

"Not yet. How did things go with Mike?"

"I reported our findings," said Iris, unpinning her hat and hanging it on the coat-tree. "He sounded interested. He said he would look into Mister Pilcher."

"And that was that?"

"What did you think would happen?"

"I don't know," said Gwen. "It sounds so anticlimactic after everything we did. In my imagination, the two of you jump straight into a squad car and roar off, sirens screaming and flashers flashing."

"We have no actual proof that Pilcher did it," Iris pointed out.

"No, but—I don't know, I expected more somehow."

"There will be," said Iris confidently. "Mike's a good man."

"He's a good man now?"

"In terms of being a detective, yes."

"You're basing this upon what, exactly?" asked Gwen.

"I am assessing him solely on what I know of his abilities, apart from whatever biases against him that I may have accumulated because of our history."

"You are being remarkably generous to him this morning," observed Gwen. "Quite the change of heart. Tell me that you haven't become sweet on him again."

"No, that ship sailed long ago," said Iris.

"Besides, you have your current man in your life."

"That plane flew this morning," said Iris.

"Oh?" said Gwen.

Then she looked more closely at her partner's face.

"Oh," she said sympathetically. "It was like that, was it?"

"It was like that," said Iris. "A good thing, in the long run. It was inspired by you, by the way."

"Me? How was I in any way responsible for this?"

"You made me realize that I wanted something better," said Iris.

"How did I do that?"

"By turning down Des," said Iris.

"My goodness," said Gwen. "I had no idea that I was setting an example. So, you confronted your unnamed paramour and threw him out on his ear instead of making love? Well done!"

"Actually, after we made love," confessed Iris.

"Oh," said Gwen. "Not quite the same thing."

"I mean, he was already there."

"I really don't want the sordid details."

"He brought a bottle of claret. And snacks."

"How thoughtful. Of both of you."

"Yes, well, it's over now, in any case."

"Are you all right?" asked Gwen. "Seriously?"

"I am, I think. Or will be. It was time."

"What now?"

"The corpse of our relationship is barely cooled, and you're pushing me onto the next one?"

"No. I mean, what do we do now? Do we still pursue our investigation?"

"I think we have to give the police a chance. We don't want them to feel like we're doing their job for them."

"That's too bad," sighed Gwen. "I made rather a loud show last night of how we were going to catch the killer ourselves."

"Lady Carolyne again?"

"Yes."

"Well, if it works out, we'll take all the credit," said Iris. "That should put a cork in her."

"If only it were that simple," said Gwen. "I wish—"

The telephone rang. She picked it up.

"The Right Sort Marriage Bureau, Mrs. Bainbridge speaking," she said.

Then her expression grew troubled.

"No, it's not—when?" she said. "Today? But I—no, no, I'm not trying to cause—Yes. Yes. Two o'clock. I'll be there. Good-bye."

She hung up and stared at the telephone.

"I have an appointment this afternoon," she said. "Can you handle the office without me?"

"Of course," said Iris. "Anything wrong?"

"So many things," said Gwen. "Well, enough gloom and doom. Let's talk about Mister Robertson. I have a candidate for him."

The telephone rang around noon. Gwen answered it.

"Right Sort Marriage Bureau, Mrs. Bainbridge speaking. Yes, she's here. One moment."

She passed the telephone to Iris and mouthed, "Mike."

"Hello, Sparks here," said Iris.

"It's Detective Sergeant Kinsey," said Mike. "I have some information for you."

"Yes, Detective Sergeant?" replied Iris, wondering at the formality.

"We've looked into your proposed suspect, and we are satisfied that he is not the killer."

"Oh," said Iris, her shoulders slumping. "Is the Yard permitted to tell me how it reached that conclusion?"

"I'm afraid not," he said. "There is one more thing. You and your partner are specifically directed not to pursue this any further. Any attempts to investigate this matter will be regarded as interference with an ongoing police matter, and will be treated severely. Are we clear about this, Miss Sparks?"

"Quite clear, Detective Sergeant," said Iris. "Thank you for your time. Good-bye."

She hung up.

"Damn it," she said. "They've ruled out Pilcher as a suspect."

"Oh, no," said Gwen. "Why?"

"He wouldn't say," said Iris. "He was being so curt. So formal with me."

"Perhaps someone was with him while he made the call," said Gwen. "Maybe he overstepped by looking into it."

"Maybe."

"What do we do now?"

"We've been officially warned away from doing anything more," said Iris.

"Say for the sake of argument that we ignored that directive," said Gwen. "What would we do next?"

"He threatened us with prosecution."

"Last night, a man threatened us with a switchblade and you didn't back down," said Gwen.

"For which I earned your well-deserved scolding. And one man with a switchblade is easier to battle than an entire metropolitan police force."

"Doing nothing for Mister Trower at this point is far worse than risking prosecution in pursuit of his exoneration."

"True enough," said Iris. "So, if we were to throw caution to the winds, then the next step would be to beard the lion in his den."

"You're going to the warehouse."

"Yes."

"Then I should—oh, blast. I have that appointment."

"Something you can't break?"

"Not without—"

She stopped.

"What?" asked Iris.

"The appointment is with my psychiatrist," said Gwen.

"You've never had an afternoon appointment with anyone since we've started," said Iris. "Why today? Why did he call you?"

"That wasn't him calling," said Gwen. "That was Lady Carolyne. Or her secretary, rather. Lady Carolyne likes to delegate her dirty work."

"What's going on?"

"She saw the article in the *Mirror*. She wasn't happy about it. She thinks my desire to clear Mister Trower is a symptom of an increased mania. That's her justification, in any case. Hence the emergency appointment."

"Since when does one's mother-in-law force treatment on one?"

"They have custody of Ronnie," said Gwen, looking down at her lap.

"What? How?"

"It happened while I was—away," said Gwen. "No, Gwendolyn, call it by its name. While I was confined, strapped to a bed to keep from doing myself an injury, injected with God knows what to make me docile. They went to court to assume custody of the sole heir to the Bainbridge holdings, and they have not relinquished it. Every now and then, they construct a new hoop for me to jump through."

"This is horrible!" exclaimed Iris. "Why have you never told me before?"

"What did you do in the war, Iris?" Gwen asked sharply, looking at her in a way that made the other woman flinch. "I don't discuss certain portions of my life with you. With anyone."

"Do you have someone advising you? Representing you legally?"

"I am still a ward of the court," said Gwen. "They appointed me a guardian, and I suspect that he is in the pocket of my in-laws."

"We should call Sir Geoffrey."

"*We* should do nothing of the sort," said Gwen. "This is none of your affair."

"I am between affairs at the moment," said Iris. "I don't mind taking yours on."

"There are no characters that you can portray nor accents you can use that will help me here," said Gwen. "I have to plough through it myself. Which is why I want to continue the investigation. I have a personal stake in showing that we were right so that I may retake the high ground that I've lost."

"Where is your doctor?"

"On Harley Street."

"Of course. That's not far from my flat. You could come by after for the post-mortem."

"I was going to come back to the office," said Gwen. "There's still time left in the day for me to get some work done. Or to stare out the window and scream at the walls. I can't do that at home."

"I had no idea. Would you like me to go for a walk and let you get in some therapeutic howling now?"

"Not today, thank you," said Gwen. "I might take you up on that offer in the future."

"Well," said Iris, glancing at her watch. "I have a rendezvous with some spivs."

"Be careful," said Gwen. "If that Pilcher fellow is there, we don't know how he'll react to your return to the fray."

"It would be interesting to see his response," said Iris.

"Even though he's no longer a suspect?"

"He's no longer CID's suspect," said Iris. "He's still mine. What do you think about him, given his conduct last night?"

"I was so wrapped up in not wanting to be on the wrong end of a knife that I hadn't really thought about it," said Gwen.

"Think about it. Put his performance through your magnifying lens. Give me the morning-after impressions."

"Performance," said Gwen thoughtfully.

"What?"

"It was a performance," said Gwen. "Both times that we've seen him, he was putting on a show of some kind."

"Well, we know he wasn't a dustman."

"Yes, and I had a nagging sense of that even then—remember my commenting on how nice he smelled? It didn't seem important at the time. So many of our clients present themselves at the first interview as something better than they are."

"Which is only human."

"Of course. The interesting thing about last night was that he backed down so easily."

"Easily?" said Iris indignantly. "We had to resort to knives and whistles!"

"Nevertheless, it was a show," said Gwen. "He wanted to present himself as something worse than he was."

"Braggadocio? Talking big in front of the rest of the spivs?"

"Men always carry on like baboons when they're in groups," said Gwen. "But our Mister Pilcher has something else which he is concealing with this display of masculine force."

"Maybe he's a poet at heart," suggested Sally, who was standing at the doorway.

"Sneak!" exclaimed Iris. "How long were you listening?"

"Just a minute or two," said Sally, coming in. "I didn't want to interrupt your analysis. Sounds like a fascinating afternoon the two of you had while I sat cajoling my Muse in this lonely office."

"We lived to tell the tale," said Iris. "How goes the playwriting?"

"I need more conflict," he said. "Have you any to spare?"

"More than you know," said Gwen glumly.

"In any case, I am the bearer of good news," he said, reaching into his pocket. "More important, I am the bearer of cash."

He pulled out a handful of bills and coins and placed them triumphantly on Iris's desk.

"Forty pounds, less my commission," he said. "The Cornwalls send their abject apologies and thank you for services on their behalves."

"No, they didn't," said Gwen.

"No, they didn't," agreed Sally. "But they paid up, so I thought I'd sugarcoat the transaction for you."

"You must tell me all the lurid details when Gwen isn't around to disapprove," said Iris.

"Sometimes I like lurid details," said Gwen.

"Nevertheless, we'll postpone the telling until we have the chance to hear it properly with drinks," said Iris, scooping up the money. "I'm going to deposit this straight away before I go shopping for stockings."

"Do you want me to go with you?" asked Sally.

"If I show up with a bodyguard, it would be extremely out of character," said Iris, scribbling on her notepad. "Here's the address. If I don't telephone here by five, send in the cavalry."

"Here?"

"Yes, here. Could you fill in for one more day, please, dear Sally? My Bar-Let would be glad of the company."

"I'll be back at some point midafternoon, so it needn't be a full shift," added Gwen.

"Well, as it happens, I have my script in progress with me," said Sally, patting a well-worn leather satchel at his side. "I shall put the time to good use. It's quiet here."

"Unfortunately," said Iris.

The waiting room at Doctor Milford's office was thickly carpeted, as was the office itself. Gwen suspected it to be sound-proofing. That and the doubled doorway to the inner officer kept those outside from hearing any shouts, sobs, or curses. The patients went in and out, rarely making eye contact with the others waiting. Conversation among them never happened, other than the muttered "Good days" springing from habitual courtesy.

There were more men waiting at this time of day, Gwen noticed. Young men, sitting rigidly upright staring into space rather than availing themselves of the magazines in the stand at the end of one of the leather-covered couches. Gwen picked up an old, well-thumbed issue of the *Illustrated London News*. It was their centenary issue from '42, with a lovely full-page black and white photo of Princess Elizabeth in her ambulance driver gear, the cap tilted jauntily on her head, her curls slightly wind-blown. There was a colour spread of the Royal Family "at home," as if being at home for them was a normal way of life for anyone else. The Queen and the two princesses wore matching light blue suits while the King was in military dress, of course. Yet it was the black and white photo of Elizabeth, the Heir Presumptive, that kept drawing Gwen back. She stared at it for a good long time, feeling inadequate.

Even before Ronnie's death, she had spent most of the war away from London. They had evacuated to the Bainbridge country estate south of Bolton, where the family owned two munitions factories. Bolton escaped the Blitz for the most part. One wayward bomb landed on an eating house near the station, killing two, but other than that, it was a peaceful existence. So peaceful that to wake up and hear nothing but birds and the distant lowing of cattle was positively surreal, knowing that the man she loved was risking life and limb in North Africa and Italy.

They had taken in children from London at the house; later from Manchester and Liverpool. They had set up a temporary school in the ballroom, and Gwen taught them how to read and write and do sums while her son ran screaming with joy with the others too young for school yet, chasing chickens and gaping at the horses.

She wondered how much he remembered his father. He had

seen so little of him, but there was a trove of letters that came weeks late. Chatty, uninformative accounts meant to cheer them both up while appeasing the censors. *I saw Bedouins riding camels! Just like in Boys' Own, only the camels are very nasty fellows who do not like one to pet them. I learned this the hard way.*

Even now, Ronnie wanted that one read to him over and over while he gazed at the photograph by her bedside.

Did he hear his father's voice? Or had the voice of the letters become Gwen's over time?

She wished there was some recording that she could play. There was a brief bit of footage from their wedding, made by one of Ronnie's friends who was an amateur movie enthusiast, but it was silent, and wearing out from repeat projections.

Her appointment time came, and Doctor Milford's secretary, Rita, showed her into his office. He sat behind his desk, studying a file, then looked up and motioned her to a seat.

"And how are we today, Mrs. Bainbridge?" he asked.

"Fine, thank you," she said.

"Let me get a few vitals, then we'll get down to the clockworks," he said, coming around the desk.

He took her pulse and blood pressure, jotted them down, then sat in a chair across from hers.

"Appetite good?"

"Yes."

"Everything else happening when it should?"

"Yes."

"How's the old perkiness? Any unusual fatigue?"

"I am working full-time and I am the mother of a six-year-old boy. Yes, there is fatigue, but nothing that I would describe as unusual."

"Mothers have more energy than all of us."

"Not true. We just need more."

He smiled at that, then continued.

"Any unusual dreams?"

There it is, she thought.

"I had one about Ronnie again," she said.

"Just the one? None besides it since your last visit?"

"No."

"Tell me."

She described it, the panic seeping into her voice as she did.

"When did this happen?"

"Last Sunday night. Monday morning, more precisely. It was odd."

"How so?"

"It felt like a warning. A premonition. Of course, that's utter nonsense, I know it, but then—"

She stopped.

"But then?" he prompted her.

"We came in to find that one of our clients had been murdered the night before."

"So I am given to understand. Did you feel that there was a connection between your dream and the murder?"

"It was an odd coincidence."

"Not necessarily," said Doctor Milford. "Let me ask—when did you first meet the poor girl?"

"Let me think. It was Monday of the week before. We interviewed her, went through possible prospects, found one we thought suitable, and put them in contact with each other."

"That's how you usually work, is it?"

"Yes," said Gwen.

"Was there anything that struck you about the woman that caused you any unease?"

"Well, I thought—in fact, we both thought that there was something shady about her. We were following up on it, but didn't hear about anything before she was killed."

"And now, according to your mother-in-law, you have decided to investigate this matter."

"Yes," said Gwen reluctantly. "That's why she called you ahead of schedule."

"Oh, she's called me about you many times," said Doctor Milford, chuckling. "You'd be in here nonstop if I acted upon every one of them, or they'd need to reopen Bedlam with a special ward just for you in a straitjacket if she had her way. I might need another for myself if Lady Carolyne keeps calling."

"I had no idea," said Gwen, the colour rising in her cheeks.

"How does that make you feel?" asked Doctor Milford, watching her closely.

"Furious," said Gwen. "Quite livid, in fact."

"What do you intend to do about it?"

"I'd like to—" Gwen started.

Then she held herself back.

"Go on," urged Doctor Milford.

"The problem is that I don't know where you stand in all of this," said Gwen.

"Given that I was hired and continue to be paid by your husband's family."

"Yes."

"You don't trust me."

"I'm sorry," said Gwen.

"No, no, perfectly understandable," said Doctor Milford. "I'd be the same if I were in your shoes. In fact, not only understandable, but in terms of self-preservation, an intelligent choice."

"Then what are we doing here?" asked Gwen.

"Excellent question," said Doctor Milford. "It is time to tell you my life story."

"Will it be very long?" asked Gwen. "You've lived a great deal longer than I have."

"Cut me to the quick, will you?" he growled in mock chagrin. "Well, let me sum up the important bits, and you can decide after whether or not you wish to continue with me."

"All right. Go on."

"I trained as a surgeon," said Doctor Milford. "I was damned good at it, in fact. When the previous war broke out, I volunteered my services immediately. I spent the next four years at various field hospitals, so close to the front lines that we caught the occasional overshot artillery, not to mention the odd whiff of gas."

"How horrible it must have been," said Gwen, shuddering.

"It was, it was," he said. "We started seeing more and more men suffering from what we were calling shell shock then and combat neurosis now. The prevailing wisdom at the time was to treat them and get them back to the front as quickly as possible. The top brass, none of whom had any background in psychiatry, saw these poor blighters as ignorant bumpkins trying to cry their way out of combat duty. They put a few of them in front of firing squads to make an example for the rest."

"How dreadful," said Gwen.

"I protested all that I could, but it was not a popular position," continued Doctor Milford. "Nor did the prevailing wisdom change much when they looked at the question after the war. There was a report on shell shock in '22 by the War Office that essentially repeated the views of the top brass. I was, quite frankly, outraged, but as a surgeon, I carried little influence. So, I went back to school and became a psychiatrist. Haven't touched a scalpel in twenty years."

"My goodness," said Gwen.

"I devoted much of my practice to ex-soldiers trying to cope with civilian life," he continued. "Saw more than my share of thousand-yard stares, I assure you. And then comes the new war, and it's happened all over again. But what a few of us realized is that it isn't only the soldiers who suffer from this. It can be anyone who undergoes a severe and sudden trauma."

"Like losing a husband," she said softly.

"Like losing a husband," he agreed. "The more intense the love, the more catastrophic the loss."

"Yes."

"You loved him a great deal, Mrs. Bainbridge."

"I did," she said. "I do."

"You would have saved him if you could."

"Yes. But I couldn't."

"Is that why you are so set on saving this Trower chap?"

He asked the question gently, but she jerked her head up as if she had been slapped.

"Do you think that's why I'm doing this?" she asked.

"Do you?" he returned.

"Doesn't his innocence count for anything?"

"It would if he were innocent," said Doctor Milford. "He doesn't appear to be innocent, however."

"Based upon what you've read in the newspapers."

"Yes," he conceded. "But do you have any information that they do not?"

"My knowledge of the man himself," she said. "And there are circumstances—"

"Such as?"

She looked at him.

"This remains confidential," she said. "Not a hint to my mother-in-law."

"That is my professional duty," he said. "Now, persuade me that this is not a fool's mission."

"Very well," she said.

She summarized the events of the previous few days. By the end of her account, he was leaning forward in his chair. She finished, and looked at him expectantly.

"Well?" she asked.

"Total conjecture and speculation," he pronounced, then he held up his hand to forestall her burgeoning burst of rage. "Yet not without validity."

"And the premonition?"

"If the dream was truly premonitory in nature, don't you think that it should have come in time to warn that poor girl beforehand?"

"I should have thought of that," she said. "It's blindingly obvious when you put it like that. So, what did that dream mean?"

"Premonitory dreams are usually disguised anxieties," he said. "Somewhere in the archives of your subconscious, your brain analyzed the visits of Miss La Salle and your devious dustman and came to the conclusion that something was wrong. It then gave you the message by means of a nightmare."

"I wish my subconscious could write things down instead," she said ruefully. "Send them by pneumatic tube or winged cupids or something."

"That would be much more convenient," he agreed. "On the bright side, you're having these nightmares less frequently."

"Have I? I hadn't noticed."

"But I have, Mrs. Bainbridge. I keep careful track of their occurrences, and they are clearly on the decline. Take that as progress."

"So, my wish to investigate Miss La Salle's death doesn't strike you as odd?"

"No," he said. "No, indeed. I have no interest whatsoever in the guilt or innocence of Mister Trower, mind you, other than the general well-meaning desire to see justice done, whatever that entails. My concern is whether or not what you are doing is based upon sense or nonsense."

"And your verdict?"

"I don't think that this is a symptom of any disease, Mrs. Bain-bridge," he said. "I shall assure your mother-in-law of that opinion."

"Then I am sane."

"Oh, my dear woman, far from it," he said, smiling.

She actually laughed at that, and it felt good.

CHAPTER 11

I ris took the Tube to Wapping Station, which put her on Wapping High Street. She walked quickly past Merle's, keeping to the other side of the street, then took the dogleg on Gamet to Wapping Wall.

The street was paved with cobblestones, with warehouses on both sides. Bridged walkways soared overhead, connecting the wharves to the buildings across the way.

The area had been by and large missed by the Blitz despite the Germans' concentration on the docks. With the exception of one that had been damaged heavily by an incendiary, the warehouses all stood tall, grey, and not overly busy despite the time of day. There weren't enough ships coming in to unload to keep the area active.

The third warehouse on the left past Monza Street was a four-storey affair, built of drab bricks whose original colour had long been lost to thick deposits of soot and grime. There was a loading bay for lorries which looked unwelcoming, and a wooden door to the right of it marked OFFICE which was locked when Iris tried it. She rang the bell and waited. A short time later, the door opened a crack and a coarse, unshaven man peered at her suspiciously.

"What do you want?" he asked.

"Archie said I should drop by," she said.

"Did 'e now?" said the man. "Didn't tell me nothin' about it."

"Tell him it's Mary," she said. "Mary from last night."

"Mary from last night, is it?" he repeated, leering. "Think that'll jog 'is memory enough?"

"He'll remember me," she said. "I'm memorable."

"Wait out there," he said. "I'll see if that's the case."

He closed the door. She heard it lock.

A few minutes later, it opened again and the man motioned her inside.

"Be quick about it," he said, scanning the streets in both directions.

She ducked in, and he closed it behind her and locked it.

"Your bag," he said, holding out his hand.

She surrendered it. He went through it, then pulled out her knife.

"What's this, then?"

She shrugged.

"Would you let your missus wander around 'ere unprotected?" she asked.

"My missus would know better than to come 'ere," he said, returning her bag without the knife. "You're safe inside. You can 'ave it back when you leave."

"Don't go playing with it," she said. "It's sharp."

"Yeah, I figured that out for meself, thanks very much," he said. "This way."

He led her down a passage into the warehouse proper. As far as the eye could see crates were stacked on pallets resting on rows of steel-framed storage shelves. Her escort led her down an aisle between the rows, stopping her at one intersection as a forklift drove through, its driver acknowledging them with a lazy salute as he passed. They reached a steel door at the end of the aisle. The man knocked three times, then four more. The door opened.

"There she is," beamed Archie. "Come in, my lovely. I didn't know if you intended to keep your appointment or not."

"I don't like to disappoint a gentleman," said Iris as he held the door for her.

"Dunno if I'd fall into that particular category," said Archie. "But I've met my share of so-called gentlemen, and they generally don't meet their own standards in my experience."

"Don't 'ave to tell me that," said Iris. "If I 'ad a penny for every blue blood who ever pinched me bum, I could retire to a life of soft cushions."

"Well, I must admit, it does present a tempting target," said Archie.

"Now, now," she said, wagging her finger at him. "Don't get fresh with me."

"You're on my turf, girlie," he said. "I get as fresh as I like with anyone what walks in 'ere."

"You must make the boys proper nervous, then," she said, glancing around.

The corner of the building had been converted to a private club-house for Archie and his cronies, many of whom were scattered about the room. One group was playing cards in the corner, while more were gathered around a snooker table, betting and commenting raucously on each shot. There was a bar at the far end, complete with a female bartender who gave Iris the once-over before returning to pouring. She was the only other woman present, Iris noticed.

Besides the door behind her, the only other exit was in the rear corner by the far end of the bar. She made a quick consult of her mental map. It had to let out at the back of the warehouse, which meant an alleyway of some kind. Were they right on Shadwell Basin? Not quite, she thought. No watery escapes here. Hopefully, none of any kind, but she didn't like the setup now that she was inside of it.

"Boys, you remember Mary?" called Archie. "Mary, friend of the late, lamented Tillie La Salle."

Iris gave a wave, and the men not too preoccupied nodded back, some checking her out in a thoroughly wolfish manner.

"Mary what?" one of them called out.

"Well, I don't rightly know, come to think of it," said Archie, turning to her. "Mary what?"

"McTague," said Iris. "Mary Elizabeth McTague is me full name."

"I don't suppose you have anything what proves that?" asked Archie.

"Proof? What for?"

"Because I wasn't born yesterday, love," said Archie.

"Right," said Iris, reaching into her bag. "If it's good enough for the rozzers, it oughter be good enough for you."

She handed over a National Registration Identity Card duly filled out in the name of Mary Elizabeth McTague, courtesy of her war work. Another souvenir that she was supposed to turn in after demobilization, but she had held onto it for unspecified emergencies, and the Brigadier had never asked for it back.

She wondered if that was a deliberate error on his part. She wouldn't put it past him.

Archie gave it a cursory glance, then handed it back.

"Miss Mary Elizabeth McTague, what can we do for you today?" he asked.

"I came for stockings," she said.

"'Ow many would you like?"

"One for each leg," she said. "But 'ow many pairs depends on the price."

"Well, we've been selling 'em for four pounds a pair—"

"Cor blimey!" she exclaimed, meaning it.

"But," he said, holding his hand up placatingly, "we have a discount for our friends, and I think we can consider you one."

"How much of a discount?" she asked warily.

"Well, it depends on 'ow friendly you'd like to be," he said.

He went over behind the bar, pulled out a long, narrow cardboard box from underneath, and opened it.

"Come inspect the merchandise," he said.

She walked over to him. He pulled out a pair of nylons and draped them across her hands.

"These are the real article," he said.

"Oh, these are lovely," said Iris, holding them up to see the light shining through them.

"Try 'em on," said Archie.

"Right," said Iris. "'Ave you got a ladies' in the place, or should I just go in back?"

"Like I said, the discount is for our friends," said Archie. "We're all friends in 'ere, aren't we, love?"

"I suppose," said Iris, looking around dubiously.

The others in the room had ceased their various gaming and drinking activities momentarily to watch the transaction with unveiled interest. Iris suddenly realized that she was on display.

"So, since you're amongst friends, try them on for us," said Archie.

"What, 'ere?" she exclaimed. "Right in front of everyone?"

"That's the deal," said Archie. "Brings the price down, depending on 'ow much approval you earn."

"I'm no dance-hall girl," said Iris indignantly. "If you think I'm going to put on some kind of show for this lot—"

"Oh, but I think you are, love," said Archie, smiling.

Only this smile had teeth in it.

Well. Do what you have to do, old girl, and maybe that will be the end of it, she thought. What's a little humiliation in the pursuit of a case, right?

"I don't 'ave nothing to 'old them up," she said.

He reached into the box and pulled out a pair of garters.

"These should do," he said, tossing them to her.

"Yeah, they'll do nicely," she said.

She kept her eyes down as the men began whistling from around the room. She reached down and unbuckled her shoe, then took it off and placed it on the bar. She took one of the stockings and began to roll it down from its edges.

"That's enough," said a voice from the back.

"What's that?" said Archie.

"I said, that's enough, Archie," the man repeated.

And Roger Pilcher walked towards the bar from the corner where he had been playing cards.

She had missed him when she came in. He must have had his back to the door.

Not good, thought Iris.

"What's this about then, Rog?" asked Archie.

"This bird you leave alone," said Roger. "She's off-limits."

"Says you."

"Yeah, says me," said Roger.

What the hell is going on? thought Iris.

"Before I beat the living Christ out of you, tell me why," said Archie.

"She 'asn't been telling you the truth about 'erself," said Roger.

Damn, thought Iris. Get ready for the forty-yard dash, girl.

She casually slipped her shoe back on.

"What 'asn't she been telling us?" asked Archie.

"It's a personal matter," said Roger. "I'd rather not discuss it 'ere."

"If there is anything you got to say about this, you say it in front of all of us," said Archie. "Spit it out while you still got all your teeth, boy."

"Remember when me and Tillie broke up?" asked Roger.

"Wasn't so long ago that I'd forget," said Archie. "What about it?"

"What I didn't tell you is that she found out I 'ad been 'aving a bit on the side," said Roger. "That's the reason why it 'appened."

"I'm surprised she din't slice you to ribbons if that were the case," said Archie. "So, what's that got to—oh, I got the wind of it."

"Right," said Roger. "This is the bit on the side. Me and Mary."

And suddenly a lifeline, thought Iris in shock. Grab it!

She walked up to Roger, her face contorted in rage.

"You weren't supposed to tell no one!" she shouted.

"Well, you weren't supposed to come around barging into me business!" he shouted back. "Bad enough you come out to Merle's, but 'ere? I told you never to come 'ere! We 'ad an agreement."

"Yeah, well, I wanted to see if you was telling me the truth about it," spat Iris. "If you really was the big man you said you was, running with Archie and the boys at all hours. I 'ad to know the truth!"

"Look around you, love. What do you see? Am I a liar?"

She turned back to face Archie, whose face had gone from puzzled anger to amusement.

"You. You're supposed to be the big boss," she snarled. "You tell me. 'As 'e been working for you all this time, or does he got another girl stashed somewhere?"

"Christ, sounds like every night with me mum and dad in the kitchen," commented one of the men by the snooker table.

"Miss McTague," said Archie. "Far be it from me to be the arbitrator of this little lovers' quarrel, but if you're asking me to vouch for 'is general whereabouts, 'e works for me, and 'as been for nearly a year now."

"And nights?"

"Some of our best work is night work," said Archie. "Stockings don't grow on trees, you know."

"Satisfied?" asked Roger.

"Well, since 'e says so, I guess I am," said Iris.

"I must say I 'ad no inkling about this from 'ow you two acted last night," said Archie. "You played it straight."

"You didn't 'ear us going at it in the street afterwards," said Iris. "Liked to 'ave waked the dead."

"Knives were out," said Roger, grinning at her.

"They certainly were," she said.

"Well, I'm glad to see true love and all that," said Archie. "So the stockings—"

"I still want a pair," said Iris.

"They're on me," said Roger.

"No," said Iris. "You're not buying your way out of this one, Roger Pilcher. I pay me own way. 'Ow much, Archie? Or do I still 'ave to put on a show for you and the lads?"

"Oh, you've put on a show, all right," laughed Archie. "Make it two and six. You can pay Louise there."

"Right," said Iris, slapping the money on the counter and taking the stockings. "It's a pleasure doing business with you. If you ever need a solid girl for any extra work, I might be interested."

"Might be a place for you," said Archie.

"You," said Iris to Pilcher. "Walk me to the train."

"All right, Archie?" asked Rog.

"A gentleman would do no less," said Archie grandly. "Are we not all gentlemen 'ere?"

"Right," said Rog. "Be back in a while."

"Take your time, my boy," said Archie. "There ain't no great demands for your services tonight."

"There ain't gonna be any from me, that's for certain," said Iris.

She rolled the stockings up carefully, then looked at Archie, winked, and put them into her handbag.

"Ta ta, gents," she said, and she sauntered towards the door, then looked at Pilcher.

"Well?" she said expectantly.

"You waiting for a 'yes, dear'?" he asked.

"I'm waiting for you to open the bleedin' door like a gentleman oughter," she said. "Show them 'ow it's done, Rog."

"Christ," he muttered, striding angrily past her and opening it.

They walked silently to the front of the warehouse, where the spiv on watch sat reading a magazine.

"One sec," said Iris. "Oy, you 'ave something of mine."

"What?" said the watchman. "Oh, right."

He pulled open a drawer and pulled out her knife.

"Careful with that," he said. "A little birdie told me it's sharp."

"So it is," said Iris. "Thanks for taking care of it. Shall we?"

"Night, Tony," said Pilcher.

"This your girl then, Rog?" asked Tony as he unlocked the door.

"Afraid so," said Pilcher. "But we all got our troubles, don't we?"

"Truer words," said Tony as they passed by him. "Night, then."

"Now," said Iris pleasantly as she took Rog's arm. "We 'ave to 'ave a little chat, lover."

"Shut it," he said.

"But—"

"I said shut it, and I meant it," he whispered urgently.

They continued on until they came back to Wapping High Street. He glanced behind him.

"All right, no one is following," he said. "Now, what the bloody 'ell are you trying to do? Get yourself killed?"

"Who are you?" asked Iris.

"I'm Roger Pilcher, and if you keep at this, I'm going to be the late Roger Pilcher," he said. "I warned you last night—"

"Who do you work for?" she asked.

"What?"

"You don't seem like CID," she continued. "Some special branch?"

"You're a madwoman," he said, shaking his head.

"Yet you came to my rescue," she said. "You could have given me up on the spot. It would have been the smartest move you could have made."

"I'm coming to regret that decision," he said. "Listen, I don't know what tree you think you're barking up—"

"I was warned away from you this morning," she said.

"From me? What for? Who by?"

"By CID," she said. "Ongoing investigation, they told me. Look, I have no intention of getting you in trouble—"

"Great," he sighed. "You're doing a fine job unintentionally then. Who do you work for?"

"The Right Sort Marriage Bureau," she said. "But you know that. You came there."

"And what's that a front for?"

"A front? What on earth makes you think we're anything other than what we appear to be?"

"Oh, I dunno," he said. "Maybe the fact that you're investigating a murder. A murder which has been already solved, in case you haven't heard. Not to mention the obvious training—you handled that knife like you were Special Forces. And the fact that you're showing up in some very odd places in character, complete with a nicely forged Ident Card, no less. You just happened to have that laying around for emergencies?"

"You never know when it will come in handy," she said. "Is your name really Roger Pilcher?"

"I could show you my ident," he said. "It's realer than yours. So, who are you working for?"

"I had some interesting experiences during the war," she said. "But I'm on my own, now. Or with Mrs. Bainbridge, to be accurate. The Right Sort is legitimate, not a front."

"Then what made you turn into Holmes and Watson?" he asked. "Or is this *Gert and Daisy Clean Up*?"

"Won't we 'ave a party when it's over?" she sang. "I love Gert and Daisy. That's the one where they catch the black marketeer, isn't it? Well, we're certainly on the right track, if that's the case. But I'm guessing that's your objective, isn't it?"

He didn't reply.

"Not CID," she speculated. "Bureau of Trade? One of Yandell's inspectors? No—they don't go in for undercover work. Ministry of Finance, however . . ."

He winced. She saw it.

"That's it, then," she said. "You're with Finance, hot on the trail of smuggled nylons—only you know about the nylons, so it can't be that. You want bigger fish to fry. Who and what are those fish?"

"Stop it," he said. "I'm no undercover."

"Why did you step in when you did, Roger Not-a-Spiv Pilcher?" she demanded. "All that would have happened is I would have shown more of my legs to strangers than I normally like to do on a first date. It wouldn't have been the end of the world."

"It wouldn't have stopped there, you see," he said. "It would have gone further once you let it start. Much further. I couldn't let that happen. Not to an innocent woman."

"So you put yourself and your operation in jeopardy to rescue me from a fate worse than death," she said. "How very gallant of you."

"You're making fun of me."

"No," she said. "I meant it. You could have left me to suffer the consequences of my recklessness. I'm grateful."

"So you'll stay away now?"

"Where were you on the night Tillie La Salle was killed?"

"Are you still on about that?" he asked, turning to stare at her in disbelief. "You were told I was in the clear."

"I was," she said. "But I don't believe everything that I am told. Where were you that night?"

"Being debriefed by my superiors," he said. "And no, you can't verify it with them, because you are not allowed to know who they are. You can bloody well take my word for it, because you have no business knowing anything else. Or even this much."

"Why did you follow Miss La Salle to our office?"

"Because I wanted to know where she was going," he said. "Then I had to see what the two of you were all about."

"Why did you care about where she was going?"

"Tillie's been up to something," he said. "Or was. I thought she was running some kind of side game, and I thought this might have been part of it."

"Side game? What was the main game?"

"She worked for Archie," said Pilcher. "That's how I got in. I romanced her, wormed my way in, made myself useful. Then she dropped me."

"Her girlfriends said you dropped her."

"That's what she told them, I guess," said Pilcher. "But something else was going on. When I heard she got killed, I thought it might have had something to do with that."

"What kind of work did she do for Archie?"

"She got information from blokes who couldn't help talking to pretty girls. Information that led to a lot of lorries getting robbed, warehouses getting looted."

"Could any of that have led to someone killing her?"

"Maybe."

"What about Archie himself?"

"If he thought she was playing him for a fool, he would have done it without batting an eye," said Pilcher.

"Maybe he did," said Iris. "Did he say anything when he heard she was killed?"

"Nothing other than surprise," said Pilcher. "He was angry. I was worried he might have thought I had done it. Exes going at it and all. I tell you, I was never more relieved when I heard they got that fellow you set her up with. Took the heat off of me."

"You're welcome," sighed Iris. "So if it wasn't you, and if it wasn't Dickie Trower—any idea where Archie was that night?"

"Like I said, I wasn't with him," said Pilcher. "So I can't tell you where he was, and I'm not about to go asking him."

"What's the big fish? You still haven't told me."

"Yeah, well, there's the problem. The big fish got away."

"What do you mean?"

"You were right about the nylons being small fry. The big money is in clothing coupons."

"Selling stolen coupons? There's enough money in that to keep them going?"

"You have no idea. Coupons go for four to six shillings apiece, and books go for up to four pounds each."

"All right, that's a lot, but to steal enough to make real money—"

"They aren't stealing them," said Pilcher. "They're fixing on making their own."

"Forgery? On how large a scale?"

"Large. They were planning on printing tens of thousands of coupon books."

"Were? What happened?"

"That's what I'm trying to find out. The new annual books get issued at the end of the month. Archie somehow got hold of a set of plates for the new coupons. I don't know if they're originals or they managed to make a mould, but they were going to put out copies that look just like the genuine article."

"So what stopped them?"

"Someone nicked the plates from Archie," said Pilcher. "Inside job, maybe a month ago. No honour amongst spivs, I'm sorry to say. The old boy may be smiling and spreading good cheer, but inside he's ready to hang people on meat hooks and roast 'em slowly."

"Could that have been Tillie's handiwork? The side game?"

"Maybe. I didn't think Tillie was that deep in that she'd have known about it, but I'm wondering about it now."

"You said she had a knack for getting men to talk about things they shouldn't talk about."

"She did, yeah," said Pilcher. "Something you have in common. But I don't think she knew about the plates."

"You knew about them," said Iris. "Why didn't you have the whole lot arrested when you found out?"

"Because I only found out about the plates after they were nicked from Archie," said Pilcher. "Without them, there's nothing to pin on him, and I'd have wasted nearly a year's work just to get them on selling nylons. That isn't exactly the big score we're hoping for. He'd be back on the outside in no time."

"What if you brought me in?" asked Iris.

"What?"

"Keep me in the fold. I could winnow out something more about Tillie, and maybe find something to help you out into the bargain."

"You have to be joking. Bad enough that you tumbled me, but now you want to double the chances I get my cover blown?"

"I know what I'm doing," she said.

"Says you."

"Besides, it would be awfully strange if that was my only appearance with you, now that our torrid affair is out in the open."

He kicked angrily at a chunk of broken brick, sending it clattering down the cobblestones.

"That's the problem with being nice to people in this world," he said. "It gets you nothing but trouble."

"Is that a yes?"

"I'll speak to my superiors tonight," he said. "If they say yes, then it's a go."

"Thank you, Mister Pilcher," she said.

"You better start calling me Rog," he said. "Mary."

"I will," she said. "I may even use some embarrassing pet name. Would you like some verisimilitude to take back with you?"

"Meaning what?"

She put her arms around his neck and kissed him, making sure to leave some lipstick behind.

"I wasn't ready," he protested as she pulled away. "I can do it better."

"Don't wipe off the lipstick until they see it on you," she advised him. "I must say, I am very impressed that you've been doing this as well as you have for so long, Rog. Keep your nose clean."

"I think I'm safer with gangsters than I am with you," he called as she headed into the station.

"That's probably true," she said. "Ta ta, lover."

She stared out the train window, trying to put her thoughts in order. Assessing her performance.

She found it wanting. Too reckless, too dependent on improvisation. And she had gone in with no backup other than—

"Damn," she said, looking at her watch.

Then she heaved a sigh of relief. It was only four fifteen. She had forgotten to call Sally and let him know that she was safe. She would have to find a phone box at the transfer station and make sure he didn't send the police into the warehouse after her.

That was not the sort of mistake she should be making. Why was she so hell-bent on proving herself today?

Was it because she had ended things with Andrew? Was she overreacting by trying to show she could out-spy the spy? And out-detect the detective while she was at it? Was she trying to solve the case so she could throw the mess in Mike's face as well?

Pathetic, Iris.

What did she have to show for her efforts? She had eliminated her top prospect for the murder, and nearly scuttled an official investigation, which was precisely what Detective Sergeant Ex had warned her against. But she might also have wormed her way closer to Miss La Salle's murderer, assuming the dead girl had indeed been double-crossing Archie.

The train pulled into Whitechapel. Iris exited and hurried to the nearest phone box and called The Right Sort. To her surprise, Gwen answered.

"I was expecting Sally," said Iris.

"He's still here," said Gwen. "He says he's in the throes of a bi-sexual love triangle which means that there are at least six possible permutations to work through. He's drawing diagrams and cursing in different languages."

"Sounds like he's in full Muse," said Iris. "How did things go with the psychiatrist?"

"He feels that our pursuit of justice is not entirely insane," said Gwen. "It gave me some hope."

"I may have to disagree with him," said Iris. "I jumped into a rabbit hole today. I landed in a pair of nylons."

"Enigmatic. Can you tell me more?"

"I don't want to hold you up from tilting with the family gorgon," said Iris. "I'm going to head straight back to the flat. But it looks like Pilcher isn't our man after all."

"What? Are you sure?"

"Unfortunately, yes."

"What changed your mind?"

"Long story," she said. "And my train is coming in. I'll tell you all about it in the morning. Give my love to Sally."

She hung up.

Because it is a woman's prerogative to change her mind, she thought.

Because today I kissed a man who I was ready to stab yesterday, she thought.

Story of my life, she thought.

CHAPTER 12

G wen hung up the telephone. Sally sat muttering at the other desk, shifting voices. She surmised from the changes in register that the love triangle involved two men and a woman. Or possibly a second woman who smoked to excess.

"That was Iris," she said. "She's safe."

"I expected nothing less," said Sally.

"She said that she's ruled out Roger Pilcher as a suspect," said Gwen. "Which narrows the field down to the rest of the city of London."

"I was at a dinner party that night," said Sally.

"All right, you're off the list," said Gwen.

"I shall rest easier knowing that," said Sally. "Will you be needing my services tomorrow while you're out seeking justice?"

"Do we seem that ridiculous?" she asked.

"Everyone and everything seem ridiculous at the moment," he said. "That's why the only serious work is to be found in the theatre."

He pulled out a manuscript, looked at it thoughtfully, then started crossing out page after page with his pen.

"You edit with great abundance," observed Gwen. "There must be something in there worth saving."

"There is," said Sally, holding up one of the exed-out pages. "The other side."

He reversed the page and fed it into the typewriter so that the blank side faced him.

"Damned shortages," he said. "It's harder and harder to get what I need, so I'm sacrificing some of my juvenilia for the greater good. It's too bad we aren't back in the Dark Ages. If I was using parchment, I could scrape it down and start over."

"If only one could do that with memories," said Gwen.

"Oh, that's good! May I steal it?"

"Be my guest."

He scribbled it on the margins of one of the used pages.

"What was the failed play?" she asked.

"One of my university efforts," he said. "Lifetimes ago. Embarrassing to look at now. Glad to be getting some use out of it finally."

"You knew Iris at Cambridge, didn't you?"

"Quite well."

"Were you and she ever—"

She thought carefully about her choice of words.

"—an item?"

"Oh, Lord," he laughed ruefully. "There wasn't a proper man at Cambridge who wasn't in love with Iris Sparks. This sad little melodrama that I am consigning to the palimpsest stage was one I wrote expressly for the purpose of casting her in the lead, with me as her romantic opposite."

"How did it go?"

"It was terrible," he said. "Written for the wrong reasons, but from the heart. I worked in as much torrid lovemaking as I could get away with. Most girls avoided me back then, big galumphing monster that I am. Not Sparks. She was fearlessly kind, if such a thing is possible. Why, I remember once in training—"

He stopped abruptly.

"Well, not my story to tell," he said. "Not in nonfictional form, anyway."

"You were in training together?" asked Gwen.

"Forget I ever said that," he said. "Please. And don't mention anything about it to Sparks."

"You were behind enemy lines," said Gwen. "You were a saboteur or something."

"Or something. I've forgotten all of it very quickly."

"A decorated hero, she said."

"She likes to puff me up," said Sally. "It wasn't as exciting as all that. Lots of sleeping in caves and cellars, trying to stay safe and warm and dry."

"Was that something that she trained to do?"

"She hasn't told you?"

"She says that she can't."

"Then I can't, either. Besides, I don't know most of it. I was away, catching colds in foreign climes."

"All this secrecy," said Gwen bitterly. "I wish that she would simply lie to me rather than drop these ominous hints."

"But she doesn't want to lie to you, don't you see?" said Sally. "I think that you've been good for her in a strange sort of way. She's someone who loves to spin tales at the drop of a hat, but she won't lie to you. You may be the first person for whom she's ever been like that."

"Will she ever tell me the truth about the war?"

"Have you told her everything about your life?" asked Sally.

"Not by a long shot."

"There you are," he said. "It will give the two of you something to do on those dreary, rainy days when Love is too tired to climb the stairs."

"Could you come in tomorrow?"

"Of course. Planning to be in the field?"

"I don't know what the plan is anymore," said Gwen. "But it helps having you here."

"I no longer unnerve you?"

"She told you that? I'm so sorry. No, Sally, you no longer unnerve me. You are a big, galumphing man, but you are a very dear, big, galumphing man."

"Thank you, kind lady," he said, taking her hand and kissing it gently. "I shall return."

"Sally," she said hesitantly.

"Yes?"

"Could you show me what your fiercest character is like? I want to borrow it."

Two trains and a bus after leaving Wapping, Iris turned onto her street in Marylebone. Her thoughts were still occupied with the day's events, but not so much that she wasn't immediately aware that she was being followed by a black Bentley with darkened windows.

She stopped walking. The car pulled up, and a uniformed officer got out, then opened the rear passenger door.

"Get in," he said.

"My mother always told me never to get in cars with strangers," she said, eyeing him up and down, searching for weak spots. He didn't appear to have any.

"But we're not strangers, are we, Sparks?" said the Brigadier, leaning forward into view.

"Will this take long?" asked Sparks. "It's been a tiring day."

"One circuit around Regent's Park should be sufficient," he said. "And I have whisky."

"Why didn't you mention that at the start?" she asked, sliding in next to him.

The officer closed the door, then got in front with the driver. There was a thick glass partition separating them.

"This will be a private conversation," said the Brigadier, noticing her glancing at it.

He was in civvies, wearing a neatly tailored grey pinstriped suit that predated the war. He had salt-and-pepper hair, and his mustache had turned a solid grey since she last saw him. He might have passed for a banker were it not for the ramrod straightness of his back. And the eyes which examined quickly, judged thoroughly, and executed unsentimentally. She wondered what the verdict would be on her. Or had the sentence already been pronounced?

He unlatched a panel in the back of the driver's seat, revealing a bottle and two tumblers. He poured for them both as the car began to move.

"You'll have to take it neat, I'm afraid," he said, handing her a glass.

"I prefer it neat," she said, taking it. "To absent friends."

"To absent friends," he repeated, tapping his glass against hers. "You're looking fit, Sparks. Those stairs are doing you a favour. Not to mention all of that traipsing about the wilds of the East End."

"You know about that."

"Merely what your former paramour told me," said the Brigadier.

"Oh, you are up to date!" she said. "Is that what you boys do when we're not around? Gossip? Did he call you from the airport, weeping copiously over his loss? Is your shoulder still damp from the tears?"

"He was rather bent out of shape," said the Brigadier. "Not how I want him going back into the field, but I believe that he will emerge from this intact. Frankly, I think that you're both better off. It was not a healthy affair, if you want my opinion."

"What if I don't want it?"

"Then ignore it."

"Consider it ignored, sir. Now, may I ask what prompted this descent from the gods?"

"Hmph. More like a rise from the depths. How nice to be tooling about in a comfy car with a pretty girl while there's still daylight to be enjoyed."

"It's even better without the smoked windows, but they do make the girl look prettier," said Sparks. "As does the whisky. Compliments aside, why are you here?"

"To see if Major Sutton was telling the truth."

"As far as I know, Andrew only lies for the Crown and to his wife," said Sparks. "Give me the particulars."

"He says that you turned down my invitation to rejoin the group."

"That, I'm afraid, was true," said Sparks.

"Why, if you don't mind me asking?"

"The war ended, didn't it? I'm quite certain I read something about it in the papers at the time."

"That war ended. The next one is in full swing. We need boots on the ground, Sparks."

"Mine are badly in need of repair."

"Your Russian and German are still fluent?"

"Da und ja, mein General-Kommissar."

"Exactly what I require. You're wasting your life at this matchmaking hobby. You could be making the world a better place."

"But I am," said Sparks. "One couple at a time."

"And when it all fizzles out, which may happen within a month at the rate you're going, where will you run to?"

"Wherever it is, I'm certain that you will find me," said Sparks.

"If your country needs you, Sparks—"

"If the country is depending on me to save them, then the straits are dire indeed," said Sparks, handing him back her glass. "I believe this is my street coming up. You can let me off here, I don't want to scandalize the neighbours. It was good to see you again, sir. Good luck with the war. I hope we win."

"Good-bye, Sparks," he said. "I may still call upon you when the situation demands. Good luck with the murder investigation. Show those amateurs at the Yard how it's done."

"Thank you, sir," she said as the car came to a halt and the bodyguard opened her door.

She walked away without glancing back, feeling his eyes on the back of her neck until she turned the corner.

Gwen sailed through the door and past Percival before the butler could even turn.

"Never mind, I know," she called over her shoulder. "The library."

She barged through the doors. Lady Carolyne looked up, startled.

"Good news, Mum," said Gwen. "The doc says I'm cured. I'm going to be at dinner tonight. Are we dressing, or is it just family?"

"You're being absurd," huffed Lady Carolyne.

"It's an absurd situation, isn't it?" said Gwen. "Now, you can keep making my life miserable, but let me remind you that Ronnie is my son no matter what you do. Let me also remind you that if you make me miserable to the point where I am driven out of here, then he will despise you for the rest of your wretched existence. I am willing to offer you some accommodation, but if you won't parlay, then it will be war between us. Don't underestimate me. Your son chose me as his wife for a reason. I've been through it the past few years, yes, but I am through it. And right now, I am famished. The talking cure has given me an appetite. I am going to dine with my son and his governess, and I hope that you will join us and have enough consideration for a wonderful and beautiful six-year-old boy who is his father to the life to make it a pleasant experience. He is fascinated by narwhals at the moment. He is writing and illustrating a picture book about one. He would love to tell you all about it."

"What in God's name is a narwhal?" sputtered Lady Carolyne.

"That is an excellent question with which to begin the conversation," said Gwen. "Although you should tone down the wording a little. Are we dining at seven? Jolly good. Oh, and Mum? Try not to drink too much before dinner. It spoils the palate."

She walked out, closing the door behind her, then leaned against the opposite wall, shaking.

"Thanks, Sally," she whispered. "That felt wonderful."

Iris came into the Bureau the following morning to find Gwen already at her desk, opening the mail.

"Good morning," she said, hanging up her hat. "You're here bright and early."

"I feel energized," said Gwen, pausing to stretch her arms out and take a deep breath. "I did calisthenics before breakfast for the first time in ages. Then I made the walk a brisk one. People were bounding out of my way on the sidewalks. I must smell like a horse right now."

"Not too bad," said Iris, sniffing the air as she sat.

"Miss Pelletier reports a good first date with Mister Carson," said Gwen, handing over a letter. "She added 'Good luck!' in the post-script."

"Encouraging on all fronts," said Iris, glancing over it.

"I've asked Sally to come in midmorning today," continued Gwen. "Only I don't know what our next step is. You were going to tell me why you ruled out Roger Pilcher."

"Here's the thing," said Iris. "I don't know if I can tell you."

"Excuse me? Why not?"

"Well—it involves a confidence. One that I am not sure that I can share."

Gwen drummed her fingers on the desk for a moment, then swung her chair to face Iris. She rolled forward until she was knee to knee with her, then leaned towards her until their faces were inches apart.

"No," she said. "That is unacceptable."

"I'm sorry," said Iris. "Knowing about it could put someone in danger."

"Yet you know about it."

"Yes, but I'm—"

"Good at keeping secrets, yes, you've told me over and over," said Gwen. "And I am sick and tired of it!"

"Gwen?"

"What you did in the war was secret," said Gwen, standing suddenly, sending her chair hurtling backwards into the file cabinet. "Well, bully for you, General Sparks. Bravo, we won, hooray for our side, and well done, a grateful nation thanks you for single-handedly doing whatever the hell you did."

"Gwen, I'm only—"

"We are partners, Iris. Partners in this business, and partners in this investigation, and you have to start treating me accordingly. You may be the one with the fancy Cambridge degree and I'm the one who never went to university and was the prize-winning duck at the funny farm, but we are in this together. Which means that I need to know any and all information that you have so that I can put my mind to it, and it's a damn good one, in case you haven't noticed—"

"I have, of course, but—"

"But it is impossible for me to do what I need to do if you withhold evidence from me. I am perfectly capable of keeping things confidential, thank you very much. I wasn't with you yesterday when you saw what you saw and heard what you heard. I would have been but for the interference of the harridan who is trying to keep my child from me."

"Who should be your first priority, don't you think?"

Gwen turned crimson.

"How dare you!" she said. "Of course he's my first priority, which is why I am trying to make this place work so that I can convince everyone that I should be in charge of his life. And right now, you are standing in the way of that, and I won't have it, Iris. Do you hear me?"

"It wasn't a degree," said Iris.

"What?"

"Cambridge. They don't let women earn degrees, no matter how much work we did. Oxford does, Cambridge doesn't. All I have for my years spent there is a Bachelor of Arts Title, known amongst the boys who never grew up as the B.A. Tit."

"Oh, dear God," said Gwen. "That's appalling. I didn't know that."

"So, as proud as I am of having gone there, and as valuable an experience as it was, I would never throw that in your face. And you're right, we are in this together, and anything I know, I will give to you, starting now. I am sorry. You'll understand my caution when I'm done explaining it, but I'm sorry for not—not trusting you, Gwen. I'm not a trusting person, so this is difficult for me. Will you forgive me?"

"The level of forgiveness will depend on the quality of the sharing," said Gwen evenly, retrieving her chair and sitting down. "Start spilling the beans, sister. Your performance will be graded on clarity, thoroughness, and presentation."

"Right," said Iris. "And when I'm done, you must tell me what essence of lion your doctor prescribed you. I want some."

She described her visit to Archie's warehouse. Gwen glanced at her legs when she described the initiation of the nylons.

"Yes, these are the spoils of war," said Iris, swiveling to reveal them. "I shall charge them to petty expenses, if that's all right with you, partner."

"Of course," said Gwen. "They're very nice. Do they really fetch four pounds? I had no idea."

"They are part of the arsenal with which we fight our battles," said Iris. "I wouldn't pay four pounds, but I understand why some women would."

She continued. When she reached the revelation of Pilcher's identity, Gwen pounded her desk in triumph.

"I said all of that male posturing was an act," she said. "We were never in real danger, were we?"

"I guess not," said Iris. "Takes some of the wind out of our heroic response."

"No, we were heroic," said Gwen. "Heroism based upon faulty knowledge is still heroism, isn't it?"

"We should give ourselves a hearty pat on the back," agreed Iris. "It was good practice for the next onslaught."

"I already had mine last night," said Gwen. "But, pray, continue."

"That was pretty much it. I proposed that I work with him. I could get inside Archie's organization, find out whatever I can. He said that he would speak to his superiors about it, and we parted."

"Parted," said Gwen, looking at her.

"Yes, we parted," said Iris innocently.

"You left out something," said Gwen.

"Nothing I can think of," said Iris.

"Something important," said Gwen.

"Nothing significant springs to mind."

"No," said Gwen. "You're still unforgiven. The whole truth, Miss Sparks."

"I kissed him," confessed Iris.

"Of course that would be the case," sighed Gwen.

"It was only to smear a little lipstick on him for our cover story," protested Iris. "It didn't mean anything."

"You've kissed three men in under a week," said Gwen. "I am including your ex-lover in the count, even though you've not mentioned anything that happened there."

"I could—"

"Nor do I want to hear any details, thank you," said Gwen.

"All right," said Iris. "At least in Mike's case, I was kissed, not kissing. Taken by surprise. His eyes were roguish, in fact."

"Nevertheless," said Gwen. "At the rate you're going, you won't be leaving any men for the rest of us. It hardly seems fair."

"You could have kissed Des by now. You chose not to. Don't complain to me."

"I get kissed every morning and night by a lovely young man whom I adore," said Gwen. "On the cheek, and yes, he is six, but I consider myself luckier than most women to be treated so."

"You are, darling," said Iris.

"All right, so if Agent Pilcher, or whatever his title is, calls, you're plunging back into the maelstrom," said Gwen. "In the meanwhile, there are other lines of inquiry we could pursue."

"For example?"

"We haven't delved enough into her personal life," said Gwen. "We learned about Pilcher, but that turned out to be a sham relationship. I wonder if she knew his identity beforehand?"

"She did have that arrest for passing fake coupons," said Iris. "I would guess that he followed up on that. What do you propose we do?"

"I feel awkward about dropping in on her family when they're still in mourning," said Gwen.

"The police do it all the time."

"We're not police," said Gwen. "It feels wrong. We didn't pump them for information at the viewing."

"We met Elsie and Fanny. They seemed to be more likely to talk. And they talked, God knows."

"We promised to give them a call," said Gwen. "Let's meet them for drinks, see what else they know. Do you have their numbers?"

"I do," said Iris, rummaging through her handbag for the scrap of paper Elsie had given her at the bar. "Here they are. I'll—"

The telephone interrupted her. She picked it up.

"Right Sort Marriage Bureau, Iris Sparks speaking," she said.

"It's Roger Pilcher."

"Oh, Mister Pilcher," she said as Gwen raised an eyebrow at her. "To what do I owe the pleasure?"

"I've got a green light from the powers that be," he said. "And Archie would like you to come in again."

"Would he? For what?"

"To run an errand, he said."

"Any idea what kind?"

"He did not share the details. He said dress like for work, but with some good walking shoes."

"Will this errand be of a legal nature?"

"I doubt it very much," said Pilcher. "Are you game?"

"I said it, and I meant it," said Iris. "When and where?"

"The warehouse at noon."

"I'll be there," she said.

He hung up.

"I have a job for Archie," she said.

"Right," said Gwen. "I'm coming with you."

"It wasn't for us. It was for me."

"Then I shall follow you," said Gwen. "Surreptitiously. I will—what's the term? Shadow? Yes, I shall shadow you."

"The problem is, you cast a rather long shadow yourself," said Iris. "If you show up to shadow me in Shadwell, you'll be visible for miles. I think this is a job interview of some kind. I don't want to muck it up by having an obvious tail. They'll think I'm working for the law."

"Then what do I do?"

"Same deal. If I don't call in by, say, three thirty, have Sally phone the Yard."

"Should they embark on a rescue mission, or shall we simply inform them to start dragging the Thames?"

"Start with the first, please," said Iris. "Here's the numbers for the girls. You go ahead and make the appointment. If it's late afternoon, leave the information with Sally, and I'll get it after I call in and join you if I can."

"Ooh, I get to do something on my own," crowed Gwen. "I'm a real detective now, Mummy!"

"Keep your whistle handy," said Iris.

"Do you honestly believe that I could get in trouble having drinks with Elsie and Fanny?"

"One never knows, do one?"

Pilcher himself opened the door to the warehouse when she knocked.

"'Allo, love," she said, planting a light kiss on his lips. "Sweet of you to meet me at the door."

"Don't get useter it," he said as he locked it behind her.

"'Allo, Tony," she greeted the watchman. "Everything all right, then?"

"Fair enough," said Tony, not looking up from a copy of *The Sporting Life*.

"Come with me," said Pilcher, leading her through the warehouse.

"This is legit?" she whispered.

"You made quite the impression on 'im," he replied. "'E wants to try you out."

"I'll try to do you proud."

"That's me girl," he said.

He rapped on the door to the clubhouse. They were admitted.

Archie was at the snooker table with two of his men, his jacket off and his sleeves rolled up. To her surprise, Elsie was there, perched on a barstool, watching the game while sipping her drink.

"Ah, there's the lovely lass," said Archie, handing his cue to one of his men. "On time, I see."

"There are times to keep a gent waiting, and there are times not to," said Iris.

"Properly said. Did Rog fill you in?"

"Only that you 'ave an errand for me to run."

"Right. Elsie!"

Elsie reached below the bar and pulled out a D. H. Evans shopping bag.

"That's the job," said Archie. "You and Elsie are gonna take that bag to New Cross Street. She's got the address. You'll go to the flat on the second storey and hand it to the bloke who opens the door."

"Does the bloke 'ave a name?" asked Iris.

"'E does not."

"Then 'ow do I know we got the right bloke?"

"Because no other bloke is going to open the bloody door!" shouted Archie. "Do you 'ave any other stupid questions?"

"One," said Iris.

"What is it?"

"I don't know what's in the bag, and I don't want to know," she said. "But I want your word that there ain't nothing that's going to blow up the bloke when 'e opens it."

Archie looked her, then started to laugh.

"Oh, that's bloody wonderful," he said, shaking his head. "Dearie, if I wanted to do someone in, I wouldn't deprive meself of the pleasure of doing it meself. And I wouldn't do it with a bomb. Bombs aren't reliable. Slit throats are. Satisfactory?"

"Very," said Iris. "Do I come back 'ere when we're done?"

"No," said Archie. "Elsie will check in with me in the morning. 'Ave a good trip."

"Ta," said Iris.

She went to the bar and held out her hand for the bag.

"Ready if you are," she said.

"I'm ready," said Elsie. "See you, boys."

Iris blew Rog a kiss. He glared.

"Oh, right," said Iris. "Not in front of the gentlemen."

"This way," said Elsie, indicating the door at the end of the bar.

It took them out to an alley in back, as Iris had guessed. Elsie led her north until they reached the basin, then headed east.

"We're not catching the train at Wapping?" asked Iris.

"Too close to the coppers for comfort," said Elsie. "We'll catch the 82 bus at Branch Road and take it through the tunnel to Surrey Docks. We can take the train from there."

"Roundabout way to go."

"That's the idea," said Elsie. "It will give us time to chat."

"About what?"

"About you cheating with me best girl's boyfriend."

"I was wondering if that was bothering you."

"Oh, I'm not bothered," said Elsie. "I'm surprised. Didn't think old Rog had it in 'im to keep a girl stashed away."

"I didn't mean to 'urt Tillie," said Iris. "It 'appened. Caught both me and Rog unexpected, but there we were, and here we are."

"I'm surprised she never said nothing about it to me," said Elsie.

"I don't know what she said or din't say," said Iris. "I don't want any problems between you and me because of what 'appened in the past. Can't change it, and she's not around for me to say sorry to, so there's nothing I can do about it anymore."

"I'm not saying there's a problem," said Elsie. "I think we can be friends for all that."

"I'd like that."

"So, I 'ave a proposition, if you're interested in making a little extra."

"I'm listening."

"Do you want to know what's in the bag?"

"Sure."

"Money," whispered Elsie. "Lots of it. This is 'ow he moves it around. 'E likes to use us girls because we don't look like spivs. The feller we're going to is a banker of sorts."

"A banker without a bank?"

"You catch on."

"So, what's the proposition?"

"There's a fair amount in there, and if we was to skim a few pounds off, they'd be none the wiser."

"Don't they count it?"

"They 'ave to move it fast, and it don't get counted until it gets to the banker," said Elsie. "I've skimmed a bit here and there before. They don't notice a few pounds out of all that's in there. What do you say?"

"I say no," said Iris firmly. "Archie's trusting me with getting this over there safe and sound, and I'm going to get it there safe and sound."

"You're missing a chance," said Elsie. "You and me, we could be in for a couple of pounds extra a week."

"I said no, and I meant it," said Iris. "Now, let's run. The bus is coming."

She held the bag tightly in her lap the entire journey. There was a box inside, she could tell that much. A shoebox, maybe. But nothing rattled inside it.

When they reached New Cross Street, Elsie leaned over and whispered, "Last chance."

"Still no," said Iris. "Which is the house?"

Elsie sighed and walked her to the address. They walked up to the second storey. Iris knocked on the door.

It swung open, and Archie stood there, grinning like the Cheshire Cat.

"Well done," he said. "Give it over."

"You're the bloke," said Iris, handing it to him.

"I'm the bloke," he replied. "This time, anyhow. Come in, 'ave a cuppa."

They walked into the flat. A porcelain tea service was set up on a card table.

"Questions?" asked Archie.

"So this was a test," said Iris. "I'm guessing there ain't no money in the bag."

Archie took out the box, opened it, and poured a pile of loose banknotes on the table.

"Well?" he said, turning to Elsie.

"She resisted all temptation," said Elsie.

"Good," said Archie, turning back to Iris. "That was the test."

"So I passed," said Iris.

"In part," said Archie.

"What did I miss?"

"You didn't give up Elsie," he said. "She told you she'd been skimming from me, but you didn't tell me about it."

"I was waiting for a moment when she wasn't 'ere," said Iris. "I din't want you to kill her in front of me. Bloodstains are 'ard to get out of clothes."

"Oh, that's real nice, innit?" said Elsie.

"Well, I'll give you the benefit of the doubt on that," said Archie. "But if you work for me, then you're loyal to me. Not to the girls you 'ang out with, not to the lad you love. It's Archie. Got that?"

"Got it, Boss," said Iris.

"Good. Milk or lemon?" he said, pouring.

CHAPTER 13

F anny answered when Gwen called.

"It's Sophie," said Gwen. "How are you?"

"Same as ever," said Fanny. "What's up?"

"Mary and I were wondering if you and the girls would like to get together later today."

"That'd be lovely. Elsie's working right now, but she's always up for a night out. Would you like to get together for tea earlier, you, me, and Mary?"

"Mary's at work, too, but I'm free. Where?"

"There's a nice shop called Nell's by the Spitalfields Market. Is three thirty good?"

"Three thirty, it is. Let me get the address from you."

"It's on Commercial Street, up from the Ten Bells."

"Got it. See you at four."

She hung up, then wrote out the information for Sally to pass along to Iris.

The telephone rang while she was putting the note on the typewriter. She answered.

"Is Iris there?"

"I'm sorry, she's out of the office at the moment," said Gwen. "May I take a message?"

"Yes. Please tell her to call Jessie."

"Jessie? Are you her friend from the Records Department?"

There was a long pause at the other end of the line.

"You know about that?" asked Jessie finally.

"We're partners," said Gwen.

"Well, she wasn't supposed to tell anyone," said Jessie. "Tell her to call me. She has my number. And tell her I'm not happy about you knowing about me."

"Look, I'm sorry if—" Gwen began, but the line went dead.

Sally showed up at one.

"How did things go with the gorgon last night?" he asked.

"I looked her in the eye and stared her down," said Gwen.

"And you've not been turned to a statue," observed Sally. "Well done."

"I should retain you as my acting coach and tactical adviser," said Gwen.

"Whatever you need, Milady," said Sally. "I see my marching orders on the Bar-Let. Are you off? Will there be danger and derring-do?"

"There will be tea," said Gwen, fetching her beret. "I may risk a crumpet, possibly two, but that will be the extent of my escapades."

"An army travels on its stomach," said Sally.

"How very awkward that must be," said Gwen.

"One gets used to it. Off to war with you, Milady. Let the crumpets sound!"

"May your Muse bless you, Sally," she replied, pulling out her bus map. "Oh, I must ask you—where exactly is the Spitalfields Market?"

The Number 8 bus took her as far as Liverpool Street Station. She walked from there. After a few wrong turns, a costermonger sent her in the correct direction. She passed by the market, a covered, red brick building that sprawled across most of a large square block, and came to Commercial Street. The Ten Bells was on the south corner opposite the market. Next to it was an eel and pie shop, with buckets of future meals in front, writhing slowly in silvery tangles while awaiting their fates. Up from that was Nell's Tearoom, with tempting arrays of cakes, tarts, biscuits, and crumpets displayed on cake stands in its windows.

Fanny was already in front, looking anxiously up and down in search of Gwen. When she saw her, she gave a cheerful wave.

"I'm early!" she shouted as Gwen crossed the street. "You're spot on time. Any trouble finding it?"

"Some, but I've been getting better at my navigating," said Gwen. "I'm thinking of trying to get a job as a conductress."

"Oh, that's fine," said Fanny. "Except when it's bad weather. You get proper soaked."

They went inside. The place was packed, mostly by women, many with small children screaming for sweets.

"Nice and quiet," grinned Fanny. "Tea?"

"Fine by me," said Gwen.

"Those cherry tarts look yummy."

"They do, but I've been in a crumpetty mood ever since you suggested tea, so I'm going to have some."

They placed their orders, then Fanny carried the tray over to a table by the kitchen door.

"This all right?" she asked.

"Suits me," said Gwen, taking the seat by the corner.

Fanny poured, then took a bite of a cherry tart.

"Oh, this is good," she sighed in ecstasy. "Try some. I'll trade you for a bite of that crumpet."

Gwen leaned forward for the offered pastry and took a bite.

"That is good," she said. "I haven't tasted cherries in an age."

"They got an in with someone, I bet," said Fanny. "Some cherry farmer out in, I dunno, Kent."

"Kent? Is that where cherries come from?"

"I don't rightly know for certain," said Fanny. "I read it in a book once. Do you know?"

"I've never thought about it," said Gwen. "They magically appeared in markets, and I ate them."

"Yeah, that magic is gone, innit?" said Fanny. "Of all the things I missed during the war, I missed cherries the most. It's still 'ard to find 'em 'alf the time."

She took a sip of tea, looking at Gwen over the edge of her cup as she did.

"There's something you wanted to talk about, isn't there?" asked Gwen.

"What makes you think that?"

"You invited me to a tearoom outside of your neighbourhood," said Gwen. "And you picked a table as far back from the window as you could."

"You don't miss a trick, do you?" said Fanny. "Yeah, there's something I wanted to ask you about."

"All right. What?"

"Des."

"Ah. I thought that might be it."

"You know how people are," said Fanny. "There's talk already."

"About what?"

"About 'im taking a fancy to you."

"There's nothing to talk about. Nothing has happened between us."

"But 'e asked you out, din't 'e?"

"He asked me to call him," Gwen acknowledged.

"And you're going to, ain'tcha?" asked Fanny, almost eagerly.

"I haven't made up my mind."

"What?" exclaimed Fanny. "But 'ow could you not? I'd go quick as a flash if 'e gave me the nod."

"It's complicated," said Gwen.

"Look, if it's me you're worried about, don't," said Fanny. "I've never got the time of day from 'im, and I'm not going to throw meself at 'is feet no more. 'E's all yours."

"He's not mine, and I'm not his," said Gwen. "But I'm glad that it won't be disturbing you."

"Well, other fish, I 'ope," said Fanny. "I'll keep looking. At least I'm not so desperate that I got to try that place Tillie went to."

"Do you think she was desperate?" asked Gwen somewhat guiltily.

"She wanted to get out of the East End," said Fanny.

"Because of Roger?"

"Oh, 'im," laughed Fanny dismissively. "She was 'appy to 'ave dropped 'im, although I din't know 'e was seeing Mary on the sly. Did you?"

"I knew Mary was seeing someone, but she didn't give me any details," said Gwen. "I thought it might have been a married man."

"Oh, she's not particular about sharing, then?"

"I don't ask," said Gwen. "I don't judge. She's my friend."

"Yeah, I know what that's like," said Fanny. "We go to church on Sundays, then chase spivs around the other six. 'Ave fun while you're young, I say."

"I can't say no to that," said Gwen. "I guess Tillie wanted to break away from that lot. Had there been anyone before Roger?"

"Nothing steady," said Fanny. "She liked to be wined and dined. She favoured Archie's lot as they 'ad the means to wine and dine 'er."

"They didn't scare her, then?"

"Not them."

"Not Rog?"

"Especially not Rog," said Fanny. "She useter say, ''Ere's me fin-ger, and that's Rog wrapped around it. Thinks 'e's using me, but I'm using 'im just as much.'"

"Sounds like they were made for each other."

"A match made in 'eaven, they was, until they wasn't. I was gob-smacked when they split, but now I understand everything."

"I wish I did," said Gwen. "That was a month ago?"

"Something like that. Then before you know it, she's dead in an alley. Not ten minutes' walk from 'ere."

"It happened near here?"

"You din't know?"

"I don't know the East End," said Gwen. "I never put a place to the name. She had gone to some café, I forget which."

"The Garland. It's over on Middlesex Street."

"So, not Shadwell, not Wapping. She didn't want to be seen."

"Like me," said Fanny. "Like to take a butchers?"

"What? The café?"

"Yeah. I'm curious. I want to know if 'er last meal was any good."

"That's—that's extremely morbid, isn't it?"

"Then I'm morbid," declared Fanny. "'Ow about you?"

"I—oh, what the hell. Now, you've got me curious. Lead the way."

Middlesex Street was to the southwest of Spitalfields Market, a one-way street with shops lining the sidewalks, with one or two sto-reys of flats and offices above. The Garland Café was topped by a bright, green and white striped awning. The two women peered through the window.

The interior was lovely. The floor was tiled in a green and white diamond pattern. The tables were covered with white cloths edged with embroidery. Waitresses bustled about, serving the late tea. The walls were covered with paintings of flowers, while artificial ones were draped along the tops.

"It's pretty," said Fanny. "At least she 'ad her last meal someplace pretty."

She started to sniffle, and grabbed for a handkerchief from her handbag.

"She was so excited and 'appy, looking forward to this," she said, crying in earnest now. "All she wanted was a decent bloke for a change, someone to take 'er away from it all. She said she was going to be set for life, and look 'ow it turned out."

"Set for life how?" asked Gwen.

Fanny waved her handkerchief around in the air.

"She said she 'ad something coming to 'er that was going to change everything, and that she was going to find a good man and settle down somewhere. She 'ad a plan."

"Something coming? Money?"

"I dunno. She never explained."

Gwen looked inside the café again.

"She wasn't killed in there," she said. "The papers said she dined alone, then stood in front, waiting. Then she left—no one saw who with. They found her in some alley?"

"Over there," said Fanny, pointing.

A narrow, dark, one-lane street peeled off of Middlesex. They ventured down it carefully.

"I read she was found on that side," said Fanny, pointing to an opening past a pub in the middle of the block. "She 'adn't gone in. The bloke must 'ave suggested they go for a pint. It wasn't 'ard to get 'er to agree to a drink. But no one in the pub ever saw 'er."

"Not too busy," said Gwen, looking around. "It wouldn't have been hard to get her alone there."

"She probably thought 'e was going in for a quick bit o' bliss," snuffled Fanny. "I 'ope she 'ad 'er eyes closed before it 'appened. Oh, Lord, I shouldn't 'ave come. It's got me all weepy. I must look a fright."

"Here, let me fix you up," said Gwen. "I'm an expert on tears."

* * *

They walked to Merle's after. Iris and Elsie were already there. Iris waved to them merrily.

"Come celebrate!" Elsie called. "Mary's got a new job!"

"What?" exclaimed Gwen.

"Keep it down, silly," laughed Iris. "Yes, I passed the—interview."

"Interview!" snickered Elsie.

"What kind of a job?" asked Gwen as Fanny headed to the bar.

Iris looked her straight in the eye with her most serious look.

"I can't tell you," she said, then she and Elsie burst into laughter.

"Remind me to box your ears later," said Gwen.

Fanny returned with two pints and handed one to Gwen.

"Next round's on me," said Gwen. "What's the toast?"

"To nylons, and all that they bring us!" shouted Iris.

"To nylons!" chorused the others.

There was more drinking and toasting, but no more useful information to be gleaned. Iris and Gwen begged off from making a night of it, seeking to escape before Archie's crew showed up.

Gwen was slightly wobbly as they left. Iris, who had seemed for all purposes several sheets to the wind, reverted to a state of sobriety.

"How do you do that?" marveled Gwen.

"I wasn't drinking that much," said Iris. "Useful technique, appearing drunk. But I didn't get much out of Elsie. Any luck with Fanny?"

"Tillie didn't seem to have any significant lover prior to Rog, so there goes that theory. She did hint at coming into something in the near future."

"Did she? I wonder what."

"Fanny didn't know. Maybe Elsie would?"

"Maybe. She's better at keeping things secret. She was there in the company of Archie and mates when I came into the clubhouse."

"Surprise, surprise."

"You sussed her out?"

"She's the smart one in that group, especially with Tillie out of the picture. I have the sense that she's deeper in with Archie than she lets on. She's never seemed exactly broken up over Tillie's demise."

"I wonder how much work Tillie did for Archie. I'll have to see what I can find out when I'm in more."

"You haven't told me what your new job is. And what Elsie's part in it was."

"Oh, the first test was transporting money. Elsie came along to throw some temptation my way. She was much too obvious a plant."

"How much money?"

"I didn't count, but several hundred pounds."

"Good Lord! It's too bad you're such an honest spiv in training. We could have gone on holiday."

"He gave me another pair of nylons in payment," said Iris. "I think he fancies me. It's too bad me and Rog are so much in love."

"Oh, the tangled webs you weave," said Gwen. "All right, let's rule out past lovers for the moment. That puts us back into nefarious activities. Could Tillie be tied into this theft of—what were they again?"

"Plates for counterfeiting clothes coupons."

"Yes. I can't say that I am very knowledgeable about counterfeiting. Does that subject fall within the vast grey area of skills you cannot discuss?"

"No," said Iris thoughtfully. "But I know a likely lad. We could visit him tomorrow morning. Meet me at the office and we'll go from there."

"Will do. Oh, your friend Miss Kemp telephoned. She needs to speak with you. I'm afraid that I let her know that I knew who she was. She sounded put off by that."

"Oh, dear. I'll have to patch that up. I was going to enlist your help in finding someone for her."

"She's our client?"

"It's been an informal barter of services rather than a full contract."

"Understood. She's been very useful. Ah, here's our train at last."

Iris saw no suspicious cars tailing her, either from the government or the underworld. She treated herself to a chop at a restaurant on the next street, taking a table where she could keep her back against the wall and an eye on the entrance. She brushed off a would-be suitor with ease, and wondered where Andrew was at that moment.

It was different to enter her flat knowing that there was no possibility of him waiting for her. The silence of absence, of desertion, filled the small rooms until she felt she was drowning in it.

She was going to have to put some serious thought into what she was doing with her life. She was upset over Gwen calling her out. Upset because everything she said was true. She wasn't used to having a female friend who wasn't in some manner or another competition. She wanted to tell her everything.

But telling her everything might drive her away.

She sighed, then remembered the call from Jessie. She picked up her telephone and dialed her number.

"It's Iris," she said. "Are you free to chat?"

"Another Friday night at home, no thanks to you," said Jessie.

"I'm working on it," said Iris. "In fact, I'm bringing in the big guns."

"What are they?"

"My partner, Gwen. She has a gift."

"Yes, I wanted to talk to you about her. She wasn't supposed to know my name."

"Sorry. We've stumbled into a situation despite ourselves, and now it's all hands on deck."

"That's the other thing. Do you know how much trouble you could have got me in, pulling the file on a dead girl?"

"That's hardly fair, Jessie. She wasn't dead at the time."

"And that makes it better? It's a good thing I didn't actually sign them out. I would have been up to my neck."

"Apologies, apologies," said Iris. "We'll try not to refer any more future murder victims."

"I suppose that sort of thing is hard to predict. Although, it's not like your girl was completely on the straight and narrow."

"Was there anything besides that one arrest?"

"Some reference to her being in with the Wapping Wall gang. Archie Spelling's boys. You've heard of them?"

"I've met them. We're all chums, now."

"You have been busy. Be careful with that lot, all right?"

"I will," promised Iris. "Oh, one more thing to satisfy my curiosity. Do you remember who arrested Miss La Salle in that case?"

"Oh, Lord, I'd have to look it up. The name was an odd one—reminded me of a fish."

"Pilcher?"

"Pilcher! Like pilchard! Yes, that was it."

"I thought it might be. All right, keep mum about our special relationship. Good things will come of it."

"Will do. How's your bloke?"

"Don't have a bloke at the moment."

"You should put your friend on the case."

"Too much responsibility," laughed Iris. "I'm hard to please. Good night, dear."

"You are about to meet someone from my mysterious recent past," said Iris as she and Gwen walked east from Mayfair the following morning.

"What's off-limits when we talk?"

"Nothing about his area of expertise is off-limits," said Iris.

"Anything about how he and I came to know each other or what we did together is."

"Not an ex-lover," said Gwen, glancing at her.

"Not this time," said Iris. "Not all of them are, no matter what you think of me."

They passed through the theatre district, taking a right from Earlham Street.

"There we are," said Iris.

J. B. SMALLEY & SONS, FINE PRINTS AND LITHOGRAPHS read the sign. The shop was painted in a surprisingly cheerful brown. The windows displayed prints of a variety of subjects and age. The two women stopped for a moment to look in the windows.

"These are beyond my budget," said Iris. "And we haven't even got to the Dorés inside. Shall we?"

Gwen was fixated on an engraving of the Roman Forum.

"Don't start," said Iris. "Work to do."

"Right," said Gwen. "Let's go in."

The interior was a gallery, a veritable maze of partitions to maximize the number of prints that could be displayed. A tall man in a cutaway suit that would not have been out of place in Ascot Downs during the previous century was discoursing in plummy tones to a pair of matrons whose handbags no doubt were sagging under the weight of the money they intended to spend there.

"That's J. B. Smalley," whispered Iris. "He's occupied at the moment. We may as well browse while we're waiting. Don't get caught by anything that will trigger the weepies if you can help it."

"That section of animal prints should keep me dry-eyed," said Gwen. "Come fetch me when he's ready."

She sauntered over to a section devoted to naturalists' depictions of creatures as they saw them or hoped they would be, going back to Linneaus. One in particular caught her eye and brought a happy smile to her face. She went over to look at it more closely.

It was a narwhal, shown improbably on top of a black rock, posing with its tail up while the ocean waves crashed dramatically about it. It had irregularly shaped spots over its plump body, and the signature tusk had a scrolled pattern along its length.

"From the Brehms *Tierleben*, First Edition," came the plummy voice from behind her. "Are you familiar with it?"

"I am not," said Gwen turning to face him. "But I know a narwhal when I see one."

"How so, if I may ask?"

"I have a budding narwhal enthusiast at home," she said. "He became quite taken with the one he saw at the British Museum. Now, he writes adventures about it. What is the Brehms *Tierleben*?"

"A zoological encyclopedia, initially published in six volumes in Germany in the 1860s," said Mister Smalley. "The illustrations were under Robert Kretschmer's supervision, but I don't think that he himself executed the narwhal. My personal opinion, only. There is no way of verifying it. This was created from the original plates, however. It's a peculiar creature, but somehow endearing."

"It is lovely in its own way, isn't it?" agreed Gwen. She glanced at the price, then sighed. "A little much for an illustration for a boy's playroom, I'm afraid."

"I do have a reproduction that I could offer for substantially less," said Smalley. "I happen to be a fellow narwhal enthusiast. I would be delighted to encourage your son in his pursuits. Would you care to come in back?"

"Yes, thank you," said Gwen. "May my friend join us?"

"Miss Sparks is always welcome anywhere in my establishment," he said. "James Smalley, at your service."

"Gwendolyn Bainbridge," she returned.

"Gracious, Jimmy," said Iris, who had watched the entire exchange. "You've got the act down perfectly. I'm impressed."

Smalley turned to her, put his finger to his lips, and smiled slightly.

"This way, ladies," he said, leading them to a door at the rear.

They found themselves in a large storage area, with shelves holding cardboard tubes labeled with their contents. There was a desk and a few chairs at one side.

"Great to see you, Sparks," said Smalley, grinning at her.

The tones were less plummy, noticed Gwen.

"Great to see you as well," said Iris. "Gwen, meet Jimmy the Scribe, one of the best forgers in London."

"Until I was forcibly retired," he added quickly. "I became a cloistered guest of the Crown for a few years until my services came back in demand."

"Jimmy forged documents for a lot of brave men and women who infiltrated Europe during the war," said Iris. "He's the best."

"I was one of many," he said modestly. "I was happy to put my skills to use for my country."

"Plus it got you sprung," said Iris.

"Full pardon, permission to take on a new life, so long as I keep on the up and up."

"This all looks quite—legitimate," said Gwen.

"A life is much easier to forge than German transit papers," he said. "I became a forger because I was a better copyist than I was an artist, but that never stopped me from wanting to live amongst these marvels. And lo and behold, I'm making better money running this shop!"

"Think how your life would have been different if you had realized that at the beginning," said Iris.

"I do," said Smalley. "But it keeps leading to the point that if I hadn't done what I did as well as I did, then I couldn't have helped the war effort as much. I would have made a terrible soldier. Now, to the topic, Sparks. You called saying that you wanted to pick my brain. What scheme are you planning?"

"Not my scheme, someone else's," said Iris. "We think there's a large forgery operation afoot."

"Making what?"

"Clothing coupons."

"Oh, that's a good target," said Smalley, leaning back in his chair and linking his hands behind his head. "Homemade plates?"

"The real thing. Purloined, then purloined again."

"Give me the rundown."

Iris summarized the details while Jimmy listened, rocking back and forth.

"I love it," he said when she finished. "No artistry in making coupons, but I appreciate the sheer scale of the enterprise. So, what do you need to know from me?"

"What do they need, where do they get it, how would we go about finding the same things and tracing it to them?"

"Is that all?" laughed Smalley. "Well, you need a printer, preferably somewhere out of the way so people won't notice it. You need ink of the right type, and you need paper, matching colour and stock. Plus people to run it, distribution, and so forth."

"There's a paper shortage," said Gwen. "There's rationing. How would they get enough?"

"Oh, there's black markets for everything," said Smalley. "The trick is getting the right kind of paper—a lot of the fake coupons I've seen are too thick, or the paper's too smooth."

"You've seen them?"

"I've been called in to consult for the government occasionally," said Smalley. "Part of the conditions of my freedom."

"Let's say that I wanted to acquire a large amount of paper without going through proper channels," said Gwen. "Where would I find it?"

"Well, I would go to people who are in the business of producing things on paper that are not so legal."

"For example?"

"Racetrack touts—tote tickets use a lot, and that's something where you cut things down to small sizes, so they'd be a good fit for making coupons."

"That's a thought," said Iris.

"And—I assume that neither of you is so delicate as to faint at this next suggestion?"

"We'll do our level best," promised Iris.

"Pornography," said Smalley. "Always around, always available. Someone keeps printing it because people keep buying it. Hell, I've got a few things here for special collectors that I would blush to show you, except the detail of the wood-cuts is exquisite."

"We'll pass, thank you," said Iris. "So, racetrack touts and pornographers should be our next direction. Sounds marvelous. Thanks, Jimmy. Grand as always."

"Likewise," said Smalley, standing. "One more moment."

He rummaged through a shelf, then brought a print over to the desk and unrolled it.

"It's the narwhal!" exclaimed Gwen. "I thought you were just making an excuse for us to come in back."

"Not an original, but a good reproduction," said Smalley. "I could let you have it at a very reasonable price."

"It's very good," said Gwen. "Yes, thank you. I'll take it."

Iris looked at it carefully.

"This is one of yours, isn't it, Jimmy?"

"It is."

"But you're no longer in the forgery business."

"A reproduction, acknowledged as such, is not a forgery," said Smalley. "I am still an artist. And I do love narwhals."

"Who doesn't? Gwen, I'll wait for you at the front."

Gwen joined her a short time later, the narwhal rolled and safely stored in a cardboard tube.

"That was useful," said Iris as they strolled back to the office.

"Now, all we have to do is dive into the worlds of racing and pornography without losing our footing or our clothing. There can't be too many places where—"

"Iris," said Gwen thoughtfully. "I think I know where it is."

CHAPTER 14

"I can't believe you wore that," said Iris.

"I'm sorry, it's my first burglary," said Gwen. "I wasn't sure what to wear."

"You look like a genteel lady housepainter."

"I didn't want to put on anything nice," said Gwen. "I imagined that there would be some crawling through attics or climbing through windows. Next time, tell me what to do."

It was seven o'clock the following morning, and the two had rendezvoused at the corner of Commercial Road and Sutton Street. The early Sunday traffic was negligible. The Roman Catholic Church on the next block had yet to open its doors.

Gwen was wearing a grey man's overall, cinched tight at the waist with piece of cord. Her top was an old muslin blouse that had spatters of paint on it. She had a straw hat over her mane, which was nonetheless impeccably coiffed.

Iris, on the other hand, wore her normal office suit, augmented by a larger handbag than usual.

"You wore that same outfit when we painted the office," she remembered. "I can still see the green streaks."

"What should I have put on?"

"Everyday clothes so you look like an everyday person, and shoes that you can run in," said Iris.

"Oh," said Gwen, her face falling. "Do you expect us to take to our heels at some point?"

"Always a possibility. Now, where is that man?"

She scanned the street in both directions.

"Maybe he disapproved," said Gwen. "Maybe he was scared off."

"Maybe I will give him a good, swift kick in his—oh, there he is."

They waited as Roger Pilcher strolled up, wearing his normal pinstripes.

"Good morning, ladies," he said, touching the brim of his trilby with one finger.

"You are late," said Iris.

"Not by much."

"If you ever again make me wait in the middle of Stepney, I shall break up with you," said Iris.

"Oh, is this Stepney?" asked Gwen, looking around with more interest.

"What's she doing here?" asked Pilcher. "Got a date posing for Van Gogh?"

"He knows about Van Gogh," said Gwen. "Completely out of character."

"So are both of you," said Pilcher. "Time to tell me what this is all about."

"Gwen had this marvelous idea," said Iris.

"More of a theory," cautioned Gwen.

"But a very good theory."

"Speculative, I admit. It needs some evidence to really make it fly."

"Which is why we're here."

"On Commercial Road," said Pilcher. "In Stepney. You still haven't told me anything."

"Well, we don't actually have anything," admitted Iris. "But we think we know where your missing plates have got to."

"You have?" he exclaimed. "Where? How?"

"Walk, and we'll explain," promised Iris.

She turned down Sutton and set a brisk pace. Pilcher had to scramble to catch up to her. Gwen matched them easily.

"So, we were thinking, what if Miss La Salle had been part of whatever group had nicked the plates from Archie?" Iris began.

"Impossible," said Pilcher. "She was my informant. She couldn't have done anything like that without me knowing."

"You see, you're not giving her enough credit," said Iris. "Tillie may not have had much formal education, but she was smart. She knew how to survive in a violent world and make her own fortune. She was able to keep Archie from finding out she was an informant and still work him for favours."

"What does that have to do with the plates?"

"They were stolen around the same time that she supposedly broke up with you," said Gwen. "She told Fanny that she was coming into something that would set her up for life. She also said that—"

She hesitated as Pilcher looked at her.

"Said what?" he asked.

"She made some rather disparaging remarks about you," said Gwen.

"Specifically?"

"That she had you wrapped around her finger," said Gwen hurriedly. "I'm sorry."

"Did she now?" said Pilcher, shaking his head. "Woman had a nerve or two. Wait. You've brought me to Martha Street?"

"Ta da!" said Iris, smiling. "Where the late Tillie La Salle worked in Tolbert's dress shop."

"Right, I knew that," said Pilcher. "Where are you going with this?"

"This is the big theory," said Iris.

"Which, as I said, needs factual evidence," added Gwen. "But I feel very confident about it."

"Will you please tell me what the bloody theory is already?"

"You tell it," said Gwen.

"No, it's yours," said Iris.

"All right. We were looking into forgery operations and how they work, and we found out that they need all the things one might expect: a printer, machines for cutting the paper to the right size, machines for binding the coupons into books, ink, and most importantly, paper."

"You're telling me what I already know," said Pilcher.

"Paper, I thought, was the key," continued Gwen. "Because there's a shortage and rationing like with most things. I was talking to this dear friend of ours, a playwright, and I think that he's really going to make a name for himself if he keeps at it—"

"Off topic," interrupted Iris.

"Yes, sorry. Focus, Gwen, focus. So, one source of black-market paper could be from pornographers."

"You know about pornography?" laughed Pilcher. "I thought you were a lady."

"Any girl growing up in the aristocracy knows where Daddy keeps the dirty pictures," said Gwen. "We would dig them out and pore over them while our parents were dining out in fancy dress."

"Never knew that. But who in all of this rigmarole sells pornography?"

"Mister Tolbert," said Gwen excitedly. "I found some risqué photos of Miss La Salle in his desk."

"When was this?"

"Wednesday last. And look what's right next to his shop!"

Pilcher looked, the two women standing on either side of him watching him expectantly.

"That's a print shop," he said slowly. "A boarded-up print shop."

"Exactly," said Gwen. "A boarded-up print shop next to a lady's dress shop that's in a terrible location for a lady's dress shop, especially since the train station closed down years ago. And there's a storage facility on the other side, which could be used for photography and paper storage and who knows what else?"

"And this is the part where you turn your back," said Iris.

"I do what?"

"You're with the government," said Iris. "We're not. We can do things you can't. Now, look the other way, lover, because we're about to commit a burglary."

"You're about to do what? Have you lost your minds? You can't just break into—"

"Please, no more noise," Gwen admonished him. "We're trying to be stealthy."

Pilcher stood on the corner, open-mouthed, as the two women ambled down the street. They stopped to look at the display windows at Tolbert's.

"Closed," commented Gwen.

"Which is why we commit burglaries on Sundays," said Iris.

She reached into her bag and pulled out a small, black leather case. She walked over to the door to the print shop, held up the padlock, and examined it critically.

"A Prentice," she said. "Give me a minute."

She unzipped the case and pulled out a pair of small, thin metal blades.

"What the hell are you doing?" asked Pilcher from behind them.

"You were supposed to stay over there," said Gwen sternly.

"But she's trying to pick the lock! How does she even know how to do that?"

"She can't tell you," said Gwen. "Gosh, that's satisfying to say."

There was a metallic clack from behind her. She turned to see Iris removing the padlock and opening the door.

"Nicely done," said Gwen.

"Prentices are easy," said Iris. "Shall we?"

They slipped inside. Pilcher stood there for a moment. Then Iris poked her head out.

"Are you coming or not?" she asked. "If not, please do us the favour of going to the corner and keeping a lookout. You aren't helping by standing around acting suspicious."

"God help me," sighed Pilcher as he followed her inside.

The shop stretched back from the street, unbroken by any walls dividing it as they had in Tolbert's establishment. It was dark—Iris and Gwen immediately produced torches from their bags and turned them on. Iris swung her beam about until it fell on a large electrical knife switch set in a column.

"Let's see what this does," she said as she pulled it down.

Enormous, round ceiling lights, protected inside metal cages, illuminated the room.

"Better," said Gwen, putting away her torch.

Large, free-standing machines loomed throughout, shining, menacing assemblies of wheels and cranks, belts and gears. Linotype machines stood against one wall; cutters and binders against another.

Iris ran her fingers lightly over the belts.

"No dust," she observed. "Everything is well-kept and recently oiled. And someone's paying the electric bill. This doesn't seem like a defunct shop to me."

"Iris, over here," said Gwen. "Paper! Lots of it."

In the back were stacked bundles of paper, square-cut.

"Rog, what colours are the coupons to be this year?" asked Iris.

"Olive and green," he said grimly.

"And there they are," said Iris, squatting by one stack and thumbing through them. "Unless they're planning on making illustrations of frogs and turtles."

"Which still proves nothing without the plates," Gwen reminded her. "We have to find them. It's an awfully big place."

"There can't be too many spots where they can hide them away," said Iris. "I would bet that they're somewhere close to the printers."

"You take that side, I'll take this," said Gwen.

"I'll just continue standing here uselessly, shall I?" said Pilcher.

Gwen went over to a work table and started pulling open drawers and rummaging through them. Iris turned her attention to a pair of sheet-metal cabinets next to an old desk with pigeonholes arranged in a hutch over it. The cabinets were locked. She looked at them contemptuously and pulled out the leather case containing her lockpicks.

"Barely worth the challenge," she muttered. "Let's—

The front door flew open with a bang. They turned to see Mister Tolbert standing in it, outlined by the morning light, cradling a double-barreled shotgun in his arms.

"What in blazes are you doing here?" he asked, stepping inside.

"I'm so sorry," said Iris, immediately raising her hands. "We didn't mean to disturb you."

"We thought you'd be going to church," added Gwen.

"Our mistake."

"Yes, we should have realized that crime and churchgoing don't generally go hand in hand. Rather obvious, when you consider it."

Tolbert looked back and forth at the two.

"The posh bird and her squeaky little maid," he said. "I should 'ave known you weren't the real goods when I first saw you."

"For a counterfeiter, you were easily deceived," said Iris. "Rog, shouldn't you be arresting him right about now?"

Pilcher looked at the man with the shotgun, then grinned suddenly.

"I don't see why," he said. "He isn't pointing it at me, is he?"

"Excuse me?" said Iris.

"After all, doesn't a businessman have the right to protect his premises?" Pilcher continued.

"Iris, why is he talking like this?" asked Gwen. "Is this some subtle stratagem to distract the gentleman pointing the Purdey at us?"

"Roger, what are you doing?" asked Iris.

"Doing?" Pilcher repeated. "What I'm doing, lover, is telling you to take your bag off of your shoulder and throw it over to me. Gently."

"I see," said Iris. "Under the circumstances, I don't seem to have any choice."

She slid her bag down her arm until the strap dangled free, then tossed it to him. He caught it, then opened it and removed her knife.

"I don't want you to start waving this around again," he said, putting it in his pocket.

"Sorry, I'm late!" cried Elsie as she burst through the door. "Did I miss all the excitement?"

"And the gang's all here," said Iris.

"It took you long enough," Tolbert said to Elsie as she closed the door behind her.

"Well, I live the furthest away, dun I?" she protested. "I came as soon as you called."

"You could live across the bloody street, and you still waste an hour figuring out your outfit," said Rog.

"You do look lovely," said Iris. "Doesn't she look lovely, Gwen?"

Gwen nodded dumbly, her eyes still on the shotgun.

"Now, I am going to walk over there by my friends," said Pilcher.

"Mrs. Bainbridge, I am momentarily going to be crossing the line of fire between Mister Tolbert and you. He is going to point that gun at your friend, Miss Sparks, so don't think of trying to make any foolish moves while I do, or he'll blast her across the room. Savvy?"

She nodded again, watching as the barrels swiveled towards Iris.

Pilcher crossed over to where Tolbert and Elsie were standing.

"Just for giggles," said Iris. "Who was closer to finding the plates? Me or her?"

"You," said Pilcher. "Now, Mrs. Bainbridge, would you be so kind as to toss your bag and that fearsome whistle of yours to me?"

"A whistle?" snickered Elsie as Gwen tossed Roger her handbag. "What's that all about?"

"I'll tell you later," said Roger, handing the bag to her. "We have to figure out what we're going to do with these two."

"You could surrender," suggested Iris. "We can offer you reasonable terms."

"Why don't you shut up?" said Tolbert. "Rog, what are we going to do?"

"I'm thinking," said Pilcher.

"If you're trying to find a way to keep us quiet, I have an idea," said Iris.

"If you're not keeping quiet when a man with a shotgun tells you to, I don't 'ave much hope of you doing it at all," said Tolbert.

"Good point," said Iris. "There's a more obvious way, however, and much nicer than the alternative of killing two innocent women, which is what Rog is considering. You don't strike me as a man who would do that, Mister Tolbert."

"In my experience, there are no innocent women," said Tolbert.

"I am open to suggestions," said Pilcher. "What's your proposal?"

"Buy our silence," said Iris. "We only got into all of this because we were trying to save our bureau from ruin after the scandal. You're about to make pots of money with this clever operation, and my guess is that you're all going to get out of the country once you cash in to avoid the wrath of Archie and his boys. Throw us a reasonable sum so we don't go belly up, and we'll keep mum long enough for you to pull it off and vanish. You can pay us from Tillie's share."

"How did you know she was involved?" asked Pilcher.

"We figured out a lot of things," said Iris. "The only thing we don't know is which one of you killed her."

"Killed Tillie?" exclaimed Elsie. "Why would we do that?"

"Didn't you?" asked Iris. "She was trying to pull out of it early. That's why she came to us. She was looking for a safe way out of Shadwell, wasn't she?"

"We didn't kill her," said Pilcher. "She was a full partner in all of this. She did most of the planning. We needed her to pull it off. Our first thought when we heard about her getting killed was that Archie got to her."

"We was proper terrified," said Elsie. "We 'ad to keep playing along, wondering all the while if our turn was next."

"Then your boy Trower got picked up for it," said Pilcher.

"Well, I am relieved to learn that you're not murderers," said Iris. "It gives me some hope that you're not going to start with us."

"The problem with your idea is one of trust," said Pilcher. "We let you go, even if we buy you off, there's still nothing to stop you from going straight to the Yard. We have no leverage."

"Our word isn't good enough for you?"

"Sweetheart, I wouldn't trust you with the secret of my middle name, much less all this," said Pilcher. "So, we're back to where we started. What are we going to do with you?"

"Look, I realize that we're not in the best position to bargain," said Iris. "But worse comes to worst, all you've got is conspiracy and forgery. Not the end of the world, I should think. But if you add murder, it's a hanging offense."

"I don't plan on doing any time at all," said Pilcher. "And I don't really mind what I have to do to avoid it."

"Keep me as a hostage," Iris urged. "Let Gwen go and keep me under wraps until it's over. She'll have to stay quiet, and you can tip her off where I am after you've taken off to South America or wherever successful thieves go to retire."

"Tahiti," said Elsie. "I always wanted to go to Tahiti. Oh! I found the whistle! You were serious about that."

"Sorry, love," said Pilcher. "It's two weeks before we can make our mint. We don't have the time to hold and feed a captive. Too much bother, too much risk you'll escape."

"She has a child, damn you!" cried Iris. "A beautiful, six-year-old boy. She is his only parent. You cannot be so cruel."

"Oh, no," said Elsie. "Look at her, Rog."

Tears were streaming down Gwen's cheeks. She started to sob openly, clapping her hands to her mouth to muffle them. Suddenly, her eyes rolled up in her head and she sagged to the floor in a heap.

"Gwen!" cried Iris, starting towards her.

"Stay where you are!" ordered Tolbert.

"But she needs help!" shouted Iris, waving her arms frantically.

"I swear to God, I will shoot you if you don't shut up!" he said, raising the shotgun towards her.

"The whistle!" Elsie screamed.

A small, silver object protruded from Gwen's mouth. A second later, a shrill, piercing blast reverberated through the shop. Everyone froze as the echoes died down.

Rog looked around, then back at Gwen, who was still on the floor, panting from the effort.

"No one ever said a woman has to own only one whistle," she said, holding it up triumphantly.

"Nice try, sweetheart," said Rog. "But there are no bobbies wandering around this area. Not on a Sunday morning."

"None normally," agreed Gwen as she sat up. "But this isn't a normal Sunday."

The three conspirators started as someone rapped politely on the door behind them.

"Hello in there!" called a man. "This is Detective Superintendent Parham of the CID. We have you surrounded. Also, outnumbered and out-armed. It would be to everyone's benefit if we can bring this to a peaceful resolution. Agreed?"

"Rog, what are we gonna do?" asked Elsie.

Rog looked around the room.

"We have hostages," he said. "We can walk out of here, demand a car—"

"They know who we are," said Tolbert. "We can't stay on the run forever. And I am not willing to get myself shot over this."

"Me, neither," added Elsie. "Especially now that I know about 'er little boy. It's over, Rog. Let's take our lumps without anyone getting 'urt."

Pilcher looked at the two women. Gwen got to her feet. Iris lowered her arms and looked at him expectantly. He reached into his jacket and pulled out her knife. She tensed, never taking her eyes off it.

"I believe this belongs to you," he said, tossing it to her.

"Thanks," she said as she caught it. "It has sentimental value."

"Probably the only thing in your life that would," he said.

He turned to face the door.

"We're coming out!" he shouted. "Don't shoot! We'll toss the gun first."

"Very good," said Parham. "Hold your fire, men. My command only."

Tolbert broke open the shotgun and unloaded the shells. Then he opened the door gingerly and threw it into the street.

"Do you have it?" he called.

"We have it," said Parham. "You are free to come out. Hands in the air, if you please."

"If we please," scoffed Tolbert.

He raised his hands and stepped outside.

"You next," said Pilcher to Elsie.

"Hug your boy for me," said Elsie to Gwen.

"I will," said Gwen. "Good luck."

She went through the door.

Pilcher turned to look at Iris.

"How did you tumble me?" he asked.

"You were the man who arrested Tillie, back when you were just an ordinary Trade Inspector," said Iris. "That's how you got her working for you."

"So?"

"So, Elsie was arrested along with her," said Gwen. "Elsie knew you were working undercover the whole time, and she's someone who would have given you up in a heartbeat if she was as loyal to Archie as she seemed."

"Unless she saw you as a means to a bigger score than what she was making from Archie," continued Iris. "Once we looked at all of you through that lens, the bigger picture emerged. Either Elsie or Tillie must have played Archie for the information about the plates. The three of you pulled off the theft, and Tolbert had the setup here and the connection to Tillie."

"Good guesswork," he said. "I still owe you a proper kiss."

"I'll put it on your account," she said. "Don't try to collect."

"Maybe when I get out," he said.

"Not likely," she said. "There's still a dead girl in all of this."

"Nothing to do with me," he said. "Good luck with that."

He gave them one last salute. Then he raised his arms and stepped into the street. They heard a brief flurry of voices and the click of handcuffs.

"Miss Sparks, Mrs. Bainbridge," called Parham a moment later. "Are you safe?"

"We are, Detective Superintendent," replied Sparks. "Come join us."

He stepped inside, followed by Kinsey. They looked around.

"It's a print shop, I'll give you that," said Parham. "But unless you have those plates, there won't be much of a case."

"Bear with me for a moment, Detective Superintendent," said Sparks, retrieving her lockpicks from the floor. She got to work on the left filing cabinet.

"Did you know she possessed this skill?" Parham asked Kinsey.

"No, sir," said Kinsey. "But nothing she does surprises me. Or maybe everything."

"I'm inclined to take those away from her after this is over," said Parham. "They aren't legal."

"Try it, and I won't be held accountable for my actions," said Sparks.

She pulled down on the handle, and the door to the cabinet swung open. She reached in and pulled out a stack of metal plates.

"Damn, they're heavy," she said. "Would you be so kind, gentlemen?"

Parham came over to take them from her. He looked at the top one carefully.

"Board of Trade insignia," he said. "That's them, all right. Well done, ladies, you've found yourselves a counterfeiting ring. We shall need you to return with us to the Yard to give your statements. You may ride with Detective Sergeant Kinsey."

"About Mister Trower—" Mrs. Bainbridge began.

"We shall discuss everything back at the Yard," said Parham.

"How do we know you won't just run off with them and make your fortune?" asked Sparks.

"The idea!" laughed Parham. "Give me some credit, Miss Sparks. I trusted you enough to bring my men here, didn't I?"

"You did," said Sparks. "But remember—we know who you are."

"She's teasing you, sir," said Kinsey. "It's her little way."

"Not a way to which I would ever wish to become accustomed," said Parham. "I will see you back at the station."

He left.

"Dear God, I'm shaking all of a sudden," said Mrs. Bainbridge.

"Delayed reaction," said Kinsey. "It isn't pleasant having a gun pointed at one."

"I don't know what you're getting on about," said Sparks. "It was mostly pointed at me."

"But that was the plan," said Mrs. Bainbridge. "You distracted him and gave me a chance to pop the second whistle into my mouth."

"How did you know the gun was a Purdey?"

"I've bagged my share of skeet," said Gwen. "I know a Purdey over and under when I see one. I can't say that I enjoyed facing the business end."

"This was a huge gamble," said Kinsey. "You couldn't be certain that the plates would be here. You might have got yourselves killed, or arrested for burglary, for nothing."

"Oh, we were absolutely certain that the plates were here," said Sparks.

"How?"

"Because I broke in here last night and found them," said Sparks. "Shall we go to the Yard now, Mike? It looks like it might be a long day."

She walked out, stopping to pick her bag off the floor and put her knife back inside.

"You can't bring that inside the office," Kinsey called after her.

"Give up, Detective Sergeant," advised Mrs. Bainbridge as she walked past him. "We've won the day. Don't spoil it."

They rode in the back of Kinsey's Wolseley. Kinsey sat up front with the driver.

"I feel like a suspect," said Mrs. Bainbridge. "It's rather thrilling, isn't it? I don't suppose we could ask you to turn the siren on?"

"Sorry," said Kinsey. "People still get in a panic when they hear sirens. Hell, they start diving for shelter when the buses change gears going uphill. We reserve it for actual emergencies."

The car turned into the entrance and came to a halt. The driver held the door for them and saluted.

"At ease," murmured Sparks as she got out. "You probably outrank me."

Kinsey led them to a bench outside of Parham's office.

"Wait here," he instructed them. "I don't know how long before we take your statements. Would you like a bit of grub while you wait? It's early for the tea cart, but we can send someone out for some pastries."

"Sounds divine, thank you," said Sparks. "I'm ravenous."

"Just a cup of tea for me, thank you," said Mrs. Bainbridge.

"Right. I shall return."

He went off in search of sustenance.

"How can you eat after everything we've been through?" asked Gwen.

"We survived," said Iris. "We must soldier on. Therefore, pastries. So, are we agreed upon our stories?"

"We are," said Gwen. "Let's hope it works."

They were each called in individually to make their statements, then returned to their bench. At several points, worried, greymustached men either in police uniforms decked in medals or in expensive Savile Row suits walked in and out.

"Board of Trade upper echelon," guessed Iris. "This must have stirred up quite the brouhaha. Some heads are going to roll."

The tea cart stopped by their bench around noon.

"Compliments of the Yard," said the lady as she handed them sandwiches on plates.

Gwen dug into hers with a will.

"Your appetite has returned," observed Iris.

"My emotions have been swinging back and forth like a sped-up grandfather clock," Gwen replied. "I feel exhilarated. And hungry. This must be like what it is to be you."

"We can't have that. One of me is quite enough."

"Some would say too many," said Kinsey as he emerged. "Detective Superintendent Parham will see you now. Follow me."

He led them into Parham's office, which was decorated with photographs of him standing with various notorious handcuffed felons and commendations from all levels, including one from the King.

Parham stood as they entered.

"Please sit, ladies," he said, indicating the chairs in front of his desk.

They did so. Kinsey stood in the corner, his arms folded.

"First, the Yard wishes to commend you on your services in this matter, unorthodox and—frankly, illegal, as they were," Parham began. "We will be mentioning your assistance in our official reports as well as the press release."

"Assistance?" Mrs. Bainbridge said indignantly. "We did everything!"

"How will you be portraying our assistance?" asked Sparks.

"As briefly as possible," said Parham. "This whole matter—an investigator for the Board of Trade betraying his sworn duties, a scheme that if successful would have undermined the public's trust in the government's administration of rationing—well, it would be greatly embarrassing to all concerned."

"You're hushing it up," said Sparks.

"Not entirely," said Parham. "It will be announced, but without a great deal of detail. The three conspirators will be prosecuted to the full extent of the law."

"What about Dickie Trower?" asked Mrs. Bainbridge.

"What about him?"

"Certainly we have established the existence of others who had motive for killing Tillie La Salle. Shouldn't that be enough?"

"Detective Sergeant Kinsey, tell them the results of your investigations."

"Sir," said Kinsey, stepping forward. "On the night of Miss La Salle's murder, Roger Pilcher was indeed with his superiors at the Board of Trade, being debriefed. The meeting took place in Westminster for several hours. Mister Tolbert was playing cards with a regular group of cronies, all of whom can vouch for his whereabouts at the time. Miss Spencer was with her family."

"Surely they could lie for her," said Sparks.

"They could," agreed Kinsey. "But we are unable to establish that."

"As far as Trower goes, we still have the murder weapon in his room," added Parham. "We have no new evidence that contradicts that which already exists. Your efforts have been valiant, ladies. I almost wish that they had borne fruit. However, the Yard in the face of everything that is known stands by its previous conclusions. Trower remains our man."

"No!" protested Mrs. Bainbridge. "You can't!"

"Enough, Gwen," said Sparks, resting her hand on her friend's shoulder. "It's over."

"We will not stop until justice is done!" shouted Mrs. Bainbridge, rising from her chair.

"Please, Mrs. Bainbridge," said Parham wearily. "Don't let your emotions get the best of you. That will be all. Kinsey, please escort them out. Get them a cab. Our expense, but bring me a receipt."

"Sir," said Kinsey. "This way, please."

He led them back to his office.

"Could you direct me to the ladies' room?" asked Mrs. Bainbridge, wiping her eyes. "I need to make some repairs."

"Down the hall, on the left," said Kinsey.

She strode angrily down the hall and disappeared.

"I'm sorry," said Kinsey. "We put as much pressure on them as we could, legally, but none of them cracked as far as La Salle went."

"I'm sure you tried your best, Mike," said Sparks. "Thanks for that, anyway."

"There's one other thing," he said hesitantly.

"What's that?"

"My clearance level was raised when I became a Detective Sergeant," he said. "I decided to do some poking around."

"Into what?"

"Some unsolved cases left over from during the war," he said.

Sparks felt a chill pass through her.

"And?"

"There was one that struck me. A man's body found in an alleyway in Brixton. Stabbing death, lots of alcohol in his system, no witnesses."

Sparks said nothing.

"There was a cursory investigation done, but it was wartime and resources were not exactly flowing to the department. The fellow turned out to have something to do with the Spanish Embassy and was believed to be a Nazi sympathizer, possibly a spy. There was a note to the file directing us to shut the investigation down quickly."

"Who from?"

"It referred me to another file that I am not cleared to see," said Kinsey. "But the photo of his face—I recognized him. He was that Spanish fellow I saw you with that night."

"But this wasn't that night, was it?" asked Sparks.

"No, it wasn't," said Kinsey. "Look, Sparks. I don't know what happened. I'm not sure that I want to know. But if this was some counter-intelligence operation, and whatever happened was on behalf of King and country—"

"This is utter nonsense, Mike."

"I'm trying to say that I think I've been wrong about you," he said. "Everything that I've done in response has been wrong, and I'm sorry."

"You based your actions upon an honest and rational assessment of what you saw, Mike. And you're still getting married."

"I could call it off," said Kinsey. "I could explain."

"Don't," said Sparks. "I'm not worth it."

"I think that you may be."

"Knowing that you think so means the world to me, Mike," said Sparks. "But it's been too long. We're different people now."

"Not so different."

"Do you remember that time we got caught by an air raid at your place during the Blitz?" she asked. "We spent the night huddling together inside a pair of blankets in that Anderson shelter, just the two of us. We made love, thinking we might die at any second, as the bombs fell so close that the debris was raining down on us for what seemed like hours."

"How could I ever forget that?"

"I was twenty-three. It was the most intense, the most exciting night that I have ever experienced, or that I ever will experience."

"We might be able to match it in other ways," said Kinsey.

"No," said Sparks. "We can't. We shouldn't. It can never be repeated. The world should never be like that again. But I want you to know that you are seared into my memory like no other person, Michael Kinsey. Go marry Beryl Stansfield and be good to her, and never think about me."

"You ask the impossible," said Kinsey.

"Always," said Sparks, smiling. "Someday, I shall get it."

Mrs. Bainbridge returned, her face composed.

"Ready?" she asked.

"Yes," said Sparks.

"I'll call for a cab," said Kinsey.

He walked them down to the entrance and held the door for them. They drove off.

"Everything all right?" Gwen asked, looking at Iris in concern.

"Yes," Iris lied. "Let's go home. It's been a long day."

CHAPTER 15

Gwen walked into the office just in time to see a dart whizzing by to her right. She stopped. Iris was standing behind her desk, another dart in her hand.

"I do hope that there is a dartboard on the other side of this door," said Gwen. "Otherwise, our security deposit is down the drain. Could you cease fire for a moment?"

Iris nodded, and Gwen peered around the door.

"Ah, there is a dartboard there," she said. "I am glad, and I am puzzled. Has that always been there and am I just noticing it now?"

"Get out of the way," said Iris.

Gwen moved quickly towards her side of the room as Iris hurled the dart. It landed just outside the outer bull's eye.

"Good shot," said Gwen. "Is this about yesterday?"

Iris walked over to retrieve the darts without answering.

"I see," said Gwen. "If it would help, I'll stand you to a game or two. I won't be responsible for the condition of the wall."

"It's not about yesterday," said Iris. "Please stop talking. I need that triple twenty."

She threw a dart.

There was a copy of the *Times* in the wastebasket, violently crumpled. Gwen fished it out and smoothed it across her desk.

"What's in here that could have set you off, I wonder?"

"Stop it."

"I am not going to sit here quietly while you're in this insufferable and possibly dangerous state," said Gwen, perusing the newspaper. "Let's see. Anglo-Egyptian negotiations, no, it wouldn't be that. The Americans have exploded another atomic bomb in New Mexico. Do you have particular feelings about the bomb? Or New Mexico, for that matter?"

A dart struck in the twenty, just above the triple ring.

"Apparently not," continued Gwen. "American wheat shipment sent to Germany to feed coal miners. A pity, we could have used that here. Trial of Nazi commander for—"

Iris drew her knife from her handbag, flicked it open, and threw it into the dead center of the dartboard, where it stuck quivering.

"And bang goes the security deposit," said Gwen. "Trial of Nazi commander for ruthless execution of eight British WAAF and FANY officers—women. They killed women. How awful."

"They knew what they were getting into," said Iris, staring across the room at her knife. "We all did."

"You were one of them."

"I was supposed to be," said Iris, sitting in her chair. "I trained with them. Special Operations. I could be prosecuted just for saying that out loud."

"You escaped. You survived."

"I never went!" shouted Iris, pounding her desk with both fists. "I broke my stupid ankle during parachute training. It was a night jump, and the chute wouldn't open properly. I was falling through the dark, trying to get it free, screaming my bloody head off, and it finally did but it slipped air and I came in too hard."

"That wasn't your fault," said Gwen.

"It was my fault that I couldn't bring myself to get back in an airplane after it healed," said Iris. "I panicked every single time.

They ruled me unfit for overseas operations. I shifted to running teams from London, got loaned out for counterintelligence, but I didn't go into battle with my friends. Marvelous women, every single one of them. Brave, intelligent, fierce women. I should have been with them. I felt like I had been given the white feather. Everyone was very understanding about it, and that made it worse. And then I found out what happened to them. They were betrayed and executed. Brutally."

Gwen said nothing, but reached out to take her hand. Iris pulled it away.

"We used to have weekly dances," she said. "We had clothes that looked like German-made clothes but were faked, right down to the labels and the stitching. We had to break them in so they wouldn't look brand new, which would have been a dead giveaway. So we had dances, and they would put German records on the gramophone and we would have a jolly old time, chatting and flirting in German, changing partners, all those handsome boys, many of whom also died in the line of duty. Even with my ankle still throbbing, I would wear those clothes and go to those dances and play my part. Two of the women wore my size. I often wonder if they died wearing something I danced in."

"Let's close up the shop today," said Gwen. "Let's find a pub that serves liquor before noon and raise a few to your friends."

"All I do nowadays when I think about them is drink," said Iris. "Thank you, Gwen, but there is not enough liquor in the world right now."

"Fine, throw all the darts you want to. Only there's still Dickie Trower sitting in jail despite our best efforts. We need a new plan."

"If our best efforts couldn't save him, what makes you think our second-best will accomplish anything?"

"We can't give up."

"We can. We put our lives on the line, and for what? Three

people in jail and the British public is safe from fake clothing coupons. Hooray and bully for us."

She held a dart in each hand, then whipped them simultaneously at the board. One of them hit the thin metal ring separating the outer bull's eye from the rest of the board and bounced off.

"Damn," she grumbled, walking to retrieve it from the floor.

"Iris, think of something," said Gwen. "You're the strategist."

"I've got nothing," said Iris wearily. "I don't know who else to question. Our covers with Tillie's friends are blown to pieces, so we can't go back. I have no more ideas, Gwen. I'm done."

"Well, I don't intend to stay here doing nothing," said Gwen, picking up her handbag.

"What are you going to do?"

"I don't know yet. But in the meantime, I'm going to visit Dickie Trower. I haven't seen him since last Tuesday. I want to tell him that we're still in the hunt."

"What's the use? You're only going to give him hope."

"Maybe that's all I can give him," said Gwen. "But at least I can give him that. Would you care to come with me?"

"No," said Iris. "I am not capable of providing comfort to anyone right now."

"Fine," said Gwen. "I will see you later. Mind the store, and try to maintain civility when you answer the telephone."

She walked out.

"Good people," muttered Iris. "Damn them all."

This time, Gwen sat on the lower level of the Brixton tram, the scenery passing by unnoticed. Ronald Colman appeared briefly in her thoughts, and she shooed him away. Des showed up next, and she lingered on him, allowing herself a momentary wallow of fantasy and regret.

Her recounting of the weekend adventures to Lady Carolyne

the previous evening had failed to impress. She came away wondering if her mother-in-law was disappointed that Gwen hadn't been killed during the endeavour. She found Little Ronnie and presented him with the reproduction of the narwhal, which she had had framed. He was delighted, and refused to let them hang it in his room, preferring to have it propped up at baseboard level in his playroom so that he could copy it properly with his crayons while sitting on the floor.

She got off at the stop by Jebb Avenue without needing any reminder from the conductress, and walked to the prison entrance with the other women as if she had been visiting there all of her life.

She signed in and waited patiently in the queue until it was her turn. She didn't chat with the others. The three that had been there the first time were not here today, and her silence and downcast expression were respected as being normal and appropriate.

Of all the places to fit in, she thought.

Her name was called, and she followed the officer to the visiting chamber.

The door on the prisoner's side opened, and Dickie Trower came in. His eyes lit up when he saw her.

"Mrs. Bainbridge, thank goodness," he said. "Tell me that you've brought good news."

He had got thinner in the six tumultuous days since she last saw him, and there was a dull bruise on his jawline that made her shudder in sympathy. He saw it and grimaced momentarily.

"One of the guards," he said. "I didn't obey an order quickly enough to his satisfaction. And I thought the Army was rough."

"I'm so sorry, Mister Trower," said Gwen. "I hate that you are in here. I wish that I had brought good news. We have put a great deal of effort into your case. We had what we thought was a promising lead, but unfortunately . . ."

"Tell me," he said. "Tell me everything."

She recounted their efforts on his behalf, starting to cry when she reached their rejection by Parham.

"I'm sorry, Mister Trower, I truly am," she said when she had finished.

"Please, don't cry, Mrs. Bainbridge," he said. "You'll get me going, and I'm trying to be strong in your presence. I cannot believe that the two of you did all of this, that you risked your lives for me. You barely know me."

"We couldn't sit idly by," said Gwen. "We haven't given up. We'll find something. There has to be something we've missed."

"Well, until then, I will cope the best that I can. I am grateful for your visit. If it wasn't for you and Mrs. Dowd, I wouldn't have seen anyone at all."

"Oh, did she come by? That was kind of her."

"She brought me biscuits, and chatted about Herbert. She thinks he misses me."

"I'm sure that he does."

"He must be so lonely, sitting in that bowl in my empty room," sighed Trower. "I hate the thought of him having no one to talk to him. Mrs. Dowd means well, but she has that house to keep up, and I doubt that she does any more than feed him, not that that isn't a considerable task."

"I'm certain that the two of you will be reunited," said Gwen.

Mister Trower looked thoughtful, then smiled at her.

"Mrs. Bainbridge, you have a son, I believe."

"Yes. Ronnie. He's six."

"May I give Herbert to him? In gratitude for all that you've done, and so that Herbert will have someone who will pay him some attention."

"Oh, Mister Trower, I couldn't possibly accept."

"No, I insist. It will be a good home for him, and I bet that your son will take to him as I did. It would do my heart mighty good to know that Herbert is bringing happiness to someone."

"How could I say no?" smiled Gwen. "Very well. Herbert shall come home with me."

"I will write you a note straight away," said Trower. "I'll send it out to the waiting room. Thank you, Mrs. Bainbridge. Thank you and Miss Sparks for everything."

"Good-bye, Mister Trower," said Gwen. "I will come back and visit you again."

Sally poked his head through the doorway, then ducked back quickly as he saw Iris, armed and ready.

"Relax," said Iris. "I wasn't aiming at you."

"I'm waiting for the 'all clear' to sound," he called from the hall. "Is it safe?"

"Stop being stupid and come in."

His hand came into view, waving a white handkerchief. Then he stepped cautiously into the office.

"A dartboard," he observed. "How civilized. Put in a snooker table and a bar, and this place might have the makings of a real moneymaker. What made that big gash in the middle?"

She held up her knife.

"Do you get bonus points for that one?"

"What brings you here today, Sally?"

"I hadn't heard from you, so I thought that I would check in to see if my secretarial skills were wanted," he said, sitting across from her in Gwen's chair. "Also, I saw the *Times*. How are you doing?"

"How do I look like I'm doing?"

"Like you are sublimating your urge to murder all of humanity."

"Only half of it. Yes, I am sublimating. Barely. It's brave of you to put yourself in my presence."

"I have a small flask of Canadian whisky from which I derive my courage. Would you care for a nip?"

"The Canadians do not make proper whisky."

"But at least they are making it. We won't get any homegrown stuff until next year."

"I'll pass."

"Suit yourself. Where is Milady this morning?"

"Doing good works. Visiting a prisoner, then something involving loaves and fishes. She wasn't clear about the details."

"Now, there's the solution to the food shortage. Thank God Jesus is an Englishman. So, she's visiting Mister Trower?"

"Yes."

"Poor sod. What's next for him?"

"Trial. Conviction. Gallows."

"Unless you—"

"No more unlesses."

He looked at her closely. She wouldn't meet his eyes, keeping hers focused on the dartboard.

"My dear Sparks," he said. "If you don't climb out of your hole and come up with a plan, you will lose the two best friends you have right now."

"The only two, and I'm already down one," she said bleakly. "Are you throwing in the towel as well?"

"You're throwing it in on yourself. Well, I'm not sure if that's possible, so let me rephrase. Remember the first time we saw each other after I came back from Italy?"

"Vaguely. I was awash in celebration."

"You were trying to drink yourself to death. You told me that you'd rather make it look like that than a straight suicide for the sake of your parents."

"I said that? I don't remember."

"I do," said Sally. "I remember everything that you've ever said."

"How sweet of you. I do remember waking in your bed, feeling absolutely wretched. And there you were on the sofa, feet dangling over the armrest. I assume nothing else happened."

"You assume correctly. And then we talked."

"We did."

"All day."

"Yes. You drove the black dog away. For a while."

"It's back?"

"It's whimpering in the corner. I am fending it off with darts."

Sally rolled forward in his chair, gripped her by both shoulders, and turned her to face him.

"I am not having that conversation again," he said. "I am not a professional. I am only qualified to be your friend, and I haven't been the best one because lately I have been so involved in my imaginary worlds that I've become neglectful of the real one. My time here as your Monster Friday while the two of you engage in feats of derring-do has chipped away at my walls, and for that, I'm grateful."

"Let go of me."

"No. Now, I don't know what to do next, but Mrs. Bainbridge is bounding into the unknown without any guidance. You are needed, Sparks. You are wanted. I will be your sounding board, and will ask both pertinent and impertinent questions to goad you and guide you along, but start putting that brilliant noggin to use or I will abandon you for a less complicated woman who will adore my talent and think that my medals imply bravery."

"Let go of me, or I will puncture you with a dart."

He slid his hands from her shoulders to her wrists.

"Go ahead and try," he said.

She looked down at her hands, then let the darts fall to the floor.

"Unfair using your superior strength," she said.

"If I fought you in a fair fight, I'd lose," he said. "If I release you, will you start thinking about this Trower problem?"

"Yes."

"Very well," he said, letting her go. "Now, think. Talk it out. Go back to the beginning. Unleash the unlesses."

"Hypothesis Number One," she said. "Dickie Trower killed

Tillie La Salle. He corresponded with her, met her, stabbed her once through the heart in a nearby alley. Then he forged a letter—no, he would have had to do that first to provide himself with an alibi—"

"Technically, not an alibi," said Sally.

"Whatever it's called. Plausible evidence for his not meeting her. And having done all of this planning, he brought home the bloody knife and stuffed it under his mattress so the police could find it easily and feel better about themselves."

"Very considerate of him," commented Sally. "So, what are the problems with that hypothesis?"

"Trower isn't the type," said Iris. "Neither the murdering type nor the type who would make the obvious mistake of bringing back the bloody knife had he been the murdering type."

"Why the latter?"

"He's an accountant. Very well-organized."

"Death by Double Entry," said Sally dramatically. "A radio play in three acts. All right, come up with an alternate hypothesis."

"Hypothesis Number Two. Someone else killed Tillie and framed Dickie Trower. We've been—"

She frowned thoughtfully.

"Go on," urged Sally.

"We've been concentrating our efforts on finding someone who had a motive for killing Tillie," she said. "Maybe we should be searching for someone who wanted to frame Dickie Trower."

"Interesting idea. How would that fit the available evidence?"

"Well, it would account for the knife. But the hypothetical murderer would have had to know about The Right Sort, because he knew enough to come here, use our stationery, and my Bar-Let, and forge Gwen's signature."

"That's a lot to know," observed Sally.

"That's why we suspected Roger Pilcher. He knew about us after following Tillie here."

"But it wasn't him."

"No, damn the luck. So someone faked the letter, then mailed it to Trower—"

She stopped, got up, and started pacing furiously around the office.

"There's something, there's something," she muttered.

Sally watched her, trying not to smile.

"The postmark!" she exclaimed.

"What about it?"

"The postmark on the letter to Trower was from the Croydon Post Office."

"He lives in Croydon."

"Yes, and the man who mailed that letter knew that. He wanted to make sure Trower got the letter in time to abandon the date."

"He could have got Trower's address from your files."

"Possibly. Or he could also live in Croydon. So: knew Trower, knew he was coming here, had access to his room, knows Croydon—Sally!"

"I'm right here, Sparks."

"He lives in a rented room in a private house. With a landlady!"

"Who could be reading his mail like a proper snoop," said Sally.

"And therefore knows about us. Our address, how we correspond, the works!"

"Or could even be his confidante, never mind the mail. Sounds like someone to investigate. Do you need me to man the telephone while you go find Milady?"

"Would you?" said Iris, dashing back to her desk and crawling under it.

"What's down there?" asked Sally.

"Petty cash," she said, opening the strongbox. "I'm taking a cab to Brixton. I need to talk to Trower and intercept Gwen."

She emerged, then threw herself on top of Sally and hugged him hard as the chair creaked in protest.

"Thank you, Sally," she said. "I do love you, you know."

She popped off him and flew out of the office. Sally watched her.

"I know," he sighed.

Iris flew down the stairs and burst through the front door. There were no more photographers lurking about—she and Gwen were last week's news. She ran to Oxford Street where the traffic was heavier and succeeded in flagging down a cab within a minute.

"Where to, Miss?" asked the cabby.

"Brixton Prison," she said. "Quickly."

He turned to look at her more closely, eyebrows raised.

"You did hear me say 'quickly,' didn't you?" she snapped.

"I did, Miss," he replied, activating the taximeter. "It's just that most people are not in a hurry to go to jail."

"Your tip depends on your speed."

"And now I have incentive," he said, stepping on the accelerator.

Gwen got off the tram on Combe Road and walked to Mrs. Dowd's house, thinking about how one might transport a fish. She didn't want to spend money on a cab unnecessarily, but the problem of carrying a fishbowl on a series of trams and buses was daunting.

She was still pondering it as she came up to the front door. She rang the bell. Mrs. Dowd opened it and looked at her in surprise.

"Mrs. Bainbridge, isn't it?" she asked. "I'm sorry. I had no idea that you were coming."

"I apologize, Mrs. Dowd," said Gwen. "I am here once again to deal with our mutual friend, Herbert."

"Herbert? What about him?"

"I was visiting with Mister Trower just now, and he kindly offered to give Herbert to my son until—well, for the immediate future. If it's not too much trouble, I would like to take him off your hands. Here is a note from Mister Trower explaining everything."

Mrs. Dowd took the note, then pulled a pair of reading glasses from her apron pocket and read it.

"Well, that certainly takes the cake," she said. "He must be giving up hope if he's abandoning Herbert. Poor lad."

"His prospects don't seem the best at the moment," admitted Gwen. "We've been trying to help him."

"You have? How?"

"We've been looking into his case," said Gwen.

"Case? Are you a detective now?"

"No, no, no," laughed Gwen. "Just someone going around asking questions and investigating matters on a strictly informal level."

"Anything turn up?"

"Unfortunately, nothing that will help Mister Trower. Hence my visit and subsequent mission to bring Herbert to his new home."

"Well, come in, then," said Mrs. Dowd, holding open the door. "Funny thing is I'll miss the little beggar. He turns out to be a good listener."

"That's good. My son is quite the talker. They should get along famously."

They went upstairs to Trower's room. Gwen looked at the fishbowl and thought about bumpy travels, sloshing water, and her dress. It all seemed a disaster waiting to happen.

"You wouldn't happen to have a box of some kind that I could carry his bowl in, would you?" she asked.

"I might," said Mrs. Dowd. "Tell you what. Come down to the parlour. I'll make you a cup of tea and you can sit while I rummage about. I think there's something in the cellar that might do the trick, but I want to clean it up a bit before you hold it against that nice outfit of yours."

"That would be lovely, thank you."

The cab pulled up at the prison gate. Iris paid the cabby with a tip that did not displease him and rushed in.

"Excuse me," she said to the guard at the visitors' queue. "I was supposed to meet my friend Mrs. Bainbridge here. Do you know if she's already gone in?"

"Bainbridge, yes," he said, consulting his list. "Visiting a Mister Trower."

"Excellent. Would it be possible for me to join them?'

"Oh, no," he said. "Only one visitor per prisoner per day."

"Then could I wait for her here?"

"Well, she left, didn't she?"

"She did?"

"She did."

"Blast. Did she by any chance say where she was going next?"

"She thanked me and said good-bye, which was very polite of her."

"Her manners are beyond compare," agreed Iris. "But did she say where she was going?"

"Said she had to see a woman about a fish."

"A fish?"

"Yes. It was a peculiar thing to say, which is why I remembered it."

"Herbert," whispered Iris. "Thank you, officer."

She turned and ran back into the street.

Gwen decided to look at the photographs on the parlour walls while Mrs. Dowd occupied herself in the kitchen. There were some paintings hanging amidst the photographs that had escaped her notice the last time she had been here. She looked at them closely, and was surprised to see *A. Dowd* signed in tiny, carefully drawn black letters in the corner of each.

"Did you paint these?" she asked Mrs. Dowd when she returned with the tea tray.

"I did. You take milk, I believe?"

"Yes, thank you. These are quite good."

"You're very kind," said Mrs. Dowd, beaming with pride. "Painting has been one of my retreats from the world. Mister Dowd used to say—well, there I go, bringing him into the conversation. I try not to speak of Mister Dowd anymore."

"I understand entirely," said Gwen, taking the cup Mrs. Dowd handed her. "I hope that you still paint. You're very talented."

"Thank you, Mrs. Bainbridge. You drink up, and I'll go find that box."

Gwen sat on the sofa and sipped her tea, idly glancing at the photographs. For someone who justifiably disliked her ex-husband, Mrs. Dowd certainly kept a lot of their photographs together on display. Remembrances of happier times, Gwen supposed. She could see how happy they had once been. There they were on their wedding day, he in a tailcoat and top hat, she in a lovely gown, her hair bobbed like they did back in the twenties. There they were dancing at some beach resort—Brighton, by the look of it. And there was the first date at that café, sitting at a table, the floor with its distinctive tiles—

Gwen picked up that photograph and looked at it more closely. The floor had a diamond pattern in the tiles. The walls behind the smiling young couple were hung with paintings of flowers.

"I was so young," said Mrs. Dowd, standing in the doorway, watching her. "Seventeen, can you believe it? He was so handsome. Such a gentleman. Or so I thought. Swept me quite off of my feet."

"This is the Garland Café, isn't it?" asked Gwen.

"Yes. Our first date."

"This is where Mister Trower was supposed to meet Miss La Salle."

"I know."

"You suggested the café to him, didn't you?"

"I did," said Mrs. Dowd, sitting in one of the high-backed chairs opposite. "I was wondering if you had gone there. I was wondering if you'd recognize it from the photograph. It's amazing what can be found right under your nose if you only look."

"You let him make the date, then sent the letter canceling it so you could meet her there instead of him."

"Yes."

"Why? What had that poor girl ever done to you?"

"Oh, her? Nothing. Nothing at all. But I had to teach Dickie a lesson, didn't I? All these years looking after him, listening to him, consoling him, keeping his room tidy and waiting even when he went off to war, nursing him after he was wounded—did you know he was wounded?"

"No," said Gwen.

"I'm not old," said Mrs. Dowd. "I am the best of housekeepers. I have memorized every magazine article that tells you how to make a proper home for your man, and I've done that for Dickie. I've been right under his nose, cooking special meals for him, letting him unburden his heart, his hopes, his dreams. And I have hopes, and dreams, and a heart of my own, don't I?"

"Of course," said Gwen, eyeing the path through the clutter of furniture to the door.

She was tired, she thought stupidly. Why was she so tired? She yawned.

"Am I boring you?" asked Mrs. Dowd, smiling.

"Not at all, forgive me," said Gwen.

"Oh, I like that. You're being polite even now. Where was I? Ah, yes. Dickie. There I was, right under his nose the whole time, and I thought he would see me, finally see me, not the housekeeper, but the woman who adored him, who would do anything for him. Then I find out about him going to a marriage bureau. A marriage bureau! He was so lonely and desperate, and yet I was here! I was here!"

The last was shouted, momentarily jolting Gwen alert. Her tea-cup rattled in her hands. She put it down on the table.

"It must have been a shock," she said.

The torpor settled into her more deeply.

"What did you put in my tea?" she asked suddenly, the horror rising in her.

"A little something to help you sleep," said Mrs. Dowd.

"You drugged Dickie. The night you killed Tillie."

"He was so upset about the letter canceling the date."

"You forged the letter."

"I did. Your custodian doesn't take good care of keeping the spare keys safe. I typed the letter and signed your name. I had one of your letters to Dickie to copy, and I am, as you've said, a bit of an artist. Another quality he failed to notice."

"Why? Why do it?"

"He was going to leave me," said Mrs. Dowd. "After all I had done for him, after all the years I had waited. So, he had to be punished."

"But me?" gasped Gwen, trying desperately to stay awake. She was having trouble keeping upright.

"He gave Herbert to you," said Mrs. Dowd. "He clearly loves you. I can't have that."

"I have a child," pleaded Gwen. "A little boy."

"He'll survive," said Mrs. Dowd. "Children are remarkably resilient. Now, go to sleep, dearie. It's better to die in your sleep. You're a big girl, and it's going to take me some time to chop you up. I don't want to make a mess in here."

The doorbell rang.

"I'm going to ignore that," said Mrs. Dowd. "I don't want to be interrupted."

The doorbell rang again, followed by an insistent knocking.

"Fine," said Mrs. Dowd in exasperation. "I'll get rid of whoever it is. You sit tight. I'll be right back."

She walked into the hall. Gwen tried to cry out, but couldn't summon the strength. She fell back against the sofa, her head colliding with her handbag.

Mrs. Dowd opened the door to see a short, perky brunette standing there, a notepad and pencil in her hands.

"How do you do?" chirped the woman. "My name is Eloise Teasley. I am conducting a survey for Mass-Observation about rationing and the response of the Ordinary British Housewife. Are you an Ordinary British Housewife by any chance, and if so, would you mind answering some questions?"

"I'm sorry, this is a bad time," said Mrs. Dowd.

"Wait," said the woman, holding up her hand. "Did you hear that?"

"Hear what?"

"Listen," said the woman, cocking her head to the side.

Mrs. Dowd listened. A faint whistle emanated from the house.

"That sounded like a police whistle, didn't it?" said the woman. "So curious. I have a friend, a very good friend, in fact, who has a police whistle. Her name is Gwendolyn Bainbridge."

Mrs. Dowd flinched. The other woman smiled broadly.

"That was very noticeable," she said. "You have to learn how not to react at the first mention of something bad if you're going to be successful. That's the first thing they taught us at Murder School. I'm going to hit you now."

"What?" said Mrs. Dowd, starting to step back, but Iris's notebook was already falling to the ground as she stepped forward to apply a very creditable uppercut to the other woman's jaw.

Mrs. Dowd's head snapped back. The momentum carried the rest of her toppling back into the hallway until she landed on the carpet with a muffled thud.

Iris stepped inside and viewed her victim. She knelt down and felt her wrist for a pulse, found one, and nodded in satisfaction.

Then she slid the metal knuckles from her fingers, kissed the top of them lightly, and put them in her handbag.

"Iris?" came a feeble voice from the parlour.

"Be right with you, darling," said Iris. "I need to secure the prisoner."

She stripped Mrs. Dowd's apron from her and quickly tied the woman's hands behind her back. Then she ran into the parlour. Gwen lay on the sofa. She raised her hand in a feeble wave, the whistle still dangling in it.

"What did she give you?" said Iris, immediately.

"Some drug. So sleepy."

"Stay with me, Gwen. I'm going to call an ambulance."

"Iris. She killed Tillie."

"I thought she might have. I'll be right back."

Gwen stared across at the photographs on the table. Mrs. and Mister Dowd stared back at her. Happiness in every picture.

They began to blur.

Iris came back, a glass in one hand, a large metal basin in the other. She put the basin on Gwen's lap, then lifted her into a sitting position.

"The ambulance is on its way," said Iris, holding the glass to Gwen's lips. "Now, drink this."

Gwen took a sip, then several more.

"What is it?" she gasped.

"Syrup of ipecac," said Iris. "It will do until we get you to the hospital for the stomach pump."

"Oh, no!"

"Things are about to become unpleasant, darling, so think of England and aim for the basin. There we go. Good girl."

Several hours later, Iris sat on the edge of Gwen's gurney in the emergency room at Mayday Road Hospital.

"Never had my stomach pumped before," said Gwen. "One more for my diary. Yippee."

"It isn't fun," agreed Iris.

"You've had it done?"

"Oh, yes."

"Can you tell that story?"

"I can, but I don't want to make you sick again."

"I have nothing left," said Gwen. "Iris—you saved my life."

"It was the least I could do after I acted so beastly to you this morning."

"Why were you there?"

"I figured out Mrs. Dowd was the most likely person to have done all this. Sally jolted me into that, bless him. I came with the intent of trying to intercept you, and maybe get her to touch something so I could get a fingerprint to pass along to that nice Mister Godfrey to compare to the unknown print on the letter to Dickie. But you did me one better in getting her to admit to the crime, clever girl."

"So clever, I nearly died."

"Nearly died is not dead. You lived to fight another day."

"I don't want to fight anymore."

"Oh, yes. You do. You have to get your son back now that we've proved you right. Look, here come Parham and Detective Ex!"

Detective Superintendent Parham and Detective Sergeant Kinsey walked into the emergency room, hats in hand.

"Well?" asked Sparks.

"Mrs. Dowd confirmed your statements," said Parham. "Her fingerprints did indeed match the one left on the letter. We will be charging her with the murder of Matilda La Salle. And dismissing the charges against Dickie Trower. The paperwork for his release will go through tomorrow morning."

"Thank God," whispered Mrs. Bainbridge.

"There's more," said Parham.

"More?"

"Pursuant to information that she provided us, we had a team dig up the gardens in the backyard," said Kinsey. "We found the dismembered corpse of a man we believe to be her late husband, Phineas Dowd."

"Good heavens," said Sparks.

"Also," he continued, clearing his throat.

"Yes?"

"Also—there was a dismembered cat."

"She really hates being left by those she loves," commented Mrs. Bainbridge.

"Ladies, Scotland Yard owes you a debt of gratitude," said Parham. "If there is any way—"

"There is," interrupted Sparks. "First, we want to be on either side of Dickie Trower when he walks out of Brixton Prison tomorrow morning."

"I think that's fitting," said Parham. "What else?"

"You have a press office."

"Of course."

"We wish to be given full credit for clearing his name, specifically mentioning The Right Sort Marriage Bureau. We want this to go to every newspaper in the city so that a press conference may be held with us when we bring him out to freedom."

"I see no reason why that can't be done," said Parham.

"Not every newspaper," said Mrs. Bainbridge. "Don't notify the *Mirror*."

Parham smiled.

"It will be my distinct pleasure to leave them high and dry," he said. "We'll see you at Brixton in the morning, ladies. Superb work. By the way, Miss Sparks?"

"Yes, Detective Superintendent?"

"The pattern of bruises on Mrs. Dowd's chin—I am not unfamiliar with them. What exactly did you hit her with?"

"Years of repression, Detective Superintendent," said Sparks. "I won't lie. It felt good."

CHAPTER 16

"It was nice of you to bring me a fresh shirt," said Mister Trower as he knotted his tie.

"My mother used to tell me, 'Always leave prison in a clean shirt,'" said Iris.

"She never did," said Gwen.

"I was very young at the time," admitted Iris. "I may have the actual words wrong."

"How did you get into Mrs. Dowd's house to retrieve it?" asked Trower. "Isn't it a crime scene? Did one of your policeman friends let you in?"

"Not exactly," said Iris.

Gwen hid a smile.

"I still can't believe Mrs. Dowd did this," he said, brushing off his jacket. "It's hard to picture her as a killer. She's always been so good to me."

"She wanted something in return," said Gwen. "And when she didn't get it, she—she's not a well woman, Mister Trower."

"If only I had known."

"If you had known, what would you have done?" asked Iris. "Returned her affections?"

"Goodness, no. I would have moved out immediately. It would have been a very awkward situation."

"You might not have made it to the front door," commented Iris.

He put on the jacket, then turned to face them.

"How do I look?"

"Very handsome," said Iris.

"Let me be motherly for a moment," said Gwen, licking her fingers and smoothing down some errant strands of hair. "There. Better. Are you ready to face the reporters?"

"I've never been in a press conference before," he said.

"You've been in combat?" asked Iris.

"Yes."

"It's worse. Keep smiling. Don't worry, we'll be with you."

The jail had set up a temporary platform outside the entrance. The warden himself escorted the three of them out. The flashes went off furiously, and the newsreel cameramen in the back swiveled their cameras and adjusted their lenses as Dickie Trower stepped up to the bank of microphones.

"Thank you," he said, then he cleared his throat. "Thank you for coming. It is a great relief to be a free man. These past several days have been a nightmare, one that I did not expect and did not deserve. It would have continued—indeed, it might have become far worse—had it not been for the remarkable efforts made on my behalf by Miss Iris Sparks and Mrs. Gwendolyn Bainbridge of The Right Sort Marriage Bureau. I had no idea when I plunked down my fee that they would not only be my Cupids, but my protectors as well. To have such fearless advocacy on such short acquaintance speaks of the greatness of their hearts."

"Well said!" shouted a spectator as Sparks and Bainbridge beamed proudly.

"I would like to extend my condolences to the family of Miss La Salle," he continued. "I never had the good fortune to meet her, but from what I heard, she was a lovely woman. May she rest in peace, and may the arrest of my—of Mrs. Dowd give them the justice that they deserve. Thank you."

"Mister Trower, what was it like in there?" called the man from the *Telegraph*.

"Unpleasant," he said. "But, in retrospect, safer than the house I had been living in."

That drew some guffaws from the reporters.

"How was the food?"

"Better than what the Army fed us, but the company was worse."

"Mister Trower, did you ever lose hope?" called a woman from *Woman's Own*.

"Never," he said firmly. "Not once I knew The Right Sort was on my side."

He reached out and grabbed the two women by the hand, then raised their arms triumphantly together. The flashes went off ecstatically.

He took a few more questions, then it was over. A few reporters made appointments with them for followup articles. Then the three walked away from Brixton Prison.

"What now, Mister Trower?" asked Gwen as they came to Brixton Hill.

"First, I am going to take a proper bath. Feed Herbert. Call my job, let them know I'm coming back. Look for a new place to live. Try and start my life up again. It won't be the same."

"But at least you'll have one."

"At least I will," he said. He took a deep breath and looked up at the sky. "God, it feels different. Same air, same sky as when you're in the yard, but no walls looming over you, no guards. Miss Sparks, Mrs. Bainbridge—I owe you a debt that I can never repay."

"We owe you one as well, Mister Trower," said Iris.

"How so?"

"We still owe you a wife. Let us know your new address and telephone when you have it."

"I will," he promised. "Find me a good one."

He flagged down a cab and sped off towards Croydon.

"He's a natural," said Iris. "He should stand for Parliament. He could run on the Reprieved Party ticket."

"I'd vote for him," said Gwen.

She turned and looked back at the prison for what she hoped would be the last time in her life. A cab pulled up in front of it.

"Look," said Gwen, tugging on Iris's arm.

A man got out of the cab, looked at the press platform which was now being disassembled, then trudged disconsolately back to the cab.

"That was Gareth Pontefract of the *Mirror*, wasn't it?" observed Gwen.

"It was," said Iris, smiling happily. "And that makes the day complete."

Gwen strode into the library without knocking. Lady Carolyne looked up at her askance.

"I wanted to let you know that I'm going to be in the papers again," said Gwen.

"Not the *Mirror*," sighed Lady Carolyne.

"Maybe not the *Mirror* this time. But all the rest. And the newsreels."

"What? What did you do?"

"We solved the murder. We proved it was someone other than Dickie Trower. We walked him out of Brixton Prison today into a full field of reporters. Our company's name has been restored. More important, an innocent man has been exonerated and freed, and we were the ones who made that happen. Most important of all—I was right."

Lady Carolyne gaped at her, which gave Gwen immense satisfaction. She turned crisply on her heel and walked out.

There were more reporters gathered in front of their building when Iris and Gwen arrived the next morning. Mister MacPherson stood in the entrance, watching them warily. After graciously answering a multitude of questions and posing for photographs, the two women escaped to the safety of their office.

"I'm not paid to be a bouncer!" MacPherson called up after them.

"We've been meaning to speak to you about the security here," replied Iris, peering down at him over the railing. "We have some concerns. Drop by later, if you don't mind."

The telephone was already ringing when they went into The Right Sort. Iris plucked the receiver from its cradle before she even reached her chair.

"The Right Sort Marriage Bureau, Iris Sparks here."

"Oh, Miss Sparks!" cried a woman's voice. "I just saw the *Telegraph*! How marvelous!"

"Yes, isn't it?" agreed Iris. "To whom am I speaking?"

"It's Miss Sedgewick. I am so sorry about my little overreaction the other morning. Can you forgive me?"

"You are forgiven," said Iris, rolling her eyes at Gwen. "It was certainly understandable."

"Tell me," continued Miss Sedgewick. "Is Mister Trower still your client?"

"He is."

"Is he still available?"

"He's been in solitary confinement for a week, so I expect so."

"Good. You must set us up immediately."

"Are you certain? Only a few days ago, you suspected him of murder."

"I know! Isn't it exciting? Let me know the moment he accepts! Bye!"

She hung up without waiting for Iris's reply.

"Who was that?" asked Gwen.

"Bitsy Sedgewick. She wants an introduction to Mister Trower. Just when I thought there would be no more surprises this week."

The telephone rang again.

"Right Sort—oh, hello, Miss Blake. Yes? Dickie Trower? I'm afraid that there is one person already ahead of you, but I can—yes, I will add you to the list. Will do. Good-bye."

She hung up, then grabbed her pad and started writing. The telephone rang again. This time, a gentleman sought to make an appointment to sign up.

The morning proved to be quite busy. They passed the telephone back and forth between desks, taking shifts answering. By lunchtime, they were exhausted and extremely happy, and the list of women interested in Dickie Trower had grown to seven names.

"We need a secretary," said Gwen thoughtfully. "And more space."

"I think you're right," said Iris.

"Well, don't ask me," said Sally, standing in the doorway.

"How do you move so silently?" asked Gwen.

"Practice, practice, practice," he said. "Catlike tread and all that."

"Are you sure you don't want the job?" asked Iris. "You already have experience and training."

"It was fine when this was a failing business," he said, coming in. "But now that you're such booming successes, the position sounds like it's going to require actual work, and I'm not cut out for that. I shall continue to be on call for collections and the odd consultation."

"Thank you, Sally," said Iris. "You've been a lifesaver. Quite literally in my case."

"I have come to bring you these," he said, depositing a pile of newspapers on her desk. "I think that's all of them. Some are worth framing. And if I may offer my own meager accomplishment in the midst of basking in your twinned radiances—I have finished my play!"

"Bravo!" applauded Gwen. "When may we see it?"

"Well, I need to have an informal reading next," he said. "A gathering of voices in my parlour so that I may hear it out loud. I'd like to ask the two of you to participate."

"I'd love to," said Iris. "Strictly a reading, though. I won't be enacting any love scenes this time."

"More's the pity," he said. "Mrs. Bainbridge?"

"Oh, I don't know," said Gwen hesitantly. "I'm no actress."

"That ain't so, and you know it, Sophie," said Iris.

"It's not in front of an audience," said Sally. "Only a few select friends. Please say that you will."

"All right," said Gwen. "Don't hold me to the high standards of you two."

"You'll be wonderful," he promised. "Ta ta, detectives."

He vanished soundlessly out of the hall.

"He must have been fearsome behind the lines," said Gwen.

"Yes."

"You calling me Sophie reminded me. I need to make a call."

The telephone rang again as she reached for it. She answered, then handed it over to Iris.

"It's a gentleman," she said. "He would not state his name."

"Curious," said Iris. "Hello. Sparks, here."

"'Allo, Mary Elizabeth McTague," said Archie.

Iris clutched the receiver in a spasm of surprise and fear.

"Hello," she said. "I wasn't expecting you to call."

"Well, I find myself in an unexpectedly peculiar position, given what I've been reading in the papers the past two days."

"What position is that?"

"I am still at liberty. Completely unarrested. And given that a couple of people very well known to me are not, I am puzzled by that. I am also puzzled that my newest employee, Mary Elizabeth McTague, 'asn't turned snitch when she was never legit to start with."

"I had no interest in seeing you go to jail if you didn't kill Tillie. You asked for my loyalty when I worked for you. I gave it. And I hear that the Yard and the Ministry of Finance want to keep the prosecution of Pilcher hush-hush, given how embarrassing it is that their prize man went rogue. Anything he can say against you is automatically suspect. They'll settle for him and the recovery of the stolen plates."

"How were you sure it wasn't me who killed Tillie? Even I'd suspect me, and I like me."

"A small detail. She was stabbed in the heart. It didn't sound like your style. You said you prefer to slit throats."

"Oh, that's rich," he said, laughing. "So, we're good, you and me?"

"We're good. But I would like to take this opportunity to tender my resignation from your organization, Boss. It was fun to be a spiv for a day, but I have my own business to run."

"I might 'ave some work for you."

"I told you—"

"It's me nephew. Bernie's not in the game, 'as a proper upbringing and education, and wants to be a school teacher. We don't know any girls decent enough for 'im, and he trips over his tongue 'alf the time when 'e meets them on 'is own. So, I thought I'd send 'im your way."

"By all means."

"And I'm sending a couple of boxes with him in my appreciation for what you've done, one for you, one for Sophie."

"I'm not sure that we should—"

"Stockings, Miss Sparks. Ten pairs for each of you."

"Well, it would be churlish to turn them down under the circumstances. How did you know Gwen's size?"

"I 'ave a knack for these things."

"You should become a hosier when you grow up."

"Always thought that would be an enjoyable profession, me being a leg man and all. Speaking of which—seeing as you and Rog ain't a thing, 'ow about you and me step out some night? I know a place with a good dance floor and a decent band."

"Legal?"

"Not completely. Interested?"

"All right, Archie."

"Friday night?"

"It's a date. I'll see you then."

She hung up. Gwen was staring at her.

"Did you just accept a date with Archie?" she asked.

"I thought it might be fun."

Gwen shook her head in disbelief, then wrote something on her notepad.

"I'm usually the craziest person in the room at any given moment," she said, tearing the sheet off and handing it to Iris. "The exception seems to be when I'm alone with you. This is my psychiatrist's name and number. Do the world a favour and call him."

"Why? I feel fine."

"You, my friend, like to put yourself at risk. Now, I have been right there with you these past several days, but that's over and done with. Yet here you are, agreeing to date a gangster who could turn on you in a second if he suspects you of being an informant."

"I don't think he will," said Iris. "And I've dated worse."

"Please. For my sake."

"Very well, since you said please. We should have our appointments back-to-back. We could make a date of it—therapy, then drinks after."

"That does sound like fun," said Gwen. "Let's do that."

"You said you wanted to make a call?"

"Oh, yes," said Gwen. "Pass me the telephone, would you?"

It was evening when she walked into the Town of Ramsgate pub on Wapping High Street. She looked around expectantly as the roar of voices subsided while the male patrons checked her out. Then she saw him, sitting in a corner. He met her eye, but gave no other sign of welcome.

She walked up to him.

"Hello, Des," she said softly.

"You called," he said. "I didn't think you would."

"I said that I would take a walk with you."

"Sophie said that," he said. "You're not Sophie."

"No. My name is Gwen Bainbridge."

"I know. I read the story. And you're not a ladies' maid. You're an actual lady."

"I never gained the title. My husband was killed before inheriting it."

"So the dead 'usband was true."

"Most of what I said was true."

"Makes the lie work better, right?"

"Des, could we take that walk, please?"

"Are you serious?"

"I am. I'd rather talk while we're walking."

"I doubt a lady's shoes are right for walking around—"

She stood back where he could see her feet.

"I brought my wellies this time," she said. "They don't flatter my legs, but you said we could see the Tower Bridge."

"Come on," he said, taking her by the arm.

They walked out the back exit. There was a stair next to the pub going down to the river.

"This is an old stair," he said as he led her down it. "It goes back centuries. They say girls useter kiss their sailor lads good-bye 'ere and swear to be true until they returned."

"And were they true? Did the sailors come back?"

"Who knows?" he said with a shrug. "It's a nice story. Gets an occasional kiss out of a girl if a lad brings 'er to the stairs."

They reached the banks of the Thames. He led her to the edge.

"You can't see the entire bridge, but there it is," he said.

She could see half of the bridge. One of the towers, the one further from the City of London, partly blocked the setting sun.

"Shall we walk a little farther?" she asked.

"What are we doing?" he replied. "What is there to talk about? You made a bloody fool out of me."

"I didn't mean to. We didn't mean to. We weren't trying to hurt anyone."

"No, but you weren't exactly trying not to 'urt anyone, were you?"

"There was an innocent man in prison. We were trying to save him."

"And it turned out to 'ave nothing to do with any of us, did it?" he said.

"No. But we didn't know that when we began."

"What about me? I was never one of your suspects. I poured my 'eart out to you, and you were only pumping me for information. I liked you. Or I liked Sophie. I don't know anymore."

"You're a decent, kind man, Des, and I'm sorry if I left you with the impression that there could be anything between us."

"Because I'm not good enough for the likes of you."

"Des, you may very well be too good for the likes of me," she said. "I have a son."

He took a deep breath.

"You do."

"Yes."

"And what's 'is title?"

"He is a future lord, which doesn't matter to me one jot, but it matters to my husband's parents. They have legal custody of him, and I am about to go to war in the courts to get him back. I am out-financed, outgunned, and outnumbered, and I cannot do anything that will jeopardize my already tenuous position. Which means as much as I would like to, I can't have—I can't get involved with any-one right now."

He looked across the water.

"How old is 'e?"

"Six. He is the light of my life, and I won't lose him."

"I've always wanted a boy," said Des. "Someone to teach the trade to, like my dad taught me."

"I know you'll be a wonderful father, Des," said Gwen. "I mean that, I truly do."

"Can't do it alone," he said.

"You know that Fanny adores you," said Gwen.

"Of course, I know that Fanny adores me," he said angrily. "If I wanted Fanny, I would be with Fanny, not wasting time on some posh—"

"If it wasn't for Ronnie, I would be saying yes to the next date, Des," said Gwen.

"You almost sound like you mean it," he said, finally looking at her.

"If you knew me better, you would have no doubt of it."

"Will it take long?" he asked. "This court battle?"

"I don't know," she said. "I don't want you to pin your hopes on me, Des. Find someone else."

"Then that's it," he said heavily. "Let me walk you back to the station."

They turned away from the river and walked to the foot of the stairs.

"Might I kiss you?" he asked.

"I'm afraid that would only make this worse," she said.

"I suppose it would."

"So let's make it worse," said Gwen.

He wasn't like Ronnie. He felt different pressed against her. He held her differently, and his scent was one of sweat and traces of oak and pine and others she couldn't identify. And his mouth—he was slow and questing and questioning, and she found herself turning the aggressor, craving him, seizing him, and pulling him to her, wanting it to go on and on until the river rose around them, carrying them both away from this wretched, terrible city.

She could not have said after how long it lasted, only that it lasted, and then it ended, it had to end whether they wanted it to or not. She rested her head against his shoulder, clinging to him, trembling.

"I can't say anything," she said. "Any words now will only be polite or stupid or completely inadequate."

"You don't need to say anything," he said. "I'll take you to the station."

She walked up the steps ahead of him. There was a moment where she stumbled on the wet stone and he caught her by the waist and steadied her, but that was all there was.

She took care to reapply her lipstick before she returned to Kensington Court.

Dinner had passed. She had no appetite for it. She went up to find Ronnie. He was in his playroom, drawing. She plopped herself down on the floor next to him.

"I have a son who is very topsy-turvy, for he plays in the drawing room and draws in his playroom," she said, giving him a kiss. "How go the exciting adventures of Sir Oswald, the heroic narwhal?"

"He's fighting a Nazi U-boat," said Ronnie. "He's poking holes in it with his tusk. It's very difficult, because he has to dodge torpedoes at the same time."

"I'm certain that he'll win in the end," said Gwen.

"Mummy? Did the playroom look like this when Daddy was a boy?"

"I don't know," said Gwen. "You would have to ask some of the older servants."

"Or Grandmother," said Ronnie. "But she's been in a bad mood. Is it because Grandfather has been away in Africa for so long?"

"That could be it," said Gwen. "I'm sure that you would be the best one to cheer her up. Will you remember to do that tomorrow?"

"Yes, Mummy."

"You are a wonderful boy. Now, you may draw until it's time for bed, but don't give Agnes any difficulties when she comes to get you ready."

"Will you come give me a kiss good-night?"

"Of course, my darling."

She left him to his work.

It was strange to think of the playroom as being her husband's twenty odd years ago. She had seen photographs of him at that age, but they were all formal poses in exquisite velvet suits. Her Ronnie had a mischievous side—there must have been much galloping about and play-fighting in that room, but he never mentioned it. Only his secret place in the attic.

He had brought her up to see it once after putting her through an over-complicated and very solemn oath of secrecy.

It's always been mine, you see, he had explained to her. *The only place in the world that's completely mine. So you understand how momentous it is that I am sharing it with you.*

I do, she said.

He had brought her up the steep, narrow steps to the trapdoor that allowed access to it, then tiptoed across the dusty floorboards, beckoning to her to do the same. Around them, steamer trunks and hatboxes were stacked to the roof-beams, old worn-out bureaus that were nevertheless too much part of the family history to discard were shoved into corners, and the entire mess was lit by a row of bare lightbulbs hanging from the apex of the roof.

Ronnie came to an armoire that must have dated back to the beginning of the previous century and carefully slid between it and the wall.

So much easier when I was young and spry, he said.

You're a pathetic wreck at twenty-two, she agreed, turning sideways and following him.

A small space, maybe six feet by four, had been cleared in front of a dormer window, which lit the area nicely. A bookcase stood by it, filled with adventure novels. There was an easel with an unfinished water colour of a biplane, and a tiny table with a pair of stools on either side.

On the table was a small box.

Oh, dear, said Gwen when she saw it. *Is that what I think it is?*

Well, now that you've seen my innermost sanctum, I'm afraid I have no other choice, he said, picking it up and kneeling before her. *Marry me, Gwen.*

She hadn't been up there since he had left the last time. She wondered if it was still intact.

She wondered if his spirit forgave her for kissing another man today.

An impulse drew her up the flights of stairs until she reached the trapdoor. It gave before her without creaking. She climbed into the attic and felt for the thin chain that turned on the lights.

She couldn't remember the layout of the trunks. There seemed to be fewer—whether it was due to Lord Bainbridge's travels or the conflation of her memories, she couldn't say.

But there was the armoire, still in place. She walked—no, she tiptoed, honouring that long-ago oath, until she reached it, then slid through the gap. Not as easily as one once had, she thought, but one has had a baby since then, and there are changes as a result.

It was all there. The book case. The easel, empty now. The table.

There was an envelope on the table.

Her hand trembling, she picked it up and held it to the light.

It had her name on it.

She didn't want to tear it open and destroy any part of it. She eased her way back into the main part of the attic, then carefully tiptoed back to the stairs, pausing to turn off the lights before she descended.

Once down, she ran the rest of the way to her room and dug a letter opener out of the desk. She slit the edge of the envelope with the care of a surgeon. Inside was a letter, and another, smaller envelope with *For Ronnie, my son* written on it.

She opened the letter and began to read.

My dearest Gwen,

I've always taken illicit pride in the fact that, unlike so many of our married friends, we never gave each other obnoxiously cute pet names. I would hate to have you crying at my funeral 'Moopsy! My beloved Moopsy' or some equally ghastly sobriquet. Gwen and Ronnie, Ronnie and Gwen— the pairing suits me fine.

If you are reading this, then I have either bought the farm or have come home and completely forgotten to destroy it. If the latter, bring it to me in a rage and devise whatever punishment you deem appropriate, and I shall humbly beg your forgiveness, and you shall sweetly forgive.

There is a will, and you and Little Ronnie will be provided for. I write this for the things that don't belong in a will. Call them wishes.

I wish that you will mourn me to the hilt, out-Niobe Niobe with your tears, and wear a stunning black dress that will be so much the envy of our female friends that they will secretly yearn for the deaths of their husbands so that they may give you a run for the money in their widow's weeds.

And then remarry, Gwen. Don't waste time wanting me alive. You're too young, too vibrant a lass to abandon the world to placate my ghost. I promise not to haunt anyone, apart from the occasional benevolent look down (I may be presumptuous as to the direction) to reassure myself that you and Ronnie are happy.

As for our son, the most important wish I have is this: DO NOT LET THEM SEND HIM TO ST. FRIDESWIDE'S! They will bully you. They will invoke family tradition. They may even stoop so low as to say that I would have wanted it. I do not. It was a miserable, cold, sadistic place, and I want our son to be joyous above all things. Keep him in London, where he can go to the museums and the zoo and the parks and have real friends, not be in some aristocratic chain-gang.

Tell him stories about me, Gwen, and not just the good ones. I don't want him to put me on a pedestal. Let him know that, all in all, I was only human, although I tried my best to be a good one. I left him a letter. Don't give it to him until he's old enough to understand. Twelve would be the right age, I think. Don't give it to him on his birthday—I'd hate to spoil it. Wait until a week or two after.

It occurs to me that I write this not knowing the outcome of this stupid war. I am maintaining my optimism. My last wish for Ronnie is an alternative. If England prevails, tell him to grow into a man who will find a way to keep others from dying in battle.

But if England falls, Gwen, tell him to join the Resistance. And if there isn't one to join, to start his own.

I have left this in our place, what was once my place. Let our son share it when he can safely sneak up those steps.

Until we meet in Heaven, I remain yours,

Ronnie

She reread it five times, laughing through her tears. Then she walked out of her room and down the hallway until she came to her mother-in-law's room. She knocked softly.

"Who is it?" asked Lady Carolyne.

"It's Gwen. I need to show you something."

"Can't it wait until morning?"

"It's something that you'll want to see. Please, Carolyne."

She heard a soft padding, then the door opened and Lady Carolyne peered up at her over her reading glasses.

Without makeup and with her hair down, she looked more human than Gwen had ever seen her. For the first time, she saw features that Ronnie had inherited. That Little Ronnie had now.

"Well?" asked Lady Carolyne.

"I found a letter," said Gwen. "From Ronnie."

"Little Ronnie wrote—"

"Our Ronnie. My husband. Your son."

She held it up so that Lady Carolyne could see the writing.

"Where was it?"

"In a place known to him and me that I haven't looked at in a very long time."

"May I read it?"

"That is why I'm here."

"Come in."

She took the letter over to her desk and turned on the lamp. She read it slowly, then read it again. When she was done, she folded it carefully and handed it back to Gwen.

"He never said anything about hating St. Frideswide's," she said. "Not once in the eight years that he was there."

"It's hard for a child to tell his parents that he hates something they gave him," said Gwen. "He would have felt that he had failed you."

"I had no idea," said Lady Carolyne. "And now, it's too late to tell him that I'm sorry."

"You can make it up to him by keeping your grandson here."

"Harold won't like it."

"There are two of us. And we have the letter."

"Do you consider us allies now?" Lady Carolyne asked.

"In this matter, yes," said Gwen. "I do intend to regain legal custody of my son. Will you be my adversary in that? I think that I have proved myself worthy, capable, and sane enough."

"Will you take us to court if we do not agree?"

"In a heartbeat."

Lady Carolyne smiled.

"We shall speak more on that when Harold returns," she said. "I make no promises. But until then, I shall look into local schools."

"Do not put him in one without consulting me," Gwen warned her.

"Good night, Gwendolyn."

"Good night, Lady Carolyne."

Iris looked up as Gwen came into the office.

"You're late," she said. "You've never been late before. Is everything all right?"

"I took a long route to get here," said Gwen. "I'm strategizing."

"Without me?"

"I may ask your advice."

"That's fine. How was your date with Des?"

"It wasn't a date. It was an apology."

"Will there be another apology later this week?"

"No. I told him that I couldn't get involved."

"Why? He seems like a decent catch."

"I'm not fishing at the moment. Not until my son is mine again."

"And then you'll call Des?"

"Iris, there are so many differences between our lives."

"Because he's a carpenter? May I remind you that Jesus was a carpenter?"

"Jesus didn't date."

"Yes, bad example, I see that, now. But why not pursue Des some more?"

"Look, say you didn't know either of us, and had interviewed both him and me and reduced us to a pair of index cards in those boxes. Would you then have matched us up?"

"No," said Iris. "But it's not a perfect system."

"Don't tell anyone," said Gwen. "Our livelihood depends on people believing that it works."

TWO WEEKS LATER

They had been working hard all morning, interviewing prospects, matching others, and sending out letters. When lunchtime arrived, Iris swiveled to face Gwen.

"Did you bring it?" she asked.

Gwen reached into her handbag and pulled out a small book of coupons. Iris produced an identical one from her desk.

"Right, here we go," said Iris, reading from hers. "'This Clothing Book must be detached immediately from the Food Ration Book; and the holder's name, full postal address and National Registration number written in the spaces provided on page 1 in INK.'"

"Detaching now," said Gwen as she pulled it out.

"They capitalized 'INK,'" said Iris. "They're very serious about it."

"Name, address, ident," said Gwen as she filled it out.

"'All the coupons in this book do not become valid at once. IT IS ILLEGAL TO USE ANY COUPON UNTIL IT HAS BEEN DECLARED VALID,'" continued Iris. "That last was completely capitalized. They're very serious."

"I solemnly swear not to use any coupon prematurely," declared Gwen, her hand on her heart.

"'This book is the property of H. M. Government and may only be used by or on behalf of the person for whom it is issued. TAKE GREAT CARE NOT TO LOSE IT.'"

"Capitalized again?"

"You better believe it, sister."

"One date with a spiv, and you think you're a gangster," sighed Gwen. "Well, we have successfully waded through the bureaucracy. Are you ready?"

"I'm ready," said Iris, rising to her feet. "Let's go shopping."

1. The Right Sort Marriage Bureau is based on actual such agencies. How does a marriage bureau work and why might someone go through a marriage bureau?

2. Miss Sparks and Mrs. Bainbridge are very different types, representing very "modern women" for their time, yet both come from the same class in a class-conscious society. How do you see the class system in their lives and experiences? In what ways are they modern?

3. London—and England overall—was devastated by World War II. How is that revealed and discussed in the book? How does it tie in to the overall story?

4. In the age of dating apps, how would a marriage bureau work? In what ways and for whom would it be more effective? Less effective?

5. How does Iris Sparks compare to women today? In what ways is she similar to contemporary women and in what ways is she a product of her era? The same for Gwendolyn Bainbridge?

6. Sparks and Bainbridge are able to parlay their personal connections and gift for guile into extraordinary access in places not ordinarily open to them. What can they do that men of the same position cannot?

7. What authors does *The Right Sort of Man* call to mind? Why?

8. Which characters—major and minor—were your favorites and why?

MINOTAUR
BOOKS

CHAPTER 1

M en find me intimidating," boomed Miss Hardiman. "That's the problem."

"Surely not," Sparks protested.

"Oh, it's been like that ever since I was little," Miss Hardiman continued, at a volume that made Sparks fear for her eardrums. And the windowpanes. "Not that I was little for long. I was the tallest early on. You have no idea what that's like."

"I never have," Sparks agreed, shrinking back at the onslaught. "But they must have caught up with you eventually."

"By that time, they had grown up terrified of me," said Miss Hardiman. "And I had got used to being the Terror of Tiny Town. I liked it, to tell the truth."

"The truth is what we require here at The Right Sort," said Sparks.

From our clients, at least, she thought.

"So, you came to London in thirty-nine?" Sparks asked, holding her steno pad in front of her, painfully aware of its inadequacy as a shield.

"Right. Perfect timing. Things went potty right after I showed up."

"Not cause and effect, of course."

"Oh, dear! You are a caution, and that's no lie! No, I showed up in July, two months of dashing about, looking for work, then came the war. I joined up right away, of course."

"Well done," acknowledged Sparks. "Where did they assign you?"

"Office jobs at first," said Miss Hardiman. "But I presented too much of a distraction, or so they told me, and not for my bombshell looks, which was disappointing. Yes, I'm joking, I know what I look like. No, I was too much of a tiger in a cage. I switched over to the motor pool, which was boring. Finally, I found my true calling."

"Which was?"

"I was an Ack-Ack Girl," declared Miss Hardiman proudly. "Started as part of a team, worked my way up to commanding my little squad."

"Really?" exclaimed Sparks, perking up. "You got to fire the big guns?"

"Oh, yes, and it was glorious! Perched up on the hilltop with the twin 525s, watching the searchlights scour the sky, trying to spot the Messerschmitts coming out of the clouds, calculating trajectories on the fly, bellowing commands at the tops of my lungs! Then BOOM!"

Sparks involuntarily snapped her pencil in two.

Gwen, where the blazes are you? she thought. I need reinforcements.

They were sitting on opposite sides of her decrepit desk in the small office that constituted the entire premises of The Right Sort Marriage Bureau. It was a humid Tuesday morning in early July, and the standing fan that Gwen had managed to sneak out of her in-laws' home pushed the thick London air only a few inches forward before it gave up, leaving the rest of the office, particularly the space around Sparks herself, unrefreshed.

Miss Hardiman had, since only one of the two proprietors was present, plunked herself down in the single guest chair directly across from Sparks. She was tall enough, even seated, to bring the top of her head in line with the dartboard that hung on the wall behind the door. This gave her the appearance of having a gaudily striped halo, the bull's-eye perched over the top of her energetically bobbing bun.

Sparks found her eyes drifting towards the bun, her hand itching for a dart.

"One moment," she said, taking the surviving portion of her pencil and sharpening it. She licked the point when she was done, a habit left from childhood.

"Right," she said. "Ack-Ack Girl. Any success?"

"Two confirmed, shared a third," said Miss Hardiman. "Do you know that we were the only women in the services who actually killed the enemy?"

Not the only ones, thought Sparks, maintaining her bland expression.

"How about you?" asked Miss Hardiman. "How did you spend your war?"

Who do you work for? shouted Carlos, his hands around her throat, her own scrabbling for the knife under the pillow . . .

"Clerical work," said Sparks. "Nothing as exciting as what you did."

"But essential, I'm sure," said Miss Hardiman with more than a touch of condescension.

"Every cog in the machine matters," said Sparks.

"Is it odd to say I miss it?" asked Miss Hardiman. "It was terrifying, but I felt I had purpose like I never had before. And now, of course—honestly, I envy you."

"Me? Why me?"

"You still have purpose," said Miss Hardiman. "You're in charge here."

"I am only in charge of myself," said Sparks. "Mrs. Bainbridge and I are equal partners and have no other employees. I'm hardly a mover and a shaker."

"But you run your own show, with no ridiculous men to boss you about," said Miss Hardiman. "That seems like paradise, in a way."

"It is different," said Sparks. "We're making a go of it, I'm glad to report."

"After all the publicity about solving the La Salle murder, I should think so."

"That's not our normal line of work," said Sparks. "It fell into our laps, much the same way a grand piano does in those American cartoons. Now, let's get back to finding you a good candidate. Would you say, given your . . . enthusiastic personality, that you would be happier with a man who stands up to it, or one who would give in to it?"

"Ohh, that's the nub, isn't it? I'd think the first, except the arguing could get exhausting over the long run. But if the lad folds the moment I challenge him, there's no fun. Could I ask for a bit of both?"

"You could," said Sparks, jotting down the answer. "Finding him is the trick."

"Which do you prefer?" asked Miss Hardiman.

"I've had fun. I've been exhausted. I'm back to fun at the moment."

"You're not married yourself, I notice."

"Correct."

"How do I know you're any good at setting people up?"

"Because we had enough faith in our abilities to do so to start a business doing it, and we've had enough success for others to share that faith. Yes, I haven't followed a flower girl down the daisy-strewn aisle myself, but I bring a particular perspective to the search, and Mrs. Bainbridge brings a different but equally useful one. We are now on the hunt, Miss Hardiman. We shall put our minds to it, and contact you with a suitable candidate shortly."

Maybe one who's hard of hearing, she thought as she rose to shake Miss Hardiman's hand.

She quashed the thought immediately.

Iris was in the middle of typing up her notes when Gwen returned, waving a pair of keys dangling from a metal tag.

"Got them," said Gwen. "Sorry I took so long. Mr. MacPherson was particularly difficult to find today."

"Where did he turn up?"

"Napping in a vacant office on the second storey, broom in hand. How did things go with the ten thirty?"

"Letitia Hardiman is now our latest client, I am happy to report. Tall, almost your height, in fact. Assertive, extremely loud. She led an anti-aircraft battery during the war, which is impressive."

"When you say 'extremely loud' . . ."

"She brought down two bombers by yelling at them."

"Hmm," mused Gwen. "We have Mr. Temple amongst our eligibles. Didn't he lose most of his hearing to an explosion?"

"I thought of him, but it shouldn't be that superficial. And with all the shouting that would come from that match, I would fear for the equanimity of their neighbors. Maybe we should match her with someone who lives in a detached house. At the end of a street. In a cul-de-sac."

"Right. Well, I'll take a look once you've typed it up. Who's next on the schedule?"

"We have a Miss Oona Travis at eleven thirty, then a Miss Catherine Prescott at noon. Nothing after that, so I suggest lunch."

"Suits me."

Iris rested her chin on her elbows for a moment. Her desk creaked, and she pulled back immediately and glared at it.

"Someone's coming up the stairs," said Gwen.

"Miss Oona Travis, I assume," said Iris, checking her watch. "She's early. Always a good sign. You take the lead on this one. I'm still getting my hearing back from the last one."

They both busied themselves with paperwork to avoid the

appearance of idly waiting for their next customer. Gwen glanced up with her best smile. Then it became real as she saw a woman standing in the doorway.

"Patience!" she exclaimed. "What a lovely surprise!"

"Hallo, darling," said the woman, coming in to receive a kiss on the cheek.

"Iris, meet my cousin Patience Matheson," said Gwen. "Lady Matheson, I should say."

"How do you do?" said Iris, coming around the desk to shake her hand.

Lady Matheson appeared to be in her late thirties, which meant that she was probably ten years older than that, guessed Iris, basing her assessment on the expertise and expense invested in the makeup and coiffure. She was dressed in a light blue linen suit with three ropes of perfectly white, perfectly matched pearls around her neck; the strands joined at a lovely ruby pendant surrounded by white diamonds.

"What on earth brought you here?" asked Gwen.

"I came to see you in your new enterprise," said Lady Matheson, looking around. "Well. Remarkable, I must say. I never thought I would see you doing this sort of thing."

"No one did," said Gwen. "Not even me. It goes to show you how unpredictable life can be."

"We've all had more than our share of unpredictability," agreed Lady Matheson. "In fact, my being here must fall into that category."

"We weren't expecting you, certainly," said Gwen. "Not that I'm not delighted to see you. It's been some time. Iris, Patience is— Well, I'm not quite sure how to describe it. She's not exactly a lady-in-waiting—"

"Oh, heaven forbid!" said Lady Matheson, giving an exaggerated shudder.

"But she works for the Queen in some capacity."

"Do you?" said Iris. "I've always found the phrase 'in some capacity' both wonderfully vague and intentionally concealing."

"How so?" asked Lady Matheson with a smile as she sat down in the guest chair.

"It's boring enough to fend off further questions while hinting at areas of occupation too mundane to warrant any interest. People, as a result, have the idea that you do something without knowing what it is, or even thinking it's something that it isn't."

"You're the one who went to Cambridge, aren't you?" observed Lady Matheson.

"Yes."

"So you think you're smarter than most people."

"Just the ones who went to Oxford."

"Lovely!" Lady Matheson laughed. "I must repeat that one to— Well, I have an Oxford friend or two, of course."

"Patience, it is wonderful to see you," said Gwen. "But we do have a client coming in."

"I could handle the interview if you want to have a cousins' reunion," offered Iris.

"That won't be necessary," said Lady Matheson. "I am Miss Oona Travis, your eleven thirty."

"What?" exclaimed Gwen.

"I am also Miss Catherine Prescott, your twelve o'clock," said Lady Matheson. "That gives us a full hour together. I know that you have the only occupied office on this level, and that the one below us is entirely vacant, but I would like to ask you to close and lock your door, if you don't mind."

They stared at her, then at each other. Iris shrugged and got up.

"That's ten pounds down the drain," she muttered as she walked to the door.

She stepped out into the hall and peered down the stairwell. There was a man in a brown three-piece suit on the third-storey landing, nonchalantly smoking a cigarette. He looked up at her, gave a quick two-fingered salute, then resumed his pose, watching the stairs below him.

Iris returned to The Right Sort and closed and locked the door behind her.

"Brown three-piece suit, brown shoes, five ten, black hair, clean-shaven, well built, mid-thirties," she said as she retook her seat. "Yours?"

"Mine," said Lady Matheson.

"Armed?"

"Possibly. I've never asked."

"Does he have a name?"

"Possibly. I've never asked."

"Patience, what on earth is going on?" asked Gwen.

"Ten pounds, you said?" Lady Matheson asked, ignoring her and looking at Iris. "What does that get one?"

"In the cases of our now mythical female customers, our efforts to find them a suitable husband," said Iris, sitting behind her desk.

"How does that fee work out per hour?"

"It varies," said Iris. "We're up to nine weddings now."

"And several promising relationships," added Gwen.

"I see," said Lady Matheson.

She reached into her bag and pulled out her purse.

"For your lost time," she said, placing two five-pound notes on Iris's desk.

"Oh, Patience," protested Gwen. "We can't possibly—"

"Yes, we can," said Iris firmly, taking the notes and stuffing them into her top drawer.

"But Iris—"

"Think of Cecil and all the other little mouths to feed," said Iris.

"Fair point," conceded Gwen.

"I thought your son's name was Ronnie," said Lady Matheson.

"It's a private joke," said Gwen.

"All right, you have our time and attention," said Iris. "Let's talk. I take it you're not here to find a husband."

"No, I've got one already," said Lady Matheson. "He's out in the country somewhere, I'm not sure which place. Probably in Scotland, blasting birdshot into unarmed pheasants."

"While you get to suffer through the London summer with us," said Gwen.

"I will be joining the royal family when they go to Balmoral," said Lady Matheson. "Might even bump into Lord Matheson if he's not too careful, but I have an errand or two to run before I do. I was having tea with Emily Bascombe on Monday and your names came up."

"Oh, how is Em?" asked Gwen. "We heard she's in the family way."

"Glowing and voracious," said Lady Matheson. "She mentioned that the two of you met at her wedding."

"Essentially," said Iris. "That was when we became friends."

"She takes indirect credit for your decision to start up this odd little business. She told me that you, dear cousin, were responsible for bringing her and George together."

"I planted some seeds that took root and bloomed quite nicely," said Gwen.

"And that you, Iris—may I call you Iris?"

"Certainly."

"That you did some digging into George's background at Emily's request."

"There were some rumours that needed debunking," said Iris. "I was able to make some satisfactory enquiries."

"And you both put your talents to use in solving the La Salle murder. We were all quite abuzz about that."

"Have you brought us another murder to solve?" asked Iris.

"Oh, dear." Gwen sighed. "I'm still not over the first one."

"No, no." Lady Matheson laughed. "This is more in your line. But before I go any further, I need to ask for your assurances that everything we discuss from this point on will be absolutely confidential."

"Of course," said Gwen immediately.

"Hold on a tick," said Iris. "You do understand that we are not legally entitled to make those assurances."

"But Iris—" began Gwen.

"Gwen, you remember how well our protests of client confidentiality went over with Detective Superintendent Parham when he came barging in here with his bully boys. Lady Matheson, if you are here to discuss any criminal matters—"

"I am not," said Lady Matheson. "At least, not yet."

"Ominously put," said Iris. "Do you expect them to become criminal?"

"I would doubt it highly, but I cannot say to a degree of absolute certainty that they won't. But if that does turn out to be the case, you have my word that you may then bring that information to the proper authorities."

"Meaning the CID," said Iris.

"Meaning the proper authorities," said Lady Matheson.

"So it may involve matters not involving the CID," said Iris. "Are we talking about international affairs?"

"At the moment, we aren't talking about anything, and I won't subject myself to further interrogation until I have Miss Sparks's agreement," said Lady Matheson, a huffy tone creeping into her voice.

Gwen was looking at her carefully.

"This involves the Queen in some way, doesn't it?" she asked quietly.

"Miss Sparks, do I have your word?" asked Lady Matheson. "I am asking on behalf of Queen and country."

"I served the King during the war," said Iris. "I suppose I ought to extend the courtesy to his missus. You have my word, under the condition that the moment things turn sour, it is no longer binding upon me."

"Done," said Lady Matheson. "And I anticipate that all of this legal-ish verbiage will turn out be quite unnecessary. Now, to the matter. We would like the two of you to vet someone, much as you did with George Bascombe."

"That sounds easy enough," said Gwen.

"Why us?" asked Iris. "Surely you have people at the Palace who can do that sort of thing."

"This is a matter of particular delicacy," said Lady Matheson. "We'd rather not have it known internally, given how gossip flies about, nor do we want the subject of the vetting to get wind of it. We don't want a word of it anywhere near the press. It's probably nothing, but we need to make sure that it's nothing and that it stays nothing."

"The 'we' in that sentence?" asked Iris. "Is it the same 'we' as in, 'We were all quite abuzz,' or a different 'we'?"

"Myself, one other person working directly under me—and the Queen," said Lady Matheson.

"Oh, my," breathed Iris.

"Patience," said Gwen. "Are you asking us to vet Prince Philip?"